Jared

By Nicole Edwards

The Alluring Indulgence Series
Kaleb

Zane

Travis

Holidays with the Walker Brothers

Ethan

Braydon

Sawyer

Brendon

The Austin Arrows Series
The SEASON: Rush

The Club Destiny Series
Conviction

Temptation

Addicted

Seduction

Infatuation

Captivated

Devotion

Perception

Entrusted

Adored

The Coyote Ridge Series
Curtis

Jared

The Dead Heat Ranch Series
Boots Optional

Betting on Grace

Overnight Love

By Nicole Edwards (cont.)

The Devil's Bend Series

Chasing Dreams

Vanishing Dreams

The Devil's Playground Series

Without Regret

The Pier 70 Series

Reckless

Fearless

Speechless

The Sniper 1 Security Series

Wait for Morning

Never Say Never

The Southern Boy Mafia Series

Beautifully Brutal

Beautifully Loyal

Standalone Novels

A Million Tiny Pieces

Inked on Paper

Writing as Timberlyn Scott

Unhinged

Unraveling

Chaos

Naughty Holiday Editions

2015

Jared

A Coyote Ridge/Dead Heat Ranch Crossover

Novel

Nicole Edwards

Nicole Edwards Limited
PO Box 806
Hutto, Texas 78634
www.NicoleEdwardsLimited.com
www.slipublishing.com

JARED – A Coyote Ridge/Dead Heat Ranch Novel is a work of fiction. Names, characters, businesses, places, events and incidents either are the products of the author's imagination or used in a fictitious manner. Any resemblance to actual persons, living or dead, or actual events is purely coincidental.

Cover Image: © marishaz (18829658) | 123rf.com

Interior Image: © tassel78 (24058168) | 123rf.com

Cover Design: © Nicole Edwards Limited

Editing: Blue Otter Editing www.BlueOtterEditing.com

ISBN (ebook): 978-1-939786-67-8

ISBN (print): 978-1-939786-68-5

Contemporary Erotic Romance
Mature Audience

Dedication

To my fearless (albeit fictional) Walker brothers
The seven of you have changed my life and will forever live on.

PROLOGUE

Two and a half years ago

"WHERE ARE YOU going?" Sable screamed, her voice grating on his last nerve.

"I'm done. Fucking done, Sable," Jared Walker informed his soon-to-be ex-wife. And that couldn't come soon enough.

The second his boss had fired him, telling Jared that he could no longer deal with his crazed wife stopping by unannounced every day trying to start a fight, Jared had decided he'd had enough. The guy wasn't wrong to fire him. Hell, he'd been putting up with Sable's bullshit far longer than he should have. She was jealous and spiteful and fucking selfish. Yes, that's what she was.

Damn it.

Everything was just so fucked up. Jared wasn't sure how things had gone to shit so quickly, but they definitely had. The woman he'd married had shed her skin not two weeks into their marriage, demanding that she be *taken care of.* The second that ring was on her finger and the marriage license was signed, Sable had changed from the easygoing, somewhat kindhearted woman to an ex-employee at the makeup counter at Macy's to a fucking diva who wanted him to make her breakfast in bed on the weekend.

Jared

No doubt about it, he'd been blinded by ... what? What the hell had he seen in her? Even now, three years later, he had no clue what he'd been drawn to other than her smoking-hot body and her Hoover-worthy mouth. Oh, and she'd given him attention—batting her eyelashes and offering her relentless come-hither stare—something he'd been missing. Or thought he had anyway. In hindsight, the lack of attention from the opposite sex had been self-imposed. Jared had just turned thirty when they met, and he'd been going through the motions, trying to figure out where his life was headed and how he wanted it to go. Marriage had certainly been an idea he was looking forward to, should he find the right woman.

Enter Sable Hillman, with her perfectly applied lipstick and fancy hair. She'd clearly walked into his life at the right time. Or the *wrong* time, depending on how you looked at it.

He was definitely an idiot.

Sable didn't want to work, but she didn't want to stay home, either. She thought they belonged to the country club elite or some shit. He could see how she'd come to that conclusion. Jared's parents were well off, and they'd set their children up accordingly. Jared had money—mostly family money—but he'd also been working since the day he turned sixteen. He hadn't had a rough life, by any means, but his father had instilled in him the need to make a good living. Damn good thing his father had demanded he have a prenuptial agreement. Jared hadn't thought it necessary, but at the last minute, he'd caved. For a second, he'd thought Sable was going to back out. He should've known better. The woman was more than willing to spend every penny he had *while* they were married. She didn't need to wait until afterward.

"Fuck you, Jared."

"No," he turned to her. "Fuck. You. And every asshole who's had the displeasure of fucking you over the last three fucking years."

Three years he'd been dealing with this shit. If it weren't for the fact Sable had gotten pregnant, Jared would've been long gone. Only he'd stayed because of his son. Derrick was the highlight of every single day. Jared went to work every morning, and when he came home, Sable generally went out while he enjoyed the peace and quiet and time he got to spend with his boy. It was the perfect routine, and since it got Sable out of his hair, Jared never complained.

"I want joint custody," he informed her as he went to the closet and began tossing his clothes out. He was packing his shit and moving out. He had no choice. He would go stay in his parents' guesthouse until the divorce was final. It would allow him to be close enough to Derrick so he could see him every other weekend and every Wednesday.

"Ha!" Sable sneered. "Like that's ever gonna happen."

Goddamn, that was going to hurt. He hated the idea of being away from Derrick for that long. He'd been hoping Sable would be level-headed about this, letting him spend time with his boy whenever he wanted. He should've known better.

Jared cast an angry glare over his shoulder. "I'll fight you for full custody if that's what you want."

"Go ahead and try it," she snapped. "Considering he's not your kid, I'm not sure that'll work out real well for you."

Jared spun around so fast Sable had to take a step back.

"*What* did you say?" The impact of her words had caused his hands to shake, and there was a red haze clouding his vision, anger and... Damn, it felt a hell of lot like fear clouded his mind.

Sable always said nasty shit to him. It seemed she got off on putting him down. Normally, he didn't rise to the bait, but *this*... He hoped like hell she was lying.

"You heard me. You think you're all high and mighty. Derrick isn't yours. You're not his father. So fuck you, Jared. You don't get shit out of this deal."

He had to sit down or his legs were going to give out. Jared managed to back up to the bed and drop down onto the mattress, staring at the woman he had vowed to love forever, a woman he no longer even liked.

Jared

"I want a paternity test," he insisted. That would prove that Derrick was his. He had to be.

Sable rolled her eyes. "I'm marrying him."

Jared tried to process her words, but they didn't make sense.

"Derrick's father. He's been begging me to leave you. I should've done it before now. And yes, you'll get your paternity test. I'll prove to you that he ain't yours."

She should've left *before now*? She wasn't the one leaving, Jared was.

"You'll have nothing," she spat.

Jared held back his retort, not sure what he could say. The woman had managed to single-handedly rip his heart right out of his chest and grind it into dust.

Derrick isn't yours.

The fact that his marriage had disintegrated ... Jared could get over.

Losing Derrick... That was a wound that would never heal.

* * *

Six months later

"Despite the fact that the paternity test states you are not the father," Edna Holloway—the expensive lawyer he'd hired—clarified, "Sable is willing to give you full custody."

Jared waited for her to continue. He was waiting for the "but." There was always a "but."

"However, in exchange, she wants twenty-five thousand dollars."

"Done," Jared said instantly.

"Jared, you should spend some time thinking about this," Edna said kindly.

"Don't need to. My name's on his birth certificate. He's my son. Find out where I need to wire the money."

Edna pulled a sheet of paper from the pile she'd brought with her. "I think we need to ask that she give up her parental rights. That will protect you going forward. She has already made it clear that she doesn't want Derrick."

And by *made it clear*, Jared knew that Edna was referring to the fact that Sable had flat out told him that she didn't have time for Derrick in her life. The man she'd claimed was Derrick's father had insisted on a paternity test, also. The results had stated he was not the father. Which meant Sable had lied once again. The new man—some rich, older guy—in her life didn't want kids, which meant Derrick had suddenly become expendable in her eyes.

"I agree," he told her. "Do what you need to do, and tell Sable I want this done immediately. While we're waiting for the legal system to putter along and do their thing, I want him living with me. In Coyote Ridge."

Since he had moved to the small town where most of his extended family lived, in an attempt to put some distance between himself and Sable, Jared had started to build a life for himself. Although he wouldn't be close to his parents, he wasn't too far away. And he had a great job. Being in Coyote Ridge would also lessen the chance of him running into Sable again.

She nodded, jotting down notes before removing her reading glasses and depositing them into her purse. "I'll keep you apprised of the proceedings. I'll ask that Sable relinquish custody over to you today." She glanced at her watch. "Why don't I try for four o'clock. Will you still be in town?"

"Of course," he said, his heart pounding. "Anything for Derrick."

Little did his lawyer know, but Jared would've given ten times that much to get his son back. Granted, there was absolutely *no* reason to let Sable know that. The manipulative bitch would only ask for more.

Jared

Chapter One

Present day, September

"A FAMILY REUNION?" Jared Walker dropped into the chair in his office and stared up at the ceiling, cell phone to his ear. "Are you fucking serious?"

For the past half hour, Jared had been humoring his cousin Travis, listening to the spiel as to why it was time the Walker family had a reunion. The last thing Jared had time—much less patience—for these days was some big-ass family get-together. At thirty-five years old and divorced, it was enough for him to deal with the day-to-day of Walker Demolition, along with being a single dad to a four-year-old little boy.

"Very," Travis confirmed, his tone gruff. "And I want it to take place next month."

Next month? The guy was getting laid too damn much these days, because now he'd lost his fucking mind and become far too optimistic. Maybe there was something to be said about the whole bisexual thing. "I think we need to be a little realistic here," Jared added.

"How long do you think it'll take to prepare?" Travis questioned, sounding genuinely curious.

Jared had no clue. He wasn't a goddamn party planner. "Do you even know where we're gonna have this thing?"

"Yep." The certainty in Travis's voice gave Jared a small measure of assurance. At least his cousin had looked that far into it.

When he realized Travis wasn't going to share the details, Jared sighed. "Where, Travis?"

"Dead Heat Ranch."

"I don't even know what that is," Jared admitted.

"It's owned by some of Cheyenne's family," Travis told him, referring to Travis's brother Brendon's woman. "Beyond that, I ain't got shit. I need you to call them, set it up."

"*Me?*" Jared sat up straight. "What makes you think I've got time to deal with this? Do you know how much business Walker Demo has at the moment?"

Travis chuckled.

Okay, so maybe he did. Jared knew that Travis probably had a finger on the pulse of every damn thing that went on with Walker Demo, not to mention the resort. And probably even the entire town of Coyote Ridge, Texas, to boot.

Unfortunately, they weren't as busy as Jared would've liked. For months on end, they'd been going ninety to nothing, and all of a sudden things had slowed drastically.

"Fine. We're not that damn busy, but still. Why me?"

"'Cause you're closer to everyone."

It was Jared's turn to laugh. "That's horseshit and you know it."

"But it sounded good, didn't it? Look, Gage just walked in and I've gotta take care of some shit. You got this?"

Another frustrated sigh escaped him, but Jared found himself nodding. "Fine."

"Thanks. Call Cheyenne or Brendon, get the information. Let me know if you need anything."

Jared didn't bother responding. He hung up the phone and dropped his cell phone on his desk, then put his head in his hands and tugged at his hair. On top of everything, he needed a damn haircut.

He sighed.

Honestly, this was the last damn thing he needed right now, but it would help to keep his mind occupied, so that was something to look forward to. When business slowed, that was when his mind started wandering, and that was never a good thing.

Ever.

Jared

Jared sat up straight and took a deep breath. Fine. He'd do it. And if Travis wanted this shindig to take place next month, Jared needed to get started now. Reaching for his phone, he had just palmed it when it vibrated. He glanced at the screen and saw that it was Cheyenne Montgomery, the very person he was about to call.

He stabbed the screen to answer, then put the phone to his ear. "Lemme guess, Travis called you?" How that was even possible with only a minute or so passing since Jared had hung up with him, he didn't know. Then again, this was Travis Walker. The guy was quite possibly not human.

Cheyenne's husky chuckle made him smile. "Of course he did."

"And to think, he told *me* to call you."

"You know Travis, always makin' sure things go the way he wants them to."

Exactly. Which was the very reason Travis should be handling this shit. "I don't know why he's trusting me with this," Jared told Cheyenne. "I get the feelin' he's gonna handle most of it on his own anyway."

"I wouldn't be so sure about that," Cheyenne said. "Rumor is, now that he's got two rug rats at home, he's havin' a hard time keepin' his head on straight already."

That didn't surprise Jared one bit. Travis Walker wasn't the easiest guy to get along with, and frazzled seemed to be the constant state he was in. Although he had toned down somewhat in recent years, which was a relief to everyone.

"I've got the number for you. Got a pen?"

Jared grabbed a pen. "Yeah."

He scribbled the number on his desk calendar as Cheyenne rattled it off. "You're gonna want to talk to Hope Lambert."

"Got it."

"She might have one of her sisters handle the details, but she's the best one to talk to first. They'll walk you through everything you need to know."

"I'll call her now."

"I'd offer to help, but I'm gonna be on the road for the next month."

Shit. That reminded him that he needed to try to coordinate schedules. A month wasn't nearly enough time to put this together and expect anyone to show up. Maybe he'd push it out a little.

"I'm sure I can handle it," Jared told her. "But if you could send me your tour dates, that'd help."

"I'll get them texted to you ASAP."

"Is this place close?" he asked. "This Dead Heat Ranch?"

"Not far. 'Bout half an hour from here, I'd say. In Embers Ridge. You know the place?"

"Yeah," he lied. He didn't know the place, but he figured a map would tell him. "You know why Travis picked it?" Jared hadn't wrapped his head around that part yet.

"You'll see when you call them."

Jared did not like the sound of that. "Should I be worried?"

"Nope. Just make sure you're clear on how many days you want."

"Days?" He flopped back into his chair and closed his eyes. "I thought this was a family reunion. An afternoon barbecue or some shit."

Another giggle sounded from Cheyenne. "I wish it were that simple. This is a dude ranch, Jared. My guess is Travis is lookin' for a solid week."

Dude ranch? Week?

The fuck?

He sighed again, this time in resignation. He wasn't going to get out of this, so he might as well step right in the shit and get moving.

"All right, I'm gonna call this Hope Lambert and see what she says. I'll let you know."

"Have fun!"

Right. Fun.

Because that was exactly what this *wasn't* going to be.

Jared

"YEP. I'LL CATCH up with you in a bit. Gonna grab a bite first," Hope Lambert said into the phone a second before she ended the call and shoved the device into her back pocket.

The sun wasn't even up and she was already two hours into her day. A colicky calf was her reason for being up earlier than usual, but Hope wasn't complaining. Luckily, their staff was on their toes, their full attention on all the animals.

However, that hadn't been the highlight of her morning. That'd come when Budweiser located a rattlesnake out near the barn. Hope didn't do snakes, so she'd pulled Grant right out of his warm bed for that one. She hadn't stuck around to see how it went, other than to find out that Budweiser hadn't gotten too close.

So much shit, not enough time.

As much as she had enjoyed the heat of the summer for the last several of months, Hope was happy that they were on the cusp of fall, which meant the long days and warm evenings would soon be behind her again. Two weeks into September and things were finally slowing down a little. And by a little, she meant significantly more so than in the extremely busy summer months. The days were growing shorter, the sun not quite so hot, the wind a little cooler, yet the work was still endless.

But with fall came preparations for winter, which was the time when there would be more attention put on the animals than on the many tourists who embarked on Dead Heat Ranch in their attempt to learn a thing or two about ranching, horses, cattle, and spending time with nature. Not to mention being entertained. And that meant, despite the days getting shorter, there would still be a lot of things to cram into a twenty-four-hour period.

Not that she hadn't been busy enough, even when the skyrocketing temperatures made certain tasks damn near impossible. But with fewer visitors, they had significantly more time to spend on the ranch. Truth be told, that was just the way she liked it.

It wasn't that Hope didn't like people or weddings or family get-togethers, she just... Okay, so yeah, that was exactly it. Hope simply didn't like people, and she wasn't a big fan of so many at one time, either. Strange characteristic for one of the owners of the largest dude ranch in the state of Texas, but there it was. Give her a horse and a few hours, Hope would gladly spend it by herself, alone with her favorite companion and her thoughts.

Fortunately, that was something she would no longer have to put off in order to accommodate the influx of tourists who had selected Dead Heat Ranch as their vacation destination for the endless summer months. With the reservations few and far between now, Hope looked forward to the chance to sit down with her sisters and understand how profitable—if she was lucky—the summer season had been for them.

Oh, and she couldn't forget the wedding. They were a little more than five weeks out from Grace's wedding—in which she would officially tie the knot with not one but *two* cowboys. Okay, maybe not officially. Grace couldn't actually marry two people, but you wouldn't be able to tell it from the ceremony. In what they hoped would be a beautiful fall wedding, there would be an exchange of rings and some sort of legally binding contract, but no one was actually getting hitched as far as the eyes of Texas were concerned. Still, the showdown required a ton of work and twice as much time.

"Hey, honey, where're you headed?"

Hope looked up to see her father standing on the porch of the main house, a steaming mug of coffee in his hand, his booted foot resting on the bottom railing, his hat tipped low, shielding his eyes from the rising sun.

"Breakfast," she told him, smiling as she took a brief detour so she could tell him good morning.

Offering a quick hug and a kiss, she patted his scruffy cheek. "Lose your razor?"

Jerry Lambert peered over at her with a sheepish grin. "Maybe." He took a sip of his coffee, watching her over the rim of his cup. "Mind if I join you?"

Jared

For the last two years, her father had spent every waking moment with his girlfriend, Jan, and they'd finally moved in together nearly a year ago. The woman's presence at the ranch put a smile on Jerry's face, so Hope couldn't help but like her. In fact, Hope considered Jan family at this point. The two of them had seemed to be quite cozy, leaving Hope to wonder whether or not Jerry and the sweet little elementary school teacher would be taking their relationship to the next level—whatever that was—sometime soon.

"Where's Jan?"

"She's gettin' ready to go to school. She's been back for a month already, but you'd think it was the first day. The woman loves her job."

Hope noticed the cheeky grin that lit up her father's weathered face. She wanted to ask him when they were going to give in and get married, but she knew not to question him. Ever since Hope's mother died when Hope was sixteen, the man had refrained from relationships with women. He'd spent the last eighteen years focused solely on his girls and his ranch—in that order.

Hope was glad he'd finally found someone who made him happy. However, not all of her sisters felt the same way she did. As it was, her sister Mercy was still having a hard time getting used to the fact that their father was in a serious relationship. No amount of talking seemed to be helping, which was why Hope had left her sister to her own devices long ago. The girl was as hardheaded as they came.

"I'd love company," Hope told her father when she pulled back and turned toward the door. "What's on the menu? Do you know?"

"I heard it was French toast," he answered, standing to his full height and falling into step with her. "Jennifer's gonna spoil us if she's not careful. No more of that veggie crap if we're lucky."

Jennifer Brathow and her redheaded little boy, Joey, had made quite the impact on the ranch when she'd come in and taken over as head chef several years back. During the holidays last year, she'd surprised them all with some heartier southern food rather than her normal organic, healthy meals. The welcome change had made the wranglers quite happy. A little begging had gone a long way, and Jennifer had continued to give them what they asked for through the colder months. Personally, Hope preferred the down-home meals because it helped her keep on the weight. Being that she worked long days, sometimes far into the evening, eating was the last thing on her mind, and when things got hectic—which was most of the time—she tended to lose weight without meaning to.

Hope stepped back out of the way so that her father could open the screen door for her, but before she could head inside, her cell phone rang. She pulled it from her back pocket and glanced at the screen.

"I'll be in in a minute," she told her father, then turned and headed down the wraparound porch, to the side of the house.

"Hello?"

"I'm lookin' for Hope Lambert," the deep, gravelly voice said.

"This is she."

There was a brief pause, then a definite sigh before the rumbling voice was back. "All right, well, I'm gonna get right to it. I don't know the first thing about what I'm supposed to ask you, but I've been tasked with puttin' together a family reunion, and the only thing I know for sure is that your ranch has been chosen as the location. Cheyenne Montgomery gave me your number. Said I should talk directly to you. So, what do you need from me?"

Hope smiled at the uncertainty in the guy's deep baritone, not to mention his incessant rambling. "Well, you could start by tellin' me your name."

A raspy chuckle sounded, and for the first time in a long while, Hope's curiosity was piqued. "Sorry. Name's Jared ...Walker."

Nope, not piqued. Her curiosity was on red alert.

Jared

"Ah, I've been expectin' one of the infamous Walkers to call me." Her cousin Cheyenne had given her the heads-up months ago, but since she hadn't heard from anyone, Hope figured they'd found another place to hold their reunion.

"Not sure whether I'm infamous or not, but I'm callin'," Jared said, sounding somewhat less confused but still slightly bewildered.

"And I can help," she assured him. "But there's a lot of things we need to cover. I was just about to grab some breakfast, and I've got some chores to take care of. I'll be glad to call you in a few hours if that works for you. If not, I can probably chase down one of my sisters, and they can help you through the process."

There was another pause, as though Jared was thinking. She didn't know the first thing about this guy, but she got the impression from the rushed tone of his voice that he didn't particularly care to sit around and wait.

"I ... uh... Yeah. Okay. Call me in a coupla hours when you have a chance. You're not that far from me. If I need to, I can always run out there and we can discuss face-to-face."

Face-to-face? Hope didn't think that was necessary. Not because she wasn't used to doing business face-to-face, but after hearing Cheyenne's colorful description of the Walkers, Hope wasn't sure she'd survive five minutes in this guy's presence. Plus, she had far too much to get done today. If she had to take the time to hold this man's hand—figuratively speaking—she would never get her chores accomplished.

"We can start on the phone to save you the trip. But once we get the basics, it probably wouldn't hurt for you to stop by and check things out." By then, one of her sisters would be taking care of the details.

"You're the boss," Jared rumbled, a smile in his voice. "I'll wait for your call."

After hanging up the phone and tucking it back into her pocket, Hope went inside the main house, suddenly realizing she had a smile on her face.

And she didn't have the faintest clue why that was.

CHAPTER TWO

WHILE HE WAITED for Hope Lambert to call him back, Jared spent a good hour and a half dealing with paperwork he hadn't had time for. Although most people he knew complained about the mundane task, Jared didn't mind it. Especially since it spoke to his sense of accomplishment. No one could deny that he was bordering on obsessive when it came to clearing out clutter. And paperwork definitely qualified as clutter. Even when it was paper*less* and came in the form of his email inbox.

Not only had he tackled the review of two bids they'd put in last week, he also responded to his mother's email, letting her know that Derrick was doing great, and they were definitely hoping to come home for Christmas this year, too. Yes, it was September and his mother was already planning holiday dinners.

"Hey, boss man," Reese Tavoularis hollered when he stepped into the small building they used for the Walker Demo office. It was basically a metal trailer that'd been set on a slab of concrete, tied down to ensure it didn't blow away in the strong winds known to blow through the area most of the year. The air conditioner was in the window of the single room, which held office furniture on one end and a small kitchenette—minus everything except for the sink and refrigerator—on the other end, near the entry door.

Redneck-chic, Jared called it.

Because the place had once been inhabited by Travis, Kaleb, and Sawyer—before they'd packed up and moved over to the Alluring Indulgence Resort—there were still three metal desks that filled the space, only one of which contained anything on its surface.

21

Jared

However, for the past couple of weeks, Jared had been attempting to change that. "You ready to plant your happy ass at that desk yet?"

Jared was hoping to train Reese as his permanent backup. While Jared's cousin, Jaxson, was known to fill in when he could, Jared wanted someone who could easily slip into the role whenever Jared needed him to.

Reese grinned over his shoulder before reaching for the coffee carafe and pouring a generous amount into a Styrofoam cup. "Man, I don't think you can handle my ass sittin' at a desk all day. I'd go fucking insane."

Jared had thought the same thing when he'd taken the job, but he'd learned that it wasn't as bad as he'd expected. Probably didn't hurt that he still spent most of his day out of the office, but still.

"One of these days, you're gonna have to give in," Jared told the other man.

Jared had hired Reese on a while back, after the younger man returned to Coyote Ridge from his eight-year stint in the air force. Reese had grown up here, which Jared considered a plus for bringing him on. Since Jared was technically an outsider—although the Walker name made him a friendly face—it helped to have someone who knew the ins and outs of the small town. Even if Reese had been gone for nearly a decade, the town had welcomed him home with open arms.

"Not if I can help it," Reese joked, moving around to take a seat at one of the empty desks.

Jared leaned back in his chair and stared at the other man. "You fit nicely in that chair."

Reese chuckled. "It's a good thing you Walker boys aren't short."

True, they weren't. Nor was Reese, coming in at six five, only an inch taller than Jared.

"What'cha got for me today, boss man?" Reese inquired, sipping slowly at his coffee as he stared at Jared over the rim of the cup.

Jared pulled up the schedule on his computer. "Brendon and Braydon are takin' care of a couple of new jobs, but I've got a pitch that needs to be done. You wanna handle that?"

"Damn skippy," Reese said with a huge grin. The guy loved the sales aspect of the job, which worked well for Jared considering he hated that shit. Put him in an office or in charge of a dozen guys on a jobsite and he didn't have a problem. Make him sell something and ...well, let's just say he could if push came to shove, but he preferred to steer clear.

Jared hit the print button, and the machine beside him whirred to life, spitting out two sheets of paper. After grabbing them, he held them out to Reese.

"I'll check back in with you later," Reese said, snatching the papers and sauntering out the door.

And that was how most of his mornings went. Jared would sit at his desk, taking care of the paperwork, while the others would prance through the building, grabbing up their assigned jobs for the day before heading right back out. They had it working like a well-oiled machine.

Speaking of well-oiled machine... Jared grabbed his Stetson, planted it on his head, and pulled his keys and phone from his desk drawer. He needed to make a quick pit stop to check on Ethan and Beau.

Less than five minutes later, he was climbing out of his truck and heading into the huge, metal mechanic shop, where he found the two men arguing about an engine they were working on. It wasn't at all surprising to find the couple having a heated discussion. Considering they were married *and* working together, Jared figured it was a wonder they both weren't walking with a limp. That much time spent with one person was more than should be allowed.

Jared knew that to be true. As much as he loved Derrick, if the kid didn't go to day care while Jared worked, Jared probably would've gone insane at this point. A little father-son separation wasn't a bad thing. Didn't hurt that Derrick loved day care. He imagined that, a year from now, Derrick was going to be over the moon to start kindergarten.

Jared

But who was Jared to interfere when Ethan and Beau made things so easy for him? Those two ran the shop better than Jared handled the other part of the business, and rarely did they need him for anything. That in itself was a plus. Since his experience beneath the hood was limited to changing a radiator hose, which he'd done years and years ago, it was probably best that Jared left the work to the experts.

Clearing his throat, he waited until they turned to look at him, then he offered a smile. "Who's winnin'?"

Ethan frowned. Beau grinned.

Yep, just as he'd guessed. Then again, Ethan was the dark-haired brooding one, while Beau was the blond giant with the quick smile. They seemed to fit each other well.

"Y'all good?"

"Never better," Ethan grumbled. "What's up?"

"Nothin'. Just stoppin' in."

"Coffee?" Beau offered, wiping his hands on a rag and moving toward Jared.

"Sure." He would never turn down coffee. He figured that had a lot to do with being a single dad and finding there weren't nearly enough hours in the day to include sleep. Caffeine was his vice.

"So, really," Ethan said, turning to face Jared after setting a wrench on one of the many toolboxes lining the wall, "what brings you by?"

It was true, Jared didn't have to check on Ethan or Beau, but from time to time, he made a point to stop by anyway. They handled the maintenance and repair on all of the heavy equipment and vehicles for Walker Demolition. Considering the sheer volume of equipment Walker Demo owned, not to mention the wear and tear the twins put on the shop trucks, they didn't have a lot of down time. Jared didn't need to micromanage, but he still liked to make sure they knew he was there if they needed him.

However, he did have a reason for being there today, and it had nothing to do with engines or equipment, or them, for that matter.

"Do you know what Travis expects for this family reunion?" Jared blurted, figuring he might as well get right down to it.

Ethan smirked. "He task you with that?"

Jared nodded, then mumbled a thanks when Beau passed over a cup of coffee.

"Lucky you," Beau said facetiously. "He tried to pin it on us, but we refused."

Yeah, well… Jared figured he would eventually get to the point when he regretted that he hadn't, but for now, it gave him something to focus on. Something other than chasing a four-year-old around all hours of the day and night.

Ah, I've been expectin' one of the infamous Walkers to call me.

Hope Lambert's raspy twang sounded in his head, and he remembered the conversation he'd had with her a short while ago.

Okay, and maybe now he was looking forward to this whole family reunion fiasco for an entirely different reason. Ever since he'd hung up the phone, Jared couldn't seem to get that sexy voice out of his head. Although it was asinine, for some reason he wanted to know what the body attached to that voice looked like.

Not that he intended to do anything about that, but he couldn't deny it was a nice distraction.

Truth was, the last fucking thing he needed in his life was a woman. He'd learned his lesson after the last one. His ex-wife had done a number on him. Theirs had been a quick courtship, which should've been his first warning that something was awry.

Jared had met Sable in a nightclub. One of those country dance halls that played more hip-hop than country music. A little eye contact from across the room and Jared had found himself invited back to her place. Sex was the appropriate next step, which had then turned into marriage three weeks later.

Jared

Needless to say, Jared hadn't seen the tornado that was Sable Hillman until it was too late. The only good thing that came out of it was his son, Derrick. From the moment Sable told him she was pregnant, Jared had been over the moon. Apparently he was the only one. During the three relatively short, although extremely painful, years they'd been married, not only had Sable been stepping out on him, she'd also broken the news to him that his son was not his son. The breakdown of his marriage was no skin off his nose, but losing his boy...

Divorcing the adulterous, manipulating woman had been easy—nothing a little money couldn't take care of—but losing Derrick... That short period of time when Jared had to be without the little boy had damn near killed him. And after having to deal with Sable's shit for years, Jared didn't want anything to do with women or the shit storm they brought with them. Which was why he'd kept his relationships impersonal and brief. A few one-nighters over the years—both parties fully on board with the plan—and Jared didn't have much to complain about.

Shaking off the thought, he looked between the two men. "You know anything about Dead Heat Ranch?"

Ethan glanced at Beau, then shrugged. "Just what I heard from Cheyenne."

"It's a dude ranch, right?" Beau questioned.

"That's the rumor," Jared confirmed. "Chey mentioned Travis wants to stay for a week."

"A week?" Ethan looked as though that was the most ludicrous thing he'd ever heard. That'd been Jared's initial reaction as well.

"Sounds reasonable," Beau chimed in.

Ethan and Jared turned to glare at him.

"What?" Beau tossed his hands up. "A week on a ranch. Horses. Cows. Chickens. No engines to fuck with. Man, seriously."

Okay, so when Beau put it that way, it didn't sound terrible. Hell, as it was, Derrick was obsessed with horses, and he figured it would be the right place to get his son some more experience with them. Jared took Derrick out to see Curtis and Lorrie's horses as often as he could, and the little boy loved it.

"I'm talkin' to them this afternoon," Jared confirmed. "I'll get more details."

"When does Trav want this to take place?" Ethan asked, shoving his hands in his pockets.

"He said next month, but I'm not sure that's doable. I'll see what they've got available."

Ethan nodded, but he still didn't look happy about the whole thing.

Jared drained what was left of his coffee. "Well, that's all I've got. I need to run out and check on a job. Y'all need anything?"

Ethan shook his head, so Jared looked at Beau.

"Nah. We're good, man."

"Cool. Let me know if you do."

Jared passed over the empty cup, then offered a quick wave as he sauntered back to his truck. Maybe he should do a little research on this ranch. See what he was getting himself into. Hell, maybe a trip over was the best way to do things. He could meet with Hope Lambert face-to-face and check it out at the same time.

Glancing at his watch, he noticed it was straight-up noon. If he grabbed a quick bite, stopped at the jobsite, he'd probably be able to make it over to the ranch right at two.

With that plan, he fired up his Silverado and laid some gravel behind him just to piss Ethan off. A quick glance in his rearview showed he'd definitely accomplished his goal. Ethan was standing in the bay door, giving him the finger and glaring at him just as he was consumed by a cloud of dust.

ETHAN WALKER COUGHED dust from his lungs as he turned back into the shop, finding his husband staring back at him with a smirk on his handsome face.

"What?" Ethan asked, throwing his hands up. "I take it you're on board with this ranch reunion shit?"

"How could it hurt?" Beau questioned, taking the empty coffee mug back to the small sink inside the shop's office.

Jared

"A week on a dude ranch?"

"Sure. Time away from here." Beau cocked his head to the side. "In case you haven't noticed, we don't get away much."

Ethan frowned. "Is that a problem for you?"

Beau was right, they didn't do much more than go to work every day, then go home, have dinner, make love, pass out, and get up the next day to do it all over again.

"I'd like to get away from time to time, sure," Beau told him. "With you."

Interesting.

Ethan had never given much thought to going on a vacation. Not that he thought a trip that included the crazies that he called family would be a vacation. Still.

"Anywhere specific you wanted to go?" he asked, curious.

"A cruise," Beau said, completely serious. "Maybe the mountains. In the winter, when there's snow on the ground. I liked Hawaii. Wouldn't mind going back sometime."

Ethan watched Beau as though he'd never seen him before. He couldn't help himself. They'd been married for almost two years now, and he was shocked that the man he loved wanted to travel. It wasn't something Ethan had ever given much thought to. But now that he was, he kind of liked the idea.

Him and Beau, alone. Somewhere quiet, with a lot of privacy.

Hmm. He would definitely have to give this some more thought.

"Come on, E. We don't have time for you to sit around with your thumb up your butt," Beau chided.

Ethan grinned, knowing Beau was messing with him. As he walked toward the truck they'd been arguing over before Jared showed up, he managed to crowd Beau against the wall. "Be careful there," Ethan grumbled softly, moving in close enough to feel Beau's breath on his lips. "You know how I get when you talk like that."

Beau laughed, then grabbed Ethan. "Baby, I'm game for whatever you've got in mind. Anytime."

Well, in that case…

Ethan kissed him.

Just before he led him to their small office, where he could show his husband just how much he intended to get done today.

"HOPE!"

Pivoting on her heel, Hope turned at the sound of her name. Even though her face was shaded by her straw hat, she still had to squint to see in the direct sunlight. That was when she noticed Grace coming her way, determination in every step of her booted feet.

"What's up?" she asked. "I was just headin' to the barn to muck out the stalls."

"That can wait," Grace stated matter-of-factly.

Great. Another fire that had to be put out before she could get her daily chores tackled. Hope was beginning to think she needed to clone herself in order to get through the day. As it was, she'd promoted Lane Miller to head wrangler because Hope hadn't been able to do the role justice with so much going on. Yet her sister was still chasing her down.

"What's wrong? Is it the calf?"

Grace shook her head.

"They didn't get the snake?"

Grace nodded. "Oh, they got it, all right."

"Then what's the problem?"

"One of the cabins flooded."

Hope stared at her sister in disbelief. "And that's my problem how? The cabins aren't my responsibility, Gracie. Talk to your man about that shit."

Grace's eyes opened wide. "I did," she said snottily. "But I thought I'd give you a heads-up since it's your fuckin' cabin that flooded."

"*What?*"

Hope was fairly certain she saw a glimmer of satisfaction in Grace's turquoise eyes. Then again, Hope had put her in her place before she had all the facts, so she probably deserved that.

Jared

"How bad is it?" she questioned, angling her boots in the direction of her cabin.

"Oh, it's bad."

That didn't tell her shit.

"Elaborate, Grace," she snapped.

"Let's just say your bedroom is underwater."

Fuck.

Not what she needed right now. She'd had some issues with the plumbing in her cabin in the past, but she'd thought it'd been taken care of.

"Is it the water heater?"

"Nope."

"One of the pipes bust?"

"Nope."

Hope glanced over at Grace, her frustration building. "What is it then?"

"Septic tank."

"Fuck." That was a nasty thought.

"You'll probably have to stay in the main house until they can get it repaired. Not to mention, it's gonna take some time to air that shit out." Grace chuckled. "Literally."

Lovely.

It took a good ten minutes of the unusually warm morning for Hope to make it to her cabin, Grace in tow. When she stepped up on the porch, Hope took a deep breath and prepared herself for the damage. As soon as she pushed open the door, she saw the water. Not only was her bedroom underwater, like Grace had said, but her living room, too.

Oh, good heavens. That was not a pleasant smell.

"I assume someone stopped the backflow?" Hope peered around, singling out the few items she had that she would've been devastated to lose. Not that she had much, but some of the things her mother had given her before she died were irreplaceable.

"Yep. Grant did as soon as he noticed."

"How'd he notice it?" Hope's cabin was the one farthest from the main house. Usually no one ventured that far, which was one of the reasons she liked it. Privacy.

"He'd been checkin' the fence line 'cause someone said there was a downed section. Let's just say he smelled it before he saw it."

Hope waded through the sewage water, which came over the toes of her boots. Everything that was on the floor was definitely down for the count, but hopefully she'd be able to salvage some of the furniture—the wooden stuff anyway. If not, she was sure she could scrounge up some extra pieces from somewhere. After all, most of what she had belonged to the ranch anyway. It'd never been her priority to fancy a place with all kinds of shit. The décor was certainly hers—most of it from her childhood bedroom, which her mother had designed herself— mostly pink and white and frilly. It wasn't necessarily Hope's taste, but it was all she had left of her mom, so she kept it.

Her bigger problem was that she would have to deal with this later. Much later. As much as she wanted to make this a priority, she had too many chores to take care of before she could focus on this.

"Grant is on his way back," Grace said from somewhere behind her. "We'll get the water out for you. And Trin said she'd help to pack up your personal things. You want any of the furniture?"

"Once it's cleaned out, I'll figure that out."

"Got it. We'll get you taken care of."

Hope nodded. She would appreciate that. Although she would prefer to handle it all herself, she knew that wasn't possible. These days, it seemed as though she was running herself ragged without any extra problems arising.

"Thanks."

"*Really?*" The disbelief in her sister's tone made Hope turn to face her.

"Really what?"

"No arguments?"

Hope peered down at the floor, pretending to look at the water.

"It'll be fine," Grace said, obviously mistaking Hope's downcast eyes for her being upset. Truth was, Hope didn't give a shit about the cabin. It was a place to sleep, but that was about it.

However, she wasn't looking forward to staying in the main house. She hadn't stayed there in... Not since she was seventeen and had insisted she have her own space. But it wasn't the lack of privacy that she feared.

No, Hope wasn't looking forward to staying in the main house because it brought back too many memories of her mother. Memories that she did her best to avoid. As it was, she'd allowed those memories to shape her world, to turn her into a hard-ass who had little time for anything more than keeping the ranch going. It was easier than letting people get close to her.

A whole lot easier.

CHAPTER THREE

AFTER LUNCH, JARED tracked down his cousin Jaxson, who handled pretty much anything Jared could throw at him. He put Jaxson in charge of the phones for a couple of hours, then hopped in his truck for the thirty-minute trip to Dead Heat Ranch.

It took a little less time than he'd expected to get to Embers Ridge, and only a few more minutes to make his way through the one-stoplight town. The place was quite possibly smaller than Coyote Ridge. On one side of the main road, there was a row of buildings—a real estate office, barber shop, hardware store, and frozen yogurt place—and on the other, what looked to be an all-you-can-eat buffet that'd been closed down, as well as a small bank. The only other thing he saw before heading down the narrow back road that the navigation system directed him to was a decent-sized wooden building boasting Marla's Bar from the sign high above the rutted gravel parking lot.

Small Town, USA.

And past the main drag, a whole lot of nothing with the exception of acres and acres of farmland. And then he saw it … the ornate iron sign for Dead Heat Ranch.

Honestly, Jared hadn't known what to expect when he pulled down the long, winding road that led through the main gates, but what he saw was pretty damned impressive. The enormous main house—which looked more like a log cabin on fucking steroids—was a definite draw for tourists. Aside from that, though, it was clear the place was a fully functioning ranch with endless miles of rolling hills surrounding it. One of the biggest he'd ever seen, in fact, and that was saying something considering the spread his parents owned in El Paso.

Jared

Heading down the gravel road, Jared passed a few dogs snoozing in the shade of the big pecan trees along the way, none of them paying him any mind. He made his way to the main house, then parked in the small lot that directed visitors to the sales office. He grabbed his Stetson as he climbed out, dropping it onto his head as he headed for the door.

Before he could get the door open, an older man wearing a straw hat, navy blue button-down, and dark Wranglers was pulling it in, welcoming him with a huge grin.

"Afternoon," the man greeted as he stepped back out of the way to allow Jared to come inside. "Name's Jerry Lambert." Jared shook the man's hand when he offered it. "And you are?"

"Jared Walker. I've got an appointment with Hope."

"Sure. Sure. Lemme holler at her, see where she's at. You lookin' to book a vacation?"

"Family reunion, actually."

"If you do it right, it'll be a little of both," Jerry said, chuckling.

Jared didn't know about that, but he smiled anyway. "Possible, I guess." When Jerry reached for his phone, Jared nodded toward the door. "Thanks. Mind if I step outside and look around?"

"Not at all. Go out through that door," Jerry told him, pointing toward a door on the far side of the room. "That'll take you around back."

"Thank you, sir." Jared left Mr. Lambert inside and stepped out onto the wide wooden porch that appeared to wrap around the entire house. It was clear that the area around the house had been designed with guests in mind. There were probably ten rocking chairs along the wall, overlooking an open grassy area with a large playscape off to the right. A little farther out and to the left was a huge swimming pool, equipped with a rock ledge and slide. It was the sort of thing you'd see at a nice resort, which, technically, this was. But the rest of the scenery was the basic things you'd see at a ranch. Barns, stables, some sort of arena, fence line as far as the eye could see. Not to mention cows, goats, more cows, and several horses. There was a large garden down at the opposite end of the house, plus laughter coming from somewhere behind him.

Jared took it all in, noticing a few people—men and women—walking around. They were dressed in regular ranch attire: boots, jeans, hats, and sunglasses. He figured most of them likely worked here. He briefly wondered if one of them was Hope. He remembered her voice from their phone call, and though he had no idea what she looked like, his imagination had conjured up a few ideas. Her voice... Lord have mercy. Sexy, raspy, and that drawl... Yeah. Admittedly, Hope Lambert's voice alone was the reason Jared had decided to deal directly with her rather than have her pass him off to one of her sisters as she'd suggested. He didn't understand why he'd done it, but here he was.

The screen door squeaked as it opened behind him, and Jared turned to see Mr. Lambert standing there. "She's a little tied up, but she said she'd be glad to talk to you if you could go over to the stable." Mr. Lambert helped by pointing in the direction he was referring to.

Jared glanced out at the oversized metal building with the doors opened wide.

"Thank you, sir." He tipped his hat as he headed for the stairs that led down to the yard.

"Oh, and if you're good with a pitchfork, grab one of those while you're in there. Help her out. She'd probably appreciate it."

The smile on the older man's face was genuine, and Jared knew he was joking but not.

"I can do that, sir," he assured the man, then turned his boots in the direction of the stable.

He was greeted by a couple of men heading toward the house, neither of them stopping to talk to him. By the time he'd reached the stable, a black lab had made his acquaintance and was steadily walking beside him.

"Out for a stroll?" Jared muttered to the dog. "Don't guess you know how to use a pitchfork, huh?" He glanced down at the dog again. "Didn't figure you did."

Stepping into the shadows, he first noticed that the air was significantly cooler, though the scent of manure and hay lingered on the damp, humid air.

"Hello?" he called out, looking around for a woman.

Jared

"Over here," came that sexy voice he recalled from his phone conversation that morning.

"Where's *here*?" he asked, moving deeper inside. There was a row of stalls on the left side of the main walkway, while two additional rows of stalls stood behind the first row. On the right side, there was a large shower area—clearly used for the horses—along with a designated area where it appeared they kept feed and supplies.

"Third stall on your left," she hollered.

As he walked, Jared took in the stable. It was clean and well-stocked, open and airy. Any animals who might've inhabited it weren't there now, but that made sense if Hope was cleaning out the stalls. From the looks of it, they housed close to a dozen horses and perhaps something smaller—goats, maybe. Since he'd already seen the big red barn, he figured they used it mostly for hay, maybe some of the larger pieces of equipment.

He took a deep breath and prepared himself for seeing this woman for the first time. He reminded himself that just because her voice was sexy didn't mean she was going to be. And even if she was, it wouldn't matter, because the last thing Jared needed in his life was a woman. It would be one thing for a hook-up, but this particular woman happened to be a relative of Cheyenne's. Which meant she was off-limits.

Then again, it had been a long damn time since he'd gotten laid. Probably close to a year. It wasn't easy to do casual relationships in a small town. There was too much gossip, too many people who knew your life story. Jared preferred to keep his trysts farther from home, and since he hadn't been doing a lot of going out lately...

Jared stopped just outside the stall, peering inside from beneath the brim of his hat.

Oh, boy.

He trailed his gaze from the woman's booted feet, up her slender legs, higher, until finally, he caught a glimpse of her face.

He was pretty damn sure that moment was when the earth stopped spinning.

If there were any such things as angels, this woman was definitely one of them. Petite, blond, compact little body. Boots, jeans, hat. Yep, she was something, all right. But what transformed her from a mere mortal to the things of the heavens was her smile.

And those eyes.

Damn.

This was not good. Not good at all.

HOPE WAS TIRED and sweaty, and she wanted nothing more than to take a shower, have some dinner, then crawl into bed. Only she didn't have a bed to crawl into yet. Nor did she have a shower that was readily available.

Shit.

She had to add *moving* to her list of things she had to get done today. Unfortunately, that wouldn't be happening anytime in the near future because it was only two and she still had shit to do, including finishing with the stalls, checking on the colicky calf, taking Ambrosia—her beloved horse—out for a quick walk, then meeting up with the ranch foreman, Grant Kingsley, to discuss an issue he apparently had.

On top of that, she had to make time to talk to Jared Walker regarding his family's reunion. In person, at that. Because clearly the man hadn't listened when she'd told him she had too much to do. His impatience must've brought him out, rather than waiting for her to call him back. Which she would've done. Eventually.

Okay, truth was, she probably would've passed him off to Faith. She *should* have passed him off already, allowing her sister to take this one so Hope could handle all the chores she already had. That's the way she usually dealt with referrals, but for some crazy reason, she hadn't. Unfortunately, she'd been taken aback by a sexy voice and found herself now waiting for the man to make his way over so she could take one look at him and be disappointed that she hadn't handed him off to Faith.

Jared

When he stepped into view, the last thing on her mind was disappointment.

Son of a biscuit eater.

Damn good thing the guy was nice to look at, because the nicely put together package that was Jared Walker took the initial sting off of what she'd planned to say to him.

"Hey," she greeted, leaning the pitchfork against the railing and pulling off her glove before reaching out to shake his hand. "Hope Lambert."

"Nice to meet you, Hope," Jared said, his lazy drawl thick, his voice low. She noticed the warmth of his big hand as it enveloped hers. Completely. As in, her entire hand disappeared inside his.

"Yeah. You, too." Hope glanced around, trying her best to remember she was a thirty-three-year-old woman and not a hormonal teenage girl. "I thought we were gonna do this on the phone." She made a show of glancing around. "As you can see, I'm right in the middle of somethin'."

And she would be for several more hours.

Jared cocked an eyebrow. "Figured it wouldn't hurt to check things out."

She was fairly certain she'd pegged his impatience accurately, but she didn't say as much. "Well, sorry to make you come all the way out here, but I've got one left after this one, and if I stop now, I won't get everything done before sundown. How 'bout I call one of my sisters, have 'em meet you at the house?"

"Not necessary," he said, his eyes locked on her face, and she couldn't seem to look away. "Point me in the direction of a fork and I'll help out."

A fork... Wait. What?

Jared cocked a sexy, dark eyebrow, then nodded toward the pitchfork.

Oh. "No, you don't have to do that," she said quickly, a little taken aback by his offer.

"I don't mind helpin' out a lady." The smirk he shot her way made Hope instantly think of hot, smoldering sex. Clearly her inactive sex life was beginning to affect her brain. "Not to mention, the guy in the office kinda asked me to."

"My father," Hope said, rolling her eyes. "Of course he did." She nodded toward the wall behind him. "Pitchfork's over there."

When he turned, her gaze dropped to his ass, and she damn near swallowed her tongue.

Now, she'd seen plenty of cowboys sporting Wrangler jeans, but never in her life had she seen a man wearing them like Jared did. He was tall and lean, with broad shoulders, a wide back, thick chest, narrow waist. Very impressive, certainly. But his ass... *That* was a masterpiece.

Hope's eyes snapped upward when Jared cleared his throat, that seductive smirk still tugging at the corners of his mouth. That was when she realized he'd turned back around. He'd busted her, plain as day, and clearly he found that amusing.

Good for him.

Nodding toward the stall, she forced a smile. "So, how many people do you expect at this reunion?"

His smile disappeared quickly, and an expression that looked a lot like confusion took its place.

"Don't know," he said, moving out of her line of sight.

After pulling her glove back on her hand, Hope grabbed her pitchfork and got back to work. "When do you want to do this?"

"Don't know," he hollered back.

"How long do you plan for the event to run?" she called out, trying to focus on the task at hand.

"Don't know."

That last one made her smile.

"What *do* you know, Mr. Walker?"

"Jared," he said, reappearing in the entrance to the stall. "There are more than enough Mr. Walkers in my family. Just call me Jared."

Hope lifted an eyebrow.

"Please," he said, that smirk returning.

"Okay, *Jared*." Hope leaned on the pitchfork. "What information do you have that'll be useful in setting this up?"

"Don't know." He smiled widely. "That's what I came here to find out."

Jared

Hope glanced toward the open barn doors. "Okay, tell you what. You help me get that stall cleaned out, and I'll take you on a tour. But that'll only buy me roughly fifteen minutes. If that doesn't work for you, then I can call my father, have him put together the information, and let my sister show you around."

The sexy cowboy tilted his head. "I'll be right over there, then."

Hope tried to hide her smile. She had no intentions of being played by this man. Sexy cowboys were definitely on her not-to-do list. At the very top, in fact. She lived and worked with them day and night, knew exactly what it meant when one set his sights on her. And it never ended in happy ever after.

And she might not know much about Jared Walker, but he definitely qualified as a sexy cowboy.

Which meant he was off-limits.

Completely.

CHAPTER FOUR

JARED MADE QUICK work of mucking out the stall, doing his best not to be affected by the soft sighs and slight grunts coming from Hope, who was working a few feet to his left. Admittedly, it'd been a while since he'd put in this type of manual labor, but the truth was, he missed it. Not since he'd left El Paso two years ago, having worked on his parent's cattle farm, had he felt like this. After he'd been fired from his job managing an equipment rental place—as a way to get additional experience while he was trying to figure out what he wanted to do—Jared had gone back to work for his father while he waited for the divorce to be final. Until his uncle called, letting him know they needed him to come to Coyote Ridge and take over running his sons' demolition business. He knew that Curtis had made the offer because Jared's father had called him, but the opportunity to get away for a while had been too good to pass up.

And when he'd finally gotten his son back, Jared had opted to stay because, one, he enjoyed it, and two, it allowed him to get Derrick far away from Sable's clutches.

It wasn't that his job at Walker Demolition was easy, but it definitely didn't require quite so many back muscles. Just being here brought back a million memories. He had loved the farm, sometimes thought about going back even. If it weren't for the fact that Sable would be all over him if he did, that was. Because of that, Jared had forced himself to stay away. Truth was, if he had to choose a profession, it would be to do *this* every day. Unfortunately, that just wasn't in his cards. At least for now.

Jared

He managed to block everything from his mind for a little while, focusing solely on the job. Before he knew it, he was finished. Propping his foot on the pitchfork, he pulled his hat from his head and wiped his brow with the sleeve of his T-shirt.

"Well, Jared Walker, looks like you do good work," Hope said, that raspy voice drawing his attention toward her.

She had lost the gloves and the pitchfork and was now standing in the doorway to the stall—all five foot nothing of her— her turquoise gaze lazily perusing the ground, probably making sure he really had done a good job.

"I've got some practice," he told her.

"Yeah? You worked on a ranch before?"

Jared found he liked looking at her. She wasn't what he'd expected. The husky tone didn't quite match the petite little thing standing before him. Hope Lambert looked sweet, almost innocent. But the way she carried herself told him she was no pushover. She was used to hard work and manual labor. If he was right, she probably spent most of her time bossing around a bunch of cowboys to boot.

"Yes, ma'am," he confirmed, never looking away from her.

There was a slight blush on her cheeks that intrigued him.

When he'd been flirting with her earlier—something he hadn't intended—he'd seen something in her pretty blue-green eyes. Something that told him to back off. Whether she'd intentionally sent him a warning or if it was involuntary, he didn't yet know. But he was hoping to find out.

After returning the pitchfork to its original spot, Jared trailed her toward a large basin sink, following her lead and washing his hands, then splashing water on his face. She passed him some paper towels.

"So, how about that tour?" he suggested.

Hope peered up at him, a smile in place. She really was beautiful in a soft, rugged sort of way. She wasn't wearing any makeup, but she didn't need any, either. He also noticed that she wasn't wearing any jewelry at all. Her hair was tucked beneath a straw cowboy hat, blond strands peeking out from underneath, curling over her shoulders, cheeks pink from hard work and the heat, but Jared was captivated by her eyes. Not only the unusual sparkling color but what he saw in them. That same warning he'd seen earlier was reflected there. He wasn't quite sure what it was all about, but he had an uncanny need to figure it out.

"Come on," she said, her eyes still locked on his face for another second before she canted her head toward the door. "Your fifteen minutes starts now. Let's go."

Jared fell into step with Hope, slowing his longer stride to match her shorter one.

"So, who is Cheyenne to you?" she asked, glancing up at him as they walked.

"She's my cousin's ... uh ... fiancée."

"So, Brendon's your cousin?"

"One of 'em, sure."

Hope grinned. "And you live close to them?"

"Moved to Coyote Ridge a couple years ago to take a job." It wasn't a complete lie. He had moved there for the job at Walker Demo. He just wasn't going to tell Hope that he'd been running from his old life, too.

"Where're you originally from?"

"El Paso," he told her. "Born and raised. I take it you've grown up here all your life?"

"Yes, sir. Born and raised right here on this very ranch." Hope's smile was radiant.

"Born, huh?"

She nodded. "Daddy spread out the hay in the barn..."

Jared could see the mischievous smirk. "Liar."

"I *was* born here, though," she said, chuckling. "In the house, not the barn. Momma had a midwife and everything."

"Well, you've got one up on me." Jared grinned down at her. "I was born in a hospital."

"Nobody's perfect." Her smile widened. "You have any brothers or sisters?"

"Four brothers, one sister."

Hope's eyes widened. "I thought *I* had a big family."

"Well, at last count, I had somewhere around thirty first cousins on my dad's side alone, if that tells you anything. Add in all their significant others, the kids…"

"Okay, so you definitely win," Hope said, chuckling.

"Cheyenne mentioned you had sisters."

"Four of them."

"You're the oldest?" he probed.

She continued to smile as they walked. "I am," she confirmed. "Then there's Grace, Trinity, Mercy, and Faith."

Interesting choice in names, Jared noted.

"And you?" Hope asked. "Oldest?"

"Yes, ma'am. Then there's the twins, Kaden and Keegan, Quinn's next, then my sister, Eve, and the youngest, Wesley."

"Twins, huh?"

"Yes, ma'am. They run in the family."

"So, I take it this family reunion could be rather large?"

"Could be," he answered. "Depends on who can make it, I guess."

"When were you lookin' to do this?" she inquired as they stepped inside an outdoor arena. "Summer months are obviously the best, unless you have an aversion to the heat. Fall in Texas… Well, you know. Some years we have a fall, others we hop right to winter. I don't suggest you get too far into the colder months. Being cooped up inside all the time can wear on the little ones."

"And the big ones," he added.

Her chuckle said she understood exactly what he meant. "True."

"Travis seems to think a month is good for plannin'," he said, watching her closely. "So I'd say October sometime."

"It's doable, I guess. A little rushed, maybe. Trail rides are good then, and so are hay rides. Provided the weather's nice, great time to spend outdoors. All depends on what we've got booked and what you're wantin' to do."

"Well ... that depends on what you're offerin'?" As soon as the words were out of his mouth, Jared realized how they might've sounded, or more accurately, what he found himself hoping for. What was worse, he didn't feel the need to take them back, because although he'd been in Hope's presence for a very short time, Jared realized that his no-woman rule was beginning to fade from the mental paper he'd jotted it on.

He watched her, noticing the way she studied his face briefly. For half a second, he thought she might play along.

She didn't.

"Well, it's a fully functioning ranch, Mr. Walker." Her eyes cooled significantly. "We've got plenty of activities the whole family can enjoy. Horseback riding, archery, swimming—although that's probably out in October. If they're interested, we can even put 'em to work while they're here."

The fact that she called him Mr. Walker made him smile. "I imagine you do," he countered, still maintaining eye contact. "And I've got a few cousins I'd like to put to work." Namely Travis and Kaleb.

Her soft laugh hit him square in the chest. There was something about this woman ... something that made him want to yank her into his arms, slam his mouth over hers and... Yeah.

And.

All the stuff Jared wasn't looking for in a woman. He didn't give a damn how pretty she was or how sweet her voice was or how fucking awesome her ass looked in those damn jeans.

He forced his gaze away to check out the arena. When he looked back, he managed to rein in his thoughts, nodding his head, signaling her that he was ready to see what else there was to see.

And he wasn't referring to her ... naked.

No, definitely not that.

Jared

HOPE DID HER damnedest to keep from glancing over at the sexy cowboy walking alongside her. She found he was easy to talk to, far more laid-back than many of their guests. He seemed to know his way around a ranch, which was a good thing. Oftentimes she had to explain to the guests what they did here at DHR, what their guests were allowed to do, and what they weren't, but with Jared, he seemed to get it.

After showing him the bunkhouses—one of which was available to guests and could hold almost twenty comfortably—and one of the thirty cabins—ranging from single room to three bedrooms—they now had available, she led him back to the main house. She'd gone over her allotted fifteen minutes, and she was trying her best not to show her irritation. When there wasn't enough time in the day as it was, Hope hated dealing with interruptions. It frustrated her to no end.

"What do you think?" she asked when they stepped up onto the porch. Budweiser, one of the Labrador retrievers, joined them, sniffing Jared's legs and boots before he earned a head scratch from the big man.

"I think it'll work." Jared squatted to pet Budweiser, then looked up at her. "I don't know anything about the length of time, how many people…"

He left the sentence hanging and she couldn't help but grin. "No worries. We can get it all nailed down. I'll have my dad get you the information you need. You can take it with you and call back when you have an idea."

Jared stood, causing her to look up at him once again, and she couldn't help but admire the straight line of his nose, his thick, dark eyebrows.

The corded muscles in his neck.

And the seductive curve of his lips.

Good gravy.

Unfortunately, she couldn't see his eyes since he'd put those mirrored sunglasses on.

Pulling herself back from the brink of insanity, Hope took a deep breath. Before she could invite Jared into the main office to get him the information he needed, Grant Kingsley and Lane Miller joined them on the porch.

"Hey," Grant greeted. "When you get a minute…"

"Sure," she said, nodding to Jared. "Jared Walker, I'd like you to meet our ranch foreman, Grant Kingsley. And this is our head wrangler, Lane Miller."

"Nice to meet you," Jared greeted, shaking both men's hands.

"Same," Lane said.

"Give me just a sec?" Hope asked Grant. "I need to pass him off to my dad."

Grant nodded in the direction of the barn. "I just saw him go that way."

Shit.

Turning back to Jared, she nodded toward the office, tried to keep her tone polite. "Come on. I'll get you set up with information. You can take it with you, then call back when you have an idea of what you need."

As they were stepping inside the office, Jared's cell phone rang. He looked to her, as though asking permission to take the call, and that warmed her for some strange reason. It was a gentlemanly thing to do, something she didn't see often these days. Not from the city boys who came to the ranch anyway. Then again, Jared Walker certainly wasn't a city boy.

Hope nodded her head, then went around to the file cabinet where they kept the brochures.

"Walker," he said into the phone. "Yeah. He okay?"

There was a brief pause that followed his concerned tone, and Hope couldn't resist looking up at Jared.

"Sure. I'll have someone come right over and pick him up." *Pause.* "Yeah. Thanks."

Hope met Jared's gaze when he hung up the phone. "Everything okay?"

Jared nodded. "Yeah. My son fell and bumped his head at day care. Nothin' major, but he's askin' for me."

Fucking fantastic. Here she'd been ogling a married man. Sounded about right.

"Do you need to call your wife?" Hope asked, trying to hide the fact that her gaze instantly dropped to his left hand to see if he was wearing a ring.

Jared

"Divorced," he replied. "But I do need to call my aunt, see if she'll swing by there and pick him up."

Hope offered another nod, then turned her attention to putting the packet of information together while he made the phone call. Her heart fell straight to her toes, and she didn't even have to guess why that was. Ever since she'd allowed herself to get captivated by Ben Ruhl, a man who'd come to the ranch as a guest a while back, and his daughter, Maddie, she'd been wary of men with children. *Single* men with children, that was. Even considering dating Ben had gone against her own self-imposed rules. Still, she'd ignored all the warnings and jumped in with both feet.

She'd liked Ben. They'd managed to spend quite a bit of time together when he and his daughter had come to visit the ranch a couple of years back. But Ben wasn't the only one she'd gotten caught up in, and that was her own fault.

At thirty-three, it wasn't like her biological clock was headed for the alarm setting, but it was beginning to tick louder than usual, and at one point, Hope had found herself quite enthralled by Ben's daughter. The thought of having a family of her own... It had appealed to her on so many levels. Unfortunately, Hope knew that having her own children wasn't a possibility, but she hadn't given up on becoming a mother.

So, when they'd broken up—if they could even consider the long-distant, brief interaction they'd had dating in the first place—Hope had made *another* promise to herself not to get involved with men who had children. This time, she swore she would hold true to that promise. No matter what. Getting through a breakup was hard enough. When she got attached to the kid ... even worse.

Once Jared finished the call, she stood up straight and held out the papers for him.

"I don't want to keep you. This is all the information on the ranch, plus some of the things we'll need to know in order to help you get the reunion set up. Once you know what you're lookin' for, give me a call. If you're lookin' to do this soon, we'll need to know, because fall is still a relatively busy time for us."

Jared retrieved the packet, his gaze never leaving her face. If she wasn't mistaken, she thought she saw the hint of awareness in those mesmerizing blue-gray eyes. Somehow, she managed to yank her gaze from his, thrusting her hands into her pockets to keep from fidgeting.

"Thanks for showin' me around," he said. "It might take me a few days to get the information, but I'll be callin' when I have the details."

"Perfect," she said, nearly tripping when she made a beeline for the door to show him out. "I look forward to hearin' from you. I mean … you know … *we* will be looking forward to it. The ranch."

Okay, so she hoped like hell he hadn't noticed the odd desperation she sensed in her own tone. She wasn't desperate. Not by a long shot. When she glanced up into his eyes, she saw something that resembled heat flaring in his gaze, and it took more willpower than she thought she had to look away this time.

"Thanks again." Jared nodded his head and pointed at her with the packet of papers.

"My pleasure."

No, no, no. That was not what she should've said. Jeezus, she needed to learn to shut her mouth. She should've said, "You're welcome." *How freaking hard would that've been?*

Too late now. Hope took a step back, allowing Jared to walk out the door, and once he'd cleared the doorframe, she quickly closed it and leaned against the wood, shaking her head in disbelief.

She had things to do, and they certainly didn't involve thinking about a sexy, Stetson-wearing, Wrangler-rocking cowboy who had heartbreak written all over his incredibly handsome face.

CHAPTER FIVE

AFTER JARED HAD left the ranch, he'd headed straight for Curtis and Lorrie's to pick up Derrick. Much to his dismay, his little boy had asked to stay there. Of course, it had taken Jared a little more than a few minutes to convince himself that was a good thing.

"Are you sure you're okay, big man?" Jared asked Derrick.

"Of course, Dad." Derrick pushed the dump truck he'd been playing with right over the toe of Jared's boots.

"Does your head hurt?"

"Nope."

"Are you sure?"

Derrick looked up at him funny. Probably wondering why good ol' dad couldn't just let it go.

Lorrie had quickly assured Jared that the bump really was nothing, but she would certainly keep an eye on it. She'd been more than willing to keep him overnight, along with Mason—Kaleb and Zoey's oldest. That change of plans had allowed Jared a few extra hours to himself, so he decided to wander over to Moonshiners to see what was going on.

As usual, the place was relatively busy on a Friday night. Some of his cousins had shown up—including Brendon, Braydon, and Ethan—along with their significant others. Once he'd received his customary beer from Mack the bartender, Jared headed back toward the pool tables and settled in an empty chair off to the side.

"Hey," Braydon greeted. "What's up, man?"

"Not a helluva lot," Jared told him, taking a long pull on his beer and watching as two guys finished up a game.

"Rumor is you headed over to Embers Ridge today. You check out that ranch?"

Jared glanced over at Cheyenne to see her smiling back at him. He lifted an eyebrow, acknowledging that he knew she'd shared the information, though he wasn't quite sure who she'd heard it from. Last he'd talked to her, he had merely inquired, not committed to going.

"Thought you were goin' out on tour?" he countered.

Her sweet smile told him he hadn't been successful at changing the subject. "Not until Monday. So? You check out the ranch or not?"

"Yep," Jared confirmed, knowing the woman wouldn't stop until he finally gave in. "Got some information."

"That place work for a reunion?"

"Probably," he admitted. Truth was, he still didn't have a fucking clue how to go about setting up a family reunion. He knew he first needed to determine a good time—for both the ranch and for his family—and then he could probably go from there. They would need to know how long they'd be there, how many guests for accommodations, etc. A dozen questions he had no idea how to answer.

Hell, he didn't even know where to start.

"So what goes into plannin' one of these?" Brendon asked.

Jared shrugged. "Not the slightest idea."

"Did you get information from Hope?" Cheyenne questioned.

Jared nodded and took a swig of his beer. "Whole packet of shit."

"Did you look at it?"

He shook his head. Truth was, Jared wasn't much of a reader. He had glanced through the material briefly, a little overwhelmed by what he'd seen inside. There were a million things they could do on the ranch for a week. Trail riding, archery, skeet shooting, zip-lining, campfires, barn games. Those were all briefly mentioned in the first paragraph of the brochure.

It would've been a hell of a lot easier if Travis wanted a fucking picnic.

Jared

Suddenly, a round of greetings sounded from the rest of the patrons, and Jared looked up in time to see the man himself walking into the bar. Beside Travis was his husband, Gage, and their wife, Kylie.

"Now that he's here, maybe we can ask him," Cheyenne said softly.

Yeah. Great. Just what he needed, to let Travis know that he was incompetent and couldn't put together a freaking family reunion without help.

Nope. No way. There was no way in hell he'd set himself up for a lifetime of harassment like that. The Walker clan loved to talk shit, and Jared had no intention of giving them any additional fodder to work with.

"Nah," Jared finally said. "I've got it covered. I'm workin' it out with Hope."

That was a whopper of a lie, but one he could probably fix. The ranch was Hope's world. If Jared needed help figuring out how to make a reunion work, surely she would have some ideas.

It wasn't because he was looking for a reason to call her.

A big hand clapped him on the back, and Jared looked up to see Travis standing beside him.

"How's it goin'?"

Jared gave a brief chin nod, then took a swig of his beer.

"Heard Derrick had an accident today," Travis mentioned.

"Yep. Nothin' major. Little bump on the noggin. Aunt Lorrie's got it covered."

"Heard that, too."

"Where're Kate and Kade?" Jared asked, referring to Travis's little ones.

"Kylie's dad and stepmom agreed to watch 'em for a bit. Kylie was desperate to get out of the house for a while. Adult conversation and all that."

"Not much adulting goin' on at your place, huh?" Jared joked.

"Funny," Travis grumbled, fighting a smile.

Travis took a seat next to Jared, only the two of them at the table. When Jared made eye contact, he saw what looked a lot like concern in his cousin's eyes. Knowing he had a snowball's chance in hell of guessing what was bothering his cousin, Jared opted not to say anything, waiting for Travis to clear his mind.

What came out of Travis's mouth next was not at all what he expected to hear.

"Since you haven't said anything, I'm beginnin' to think you don't know. Which is the only reason I'm bringin' it up."

Jared frowned, waiting.

"Sable's lookin' for you."

That got Jared's attention, and he sat up straight, his beer all but forgotten. "What do you mean?"

"When you were gone this afternoon, Jaxson got a call from some irate chick who was lookin' for you. Said it was imperative that she speak to you right away. He knew who it was but wasn't sure how to handle it."

"Why didn't he contact me?" That seemed like the logical thing to do.

Travis ignored his question but continued, "Jaxson called me."

"What did she want?"

"Jaxson doesn't know for sure. He got her number and told her you'd call her back. I told him to let me talk to you first."

Fuck.

The last damn thing Jared needed was his fucking ex-wife hunting him down. He'd moved on long ago, and he and Derrick were doing great without her. It'd been almost two years now, and he damn sure didn't need her poking her face back in his business.

It had been difficult enough when he'd learned that she didn't want to be a mom and had easily handed the little boy over to him. Well, maybe not easily, but in exchange for twenty-five thousand dollars, the bitch had been more than willing to let Jared play daddy—her words.

Jared

In order to protect Derrick, and Jared, his lawyer had the presence of mind to insist that Sable give up her parental rights, allowing Jared to have sole custody of the little boy. Although Derrick wasn't biologically his, based on the DNA test Sable had had done, that didn't change the fact that Jared was Derrick's father. According to Sable, Derrick belonged to a guy she'd been sleeping with. A guy she'd left Jared for.

Sable finally admitted she didn't have a clue who Derrick's biological father was. The woman wasn't known for keeping her legs closed, married or not.

Not that any of that mattered to Jared. Derrick was his little boy. He was the reason the sun rose and set each day. And Jared damn sure wasn't going to allow Sable to come back in and fuck shit up. If she wanted to be a mother, she should've thought about that a long damn time ago.

"Fuck," Jared muttered.

"I thought you should know. I've got eyes and ears out. If she shows up in town, I'll know."

Jared didn't know whether that would happen or not. It all depended on what Sable wanted. If he had to guess, she was in between men and feeling sorry for herself. That was usually the only time he heard from her. Or, of course, when she needed more money.

"In the meantime, I've got Mom and Dad payin' close attention. They'll make sure you know anything they know."

"Yeah, thanks." Jared's head was still spinning with all the information.

"So…" Travis began, taking a sip of his beer, then setting it back on the table between them. "How's it goin' with the family reunion?"

At the moment, Jared wasn't sure which of those topics he didn't want to talk about more.

"A FAMILY REUNION? Thirty first cousins? Are these people married? Do they have kids?" Mercy's voice had risen into the dog-whistle range.

Hope stared at her sister. "I'm sure they won't *all* be here."

"But what if they are?" Mercy countered, looking a little panicked. "I mean, if they've got families of their own... Multiply that by three, on average... I don't know if we've got room for that many people. How will we feed them all?"

"We've got room," Hope assured her. "And we'll have plenty of food on hand. Plus, it'll be good for business."

"How long'll they be here?" Mercy inquired.

Hope shrugged. "I'd guess a week." She didn't know for sure, but if there were that many family members, it only made sense.

"If we even have a week we can squeeze them in," Faith noted. "I assume we're talkin' around a hundred people or more. That'll fill up most of our cabins and all of the main house."

"It'll be tight," Hope added, "but it's not impossible."

Hope had come to the recreation center to check in with her sisters after she'd showered and grabbed a bite to eat. Gracie and Faith had somehow worked their magic and had a lot of Hope's clothes transferred to the main house in one of the guest rooms that offered a little privacy. It actually wasn't too bad, but Hope fully intended to get moved into another one of the cabins as soon as she possibly could. Unfortunately, the ones she had to choose from were all currently occupied, or reserved, so she would have to wait.

Since her schedule had been opened wide thanks to her sisters' good deeds, Hope had decided to seek out Grace and Faith to thank them. Unfortunately, she hadn't found Grace, but she had run into Mercy and Faith. How they'd gotten on the topic of Jared Walker, she wasn't quite sure, but now she couldn't seem to change the subject no matter how hard she'd tried.

And she had certainly tried.

Shit, for the past few hours, Hope had done her level best not to think about the brooding cowboy with his devilish smirk and bedroom eyes. The same cowboy who had a little boy.

55

Jared

Yep, that quickly put a damper on her libido. The thought of spending time with another kid only to have that kid ripped out of her life… Hope wasn't interested, thank you very much.

"Has he called you yet?" Mercy inquired, reaching for her beer and tilting the bottle to her lips.

"No." Hope reached for her own beer. "And I don't expect him to. At least not for a few days. I gave him the information packet, so I'm sure he'll have to talk to his family. And he's not gonna call me. He'll call the ranch office," she added, glancing over at Faith. "I figure you can help him with anything he needs."

"Or he'll call and say they want to book the first week of October," Mercy grumbled. "We need more time than that to get things ready."

"And we won't refuse his business," Faith answered with a little impatience in her tone. "If we can accommodate a hundred people, we'll make it happen. If not, we'll suggest a different date. However"—her eyes locked on Hope's face—"I don't have time to handle that right now. I'm tryin' to handle the insurance claim on the cabin."

"I'm sure he won't call right away," she countered. Hope wasn't going to be placing any bets on Jared calling to set up that quickly. Although impatient, he didn't seem like the type of guy to make decisions without knowing all the details. If she had to guess, he would be working through the logistics before he called back.

Or he wouldn't. She would have to wait and see.

Hope took a sip of her beer. "You seen Gracie?"

Faith nodded, then smiled. "She was headin' out to the barn when I saw her about half an hour ago."

The barn? What would Gracie be doing—

"With Grant and Lane," Faith added helpfully.

Hope shook her head. Of course her sister would be going to the barn with her men. Which meant no one else should be going out to the barn. No reason they should be subjected to … that. Hell, Hope remembered the day she'd accidentally rolled up on the three of them at Grace's cabin. Needless to say, Hope had made a point to schedule her visits since that day.

The thought made her laugh.

"So, tell me about Jared Walker," Faith prodded.

"Nothin' to tell."

"And that right there means there's a lot to tell," Mercy quipped. "Is he hot? I've seen Cheyenne's fiancé and ... holy hell. Did you know he's got an identical twin? I mean, God was in a great mood that day."

"Whatever." Hope knew her sisters were teasing her. They always did. Good grief, when she'd been seeing Ben for that brief period of time, they'd given her endless shit about it. And Ben was a tried-and-true city boy. They'd had very little in common, but that didn't stop them from talking for hours.

"I heard he has a killer ass," Faith stated.

Hope felt her cheeks heat; the memory of getting caught staring at that killer ass beat against her brain. Yep, killer was a nice way to sum it up.

Mercy chuckled. "Cheyenne said he's single."

"And that means what to me?" Hope didn't care if he was single, although she already knew he was thanks to her awkward questioning earlier. The guy probably thought she was sitting around lusting after him.

She wasn't.

"Woman, your face is going to burst into flame at any moment," Faith said with a giggle.

Hope was surprised it hadn't already.

How the hell had she gotten to this point? Her day had started out simply enough, then Jared Walker had walked onto the ranch and...

And what?

He'd sparked the dry kindling of her libido?

Okay, maybe a little.

But she had a surefire way of putting that out. It required half an hour with her battery-operated boyfriend, and she'd be good for another year or two.

"She's smitten," Faith whispered.

"*She* is *not* smitten," Hope denied.

"Oh, you definitely are," Mercy insisted. "And to think, if all goes well, this cowboy's gonna be spendin' a week right here on this ranch. What're you gonna do then?"

Jared

That was a question Hope had already asked herself. More than once.

And she still didn't have a damn answer.

Not one that made sense anyway.

CHAPTER SIX

"I WANNA HELP!"

Jared grinned at Derrick, watching as his son picked up a screwdriver Jared had set on the ground near all the other tools he knew he needed.

"Yeah?"

Derrick nodded. "Yep. I can put the screw in."

"Come on, big man, let's do this," Jared said, swooping Derrick up in his arms and carrying him over to the two-by-fours he'd managed to connect.

He dug an extra screw from his pocket, then plopped down into the grass with Derrick in his lap.

"Wet's do this!" Derrick squealed.

Holding the sharp end of the screw against the wood, Jared sat patiently while Derrick stabbed the other end (along with Jared's hand) numerous times as he attempted to complete his task. Since this particular screw didn't matter, Jared didn't worry about how well Derrick did, just that he enjoyed doing it.

With a little help from Jared, Derrick managed to get the screw into the wood—or the tip of it anyway—which was all he seemed to care about. When he saw that the little silver piece was standing on its own, Derrick hopped out of Jared's lap, dropped the screwdriver, and started dancing around.

"Did it! I did it!"

"You definitely did, big man. Now what d'ya say we grab some lunch?"

"SkeddieOs! SkeddieOs!"

"SpaghettiOs, huh?"

Jared

Derrick nodded, grabbing Jared's hand as he tugged him toward the house.

With more patience than he ever thought he would have, Jared got Derrick settled at the table, pulled a can of SpaghettiOs out of the cabinet, and got to work heating them up.

"Dad, can Mason come over?"

Jared peered at Derrick over his shoulder. "I'll have to call his dad to see," he explained.

"Where's your phone? I wiw get it!"

And off Derrick went to find Jared's cell phone. He definitely didn't mind the idea of Mason coming over, especially if that meant Kaleb would join him. Jared wouldn't deny needing help to get the swing set put together. At this rate, if he had to do it by himself, Derrick's little butt wouldn't see a swing until he was five.

"Here ya go, Dad! Your cew phone."

Jared took his phone and set it on the counter while he pulled the food from the microwave, stirred it, then set the bowl down, urging his son back up to the table.

"Miwk, pwease," Derrick called out as soon as Jared got back to the counter.

Without hesitating, he grabbed a cup, filled it with milk, then delivered it back to the table.

"Thanks, Dad!"

"You're welcome, big man."

It was a little awkward to hear Derrick call him Dad considering he'd been calling him Daddy for so long. Apparently, another kid at Derrick's day care called his father Dad, and Derrick had taken to doing the same thing.

"Caw Mason!"

"What d'ya say?" Jared replied.

"Pwease!"

Grabbing his phone, he pulled up Kaleb's number and hit the call button.

"If you're askin' for me to bring this crazy, rotten kid over, I'll be there in about ten minutes."

Jared laughed at Kaleb's greeting. "He drivin' you nuts?"

"Good grief," Kaleb said on a sharp exhale. "The boy won't sit still."

"Well, if you're up for it, I could use some extra hands to help with the swing set."

"That works perfect. Zoey took Kellan over to V's, so it's just me and Mason. Lemme get some shorts on the kid and we'll be right over."

"See ya in a few."

"Is he comin'?" Derrick hollered as soon as Jared put the phone down.

"He's comin'," he assured his son.

"Yay!" Derrick fist pumped the air. "Wiw you have the swing set finished? We wanna swing."

"It'll be a while, but I'll get it done." Jared leaned over, putting his elbows on the counter while he watched Derrick shovel SpaghettiOs into his mouth—the Os usually made it, but the rest was dribbling down Derrick's chin.

Derrick turned serious eyes on Jared. "Well," he said, struggling to get his tongue around the L sound, "if you need help, Dad, just wemme know. I'm the big man now, so I can get it done."

Jared chuckled, his heart swelling at least three sizes as he stared at the greatest gift he'd ever received. "I'll remember that."

Four hours later, with the boys safely watching *Paw Patrol* in the living room, Jared hooked the last swing.

"You think it'll hold?" Kaleb asked, a smirk hidden behind the lip of his beer bottle.

"Since you were the one doin' most of the work, I'm kinda leery about it, too," Jared deadpanned.

"Well, why don't you sit your happy ass down there and test it out?" Kaleb taunted, still grinning.

Jared pretended to think about it but then turned and headed to the back door. He stuck his face up to the screen and whistled.

Within a second, two munchkins came barreling toward him, barely giving him enough time to pull the screen open.

"Is it done? Is it done? Can we swing?" Derrick hollered.

"Can we swing?" Mason echoed, mimicking Derrick.

Jared

"Y'all can swing," Jared confirmed.

Kaleb set his beer on the platform by the slide, then helped Mason and then Derrick into the swings. Jared chuckled when Mason began violently kicking his legs in an attempt to make it move with no luck.

With beer in hand, Jared moved around behind the boys while Kaleb did the same. They proceeded to pull the swings back, then gave them a gentle nudge forward. Mason and Derrick squealed with excitement.

"So, you get any more details on this ranch idea for the reunion?"

Jared took a swig of his beer, gave Derrick another push, and glanced over at his cousin. "I checked it out yesterday. Nice place."

"Cheyenne was tellin' Zoey about it a while back. She also happened to mention she had five cousins."

Jared heard the amusement in Kaleb's tone.

"*Female* cousins," Kaleb added.

"Yep, that's what they say." Jared feigned disinterest. Truth was, he'd spent far too much time already thinking about one of Cheyenne's female cousins ever since he laid eyes on her yesterday.

Hope Lambert was a woman that no red-blooded man would forget after meeting her.

"I know that look."

Jared snapped his eyes over to Kaleb. "What look?"

"*That* look." Kaleb pointed with his beer bottle.

"Man, I don't know what you're talkin' about."

"You forget I've got six brothers. Every last one of 'em fell in love *after* I did. I watched it happen." Kaleb was grinning from ear to ear. "I know the first signs when I see 'em."

Jared snorted. "You're outta your mind."

Derrick snorted, copying Jared. "Yeah! You're outta your mind!"

Mason followed suit. "Outta mind!"

Kaleb shook his head because he knew as well as Jared that they'd be listening to that for hours to come. But the grin never left his face.

Jared could've told him there was no way in hell he would ever fall in love with a woman again. He'd been burned too badly. Not interested.

He didn't give a good goddamn how fucking hot Hope Lambert was. Falling in love with a woman wasn't in his life plan.

HOPE MADE HER way to the dining room for dinner. She'd managed to sneak in a shower, pull on a pair of shorts and a T-shirt, pile her wet hair up on her head, and decided she was done for the day. Sure, she'd gotten her chores completed, but when she said done, she meant done. Anything else that came up tonight was going to be Grant's problem.

"There's still some left," Jennifer called from the kitchen. "But you better hurry."

Hope mussed Joey's hair as she passed the little boy on her way to get the leftovers. "What's up, shorty?"

"Hi, Hope," he said, never taking his attention off the macaroni and cheese on his plate.

Stepping into the kitchen, Hope inhaled the incredible smell.

"Chicken-fried chicken and cream gravy. Probably some mashed potatoes left, too."

"You know, Jen, I think you're spoilin' these boys. You surprise them with this all the time, and they'll start refusin' to eat the bird food."

Jennifer laughed. "It's not bird food."

"Coulda fooled me."

"Well, if you wanna know the truth, I only keep making it 'cause you're lookin' a little skinny."

Jared

Instinctively, Hope glanced down at her body. Her clothes were a little big, but not too bad. She'd probably lost three, maybe five pounds recently. Far more than she should have, but no matter how hard she tried, she couldn't seem to keep the weight on. Some people didn't understand how that could be a problem, but Hope felt it when she lost too much weight. She never felt good; she was always tired. It was a vicious cycle she seemed to be caught up in.

"Oh, and I saw that handsome cowboy you were chattin' with yesterday."

Hope shook her head as she spooned potatoes onto her plate. "He's lookin' to host a family reunion here on the ranch."

"Mm-hmm. I saw the way he was checkin' you out."

Swinging around to face her friend, Hope snorted a laugh. Very unladylike, but she couldn't help herself. "He was not."

"Oh, he most definitely was," Jennifer told her, extremely serious.

"Whatever." Hope grabbed a fork and took a bite. She was too hungry to wait until she sat down.

"So, who is he?"

"Jared Walker. My cousin Cheyenne's engaged to his cousin Brendon."

"Sounds to me like maybe good ol' Chey sent Jared your way for a reason."

Hope hadn't thought of that, but she seriously doubted it. Then again, Jared did seem completely beside himself when it came to getting this reunion nailed down.

Not that any of it mattered. She needed to get her mind off the man, and Jennifer certainly wasn't helping matters. Which was why Hope decided to change the subject.

"What about you?" Hope pointed with her fork. "I saw you and Zach talking the other night."

Zach McCallum was the ranch's on-hand medic. From what Hope could tell, the man did not try to hide the fact that he had a crush on the sweet chef.

As she expected, Jennifer blushed but quickly turned away. "We're friends."

Right. Friends. Because friends made you blush like a virgin. Uh-huh.

Hope chuckled. "I'll catch you later. Come out there if you can take a break in here."

"I gotta get breakfast started. I like to be prepared when I get up in the morning. That way I can serve any early risers."

"No worries. Talk to you later," she said as she carried her plate of food into the dining room.

Since it was late, the dinner rush had long since faded, and there were only a few guests sitting at the tables—a couple of guys playing checkers, two women drinking coffee and talking animatedly. Hope didn't want to interrupt or look as though she was eavesdropping, so she stepped out on the back porch to finish her food.

Leaning against the rail, she peered into the twilight. Since it was only September, the sun was still lingering a little longer in the evening than it would in the coming weeks. Hope liked that part of the year, when the days didn't feel quite as never-ending. Since she worked such long hours, she generally forced herself to quit early when it got dark.

She hopped up on the rail and continued to eat, catching a glimpse of the few people who were still wandering about. Most of them were wranglers who were heading to the bunkhouse for the night, some probably heading to the bar in town. Even with those people, it was peaceful out here. She could hear the crickets chirping, a few birds that were up past their bedtime singing in the trees surrounding the house. Every now and then, she could hear the click of a bat as it swooped past.

God, she loved it here.

It wasn't hard to see why, especially on nights like this. Hope had worked hard to convince herself that this ranch was all she needed. Well, the ranch and her sisters and her dad. They were all that mattered in her world. She had long ago given up on a happily ever after for herself. Then Ben had come into her life, and she'd considered it only to end up heartbroken one more time.

Jared

Hope knew she wasn't cut out for romance. She simply couldn't do it. The few guys she'd dated in the last few years didn't seem to understand her commitment and dedication to this place. The only thing she could probably look forward to was a casual fling here and there. Not that she was openly looking for one, but if the stars aligned just right and she found herself with the right man, she could probably see a few nights of hot, sweaty sex on her horizon.

Of course her thoughts instantly drifted to Jared Walker.

She wasn't sure what she was going to do about that man. She didn't know enough about him to even say she was interested. Other than his rugged good looks and his gentlemanly manners, that was. If she had to make a decision based on that, sure, she could see herself getting naked with him. Maybe.

She chuckled to herself.

Right.

Because she was some kind of wild woman who went looking for men. She couldn't even pretend that was true. Even though, sometimes, she wished she were.

CHAPTER SEVEN

THE WEEKEND PASSED without incident. While he didn't spend his days at the Walker Demo office, Jared ended up spending most of his time in his yard. Technically, the house didn't belong to him. It belonged to his aunt and uncle, who had built the place for their son, Kaleb, years ago. But when Kaleb decided to move in with his then fiancée, Zoey, Kaleb had kindly given up his bachelor pad. And it worked for Jared and Derrick. The rustic, two-bedroom cabin was just what the two of them needed.

Plus, the huge yard. Definitely needed that.

Once the swing set was up and functional, Derrick hadn't wanted to do anything else. So, Jared pulled out a chair, slathered Derrick with sunscreen, put the sprinkler nearby, and let Derrick go to town. They wouldn't have too many more days of that what with fall rushing up on them. Since the temps were still hitting the high eighties, it was working for now.

Aside from that, Jared had done little else.

Well, unless thinking about Hope counted.

For some unknown reason, the woman had plagued his mind. At one point, she'd even showed up in his dreams. It had been a sexy dream, he had to admit.

Which was the very reason he was calling her now. He needed to put this absurd infatuation to rest, and the only way he knew to do that was to set up a time to meet to go over the details of the reunion. Once they got this shindig out of the way, he would have no reason whatsoever to think about Hope Lambert or her sexy voice or wicked curves or stunning smile.

Fuck.

Jared

After Sunday dinner at Curtis and Lorrie's, Jared had taken the opportunity to talk to some of his family members to see what, if any, dates might work for them in the coming months. Turned out, the idea of a week at a dude ranch appealed to more people than he'd thought it would. However, since no one had given him any input as to when a good time for it would be, he'd left with pretty much what he'd started with. Nothing.

"Hope Lambert," the raspy voice said in his ear.

"Hey," he greeted. "It's Jared Walker."

"What can I do for you, Mr. Walker?"

The fact that she still insisted on calling him that made him smile.

"I wanted to see if I could swing by the ranch this afternoon to talk about the reunion."

"There is always someone in the office during the day," she replied. "Just stop by. My dad or my sisters will be happy to help you out."

Ahh. She was going to play it that way.

"I want to work with you directly," he said, keeping his tone matter-of-fact. He'd had to do it numerous times in his line of work. Often, one of the general contractors wanted to pass him off to someone else. Jared generally refused. He could get more accomplished going straight to the source.

There was a brief pause, followed by, "Well ... I ... uh... Sorry, but today's not a good day. Mondays never are. I've got a ton of stuff to take care of. Even if I could meet with you today, I wouldn't be free until late..."

"Late works," he said, probably a little too quickly. "How about dinner?"

Okay, he really hadn't meant to ask her out.

"Um ... I don't think that's a good idea."

"You don't eat?"

Hope chuckled. "Yes, I eat."

"Then why isn't dinner a good idea?"

"I ... uh..."

"Dinner, Hope. We'll talk about the reunion. I've got some questions."

This time the pause lasted long enough to make it uncomfortable.

"Hope? Are you there?"

"Yeah." A heavy sigh sounded in the phone. "I really think it'd be better if we meet later in the week. Or, better yet, you can email me your questions."

"Are you scared of me?" he taunted, knowing that she was purposely blowing him off.

"What?" She sounded affronted. "No. I'm just ... busy. Really busy. I don't have time for—"

He pushed, purposely cutting her off. "That's it, isn't it? You're scared of me. Worried that one dinner and you'll fall in love, beg me to marry you..."

"I most certainly will not," she countered with a snort, but Jared could tell she was amused.

"Good. Then I'll pick you up at seven."

"Mr. Walker..."

"Jared," he retorted.

"*Jared*, I..."

Realizing she was still trying to come up with a way to brush him off, Jared decided to take the decision from her altogether. "I'll see you at seven, Hope. And I'm lookin' forward to it."

Rather than waiting for her to fumble more, Jared disconnected the call and smiled to himself. Sure, that might've been a little high-handed, but there was something about this woman. Something that made him want to pursue her despite the fact that he knew better.

He didn't often find himself in this predicament. He could probably count on one hand how many times in his life he'd had to put real effort into pursuing a woman. It was rare. In fact, it might've happened once. Twice at the most.

But he liked it.

Jared definitely liked the fact that Hope wasn't giving in. Now, whether or not that would ever happen, he wasn't sure, but he damn sure was looking forward to trying.

Jared

Then again, once he got her—*if* he got her—he had no fucking clue what he was supposed to do with her. Sex was certainly up there on his list of things he wanted to do, but other than that, there really wasn't much he could give this woman. He was a single dad, and he'd made a vow to himself that no woman would ever interfere with his relationship with Derrick, nor would any woman come before his son. The kid was his whole reason for breathing. He looked forward to every single second he got to spend with the boy, which meant there really wasn't any room for a woman in his life.

Yet he wasn't compelled to call Hope back and cancel.

And he wasn't sure what that said about him. Or his intentions.

Granted, he'd have to think about that later, because right now, he needed to give Kaleb a call. See if he would mind watching Derrick for a few hours tonight.

HOPE PACED THE small guest room. She had finished up for the day, working a little longer since she supposedly didn't need to eat dinner yet. Then she'd gone up to her room, hopped in the shower, and pulled on a T-shirt and a pair of shorts.

Now, with Canaan Smith crooning from the speaker on the nightstand beside the bed, she was pacing in front of the small closet that held a few of her clothes. Luckily, Faith had thought to bring Hope's sensible clothes—jeans, T-shirts, a couple of blouses, boots—which meant Hope didn't have to bother with getting dressed up for this...

Whatever *this* was.

She still could not believe Jared had *insisted* that she go on a date with him.

A freaking date.

Then again, she couldn't believe she'd allowed the sweet-talking cowboy to talk her into it.

But it wasn't a date.

It was dinner. That was all. Dinner where they would talk about business; she would make sure of it. So maybe they'd have dinner. It wasn't like she couldn't survive an hour in his company. She could talk about the ranch until she was blue in the face.

Snatching a pair of jeans, Hope glanced down at them before shoving them back in the closet and pulling out another pair. A nicer pair.

Crap.

Why was she doing this to herself?

The last time she'd been on a date had been with Ben. Two years ago? Something like that. And not once since then had she even worried about her nonexistent social life. So what if she hadn't had sex in two years? Didn't mean she was going to have sex with Jared Walker.

Dinner, she reminded herself. A business dinner.

Maybe she should invite her father.

No. That would definitely be weird.

Throwing the jeans on the bed, Hope headed back to the bathroom to pull the towel off her head. Her hair tumbled down just past her shoulders and she frowned. No way could she go looking like this. Even if it wasn't a date, she didn't want to look like a drowned rat.

Which meant she had to put a little effort into getting herself presentable.

For the next half hour, that was all she focused on. After blow-drying and straightening her hair, she swiped some color on her eyelids, then brushed mascara over her lashes, topping it off with a subtle gloss on her lips.

That was as good as it was gonna get.

After pulling on her jeans and finding a shirt that she didn't normally wear when she worked, Hope studied herself in the mirror.

God, she hated this.

She hated that she was actually looking forward to seeing Jared again. She hated that she was almost nervous about going out with him.

Jared

There were a million reasons she should've called him back and told him that she couldn't do this. Instead of listening to the voice of reason all but screaming in her head, she had pretended that this really was a simple business meal and after they talked about his reunion, she would be back here, gearing up for another busy day tomorrow.

"You're overthinking this," she muttered to her reflection.

What if she really was? What if Jared simply wanted to take her to dinner to talk about the logistics of his family reunion? After all, he really did seem perplexed when it came to how to go about setting this up. She should've told him she could easily handle all of the details, right down to sending out an email invite to anyone and everyone he wanted to show up. They'd done that before, and it usually worked out well because they managed everything from their end. No surprises.

But she hadn't done that.

And if she could do it all over again, she wasn't sure that she would, either.

Half an hour later, after Misty, the housekeeper, had so kindly knocked on her door to alert her that Jared was there, Hope was once again mentally chastising herself.

She still couldn't believe she'd agreed to this.

Here she was, strapped into the passenger seat of Jared's fancy Chevy Silverado truck, letting him whisk her away from the ranch so they could have dinner together. Clearly she was losing her touch. Turning down dates had become one of her specialties, something she exceled at.

She still wasn't sure what had happened here.

Shit. Dating so wasn't her thing. She should be at home with a bowl of popcorn and a movie.

With her pajamas on.

Getting ready to call it a night.

After all, that was the extent of the excitement in her life. That and flooded cabins. At least when it came to *after hours* anyway. The rest of the time, she was working, something she enjoyed immensely and had made her entire focus for years.

Somehow Hope had clearly failed today because she'd allowed this smooth-talking cowboy with the sexy voice and the sparkling eyes to persuade her to have dinner with him.

A freaking cowboy, for chrissakes.

The irony was not lost on her.

She couldn't help but notice that the truck smelled new. How was that even possible? He had a kid. Shouldn't there be toys strewn across the backseat? Maybe some old fast-food wrappers on the floor? Nope. No toys, no food, but there was a car seat in the backseat. Other than that, there wasn't so much as a piece of trash anywhere. And it'd been vacuumed recently.

Why did it matter? She didn't care how Jared kept his truck. Or that it smelled like him. Something musky, spicy. Sexy.

Uggh.

While she continued to stare out the window, Hope pretended not to notice the way Jared briefly glanced over at her. She could feel the intensity of his gaze every single time.

Jeezus. She was in trouble here.

At least she'd been the one to insist on the restaurant. And restaurant was putting it kindly. Where they were going was really nothing more than a backwoods bar that served up some appetizers and burgers to go along with the beer. Not one of those fancy places with candlelight and tablecloths. This one had peanut shells on the floor.

Peanut shells.

Hopefully he didn't have a peanut allergy.

Then again, if he did, maybe they'd turn right back around, and he could take her home.

So, yeah. This was a win-win for her. As far as she was concerned, that made the score even to this point. She'd show Jared what she thought of his high-handed insistence. He thought he was smooth, not asking. Well … she was the master of avoidance, and he was not going to get one over on her.

No matter how much it had turned her on when he'd gotten that demanding edge in his deep voice.

Jared

"You look fantastic, by the way," Jared said as he drove, looking at ease in the driver's seat of his impressive truck—the kind with fancy leather seats and all the bells and whistles. One hand casually resting along the top of the wheel, his other arm propped on the console between them.

"Thanks," she said, surprised by the compliment.

Not that she hadn't had her fair share of them, but since she'd grown up on the ranch, they were generally few and far between. Her father had threatened to castrate any man who so much as looked at one of his daughters, and for the most part, that had been effective in keeping the wranglers focused on work. As for those few who had been stupid enough over the years, their compliments were usually accompanied by a wink and one of those crooked, come-hither grins notorious to cowboys. The kind that made women want to strip right out of their boots and be ravished.

Yeah, well, she'd been there and done that. And the ravishing was generally little more than some heavy petting, a few grunts and groans, then a grand finale. For him.

It was safe to say Hope hadn't had the most impressive sex life, but she didn't dwell too much on that. She had more than enough shit to do to worry about getting laid. Her nightstand drawer was well stocked with batteries, and her vibrator was very much her best friend.

She didn't need a man.

"And me?" Jared asked.

Hope glanced over at him, confused.

His sexy grin widened when she frowned.

"You're supposed to say, 'You look nice, too, Jared.' That's the way this datin' thing works, right?"

"I never would've taken you for the insecure kind," she quipped.

His grin widened, his eyes heating. Yeah, she doubted he had an insecure bone in his entire body.

"Plus, this isn't a date," she assured him.

"Oh, it's a date," he argued.

She was getting a lot of that from him. Seemed Jared had an agenda all his own, and Hope was beginning to feel a little off-kilter about it all.

They pulled into the gravel parking lot of the restaurant/bar, and Hope half expected him to balk at the place. Instead, he smiled to himself, then climbed out of the truck after telling her to stay put.

She did not stay put.

Rather than allow him to open her door for her, Hope hurried out of the truck and met him as he came around the front of the vehicle.

What she'd expected to happen and what happened were two very different things, and that off-kilter feeling turned into full-blown vertigo when Jared trapped her between his big body and the grille of the truck.

He smelled good.

Like, really good.

"I'm not sure you understand how this works," he said, his tone low, seductive.

And damn it all to hell, he was still smiling.

"Then tell me how it goes," she said, trying to keep her temper in check while fighting her body's ridiculous response to his nearness.

He was right about one thing, this wasn't how this worked, but it was still to be seen as to who would get their way. As much as Hope didn't want to relinquish control, she was beginning to get the impression that Jared Walker was not the laid-back, passive country boy she'd pegged him to be.

And fuck a duck, she actually liked that.

A lot.

CHAPTER EIGHT

JARED HAD KNOWN from the moment he laid eyes on this woman the first time he'd come to the ranch that she would be a handful. She was proving that now, and he was fairly certain she was pushing him on purpose. What Hope didn't know was that he didn't mind. That was one of the things that turned him on about her. And the more she pushed, the hotter he found her.

Then again, he wasn't going to tell her that her little plan was backfiring in her face, either. He'd have a far better time sitting back and letting her figure that out on her own.

As he crowded her between his much bigger body and the grille of his truck, Jared let his eyes caress her face. She was wearing makeup, he noticed. Very subtle, but it highlighted her eyes and made her lips glisten in a way that practically hypnotized him. Beautiful was a word that didn't even begin to describe this woman.

"Are you allergic to peanuts?" she whispered.

It took a moment for her words to process; he'd been too caught up in the heat generating between their bodies. Or maybe that was coming from his engine.

"I … uh… No, I'm not allergic."

"What about your son?"

Now he was really confused. "No."

"Good. Then we can go in."

The way she said *good* did not actually sound good. She sounded somewhat disappointed. Did she want him to be allergic to peanuts? Or was she simply hoping they wouldn't have to go inside?

Ding, ding, ding.

Based on the gleam in her eye, Jared knew that Hope had been hanging on to one last ... well, hope. If he or his son were allergic to peanuts—which he assumed this restaurant had, probably on the floor—then she could back out kindly, and he would take her home.

Sorry to disappoint, sweetheart. Hope wasn't getting off the hook that easily.

Jared stared back at Hope for a moment, replaying the last few seconds. He briefly wondered if he would ever understand the way her brain worked. Rather than try, he took her hand and linked their fingers together before turning toward the door. When she tried to pull away from him, he held firm, enjoying the way her small hand fit perfectly in his. If Hope really wanted to get away, she could, but he didn't think that was the case.

She proved him right a few seconds later when she quit trying and sighed.

When they reached the door, he pulled it open and allowed her to walk ahead of him.

His smile returned when he got his first glimpse of the *restaurant* Hope had wanted to come to. A second later, his assumption about peanuts proved to be true.

Then again, he wasn't all that surprised considering the sign out front said Marla's Bar, not restaurant. Jared had known from the second she made the suggestion that this feisty little cowgirl was trying to turn the tables on him.

"This is nice," he said, watching her face as she stared back at him, clearly confused by his response. "Do we seat ourselves?"

"Yeah," she huffed. "At the bar."

"Lead the way," he encouraged, grinning widely.

Before Hope turned away, Jared noticed the way she rolled her eyes and inhaled sharply.

Two could play this game.

He couldn't help but let his eyes slide down her body, admiring the fit of that white T-shirt, along with the snug jeans that accentuated her phenomenal ass. She was tiny, but he knew better than to underestimate her. There was something fierce inside that small package.

Jared

Once they were seated at the bar, Jared took a moment to look around. This was probably the most rustic place he'd ever been to. Certainly what he'd expect to find in a small, backwoods town in Texas. Embers Ridge was a lot like Coyote Ridge in size, which he actually preferred. And from what he could tell, the few businesses they had rivaled those in Coyote Ridge as well.

Not that he was bothered by that fact; it just wasn't the sort of place he would've chosen for a first date. This place reminded him a lot of Moonshiners. The wood-paneled walls and hardwood floors were fitting, and the animal heads—those were the one thing Moonshiners lacked, which meant the most-rustic award went to Marla and her bar—that decorated it were a nice touch. It appeared that this particular establishment hadn't gotten the memo about no smoking indoors, because it was still allowed, apparent by the haze and the overwhelming stench that lingered.

But Jared hardly noticed anything other than the sexy woman now seated beside him, currently ordering a beer and a cheeseburger, as though she did it all the time. She probably did.

"I'll have the same," he told the bartender, smiling kindly.

The look he got back was one of amusement, and he got the impression the bartender knew Hope. She probably figured Jared would be out on the curb before the night was over. If Hope had her way, he figured that would be the case as well.

What they didn't know was that Jared wasn't the type to back down from a challenge. He'd spent the better part of the last several years recovering from a bitter divorce battle with his ex-wife, not to mention raising the little boy that his ex had tried to take away from him. It would take a hell of a lot more than a redneck bar and peanuts on the floor to discourage him.

Despite all that, Hope was a breath of fresh air. Even if she was ornery as hell.

He could deal with ornery over bitchy any day of the week. And tonight, he had every intention of winning Hope over. It looked as though they would be spending a little time together while they worked on getting the family reunion set up, but Jared didn't intend to make all that time about work, so he had to make the most of it.

"You dance?" Hope asked him after the bartender brought over their beers.

"I hold my own," he replied, sipping his beer as he spun around to get another look at the dance floor. He glanced back at her. "Why? You askin'?"

The corners of her soft pink lips curved up. "Not in this lifetime."

"What do you want to bet that by the end of the night, I'll get you on that dance floor?" he wagered.

Hope's golden eyebrows lifted. "I'll take that bet."

Jared didn't bother to place the bet on whether or not he would end up in her bed before he went back home, but he was already trying to find a way to make that happen.

More than once if he had his way.

SITTING AT THE bar made it nearly impossible for Hope to face Jared, which turned out to be a good thing. It kept her mind from wandering to things better left alone.

Like how it would feel to have those lips on hers. When he'd been so close to her out in the parking lot, it'd taken a tremendous amount of effort not to stare at them, not to think about him kissing her. Would they be as soft as they looked?

Or what about his hands? She could practically feel them sliding over her skin, warm, strong, demanding…

Lord help her.

Hope had mentally kicked herself for thinking those things when he'd trapped her between his extremely impressive body and the grille of his truck a short time ago. Rather than hate that he'd gotten her in such a vulnerable position, Hope had actually enjoyed it.

Jared

Though she wouldn't admit that even if there was a gun to her head. She'd worked hard to establish a reputation for being no-nonsense and in charge. She'd learned early on that it was exactly what her sisters needed. In order to allow them the ability to grow up without having to spend all their time working, Hope had tried to take on some of that burden. Sure, it might've hardened her a bit, but that wasn't a bad thing.

Plus, she had to show backbone in order to work with men all day. One show of weakness and she would've lost all the respect she'd worked so hard to earn.

Didn't mean that she wouldn't mind being the submissive one from time to time. It was quite possible that Jared knew that. And if he didn't, he'd probably figure it out rather quickly if he kept the whole alpha thing going.

She was a lost cause. No doubt about it.

Which was why Hope had assumed that sitting at the bar would be the safe bet. Sure, they were close enough that their legs touched from time to time, but she didn't have to look at him. Or so she thought, right up until she realized she could see him in the mirror above the row of liquor bottles on the wall.

Aww, crap. Their eyes met in that damn mirror, and Hope felt a flash fire ignite in her veins. This man was proving to be far too much temptation for her undersexed body. She needed to get this moving along so she could go back to the safety and security of her bedroom. Alone.

"Have you determined a good time for your family reunion?" she inquired, sipping her beer and staring down at the scarred bar top to keep from looking his way.

"I have," he said, his tone far more confident than it'd been the last time she'd asked that question.

Unfortunately, that confidence had her swinging her head around to look at him. "You have?"

His smile was slow and…

Whatever.

"When?" She might've sounded a little like a frog just then.

"October twenty-ninth through November fourth."

80

Hope nodded, as though that made sense. A week at a dude ranch was actually about the right length of time to enjoy all of the amenities. "I'll have to check the schedule to see if we can accommodate that." She wouldn't really. She knew they had it open, because she had made a point to check which weeks *weren't* available. Halloween week was wide open. He wasn't giving himself much time to plan, but she assumed, with thirty-something first cousins, he would have quite a bit of help.

The smile he gifted her with was a knowing one.

"What? Why're you lookin' at me like that?"

"I actually called the office earlier and spoke with your father. He checked the schedule and assured me that you'd be able to accommodate roughly one hundred guests during that week."

Well. Hope didn't know what to think about that.

"I figured I had to get the basics in line so we could start working on the rest."

Hope nodded, then took a long swig of her beer. "Maybe you should work with my father on getting this set up."

Jared immediately shook his head. "Sorry, sweetheart, you're not gettin' rid of me that easily."

"I'm not tryin' to get rid of you." She was definitely trying to get rid of him. "I just figure my father might have more time to help you get everything in order."

Jared tipped his bottle to his mouth, and Hope's eyes were drawn to his lips once again. He had nice lips. Firm lips. Sexy lips.

Shit.

"He actually offered to help," Jared explained after taking a pull on his beer. "I told him I'd prefer to work with you."

"Why me?"

The amusement dropped from his expression, and when their eyes met, Hope felt like something punched her in the solar plexus. Something that felt a hell of a lot like ... pure, unfettered lust.

When his big hand landed on her thigh, then pressed down as he turned her to face him, her breath caught in her throat. What the hell was he doing? And why the hell wasn't she pushing him away?

Jared

"I've been thinkin' about you since last week," he said softly, his mouth only inches from hers when he shifted on his stool to get closer.

"Yeah?" Yep, that was her sounding all breathless.

"Oh, yeah. And I've decided I want to get to know you better."

"What if I don't want to get to know *you*?" Well, if that was the case, someone should probably alert her rapidly thrumming pulse and the gravel in her throat, because she definitely didn't sound like she didn't want to get to know him.

And yes, just as Hope suspected, Jared noticed.

"If I thought that was the case, I wouldn't be here now."

Was he getting closer?

Hope swallowed hard.

"But we'll be working together," she said, trying to come up with a way to get out of this.

"We will. So what'll it hurt?"

Did he expect her to answer that? Because she had a dozen answers on the tip of her tongue.

"How about we don't put any pressure on this, Hope? We've got a month and a half to plan the greatest family reunion in the history of family reunions, and when that's over, if you want me to go away and never come back, I'll do that."

This was completely unfair. He'd clearly given some thought to this already, and she felt … blindsided.

Okay, maybe she wasn't entirely out of the loop. She had *met* him. That momentous occasion was ingrained in her brain. There had been something about this man that she couldn't stop thinking about ever since he'd showed up at the ranch three days ago. Wow. Had it only been three days? And to think, she'd spent that much time trying to stop thinking about this cowboy. Trying and failing.

Maybe Jared was onto something. Maybe they could pursue this while they were spending time together anyway. Like he'd said, what could it hurt?

The rational side of her brain told her that if they did pursue this—whatever they were doing here—then this could only be about…

"Sex," she blurted.

His dark brows lifted, and a smile that Hope decidedly categorized as sinful appeared on his lips. "I like the idea of it, yeah."

"No... I didn't... I meant, we shouldn't ... have it," she whispered back. That was a lie. They should have lots and lots of it.

God, she was a mess.

Jared leaned in closer, his lips only a fraction of an inch away from hers. If he wanted to kiss her, he could've so easily done it. Hope was trying to keep it together, but the heat emanating from this man and his intoxicating scent, mixed with the adrenaline fueling her rapidly pounding heart, was making it hard for her to think.

"We should have lots of it," he breathed against her lips. "As much and as often as possible."

Hope tried to shake her head, but that caused her lips to brush against his and her thighs to clench together.

"Is there someone else?" he questioned.

Hope shook her head.

"Then what's stopping us? No strings, Hope."

"Only sex," she managed to say.

"If that's what you want."

How had they gotten to this point? Three days ago she'd met the man for the first time, and now she was sitting here on the barstool in her favorite bar ready to drag him out to his truck and ... ride him.

Oh, hell.

"What d'ya say, Hope?"

Hope swallowed hard, licking her lips ever so slightly, gearing up to say...

"Here's your burgers, lovebirds. Anything else I can getcha?"

Relief, sharp and all-consuming, swamped her, nearly causing Hope to fall off her stool.

CHAPTER NINE

JARED HONESTLY WASN'T sure what just happened.

One minute he was pledging to win Hope over, and the next he was committing to endless amounts of no-strings sex with the woman. Shit, he hadn't even kissed her yet.

As intriguing as the idea was—both endless sex and kissing her—he needed to do a quick rewind and figure out just how they'd made it this far this quickly. While Hope turned around and faced the bar, Jared took a deep breath and gave a little attention to his burger while signaling the bartender for another round.

"What just happened?" Hope muttered, casting a sideways glance his way, letting her hair fall over her face on the other side, shielding her from the bartender.

Jared grinned. Good. She was feeling it, too. "I'm pretty sure you offered unlimited sex."

"Oh, God." She grabbed her burger with both hands, leaned forward, and took a bite probably twice the size of her mouth.

He couldn't help but laugh.

She, however, did not find his reaction at all amusing based on the way she grimaced.

This was quite possibly the weirdest situation he'd found himself in, and truth was, he damn sure wasn't a saint. He'd had more than his fair share of one-night stands in his lifetime, but usually the proposition came *after* dinner or drinks or ... or something more than simply sitting on a barstool.

Then again, he hadn't met a woman like Hope Lambert before. There was something about her, something that intrigued him, made him think that not all women were the devil and out to string a guy up by the balls.

Jared ate a couple of French fries while he waited for his beer. He watched as Hope dutifully ate several bites of her burger and finished off what was left of her beer before daintily wiping her mouth with a napkin.

Damn, she was pretty.

She shot another sideways glance his way. "You know we can't have sex, right?"

Her words were spoken so softly he barely heard them over the music coming from the jukebox in the corner.

"Oh, I beg to differ. It's quite possible."

She looked at him fully. "I don't even know you."

"But you will."

"But I won't have sex with you until I do."

"No one asked you to."

"Oh." Her eyes widened, but their conversation was cut off when the bartender returned, setting their beers on the bar in front of them.

For the next few minutes, they ate their dinners quietly, neither of them saying a word. Jared wasn't sure what to say that would make this less awkward. Part of him wanted to toss her over his shoulder, carry her fine little ass out to his truck, and do some things to steam up the windows. The other part of him wanted to wait this out, to see what Hope would say once they were finished.

He got the feeling she was going to do a lot of backtracking. Well, he was ready for her. No way was he going to let her get out of this. They might not have sex tonight, or hell, even this week, but it would happen. And it would be fucking incredible.

Jared

As he pushed his plate away, his thoughts instantly drifted to Derrick. His little boy was currently at Kaleb and Zoey's house, probably already lying down, watching television after playing with Mason for a couple of hours. His cousin had so kindly agreed to watch him so that Jared could take Hope out, under the guise of talking about the reunion. That little detail alone meant that Jared wouldn't be spending the night away from home. In fact, he would have to call it an early night in order to get back to his son.

And that quickly put a damper on the lingering sizzle between him and Hope. As much as he wanted to take her up on her offer—it was definitely an offer, he could see it in the brilliant blue-green of her eyes—tonight wasn't going to work for him. The first time he took her, he had every intention of giving her his undivided attention. He needed a hell of a lot longer than a couple of hours.

So the sex would have to wait.

Refusing to let that knowledge bring him down, Jared finished his burger, and when the plates were taken away, he turned to Hope.

"Dance with me," he said softly.

"Is that a request or a command?" she countered, peering at him sideways.

"Whichever you prefer," he told her truthfully. "I'm rather adept at both."

Hope laughed, as he'd intended. Then, to his shock, she actually got down from the barstool, took his hand, and led him to the center of the dance floor. Well, technically, it was nothing more than a ten-by-ten area that had been left empty for this purpose.

"For the record," she told him, "I'm the one who got *you* out here. Not the other way around."

Jared laughed. He knew she was referring to their earlier bet. And in a way, she was right.

Jared pulled her against him, thankful for the slow song coming from the speakers. Their boots moved smoothly on the dusty floor, their legs bumping occasionally as they two-stepped.

"You know we're never gonna get this reunion planned if you keep doing this," she said, peering up at him.

He loved how small she was, how easily he could hold her to him. "Doing what?"

"Dancing, flirting, telling me we're gonna have sex."

Jared leaned in closer to her ear under the guise of holding her tighter. "Well, darlin', we're never gonna get *any*thing done if you keep saying that word. When those three letters roll off your tongue, I want nothing more than to strip you naked and feel your soft skin beneath my lips."

Hope's sharp inhale told him he'd hit his target. She pulled back and stared up at him. The heat glimmering in her eyes said she liked what she heard.

"We're really gonna do this?" she questioned breathlessly.

Jared stopped moving and lifted his hand to the side of her face. He brushed his thumb over her cheek while he stared into her beautiful eyes. "You tell me, Hope." Damn, he was as breathless as she was. "It's been a long time since I've felt like this."

He wasn't sure what exactly he was feeling, though. Lust? Abso-fucking-lutely. Hell, his dick was rock hard and ready. He wouldn't have a problem pulling her into the bathroom and sinking deep inside this woman right now. To hell with getting to know her.

"I'm not looking for a relationship," she said.

"Good. Me, either." It was the truth.

"And when the reunion is over, this has to be over, too."

Jared nodded. He could agree to that.

Her gaze slid to his mouth, and Jared knew she wanted him to kiss her. And he wanted that more than he wanted air, but not here. With the way he was overheating, one kiss was going to lead to some rather inappropriate groping, and he did not need an audience for that.

Jared

HOPE THOUGHT FOR a second that Jared was going to kiss her on the dance floor. In fact, she was prepared for him to do just that. So when he pulled away and made a beeline for the bar, tugging her along behind him, she was a little shocked. Even a little disappointed. Her head was still spinning when Jared pulled her out to the parking lot after dumping several twenties on the bar to pay their bill.

Okay then.

She could feel the electricity that arced between them as he made his way over to his truck and directly to the passenger-side door. Maybe he was too much of a gentleman to make the first move. No, that couldn't be it. Sure, he was a gentleman; that wasn't being refuted. However, he had a devilish side, and if she had to guess, it overpowered the gentleman when need be.

Rather than open her door, though, Jared once again shocked her by pinning her up against the door and crowding her. He was so close she had to look up to see his face. What she saw in his eyes made her body burst into flame. But still, he didn't kiss her.

"Jared…" She was on the verge of begging.

"This scares me a little," he whispered.

Hope offered a questioning look. She had no idea what he was talking about.

"I'm not sure I've ever been this hot for a woman before. You make my dick so fucking hard."

Wow. And that made her body burn hotter.

They were players, Hope. Every last one of them.

Those were Cheyenne's famous last words. She'd been talking about the Walkers.

Until they set their sights on someone. And heaven help me, it's so worth it. They're relentless when they want something. Just ask Zoey or V or Kennedy or Jessie or Kylie.

Hope heard the conversation so clearly in her head.

And God, you can only hope that one of them doesn't set his sights on you. You won't survive it.

She forced herself to search Jared's eyes, trying to read his mind, his intentions.

"I can't even tell you all the things going through my head right now."

Hope smiled. "Dirty things?"

"God, yes." More heat flared in his smoky-blue eyes.

Cheyenne was probably right. She wasn't going to survive this, but she couldn't seem to stop herself from wanting him. Desperately.

Rather than respond, Hope flattened her palms on his chest and slid them up to his neck. He was a full foot taller than her, which made looking up at him almost uncomfortable.

"Fuck."

And then it wasn't uncomfortable, because Jared lifted her up, forcing her legs to wrap around his waist seconds before his lips came down on hers.

Heaven almighty. And there she was, crushed between his huge body and his truck, clinging to this man as though her life depended on it. The kiss stole her breath. It should've been a full-on thrashing of tongue and teeth, but no... Jared Walker had the self-control of a damn saint. He didn't try to devour her in one bite. His lips brushed hers, his tongue sliding softly into her mouth, hesitantly twining with hers. A rough groan rumbled in his chest, and Hope knew she was never in a million years going to survive the intensity of what this was between them.

It was the kind of magnetic, unstoppable attraction that you read about in romance novels. So hot, so powerful it made you do crazy shit. Like make out with a practical stranger in a damn parking lot, in a very small town, where, tomorrow, word would've spread far and wide. Yep, Hope figured by sundown tomorrow, half the ranch would've heard that she and Jared were getting frisky on what wasn't even supposed to be a date.

However, the more he kissed her, the less she cared.

Hope wrapped her arms around his neck and shifted her head slightly to deepen the kiss. And then, much to her total horror, she practically tried to climb his body. She ground herself against him until he was pressing her up against the truck door, the hard ridge of his erection providing delicious friction right where she needed it most.

Jared

"Jared." She couldn't stop the whimper that escaped her. When his mouth trailed down to her neck, Hope held on tighter as her body threatened to detonate from the erotic dry humping that was taking place right here in the parking lot of Marla's Bar.

"Fuck ... I would give my fucking right arm to be inside you right now," he groaned.

Yep. That did it.

Without warning, an orgasm the likes of which she'd never experienced ripped through her, causing her to cry out. Thankfully, she pressed her face into his neck in time to muffle the sound, but no doubt he knew what had just happened.

"Holy fuck, woman. That was... Holy fuck."

Yeah, holy fuck was right.

She didn't have too much time to be embarrassed, because Jared's mouth was on hers once again, and somehow, he brought her back down slowly.

"You okay?" Jared's voice was edged with what she could only assume was restrained passion.

"Probably better than okay," she told him, sliding down his body and to the ground. "I've ... uh ... never done that before."

Jared leaned in, one hand planted on the truck door, the other tilting her chin up. She stared into those mesmerizing eyes and held her breath.

"I don't have any problem with being your first." There was a hint of cockiness to his tone, but Hope had expected as much.

Unable to look away, she simply stared at him for what felt like forever. He didn't say anything, either; they just stood there, their eyes locked together. And it was in that moment that Hope knew the next few weeks were going to be by far some of the hottest she'd ever experienced.

More importantly, she was okay with that. Looking forward to it, actually.

Who would've thought?

CHAPTER TEN

JARED WOKE BEFORE the sun was up. After taking Hope back to the ranch, walking her up to the front door, giving her a relatively chaste kiss good night, he had managed to get back to Coyote Ridge in time to pick Derrick up before the boy fell asleep. Not because Zoey hadn't tried.

"That kid's got some serious willpower, Jared," Zoey *informed him when he stepped into the house. "I told him he should close his eyes and his daddy would be there to pick him up and take him home..." She stepped toward the living room and pointed.*

Derrick's eyes left the TV, shifting toward Jared. Seconds later, he had launched himself into Jared's arms.

The little boy grinned at Zoey. "See, I towd you I couwd stay awake."

Zoey patted his back and kissed his head. "And you definitely did. You were right." She smiled up at Jared. "Teach me to make a bet with the kid."

Thankfully, once they got home, Derrick had been wiped out and went to bed without complaint—something he did frequently since he refused to take a nap. At that point, Jared had forced himself to go to his room and close his eyes.

He wasn't sure how that had worked out. At the moment, he felt as though he hadn't slept a wink. He couldn't stop thinking about Hope—or dreaming if he *had* managed to fall asleep—about the way she'd come apart in his arms.

"Damn," he said on a whispered breath.

Jared

Rather than get up and get his day started, he opted to lie there in the dark, once again reliving that kiss from last night. Of course, his dick was reliving it, too, and he had no choice but to take care of business. Sliding his hand into his boxers, Jared fisted his cock as that kiss played in his mind. The way Hope had wrapped her legs around him, grinding her pussy against his aching hard-on. It'd taken every ounce of willpower he had not to come in his fucking jeans. She'd been so damn hot, taking what she needed from him.

He stroked himself faster as he thought about all the things he wanted to do to Hope when he finally got her alone. He could practically picture her riding his cock while she stared down at him...

"Fuck..." Jared closed his eyes as he came in a rush. It took him by surprise, actually.

Although he'd been with a handful of women since his ex-wife, he'd never been able to come like that. Not even with Sable. It was as though he was going through the motions, sating the urge, but never quite getting the relief he needed. And though his hand wasn't what he wanted at the moment, the memories of Hope from last night did it for him.

He only hoped he had a little more restraint when it came to the real thing. Otherwise, this was going to be one embarrassing affair.

Two hours later, after Jared dropped Derrick off at the day care, he headed to the office. As usual, he was the only one there. After taking care of a couple of phone calls and clearing his inbox, he pulled out the packet Hope had given him the other day. The brochure for the ranch. He'd seen that there was a checklist included, and he was interested in what the next step was. He'd already determined the location and the date, so that was a start.

According to the checklist, he needed to gather the information for the guests. Luckily, Lorrie already had all of that information. It wasn't the least bit surprising, either. She was probably the most organized person he knew.

He turned to his computer and located the email he'd received from Lorrie yesterday. He clicked on the attachment and found a spreadsheet with every damn thing he could possibly ever want to know about the Walker family. Names, birthdates, ages, addresses, phone numbers, anniversary dates... Shit. This was going to take some effort based on the sheer number of people, but Aunt Lorrie really had done the hard work. He at least knew how to contact everyone.

Because he wanted an excuse to talk to Hope, Jared decided to call her up and ask a couple of questions. Rather than call the ranch office, he called her cell phone.

"Hope Lambert," she answered in that sexy voice of hers.

"Hey."

"Jared." She didn't sound the least bit surprised to hear from him. "To what do I owe the pleasure?"

"Got a couple of questions for ya," he told her simply.

"Yeah? Well, if they involve what color panties I'm wearing, you'll have to call me later."

Damn. He swallowed hard. "Uh ... well, I'll definitely be calling later about that, but right now, I had a question about the reunion."

She chuckled, sounding somewhat embarrassed. "Of course you do."

"So, now that I'm absolutely *not* thinking about what color your panties are..." Red? Black? White? Oh, damn. He took a deep breath. "I'm trying to organize this list of family members. Any suggestions on how to handle this many people?"

Her voice sounded muffled when she said, "Yeah, hold on. I'll be right there." It was clearer when she added, "Sorry about that, Jared. I had to find somewhere more private."

So she'd teased him about her panties while she'd been with someone?

"My suggestion," she continued seamlessly, "is that you assign one person for each family. For example, maybe have the oldest child from each of your dad's siblings get the information you need. You can delegate some of the duties to them. Especially since you're trying to get this accomplished in such a short amount of time."

Jared

"Great idea." He was still thinking about her panties.

"You have to get the invitations out first. Letting the family know about the get-together is the most prudent. Once you get a head count, you can work on everything else. The rest, since you're having it here, will consist of minor things."

"Such as?" Jared simply wanted to listen to her talk. He had the checklist and got the gist of it from skimming, but hearing Hope's voice did something for him.

"Such as any dietary requirements. Any awards or trophies if you plan on having various games during the reunion. Getting the necessary releases signed for things here at the ranch such as horseback riding and zip-lining. That sort of thing."

"Looks like I've got a lot to do."

"It won't be easy," Hope stated.

"But you'll be there to help me, right?"

"I'll definitely be here," she said. "You're welcome to drop by anytime you want."

"Tonight?"

Hope chuckled. "Except tonight. I'm actually in the process of moving."

"Moving? Don't you live on the ranch?"

"I do. Last week my cabin flooded. Septic tank issue. Ruined almost everything. I've been staying in the main house for a few days." Her voice lowered slightly. "Not a lot of privacy going on there."

Jared could imagine.

"There's another cabin available, but I can't get completely moved in until Friday."

"Was that an invitation?" he teased.

"For Friday...?" She paused briefly and Jared found himself holding his breath. "Yes."

Damn. He hadn't expected her to be so matter-of-fact.

"That is, if you want to come by."

Jared realized she'd taken his silence to mean he wasn't sure.

"I definitely do," he told her. Now he had to work on finding a babysitter for Derrick.

"Okay then." He could hear the smile in her voice. "Well, I better get back to work. Feel free to call me if you have any more questions. And check out that packet I gave you. It's got a lot of information in it."

"I've got it right here," he told her. "I simply wanted to hear your voice."

This time it was Hope's turn to be silent.

And once again, Jared was holding his breath.

"I'll ... uh..." Hope chuckled. "I'll see you on Friday."

Jared grinned, exhaling roughly. "I'll bring dinner."

"Sounds like a..."

Come on, say it. Say it.

When she didn't, Jared urged her. "A *what*, Hope?"

"I was gonna say date."

"That works for me," he told her, feeling as though he'd managed to get his foot in the door with this woman. "See you on Friday."

Jared hung up, then stared at the wall. He couldn't wipe the smile off his face.

While he contemplated how he'd managed to get in over his head with the angelic cowgirl, he pulled up his email. He scrolled through, checking to see if he'd received anything on the one bid he was waiting to hear back on.

Unfortunately, that email wasn't there, but another one was.

From Sable, with the subject line of: *If you care anything about Derrick...*

Jared double-clicked to open the email.

Jared,

It's time you and I sit down and have a serious conversation. I've been trying to call you, but that crazy-ass family of yours keeps sticking their nose into business that doesn't pertain to them. This is about my son.

Jared noticed the "my" in that statement. Legally, Derrick was *his* son.

Jared

I'm done playing games with you. I wanted to give you one last chance to talk to me before I contact a lawyer. I've changed my mind on handing my son over to you. I want him back. I needed some time to get my life together and I've done that. So, unless you and I can come to some sort of agreement, it looks as though I'm going to be a part of your life again. If, that is, you can convince a court that you even deserve to be Derrick's father. And in case you're thinking about deleting this, I want you to know, I will be seeking sole custody of him. Think about that. I'll give you two weeks, Jared.

Always yours,
Sable

Jared sat there, completely stunned, rereading the email over and over again. He tried to rein in the fury that seemed to soar in his veins.

It was a wonder he didn't break the computer.

I SIMPLY WANTED to hear your voice.

Even two hours after Hope got off the phone with Jared, she couldn't stop thinking about what he'd said.

Then again, she couldn't stop thinking about what *she'd* said.

She was going to see him on Friday.

Friday.

That was only three days away, and she wasn't sure she could handle the stress of anticipation for that long. She was going to spontaneously combust.

Part of her wondered if Jared Walker was for real.

The guy was intensely attractive, perhaps the best kisser in the entire universe, and he managed to easily balance his dirty talk with sweet words. From her experience, men who could manage all of that didn't exist. Something had to be wrong with him.

Hope wanted to get him naked. So, of course, she could check for herself.

"Hey, Hope!"

Shit.

Spinning around and dropping the brush she'd been using to groom Ambrosia, Hope saw her sister Faith standing only a few feet behind her. She'd been so caught up in her own thoughts she hadn't heard her come in.

"A little jumpy there, are ya?" Faith asked, studying Hope's face a little too intently.

Hope shrugged. Anything she said would only look defensive, and Faith would be all over it in a second.

"What's up?" She bent down and retrieved the brush, then moved out of the stall.

"I was talkin' to Dad earlier. He told me about the family reunion scheduled for late October. I need to know when they'll be paying the deposit."

Hope put the brush back where she got it from. "They're still working out the logistics."

"So you haven't quoted them a price yet?"

"Not yet. Once they tell me how many people, I can get it pretty quickly. Why?"

"Just wanted to stay on top of it."

"As soon as I know, you'll know."

Hope turned to see her sister staring out through the stable doors. She followed her gaze and noticed Faith was staring at Rusty Ashmore, one of their best wranglers. Didn't surprise her.

"Have you asked him out yet?" Hope asked, not waiting for her sister to respond as she headed back to the main house.

"It's not like that," Faith stated, running to catch up.

"I think you've said that before. For, you know, like, the past *three years.*"

"And I meant it. Then *and* now."

Jared

Hope couldn't give Faith a hard time. She'd learned long ago that she would be a hypocrite if she teased her sisters about the men they *didn't* go after. After all, she was guilty of not going after what she wanted. That didn't mean she wasn't happy, because she was. She had everything she needed right here on this ranch.

Well, except for maybe Jared Walker.

But, in her defense, he was new and sparkly and exciting. His luster would eventually dim, as did all the others, and she'd be right back, her sole focus being the ranch and all that it entailed. That was the way it'd been for her ever since her mother died. She'd made a promise that she would fill those giant shoes as best she could by taking care of her sisters and ensuring the ranch ran the way her father wanted it to. As time went by, she'd grown into that role. And she liked it.

Sure, it was a little lonely at times, but Hope wasn't worried about being alone. She found it much easier to be alone than to sit in the wings, waiting for the other shoe to drop. She hadn't had but a couple of relatively serious relationships in her life, but she'd learned from them. No matter what, she ended up alone, so it was just easier not to get her hopes up.

Maybe that was what she liked about Jared. He didn't beat around the bush. He wanted sex from her. That she could handle. She was almost thirty-four years old, completely capable of making good decisions for herself. No reason she couldn't have a brief affair with him.

But she hadn't been entirely truthful with him last night. When they agreed to proceed and address this crazy sexual chemistry they had, she'd told him that once the reunion was over, they'd call it quits. She might've fudged a little on the timing, because she had absolutely no intention of letting it go on that long. For one, the man had a son. If she stuck it out until after the reunion, there was a serious chance of her meeting that little boy, and she didn't want to do that. Not to herself, not to Jared, and certainly not to some little kid who she knew she would want to spend time with.

Her heart couldn't handle that again. She could remain aloof and detached yet still enjoy some physical gratification with a sexy-as-shit cowboy, but that was as far as she was going to let it go.

"You have dinner yet?" Hope asked Faith.

"Nope. You?"

Hope shook her head. "Come on, let's grab a bite. I think I'm gonna call it a night."

And hopefully, unlike last night, when she'd been too keyed up to sleep, she'd manage to catch a few z's before she had to get up and do it all over again tomorrow.

CHAPTER ELEVEN

JARED STARED ACROSS the table at his cousin, waiting for Travis to respond. He'd done his best to lay out his plans for the reunion, and he wanted to ensure he was on the right track. It wasn't that he doubted his abilities, but he knew Travis. If the man wasn't happy with the way things were going, he would take over, and Jared wasn't about to let that happen.

"I think it's a great idea," Travis said, staring at the sheet of paper Jared had printed out for him. "But why me? Why not rope Zane into handling this?"

"You're the oldest. It's the easiest way to divvy it up."

Travis lifted his eyes, meeting Jared's gaze. "How many people do we have coming to this?"

Jared shrugged. "I don't have a firm count yet, but I'd say around a hundred."

"Damn. And the ranch'll hold that many?"

"That's what I'm told."

"You figured out a cost yet?"

"Working on that next. As soon as I can get Hope a firm head count, we can determine lodging and all those costs. Food, entertainment, and the like." In fact, he was planning to talk to Hope when he saw her tonight. Okay, maybe he wasn't exactly going to talk about pricing tonight, but in the very near future he would.

Travis nodded. "I'm covering the cost of this. Make sure everyone realizes that. They'll only need to cover the cost of getting to the ranch."

That was a generous gesture on Travis's part, for sure. "I'll do that."

"So we're all set then?"

"For October twenty-ninth, yes." Jared knew Travis had been anticipating sooner, but he couldn't make that happen. He did have a full-time job to do in between trying to figure all this reunion crap out. Not to mention, the bullshit his ex-wife was trying to stir up. Jared wasn't sure how much worry to give it. He only knew that ignoring her wouldn't make her go away.

Travis set the paper down on Jared's desk and leaned back in his chair. "You hear from Sable?"

Staring at his cousin, he contemplated how much he wanted to tell Travis. Being that Jared had been in Coyote Ridge for almost two years, he'd seen Travis in action. The man took the saying "take the bull by the horns" to the extreme. That could probably work out in Jared's favor right about now.

The usual anger he felt when he thought about that woman was right there, heating his skin and pissing him off. "Yeah."

Again, Travis stared at him, clearly waiting for Jared to elaborate.

Reaching in his top desk drawer, Jared pulled out the email he'd printed. He leaned over and passed it off to Travis.

Jared leaned back in his chair, waiting patiently. He hadn't mentioned the email to anyone yet. He'd been trying to figure out what the best plan of action would be. He needed to contact his lawyer, see if Sable had any leverage here. She'd given up her parental rights, and from what he knew, their agreement was ironclad. But when it came to stuff like that, Jared figured there was a lot of gray in a world that definitely wasn't black and white. Especially if Sable was claiming she had needed time to get her shit together before she could be a good mother to the boy.

It was a crock of shit, that much he knew for certain.

"Lemme ask you somethin'," Travis prompted, peering up from the paper.

Jared lifted one eyebrow.

"If Sable comes back around, you have any plans to let her into Derrick's life? Clearly she's gearing up for something."

Jared

He should've expected that question. Hell, he'd thought about it more times than he cared to admit. The problem was, Jared didn't know if there was a right answer for it. The woman was Derrick's mother. "My first answer is no," Jared explained. "But I guess it would depend on what she wants."

"Say she wants you back."

"Oh, fuck no," Jared snapped, sitting up in his chair. "That's not even an option."

Travis didn't seem a bit surprised by that. "Okay. Say she just wants to be with her son." He lifted the paper. "And she's really gotten her shit together."

"I don't trust her, Trav," Jared told him honestly. "I don't trust her not to walk out on that little boy again. Do you know how long he cried for her? It broke my fucking heart. He wanted his mother, and she didn't want to have anything to do with him. I can't let her do that to him again."

Travis got to his feet. "That's what I needed to know."

Jared stood. "No way, man. You don't ask me somethin' like that and then walk outta here. What're you thinkin'?"

At least Travis had the decency to look him in the eye. "I'm not thinkin' anything. Not yet anyway. I just want you to remember that in the future." Travis waved the paper. "I'm takin' this with me. Let me do a little diggin' before you respond."

Jared nodded.

"Sable's comin' back, Jared. She's trying to insinuate herself in your life."

"What? Who told you that?"

"No one," Travis stated firmly. "But she's threatening you, hitting you where it hurts. She knows you'll do anything for Derrick. My guess is she's either outta money or she's rollin' solo and needs... I'm not gonna say it."

"Dick?" Jared had no problem saying it. That was exactly what Sable was after. Only she wanted a dick with money attached to it. She'd thought she would get that with Jared in the beginning, but he'd had none. Or so he'd convinced her. When she had signed the prenup, she honestly didn't realize all that she'd be giving up. In the end, she had gotten what she'd wanted. When it came to Derrick's happiness, Jared would've given her every fucking penny he had.

"It's not my place to tell you what to do, so I won't. But if you need someone to talk to, I'm here."

Jared nodded. He knew that. Although he'd grown up in El Paso, his father the only Walker who had moved out of Coyote Ridge, Jared was still close to most of his cousins. Especially Travis since they were relatively close in age, Travis being three years older.

"Lemme know if we can help with the reunion."

"Oh, now you offer," Jared called after him.

Travis grinned. "Somethin' tells me you ain't as willin' to give up the job as you're pretendin' to be."

Jared flipped his cousin off because, damn it all to hell, the asshole was right.

"See ya," Travis hollered as the door shut behind him.

"IS THAT IT?" Lane asked when he and Grant set the couch down against the wall.

"Looks like it," Hope told him, glancing over at the clock on the wall.

"You got a hot date or what?" Lane questioned. "About the fourth time you've looked at the clock in the past fifteen minutes."

Hope glared at her soon-to-be brother-in-law.

Lane grinned from ear to ear, putting his hands up in mock surrender. "Got it. Hot date. We'll just be gettin' outta your hair then."

Jared

"Shut up, Miller." Hope had known Lane would tease her relentlessly, and yes, it was her fault. She had been glancing at the clock ever since Lane and Grant stopped by with the furniture she'd asked them to bring.

"You check everything else out?" Grant asked as the pair moved toward the front door. "Make sure it was workin' all right?"

"All the necessities, yes." Hope knew they'd worked double time to get the cabin cleaned and ready for permanent living—new shower curtain, full-size refrigerator, that sort of thing—as best they could. They'd had to remove the furniture that'd been there to make room for Hope's, and that was all done after the guests had vacated at ten o'clock this morning. It would've been better if she could've given them another week to work on it, but as she'd expected, staying in the main house was too difficult for her.

For one, her father and Jan were staying there. Granted, the master bedroom was off in its own wing of the house, sectioned off from the guests, but still. It was a little disconcerting to know that her father and his girlfriend...

Yeah, she did her best not to think about that.

"All righty then," Grant said. "Holler if you need anything else."

"Thank you both," Hope told them when they stepped out onto the porch. "I really do appreciate it."

"Uh-oh," Lane grumbled with another of those face-splitting smiles. "Who's the hot date with?"

Hope frowned, confused.

"You're bein' far too nice. Must be lookin' forward to the date."

"Shut the hell up and go home," she ordered, trying to keep her face stern. She was usually good at it, but Lane somehow managed to make her smile. Hope understood why her sister had fallen in love with the guy. Hell, she understood why Gracie had fallen in love with both of them.

For the longest time, Hope had watched the three of them sneak around as though no one was wise to it. Of course, Gracie had been concerned with how their father would react. After all, Lane and Grant were both employed by the ranch, and their father had ordered the employees to stay far away from his daughters. In the end, love won out. And Hope was glad that it had. The three of them deserved to be happy.

Not that she would ever admit that to anyone. It would ruin her reputation.

Grant grabbed Lane and pulled him toward the truck. "See ya tomorrow."

Hope offered a quick wave but then hurried back inside.

It was already six o'clock. The text she'd received from Jared said he'd be there at seven and he'd be bringing dinner. He had asked if she had a problem with steak. She'd told him no. He hadn't told her where he was getting food, only that this time he was going to be the one making the decision on where. Something about not trusting her choice in restaurants.

That meant she had an hour to get the sheets on her bed and to take a shower. Aside from the furniture and a few of her clothes, the rest of her stuff was at the main house, and she would work on getting it all moved back over the weekend when she had time.

For right now, she didn't figure she needed much more than herself.

Oh, and the box of condoms she'd picked up when she went into town yesterday. If things went the way she thought they would, she'd definitely be needing those.

CHAPTER TWELVE

ALTHOUGH IT TUGGED at his heart to leave Derrick at Travis's for the night, Jared managed to finally leave. Probably didn't hurt that his boy practically pushed him out the door.

"Bye, Dad," Derrick said, wiggling for Jared to put him down. He'd purposely picked the kid up for a hug, knowing that once Derrick was inside, he wouldn't see him again.

"You gonna be good?" Jared asked.

Derrick turned toward him, cupping his face, his expression serious. "I'm awways good."

Travis's laugh could be heard as he made his way into the foyer. "Always."

Jared grinned. Right.

"He'll be fine, Dad," Travis teased. "Don't worry your pretty little head."

Jared fought the urge to flip Travis off. He turned to Derrick, cupping the back of his head and pressing his lips to Derrick's cheek. "Later, big man. Seriously. Be good."

Derrick nodded enthusiastically and practically jumped out of Jared's arms, making a beeline for the kitchen. Jared heard the door squeak open and then Derrick's excited squeal.

"Kate's in the kitchen. They're making cookies." Travis grinned. "Have fun tonight. Don't do nothin' I wouldn't do."

Jared cocked an eyebrow. "You know, coming from you, that's not exactly a warning, right?"

Travis smirked. Oh, he definitely knew.

Yep. It was very clear that Derrick was more than excited to spend the night with his cousin tonight. Derrick loved being at Kaleb's, but he was always over the moon to go to Travis's and play with Kate.

So, after grabbing dinner as he'd promised, Jared made his way to Hope's, arriving at seven o'clock on the dot. As he pulled down the narrow dirt path that bypassed several cabins, he found the one with the number four on the outside. Looked like there were nearly two dozen spread out on this side of the ranch, several hidden back in the trees that ran along the eastern side of the property. He didn't know how many they used for guests and how many were occupied by those who worked on the ranch, but it appeared they had enough to go around. There was a black Chevy that'd seen its fair share of life on the ranch parked haphazardly beside it, and the front porch light was on, so he assumed he was at the right one.

It took him all of a minute to grab the food and make it up to the porch, another minute for Hope to come to the door. The instant he saw her, he damn near swallowed his tongue.

Standing just inside the screen door was quite possibly the sexiest woman in the world. She was wearing some kind of flowy shirt with thin straps that showed off her tanned shoulders, her silky blond hair concealing only a portion as it hung down. The short denim shorts she wore gave him an eyeful of her equally tanned legs. As soon as she pushed open the screen door, he stepped inside, and his nostrils were instantly tickled by the sexy perfume she was apparently wearing. Or maybe that scent was coming from the candle burning on the kitchen table.

"Hey," she greeted softly, smiling up at him as she closed the door behind him.

He cleared his throat because, yes, he couldn't speak.

Thankfully, she took the paper sack from his hand and put it on the table beside the candle. Before she started to unpack their dinner, Jared reached for her, unable to stop himself.

Her quick inhale told him she wasn't expecting it, but she moved closer, willingly letting him tug her toward him. He took a few seconds to drink her in, lazily gazing down her body, then back up to meet her eyes. "I ... uh... Christ, woman, you look amazing."

Jared

Hope's smile made his dick twitch.

"Forgive me for being so forward," he said politely but then pressed his lips to hers.

He'd thought about kissing her again for the past four days. He wasn't sure he could make it through a meal without tasting her at least once.

Her soft moan was music to his ears. The way her hands fisted in his shirt, pulling him closer, had Jared deepening the kiss. And then, very much like the last time he'd seen her, Jared hoisted her up, forcing her to wrap those smooth legs around his waist.

"We should probably eat," he mumbled as she bit his lower lip.

"Probably," she agreed but never stopped kissing him, inhaling him with the same urgency he was showing her.

"What is it about you?" he questioned, rhetorically, of course. There was something about this woman that caused him to lose all control. Even before that first kiss they'd shared at the bar, Jared could think of doing nothing but touching her, kissing her. And since… He wanted to make her come; he wanted to hear her cry out his name as she came on his cock.

Hope's finger slid into his hair, tugging to near pain as he kissed her harder, deeper. She thrust her tongue against his, their teeth clashing as they attempted to devour one another. Unable to resist, he ran his hand up the underside of her leg, his fingers dipping beneath the edge of her shorts.

Her skin was so smooth, so soft. He wanted to run his fingers over it for hours. She smelled like heaven, tasted even better. Jared knew he should stop, but he couldn't.

"I didn't mean for this to happen," he told her truthfully.

"I'm not complainin'," she whispered. "Dinner's overrated anyway."

Yeah. What she said.

"Aww, God. You're wet for me."

Hope moaned softly when he slid his fingers beneath her panties, teasing her. Damn it. He couldn't force himself to pull back, to press pause. He didn't want to.

When Hope shifted, trying to get his fingers where she wanted them, he took that as a sign to continue. Jared walked around to her couch and sat down with her straddling his lap. He gripped her ass, pulling her so that she was once again grinding against him.

"Tell me to stop, Hope," he urged. Heaven knew he wasn't going to be able to do it.

"I don't want you to stop."

Okay, well, there went that idea.

Jared slid his hands up underneath her shirt, stroking the smooth skin of her stomach, then higher. He lifted her shirt, taking in the soft pink bra she had on and what looked to be a colorful butterfly tattooed on the upper swell of her right breast. Granted, he saw it only briefly because he closed his eyes when he leaned forward and took her breast in his mouth, sucking her through the satin.

Yep, they'd gone from zero to sixty in a minute flat. If she didn't put the brakes on, they were going to careen out of control. He wanted her so fucking much it hurt.

"Jared... Oh, yes... Yes." Hope held his head against her as she moaned.

He teased her nipple through the fabric, then pushed her bra up and gave her his full attention. First one pebbled tip, then the other. She was still grinding against him, the warmth between her thighs driving him wild. If it weren't for his jeans and her shorts, he could've easily slid up inside the heaven of her body.

Releasing her from his mouth, Jared kissed her again, holding her head as he attempted to slow things down. He'd known that this thing between them was explosive, but he honestly hadn't intended to get down to business quite this soon. Sure, in his fantasies, maybe. But the gentlemanly side of his brain told him he needed to chill.

Only he couldn't seem to stop and Hope didn't seem to want him to.

Jared

Hope's hands tugged his T-shirt out of his jeans, then lifted it up and over his head. He groaned low in his throat when her mouth slid down his neck to his chest. Her hands wandered over his stomach, soft and silky smooth. He stroked her back, his eyes rolling back in his head. Her touching him... More than he could process right now.

"Nothing wrong yet," she mumbled.

"Huh?"

"Nothing."

"Hope..." He wanted to tell her they should stop, but his brain wouldn't relay the information to his mouth. Apparently his dick was in charge, and no way was he going to stop if that was the case.

When she reached for the button on his jeans, he knew there was no turning back.

"You sure about this?" he asked, his hands cupping her breasts while she attempted to undress him.

"Absolutely. Lose the clothes, Walker."

Well, he always had been good at following directions.

THE INSTANT SHE saw Jared standing on her front porch, so overwhelmingly tall and sexy, Hope knew exactly where this night was headed. And when he reached for her as though he couldn't keep his hands off, she gave in to her overwhelming urges as well.

Since the night at Marla's, she'd thought about him at least a dozen times. No, make that two dozen. Per day.

For whatever reason—lack of sex, hormones out of whack, you name it—Hope simply couldn't stop thinking about him. More accurately, she couldn't stop thinking about getting him naked.

110

And though she'd almost had herself convinced that there was something wrong with him—had to be because this man was too good to be true—she couldn't find anything at the moment. She'd happily keep searching, though.

Oh. Boy.

And now that he was here...

She couldn't get enough of this man. Especially now that he was shirtless. As her sister had said, God had been in a damn good mood the day He made Jared. Damn good mood. The man was perfect in every possible way. All hard angles covered by smooth, tanned skin. He had soft, dark hair covering his chest, which she liked. A lot. There was something about a man with hair on his chest.

Jared chuckled as she tried to release him from his jeans. With her sitting on his lap, that wasn't going to happen easily, but she didn't want to stop. She wanted to feel him inside her right now, and if she had to wait another minute, she was going to scream.

"Stand up," he instructed.

Hope crawled off of him and got to her feet, watching him, waiting for... She didn't know what she was waiting for, but she needed him. Right fucking now.

He seemed to know that, because Jared's eyes locked on hers, and then he was removing her shirt, working the button free on her shorts. He even managed to get them off of her with little movement, relieved her of her bra and panties before pulling her back onto his lap, once again straddling his hips.

"You have too many clothes on," she told him. She was stark naked, and he had on his jeans and boots.

When he produced a condom, a sigh of relief escaped her.

"In a hurry?" he teased.

His gaze was smoldering as he looked at her, his eyes slowly caressing her overheated skin.

"More than you know." Why the hell shouldn't she be honest with him? It was clear what they were doing. It wasn't often that she had the chance to tear off some sexy cowboy's clothes in her living room.

Jared

"I thought you said you wanted to get to know me first," he said, his voice gruff.

"I decided I know all I need to know." Not quite the truth, but no way was she going to put this on hold. They had plenty of time to get to know each other. And if they didn't, it really didn't matter. The chemistry at work here clearly wasn't built on friendship and understanding.

Jared lifted his hips, forcing his jeans down to his thighs, and in an instant, he had the condom rolled over his length while Hope stared down at him. The man was … extremely well-endowed. Thankfully, she didn't have time to contemplate the mechanics of how this was going to work, because Jared pulled her back to him, their lips melding together, and Hope was once again in charge.

She lifted up at the same time she reached between her legs, guiding him right where she wanted him most. It took a moment, but she managed to work herself down on him, taking most of him inside her with little discomfort.

"Yesssss." He felt so damn good. So freaking good. It'd been so long… He stretched her, filled her, caused a fiery storm to ignite in her womb, ratcheting up her need tenfold.

"Relax, Hope…" He pulled his mouth from hers and glanced down to where they were now joined. "Darlin'… Oh, fuck yes… You're so damn tight."

It sounded almost as though he was trying to warn her, but she ignored him. Instead, she lifted up slightly, lowered herself back down. All the while watching him watching her. It was sexy as fuck. It was like she'd gone to the all-you-can-eat buffet and started with dessert first. And in this case, Jared Walker was the sweetest chocolate ever made.

Jared's hands moved to her hips as he began guiding her, rocking her onto his erection, giving her a little more with every upward stroke. When he lifted his eyes and met her gaze, she saw everything he wanted her to see.

"You riding my dick… Best feeling ever. Don't stop, Hope. Ride me, darlin'."

Oh, boy. If he kept that up, she stood no chance against him.

Hope couldn't keep from staring at him while she took her pleasure from his body. The heat of his hands on her hips, the warmth of his gaze as he watched her breasts, the exquisite friction…

"Keep goin'," he urged. "You're not done yet, Hope. You're so damn beautiful. And you feel so fucking good. So soft, so hot, so wet. God, yes."

Hope squeezed her inner muscles, watching the way his eyes rolled back when she did. Yeah, he definitely liked that. She probably could've done that all night long, but she suddenly needed more. She was riding that fine edge, the unmistakable hum of an impending orgasm beginning in her core. She was going to come, no doubt about that.

Jared must've sensed that she was close, because he wrapped his arms around her, pulling her against him, her breasts crushed to his chest, his mouth meeting hers again. And while he kissed her hard, Jared held her to him, thrusting his hips upward to meet her.

"Yes," she murmured against his mouth. "That… Oh, God… Keep … doing … that…"

Before she had a chance to warn him, Hope's entire body ignited into a firestorm of sensation, her orgasm ripping through her, hot and bright and so damn incredible.

"You comin' for me, darlin'?"

"Oh, yeah," she managed to groan, her body drawn up tight as she crested again thanks to the incredible thrusting of his hips.

"Can you come for me again?"

"If you … keep … doing… Oh, God, Jared!" How he did it, she didn't know, but suddenly Hope was soaring once again, but this time, he went right over the edge with her.

Chapter Thirteen

JARED DID HIS best to catch his breath, but it wasn't easy. Whatever had just happened between him and Hope... Holy. Fuck.

Quite possibly the best orgasm of his entire fucking life.

He ran his hand down Hope's back. She was still lying against him, still straddling him, still sheathing him inside her warm body. And the hell of it was he didn't want to move. He wanted to remain right there forever. Or for at least another couple of hours so that he could do that again.

"That was ... surprising," Hope said, smiling when she sat up to look at him.

Jared smiled, too. He couldn't help himself. "Surprising, huh? I could've come up with a million different adjectives."

"Yeah?" Her eyes glittered with amusement. "Such as?"

"Incredible. Mind-blowing. Amazing. Fan-fucking-tastic. Best sex ever."

Hope laughed and this time he dislodged from her body, his cock far too sensitive after that explosive ordeal. Before he was ready, Hope climbed off of him and began retrieving her clothes from the floor around them. While she dressed, he went to the bathroom to dispose of the condom. Telling himself he was giving her a little privacy, he closed the door and took a moment, staring at himself in the mirror above the sink.

He looked like a man who'd been fucked within an inch of his life.

Which was probably true. Sweet little Hope Lambert had completely and totally rocked his world.

Okay, so maybe he'd figured that would happen if he was really, really lucky. He wasn't sure he'd done enough good deeds in his life to deserve this. Then again, he wasn't going to get all sappy, either. Sex was sex. Sex with Hope was... Well, maybe it was more than sex. It was mind-blowing, as he'd told her. But he had to remember that there wasn't anything else for him here. Hope had already told him that it couldn't be more. She wasn't looking for a relationship.

Then again, neither was he.

"Holy fuck," he whispered to his reflection.

Not wanting to dwell on the crazy sensation tormenting his insides, he cleaned up and righted his jeans before stepping out to find Hope placing the food he'd brought on plates. She was so fucking sexy. He honestly had thought she couldn't look better than she had the day he met her when she'd been wearing a T-shirt, jeans, and boots, her straw hat on her head, but fuck if he hadn't been dead wrong. She looked incredible wearing those short jean shorts and that flowy shirt that offered a hint of her tanned stomach or even her back, depending on which way she moved.

"Hungry?" she asked, smiling over at him.

"Starving." He simply didn't know what he was hungry for. Food or her.

Definitely her.

"Come on then. Sit down. You want a beer?"

"Sure."

After tugging his T-shirt back on, Jared claimed one of the chairs at her table, but he waited until she sat down before doing the same.

"This gentlemanly thing"—Hope waved her hand at him—"is it hard to do?"

"What gentlemanly thing?" Jared picked up his fork but kept his eyes on her.

"Opening doors, pulling out chairs..."

"I guess I don't even think about it. It's the way I was raised."

"I like it."

Jared grinned. "I figured you'd be used to it. Workin' on the ranch and all."

Jared

"The term *cowboy* is not synonymous with *gentleman*. At least not always. A lot of the cowboys I encounter prefer the look to the real deal."

"Is that right?" Jared took a bite.

"Yep." Hope put her hand on her beer bottle. "And I'm not making fun of you by any means. I really do like it. Unfortunately, it's a rare trait these days."

"Not in my family," he told her. "My father would tan my hide if I didn't treat a woman with respect."

Hope's cheeks turned a pretty shade of pink.

"Why're you blushin'?" he inquired.

"I was wonderin' if your daddy would consider what we just did respectful."

Jared dropped his gaze to his food. Now he was the one blushing, and wasn't that just stupid. He did not blush.

"Again," Hope said, "not making fun. I'm actually lookin' forward to doin' it again. Soon."

It was a close call, but he managed not to choke on his steak. "Good to know."

"Since we seem to be doin' things backwards, tell me about yourself."

"What do you wanna know?"

"You said you were raised in El Paso. You've got four brothers, one sister, all younger. I'm assumin' your folks are still alive because you mentioned your father in present tense."

"They are," he confirmed. He remembered his first trip to the ranch, when they'd had a brief but somewhat personal conversation. "You've got a good memory."

"So I'm told." She smiled and took a swig of her beer. "What is it that you do?"

"I run Walker Demolition. When my cousin, Travis, built his sex resort, he needed someone to take over the family business."

Hope's eyes widened and she snorted. "Sex resort?"

"Cheyenne never mentioned it?"

"Nope. She must've left that part out."

116

He grinned while he chewed. "Yep, Coyote Ridge has its very own fetish hotel. Four of my cousins work there full-time. My uncle Curtis was the one who convinced me to take the job at Walker Demo when Travis wanted to step away. It required me to move from El Paso, but I was…"

Shit. He really didn't want the conversation to take this turn.

"Divorced?"

Okay, well, looked as though he didn't need to explain too much. "Yeah. Divorced. I needed to get away for a little while."

"Are you plannin' to go back?" Hope looked both casual and curious as she continued to eat while managing to interrogate him at the same time.

"To El Paso?"

She nodded.

"No. At least not anytime soon. I like Coyote Ridge. Derrick—my son—likes it there."

"How old is he?"

"He turned four on May sixth."

"Does he live with you?"

Jared met Hope's gaze, trying to determine how much information he wanted this woman to have. He liked her. Really liked her. But she had already told him this was a temporary thing, and in order to fulfill that obligation, Jared knew that they couldn't share too much about themselves.

"Sorry. I didn't mean to pry."

He picked up his beer bottle but didn't take a drink. He held her stare for several silent seconds. "Hope, I'll tell you anything you wanna know. But if you want this to remain casual…"

"You're right." She put down her fork. "I don't really want to know."

Jared expected to hear those words. They'd agreed to this up front. What he didn't understand was why he was suddenly overcome with disappointment.

"This is about sex." Hope's smile once again lit up her face. "So finish that up so we can get back to it."

Well, then.

117

Jared

Disappointment all but forgotten.

HOPE KNEW SHE'D been digging too deep. Jared was right about them needing to keep this somewhat casual. Granted, the sex wasn't casual by any means, but yes, if she got to know him too well, there was a good chance she might start to like him. Well, more than she already did. As friends. She refused to like him more than that. She didn't mind a friends-with-benefits type deal going on, as long as neither of them expected more in the end.

It wasn't easy, but she managed to focus on eating in silence for a few minutes. When they were both done, she rinsed the dishes and put them in the dishwasher while Jared put the empty containers back into the paper sack.

"You want another beer?" she asked, wiping her hands on a dish towel before turning back around to find him standing less than a foot away.

"I don't want another beer." His voice was deep and dark and so damn sexy. It matched the intensity in his eyes.

"Then what do you want?" She hardly got the words out; her heart rate was already accelerating as he moved even closer. Then closer still. She gripped the edge of the counter behind her, his large body boxing her in. And then she was looking up into his face, studying his features, trying to see what his intentions were.

Jared stared down at her, not saying anything. His hands were on her hips, but they slowly worked their way up, once again removing her shirt. Hope didn't stop him. She didn't want to stop him. His touch felt so good. Although she tried to play the part, she hadn't been with a man since Ben. Two years was a long time to go without the intimate human contact that Jared was providing. She never wanted him to stop.

Hope swallowed hard when he reached around and deftly unhooked her bra. His work-roughened fingers sensually scraped down her arms as he slid it from her body. Still, he said nothing. The only sound was her ragged breaths as she waited for whatever he would do next.

Then he was once again picking her up, but this time he deposited her on the counter, his hands roaming up to her breasts, cupping them firmly. Hope got the sense that he was trying to refrain, trying to take things slower this time. Only she didn't want slow. She wanted this man to lose every last ounce of his control.

She couldn't look away from him. There was a muscle flexing in his stubble-lined jaw. He looked to be trying to hold back, his eyes moving over her face as though he was trying to memorize every feature.

And wasn't that sexy as hell. Watching this man who seemed solely focused on her, wanting nothing but her, thinking of no one but her.

He was good.

Damn good.

The seduction thing... Jared Walker was a master of it.

Similar to earlier, Jared managed to rid her of her shorts and panties in record time. The tiled countertop was cold against her butt, but Hope didn't dare move. She couldn't. She was riveted to this moment, never wanting it to end.

Once again, she tugged at his shirt, wanting him to remove it so she could look at him the way he was looking at her. The man was masculine perfection. All ripped with muscle and smooth, firm skin. It was evident he didn't work out in a gym. His muscles were the kind earned from hard manual labor. She wasn't sure what it was he did at Walker Demolition, but whatever it was, he managed to stay in shape.

This scene was playing out much the same as earlier. Not that she cared. The only difference was they were in the kitchen this time and not on the couch. However, the same overwhelming magnetism was still there, pulling them together.

Jared

Fumbling a couple of times, Hope managed to unbutton Jared's jeans, never breaking eye contact. They were both breathing hard at this point, but still, they seemed to be holding back, and she wasn't quite sure why that was.

Jared's hands slid like water over her skin. She wanted more, but she didn't want to break whatever this was between them. She'd never experienced this type of intimacy when it came to sex. Not a word spoken, but so many things were right there, most of them in the way Jared looked at her. There was no doubt that he wanted her.

Once again he retrieved a condom from his wallet, and she briefly wondered how many he carried in there at one time, but she didn't ask. Truthfully, it didn't really matter. As long as he was prepared, she was good. And if he wasn't, she had her own stash they could use.

"Let me," she offered, taking the condom from his fingers. She quickly opened it, then rolled it over his length. He was hot and hard and smooth in her hand, silk over steel.

"Hope..."

As soon as he was covered, it was as though something snapped. His mouth slammed down on hers, her arms swinging around him, pulling him closer while he shifted her so that she was hovering on the edge of the counter when he entered her.

"Oh, yes..."

The kiss was brutally hot, yet Jared remained in control the entire time. He didn't fumble, didn't slobber on her like some men did. No, he worked her mouth with his tongue, making her melt beneath the onslaught of need that caused all of her nerve endings to come to life. Similar to the way he was fucking her. It was hot and wild and... This was perfection in every way.

"Can't get enough," he groaned, nipping her lip as he shifted her, changing the angle, making her cry out in exquisite ecstasy.

"Harder," she urged.

Jared delivered, his hand at her back holding her in place while he plunged inside her over and over, deeper and deeper.

The only thing she could do was dig her fingernails into his back and give herself over to the incredible friction that was quickly pushing her closer and closer to release. His arms tightened around her, his tongue thrashing against hers as he continued to thrust his hips forward, filling her again and again. Hope couldn't hold back any longer, and when she cried out, Jared swallowed the sound, his rumbled groans vibrating against her as he continued to fuck her, never relenting. It became clear that he wasn't going to settle on merely one orgasm, and the way he was using her body would surely push her over the edge one … more … time…

"Jared!" Hope grabbed him as her body exploded, harder than the first time.

It was then that he slammed into her several more times, still holding her tightly as he chased his release. And the roar that followed was likely the sexiest thing she'd ever heard.

Jared

Chapter Fourteen

THE FOLLOWING MORNING, Jared woke as the first rays of the sun began trickling into the room. He took a moment to orient himself, remembering that he was in Hope's bed. Her warm body was still curled up next to him. He grabbed his phone from the nightstand, glanced at it to ensure he hadn't missed any calls or texts. Nope. Nothing. He knew he had to head back to Coyote Ridge so he could pick up Derrick, but he couldn't bring himself to leave just yet.

Not without having this woman one more time before he did.

After they'd fucked in the kitchen, Hope had pulled him into her bedroom, where they had stretched out on her bed. He hadn't been able to resist kissing her until they were both too tired to stay awake a second longer.

But now he was awake again and he was ready for round three.

Doing his best not to rouse her, Jared pushed the sheet down, revealing her sweet little body to his hungry gaze. He could see Hope's toned muscles beneath all that soft, golden skin. It was clear she spent a lot of time outdoors. The freckles on her shoulders and the few scattered across her nose told him she'd logged plenty of hours in the sun. She was a little on the skinny side, but he didn't hold it against her. It was clear she worked hard, and if what Cheyenne had told him was true, she spent more than her fair share of time running this ranch.

He wanted to spend more than his fair share of time exploring every inch of her. His mouth watered with the need to taste her.

It took a little effort, but he managed to move down so that he was perched between her legs, brushing his lips over her breasts, her belly, her hip before settling into place. He kissed the inside of her knees, watching to see if her eyes were open, then slowly moved up her thighs. Nope, still closed. Before he reached his target, he felt Hope shift, her legs spreading, providing him better access.

Not one to bypass an opportunity, Jared took complete advantage, running his tongue over her delicate skin, licking her gently. She was completely bare, and even now, though her eyes weren't open, he could tell she was wet and ready for him. That alone made his dick harden more than it was already.

He ignored his body, choosing to focus on hers. Jared used his fingers to open her so he could slide his tongue against the soft, pink flesh. He lazily licked her, teasing her clit briefly, gently ringing her entrance.

"You could wake me up like this every single day for the rest of my life… Oh, jeezus, that's good."

He knew she didn't mean that the way it sounded—the rest of her life was a long damn time. But today, he could definitely help her out. Without rushing, Jared fondled and teased, dipping his fingertip inside her while he suckled her clit. He didn't stop until Hope's fingers were wound in his hair, holding him to her. She clearly enjoyed his ministrations, so he continued, focusing on the swollen bundle of nerves. He worked her until she was writhing on the bed, pulling his hair.

"Don't stop," she whispered. "Don't ever stop."

Jared put forth a little more effort, wanting to make her come before he gave in to his body's need for her.

"Oh, yes… Oh, yes… Oh… Jared!"

He gripped her hips, fusing his mouth to her as she came in a rush. He let her ride out her climax, gently lapping at her, enjoying the way she tasted on his tongue.

When he looked up at her, he saw she was holding a condom in one hand, a gorgeous smile on her face, her blue-green eyes glittering.

Jared

A few minutes later, when he plunged deep into her body, Jared knew there was no better way than this to start the day. Or any day, for that matter.

WHEN JARED LEFT, after he'd thoroughly kissed her on her front porch, Hope had hopped in her truck and made a beeline for the main house. It was later than she normally started the day, but considering how she'd spent the last hour, she didn't much care. So she pretended that it was early and wandered into the kitchen, snatching a couple of biscuits before smothering them in sausage gravy. She ate right there, standing by the stove, hoping no one would interrupt.

With luck on her side, she wolfed down her food, rinsed the plate in the sink, and then slipped right back unnoticed, making her way to the barn. Only then did she breathe a sigh of relief.

"Had company last night, did you?" Mercy called out, sauntering out from beside the house.

Hope jumped, her hand going over her heart. "You scared me."

Mercy grinned, clearly pleased to know that.

"So that's a yes? Company?"

Crap. Of course her youngest sister would be the one to notice that. Of all of them, Mercy was the one who gave everyone the most shit. She was also the one who loved sticking her nose in everyone else's business but made sure to keep any prying eyes off of whatever it was she did in her spare time.

"Good morning, Mercy," Hope said, refusing to let her sister spoil this for her. Seriously, no one could spoil this day for her. After the way Jared had woken her up... Nope, no one.

"He's a hot one," Mercy said as she fell into step beside her. "Jared Walker, right?"

Hope glared at her sister but didn't respond.

That only caused Mercy to laugh. "That's what I thought."

Hope spun around, suddenly needing to ensure Mercy didn't go running her mouth. The last thing she needed was for anyone to think that she was dating this man. What they had going between them was uncomplicated. When other people started talking about it, complications were sure to arise. Hope didn't want to take that risk.

"He's just a friend," she explained.

"Friend with benefits?"

"Yes." Might as well tell the truth. "But that's all it is. Nothing more. So, please, can you just leave it alone?"

"I'll think about it. But probably not."

Hope sighed, then turned and continued toward the barn. She had things to do and probably should've bypassed breakfast, but she'd been too hungry to function. After Jared had given her another couple of orgasms this morning, it was a wonder she had enough strength to walk, let alone work.

"So, when's he comin' back?" Mercy asked, clearly ignoring Hope's request to leave it alone.

Hope shrugged. She wasn't sure when she was going to see him again, but as soon as he was out of sight, she'd told herself she needed to wait at least a week.

Granted, a week felt like an incredibly long time, especially when she was sure that man had become her newest addiction. Still, this sex thing was only going to work if they managed to keep some space between them.

Not that she'd told him that, but Hope knew that Jared understood. Since he had a little boy at home, it wasn't like he could do a lot of sleepovers anyway.

"Well, if it's any consolation," Mercy said when they reached the porch, "it sure is nice to see a smile on your face."

Hope faced her sister once again, completely taken aback by the comment. Mercy was serious. There wasn't a single teasing note in her voice, which was surprising. Mercy was the most obnoxious, always getting in everyone's business. Hope figured it was her way of keeping people from getting into hers.

"It's been a long time," Mercy said softly. "You deserve to be happy."

Jared

But before Hope could say anything more, her sister spun around and left her standing there, jaw hanging to the ground.

MERCY SET OFF for the mechanic shop, needing to stop by and grab something before Cody Mercer arrived for the day. She'd been steering clear of him for ... a long time now. It seemed to be getting easier, but she was starting to believe that was wishful thinking. Or maybe the opposite.

For the longest time, Cody had pursued her, and truth be told, Mercy had liked him. Oh, who was she kidding? She still liked him, although she'd rather die than have anyone figure that out. Especially Cody. If the man knew that she liked him, Mercy figured he would finally move on. That was how it worked, right? He chased her, she gave in, he walked the other way.

And they both knew she'd given in. It had been wild, too. But because she had pretended it was meaningless, Cody continued to be interested. But Mercy wasn't ready for him to stop being interested. Not that she made a habit of being a dick tease. That certainly wasn't the case. It hadn't been her plan in the beginning, either, but the second she'd realized things between them could get really serious, she'd panicked.

Think about it. His last name was Mercer. Her first name was Mercy. Uhh... No freaking way could she ever let it get serious with him. She was not going to be Mercy Mercer.

Which was why she was slipping into the building after glancing inside to ensure it was empty. She needed a wrench, but she hadn't wanted to ask him for it. She refused to talk to him unless it was absolutely necessary. And this wasn't one of those times.

It only took a minute for her to find what she was looking for. She started for the door at the same time someone turned the knob on the outside.

"Shit," she mumbled. *Please God, if you're in a good mood today, don't let it be Cody.*

Clearly He wasn't in a good mood, because the man who stepped through that door was none other than the bane of her existence. All six feet of him with those gorgeous emerald-green eyes that were instantly on her.

"Hey," he greeted, looking away. "Need something?"

"Nope," she said, inserting a ridiculous amount of cheer into her tone. "I found it."

Knowing there was no way this wouldn't be awkward, Mercy launched herself toward the door. She thought she was home free until Cody called out after her.

She paused, the door open, one foot outside. Damn. She was so close to freedom.

"Are you still seeing that guy?" Cody asked.

Mercy knew which guy Cody was referring to. His name was Daniel, and she wasn't seeing him, but no one knew that. The first time Cody had jumped to that conclusion, Mercy had learned it was an easy way to get him to back off. Since Daniel was nothing more than a friend, letting Cody assume that she was dating him had seemed harmless at the time.

Rather than answer—she didn't want to lie to him—she turned and met his gaze, giving him her best *what do you think?* look before practically leaping out the door and letting it close behind her.

CHAPTER FIFTEEN

"YEP. THAT'S WHAT I heard," Jaxson said, leaning his chair back on two legs.

Jared watched his cousin carefully. "You're worse than a goddamn girl, you know that?"

Jaxson chuckled, then dropped his chair to the floor. "Maybe, but it's still true. No sense trying to deny it."

"True or not..." Jared wasn't sure how he'd gotten caught up in this conversation. When Jaxson had come into the office to tell him about the latest rumor—apparently Jared was in a hot and heavy, not to mention very serious, relationship with a woman in a neighboring town—Jared knew he should've thrown him out right then. "Let it go."

"You like her, don't you?" Jaxson used that annoying teasing voice, like one of his brothers would've used to piss him off when they were kids.

Jaxson was Maryanne's oldest son. And since Maryanne happened to be Jared's father's youngest sister, Jared was no doubt going to have to work with the man through this reunion ordeal. Never mind the fact that Jaxson filled in at Walker Demo when needed. He refused to take on a full-time job because he preferred his jack-of-all-trades lifestyle, which he'd turned into a fairly lucrative business as a handyman in Coyote Ridge.

"I do like her," he told Jaxson, knowing if he denied it, the man wouldn't stop. "But that doesn't mean you have to act like a ten-year-old. Don't you have someone's pool to clean or somethin'?"

Jaxson grinned. "As a matter of fact..."

"No married women, Jaxson," Jared warned as his cousin headed for the door.

"I've got some morals, thank you very much."

"Just not all that many."

"True. But you don't hear the ladies complainin'."

"I don't hear 'em singin' your praises, either."

"That's because you're not in the same room. Trust me, there's an awful lot of 'oh, God, Jaxson, you're so good at that' going on."

Jared waved him off with a choked laugh. "Go on. Get outta here. Oh, and thanks for helpin' out. I appreciate it."

"Anytime!" Jaxson pushed open the screen door. "Oh, hey, Trav. What's up?"

Jared heard the rumbling sound of voices when Jaxson stepped outside, but he didn't hear what they were saying. He didn't much care, either, since Jaxson was probably sharing the most recent rumor that Travis would want to confirm in five…

Four…

Three…

Two…

"Hey," Travis greeted, his tone somber when he stepped into the office. "Got a sec?"

Jared nodded, then leaned back in his chair. He'd been waiting for Travis to get back with him before he reached out to Sable. It wasn't that he wanted to give in to her demands, but he did need to see how serious she was about trying to take Derrick from him.

Travis perched on the edge of the desk across from him. "I don't have much news, but I did call in a couple of favors. I've got people looking into what Sable's been up to for the past two years."

Jared sighed. He knew that was probably a waste of time. Hell, he knew what she'd been up to. Probably screwing any man who could get it up for her. That was the way she worked.

"I do know that she hasn't married," Travis told him.

"I knew that. The guy she said was Derrick's dad kicked her to the curb when he found out the truth. The other was an old, rich guy who probably saw her comin' a mile away."

Jared

Travis nodded. "I also know that she's been stayin' at her parents' place these last few weeks."

Jared sat up. "Really?" That was interesting considering Sable didn't get along with her folks.

"I think it's safe to assume she's run outta money," Travis noted.

"Sounds like it."

"Which means she's comin' after you for more. Probably trying to squeeze you for whatever she can. Since she knows what Derrick means to you—to this whole family—she's gonna put the hurtin' on but good."

"I need to call my lawyer," Jared told him.

"Probably. At least to get an idea of what Sable's chances are of gettin' him back."

Slim to none, Jared hoped.

"With the rumors runnin' through town," Travis continued, "she's gonna be pissed if she does show up here. I think she thinks she has you by the balls. If she finds out you're seein' someone…"

"I'm not." Jared sighed. "It's not serious, but yes, I'm seein' Hope. That stays between you and me, Trav."

Travis nodded.

"I'm not too worried about Sable," he lied.

"You shouldn't be." Travis stood up. "The two of you have the support of this entire family, Jared. We're not gonna let her come in and fuck this up for you. That's the way family works."

Jared had to look away. The fact that Travis and the rest of the family had his back made a world of difference.

"Should I call her?"

Travis shook his head. "Nah. Email her back. That way you can say you contacted her within her time frame. She'll respond, but again, just drag it out. Once she realizes she ain't gonna get money here, she'll move on to the next guy."

"I don't want her anywhere near Derrick," Jared told him, maintaining eye contact so his cousin could see the seriousness in his eyes. They'd had this conversation the other day, and Jared had told him he didn't know what he wanted. Now he knew.

130

"Understood. She won't get near him, I guarantee that." With that, Travis nodded, then headed for the door. "You hear from her, let me know. I'll do what I can from this side."

"I appreciate it," Jared called out.

"That's what family's for," Travis answered, the screen door slamming behind him.

When the office was empty, Jared turned to his computer. It seemed that he'd spent more time this week fighting off his family and their accusations that he'd found some woman in a neighboring town than doing anything else. Sure, he'd spent the night with Hope last Friday, but heaven almighty, how the hell had it spread through town so quickly?

Well, technically, the rumor didn't include Hope's name. Apparently, whoever started it didn't know *who* Jared was spending his time with, but they'd been pretty adamant he'd been spending it with someone.

Small towns.

That was one thing he definitely missed about El Paso. It wasn't small enough for everyone to know everyone. He'd been a mere number for the Census Bureau. But here in Coyote Ridge, he was a Walker, therefore he was on the top of the gossip list.

Jared glanced at the clock. It was already two thirty. Seemed every day this week he had been counting the minutes, wondering if Hope was going to break down and call him. Up to now, she hadn't so much as sent an email or a text message. Then again, he hadn't sent her anything, either. He'd been hoping she would make the next move.

Fact was, he was going batshit crazy waiting for her. He wanted to see her again, wanted to get his hands on her again. Hell, he sometimes feared that he'd dreamed what had happened between them. They'd damn near burned up that tiny little cabin of hers that night.

Jared

"You're a fool," he muttered to himself. He wasn't supposed to be worried about a woman. Any woman. He needed to focus all his energy on taking care of Derrick and avoiding Sable at all costs. The little boy was all he needed in his life. Him and his family, that was. Jared damn sure didn't need some woman in his life, insisting that he spend time with her, take her out, romance her, and all that shit.

So why the fuck couldn't he get Hope Lambert out of his head?

He had a feeling he knew that answer already.

One, the sex was off the fucking charts.

And two, the woman didn't seem to give a fuck if he was wining and dining her. Hell, if he had to guess, she hadn't thought about him once since he left her house on Saturday morning.

He should've been happy about that.

Key word being should've.

GRACIE LEANED BACK, propping her feet up on the desk in the small office they all shared. Hope had been trying to knock out a couple of things before she got back to her chores, but her sister didn't seem to care that she was busy.

"When're you gonna see him again?" Gracie asked.

"I'm not," Hope said simply. Truth was, she didn't know if or when she would see Jared again. She had a feeling she would for the simple fact that he was planning a family reunion at the ranch, but as far as casually, Hope wasn't sure that was going to happen.

She'd bitten off more than she could chew when it came to Jared, and she knew that after only one night with the man. As much as she wanted to be the casual-sex kind of girl, she couldn't do it. Her heart was already getting invested, and that wouldn't do anyone any good. She hadn't been lying when she told Jared she wasn't looking for a relationship. Certainly not with a single dad.

Apparently, her brain and her heart weren't on the same page. Her heart wanted to put up a wall, protect her from future heartache, but her brain wouldn't shut off. She thought about Jared constantly. Probably would've been a hell of a lot easier *not* to think about him if her sisters would mind their own damn business.

"Why the hell not?" Gracie didn't move, didn't seem fazed that Hope wasn't interested in talking.

"Because." That was all she had.

Gracie chuckled. "Oh, you're so full of shit."

Hope lifted her gaze to her sister. "It's not like that. He's hiring us for his family reunion."

"Oh, and now you get down and dirty with all the folks lookin' to schedule an event here? That's quite a sign-on bonus, don't you think?"

"Shut up." Hope turned her attention back to the computer. "I've got stuff to do, then I've gotta go check on the calf."

"I'll be more than happy to do that for you."

"Yeah, thanks." That would definitely make Hope's afternoon easier. She had too much shit to do as it was.

"Under one condition."

Hope shook her head. "Forget about it. I'll get it taken care of."

"What's wrong with this guy that you don't wanna see him again?"

"I never said there was anything wrong with him." Or that she didn't want to see him again. More like she *shouldn't* see him again.

"So, what? You just ignore him so he'll go away?"

Hope turned her chair to face Grace, then dropped her arms onto the desk. "What do you want from me, Gracie? Don't you have a wedding to plan?"

"All taken care of." Gracie grinned. "See, I've got these amazing sisters who love me enough to make my special day perfect."

Hope rolled her eyes.

"Don't you ever wanna get married?" Gracie's tone was less teasing.

Jared

Frowning, she shook her head and turned back to the computer screen. "Not in my life plan."

"So what is? Running this place until you're old and wrinkled?"

"Yep. That's my goal."

"You're nuts."

"And I'm also busy," she told Gracie seriously.

"Yeah, yeah, yeah. Always busy." Grace dropped her feet to the floor. "Hope, you really need to get a life."

"I have a life, thank you very much. And it involves taking care of this place. It ain't gonna run itself."

"Nope, it's not. That's why the rest of us are here. We bust our asses day in and day out to help run it. Doesn't mean that's the only thing we do."

Hope cocked an eyebrow. "Really?" She snorted. "I seem to recall you turnin' tail and runnin' when a coupla cowboys came chasin' after you. I don't think you're the one I should be takin' romantic advice from, quite frankly."

"Well, you should take it from somebody. Or, seriously, you're gonna wake up old and gray and wrinkled. No babies, no husband to share your bed with. You'll be all alone and ... old."

Hope had heard this spiel from too many people over the years. Her sisters were always giving her a hard time. A couple of times her dad would weigh in on the subject as well. It was tiring. "I couldn't think of a better way to spend my life." It was probably the biggest lie she'd ever told.

"All right. You win," Gracie huffed. "I'll quit."

"Thank you. Now go check on the calf," Hope ordered.

"Sure. But then I'm headin' home early today. I've got a coupla cowboys who'll be wantin' dinner, and I fully intend to feed 'em when they get home."

"You don't cook," Hope reminded her sister.

"Who said anything about food?"

Hope was still laughing when the screen door slammed behind Grace. Her sister was something else. And no, Hope didn't much care for all the lectures she'd received over the years, but she knew her family meant well. They loved her and this was their way of showing it.

Leaning back in her chair, Hope stared at the computer screen. She hated that she had the sudden overwhelming urge to call Jared, to invite him over, to spend a couple of hours with him. Naked, of course. But sure, they could do some talking during that time. There wasn't anything wrong with that.

Except Jared had a life. He had a son. He had better things to do than come out to the ranch for a booty call. And no way was Hope going to him. Hell, she hadn't taken time off in… God, maybe she had never taken any time off. She didn't know, honestly.

What she did know was that if she ignored this ranch for even a minute, she'd spend the next week trying to play catch-up. She'd hired a few extra hands last year just to keep up with the work they did have. Granted, turnover on the ranch was great. Those who thought room and board meant easy work had another thing coming. Sunup to sundown, that was the way things ran around here. Considering this was the first weekend when they hadn't been flooded with guests, she really couldn't afford to get sidetracked.

Not even by a sexy, Wrangler-wearing, orgasm-inducing cowboy who knew how to play her body like a violin.

Nope. Especially not by him.

Hope shook her head in disbelief.

Because yes, she got the sneaky feeling she was going to call him.

Her body wanted a replay. That was the only reason. Really.

CHAPTER SIXTEEN

"HEY," JARED SAID as he held the phone to his ear, a smile plastered automatically on his face.

"Hey," Hope said, her voice soft, sweet.

She was the last person he'd expected to call him, although he wasn't disappointed in the least.

"What's up?" he asked, glancing in his rearview mirror to where Derrick was sitting in his car seat, watching the iPad he had in his hands, headphones on his ears.

"I was wondering if maybe you could stop by the ranch for a bit."

"Stop by?" Jared chuckled. "For any particular reason?"

"Yes."

She didn't elaborate, which intrigued him.

"Do I have to guess?" he teased.

"No. I ... want to see you."

"Do you now?"

Hope huffed. "If you don't want to stop by, just say so."

"Something you want to talk about?" he asked, changing his tactic.

"Yes."

"If it involves naked talking, I'm there," he told her, once again glancing back at Derrick, making sure his son couldn't hear him.

"That's exactly the kind of talking I'm hoping for."

"Well, hell, woman. Why didn't you just say so? I've got somethin' to take care of, but I can be there in ... probably three hours." That would put it just after dark. "That work for you?"

"Yep," she said sweetly. "I'll be down by the lake."

The lake?

This sounded promising.

"See you then," he told her, then waited until she disconnected the call.

Jared glanced in the rearview mirror again and found Derrick looking up at him as though he'd sensed him watching. A grin split the little boy's face as he held up his iPad, pointing to something on the screen.

Looked like Jared was going to have to find a babysitter.

* * *

It was a little more than three hours when Jared finally made it out to the ranch. He stopped one of the wranglers he saw wandering by and asked how to get down to the lake. By truck, it only took five minutes to get there, and when he did, he found Hope's truck parked on a section of land that dammed off the water.

He pulled in behind her, put it in park, and then hopped out. He took a look around before wandering down toward the water.

Sure enough, there was Hope, sitting on the small fishing pier, her feet dangling in the water. It was nice out tonight. Not too hot, not too cold. The weatherman kept threatening that a cold front would be blowing in any day now, hopefully dropping the temperatures a good ten degrees, but until it actually happened, Jared would remain skeptical.

"Hi," Hope greeted him when she turned to look his way.

"Hey."

"Have a seat." She patted the wood beside her.

Jared eased himself down, hanging his legs over, careful not to get his boots in the water.

Jared

And just like the last time he saw her, Jared was instantly overwhelmed with the urge to touch her. He'd honestly never felt this sort of unrestrained lust when it came to a woman. Hope Lambert did it for him. He thought about her endlessly. Day, night. Didn't matter. Even on the drive out, he'd imagined the many different ways he could greet her. The main one being with a smoldering kiss that would set them both aflame. Somehow, he managed to refrain.

In the dark, the two of them stared at one another briefly before he spoke. "I should probably be offended that you're using me for sex..." he teased, keeping his voice low.

"But you're not?" she asked.

"Offended? Not at all. Not when I see you. It takes a lot of damn effort to keep my hands off you."

"Why would you want to do that?"

Jared shrugged. "I figured you'd wanna talk."

They were silent again, still staring.

"How was your week?" she finally asked.

Jared shrugged, leaning back on his hands as he stared up at the sky. "Same as last week. Busy. No major fires to put out, so that's a plus." He peered over at her. "What about you?"

"Good. Things are slowin' down a little now that we're not in peak tourist season."

"What do you do in that downtime?"

"Depends. Chores come first, takin' care of the animals, you know? My sisters get to help more when we have fewer guests. We've got a small store on the property, which doesn't have to be open as much." She smiled, pushing a strand of hair behind her ear. "Like you, we have the normal disruptions. Problems with water, broken tractors, equipment failures. That sort of thing."

Jared stared out at the water, enjoying the sound of her voice. When he looked over, he found Hope staring at him. He could see the heat in her eyes. How they'd managed to make it these few minutes without mauling one another, he wasn't sure. He did know that it wouldn't be much longer before that happened.

Hope finally spoke. "I don't wanna talk anymore, Jared."

138

Damn, she was so beautiful. Her long blond hair glimmered in the moonlight; her turquoise eyes practically glowed.

She moved closer and Jared remained perfectly still, refusing to reach for her. He didn't trust himself. But then Hope straddled his thighs, and he wrapped his arm around her, holding her close, not wanting her to go into the water.

"This thing between us…" Hope smiled as she got settled. "I like where it's going."

Jared cocked an eyebrow.

"This only-sex thing," she explained. "We've got a month of it before your family reunion. I thought maybe we should come to an understanding."

Jared brushed her hair back behind her ear. "What's that?"

"I've come to accept that sex with you is … phenomenal."

"You don't say." He grinned, letting his hand drift up her thigh. Tonight she was wearing a dress. Nothing fancy. A little more than a sundress, probably. She had on a lightweight sweater over it, probably due to the cooler air coming off the water.

"I do say. But I think it'll be easier if we don't play any games."

"Like sex games?"

Hope chuckled, shifting closer, grinding against his rapidly growing erection, her fingers cool against his cheeks. "I like sex games."

Yeah, he suspected she really did.

"But those aren't the games I'm referring to," she clarified. "I was thinking more along the lines of who's gonna call who."

Jared hadn't called Hope, nor had he texted her, for the simple fact that he wanted her to make the next move. It hadn't been a game he was playing, but he could see how it might seem as though he were. His real reason had been because he wanted her to be sure this was what she wanted. He'd met women before who had agreed to only sex; however, after the first rodeo, they were moving on to planning the wedding and whatnot.

Although Jared was interested in something more than sex with Hope, he certainly wasn't entertaining any notions of happily ever after. Not this early on anyway.

Jared

Hope said she wanted this, but Jared hadn't wanted to assume anything.

"So, we'll what? Have a standing date?" he asked, grinning.

"Something like that." Hope leaned forward and brushed her lips against his. "You know, before you got here, I had this whole conversation planned out, but now that you're here, I really just want…" She leaned in closer to his ear, her breath warm against his cheek. "I really want to feel you inside me."

Jared curled one hand around Hope's head, bringing her mouth to his while his other hand slid beneath her dress, his fingers eagerly seeking her pussy. Oh, damn. The woman wasn't wearing panties. She'd obviously known exactly what she wanted when she invited him down here.

He teased her clit by grazing it with his thumb repeatedly, his tongue driving into her mouth as she latched on to his shoulders. As much as he liked her adventurous side, the hard wood planks of the pier weren't going to make this easy. Rather than tell her that, Jared shifted, getting to his feet as she wound herself around him. He had to move his hands to hold on to her, but she didn't seem to mind.

The only reason he pulled his mouth from hers was to ensure he wasn't going to take a walk off a really short pier as he tried to make his way up to his truck.

Thankfully, that trek didn't take him long at all.

WHEN JARED OPENED his truck door and pulled her inside with him—thankfully he'd opted for the backseat—Hope didn't say a word. It wasn't until he had the door closed, her perched on his lap, and was once again kissing her that she had to put the brakes on.

She peered around briefly, noticing there was no car seat in the back this time. It was a solid reminder that this man had a kid and she had to be extra careful with how far she let this go. Emotionally, of course. Sexually... Well, it was far too late for that because Hope was jonesing for this man.

"Were you worried someone would see us out there?" she asked, meeting his gaze.

Hope saw amusement reflected in the smoky blue depths.

"No," he told her. "That's the least of my worries."

"You don't mind an audience?" She meant it teasingly, but the heat that backlit his eyes told her that he hadn't taken it that way.

"My cousins run a fetish resort, Hope. I don't have a whole lot of limitations."

For some reason, that drew her up short. She hadn't thought about how many women he might've been with over the years. And no, she hadn't thought he'd been celibate since his divorce, but...

"I haven't taken any women there," he said, brushing his lips over hers. "In case that's what's going through that pretty head of yours. However, I have gone. I've checked it out, spent a little time ... watching."

"So that really is a thing? Watching?" Hope slid her sweater off her shoulders, revealing the strapless sundress she'd put on. She'd had one thing in mind when she had dressed—ease of removal.

Jared's eyes dropped to her mouth, her body warming as his hands grazed over her slowly.

"It's definitely a thing. So, if you'd ever like me to take you, just say the word."

Her? At a sex resort? Hope fought the urge to snort. Sure, she enjoyed sex as much as the next woman, but she couldn't imagine...

"Scoot back, just a little," Jared ordered.

Jared

Since Hope was facing him, straddling his lap, she had to move her butt toward his knees, her back against the front seat, in order to do what he asked. The backseat was much bigger than she'd thought it would be. Considering Jared's knees weren't up by his ears, there was quite a bit of room.

"Now put your feet up here," he instructed, patting the seat on either side of his hips.

Hope did.

Jared seemed to want to take it from there, so she sat there, reaching behind her head to hold on to the headrest, watching him while he put his big hands on her knees, pushing them wide, exposing her as he pushed her dress up to her waist. But he didn't stop there. With her arms stretched back, her breasts were thrust forward. He reached up, pulling the bodice down until her naked breasts were exposed.

She really was glad she had foregone the bra.

His fingers drifted lower, sliding over her bare mound, and she sucked in air as the intense sensation made the hair on the back of her neck stand on end.

"I like how wet you get for me," he said, his eyes flicking up to meet hers briefly before trailing ever so slowly back down. The heat of his gaze made her insides tremble, her womb contract. The man knew how to stoke a fire, that was for sure.

And when he met her eyes again, he held her gaze as his hands roamed, his fingers lightly grazing her skin.

Hope had never had adventurous or extremely verbal lovers, but Jared Walker seemed to be both of those. She tried to tell herself that was why she wanted this. Why she was looking for no strings for the next month. It certainly didn't hurt.

Jared's thumb slid through her slickness, grazing her clit, then gliding lower. Never once did he take his eyes off her face. It was as though he enjoyed watching her reactions. And she was certainly having those in spades. The man was wicked with his fingers, as well as other things. Like his tongue.

The mere thought sent a tremor through her.

His other thumb brushed over her bottom lip. "One of these days, I want to feel your sweet lips on my dick."

142

Heat exploded inside her. The thought of sucking him into her mouth, watching him the way he was watching her now... "Why wait?"

"'Cause I'm not done with you yet."

Hope's head fell backward when he pushed one thick finger inside her. "Ohhhh." She arched her back, trying to take his finger deeper, wishing he would add another.

"I could sit here and play with your pussy all night," he told her. "It would be so much better if I could taste you, slide my tongue right here..." He demonstrated with his finger. "I want to make you come again with my mouth, Hope."

Lifting her head, she met his gaze, doing her best not to rut against his hand.

Jared added another finger, fucking her slow and easy with two deliciously thick fingers while his thumb circled her clit, over and over.

"Why didn't we do this at your place?" he asked.

Hope shrugged. "I was hoping for ... adventure, I guess."

She hadn't wanted Jared to think she was boring, actually. They'd had sex on her couch, on her kitchen counter, and even in her bed. Those were all relatively safe places. She wanted to experiment, especially if she only had one month with him.

Jared twisted his hand around, driving his fingers even deeper as he pulled her mouth to his. "I definitely think a trip to AI is in your cards."

AI... Right, Alluring Indulgence. The sex resort.

She didn't know about that, but she didn't tell him as much. However, it had piqued her curiosity.

What could it hurt? She wouldn't be seeing him after his family reunion, and she wouldn't be seeing anyone at the resort after they went there either. Of course, Cheyenne was her cousin. As far as Hope knew, the woman was going to marry a Walker. If she was invited to the wedding—which she definitely would be—perhaps she would run into Jared again. That might be awkward.

"Would you like that, Hope?" Jared was pumping his fingers into her, deeper, faster, pushing her closer and closer to the edge. "I can show you what real adventure is."

Jared

Hope dug her fingernails into his shoulders, trying to hold on as he finger-fucked her. It felt so damn good.

"I won't let another man touch you, though. I'm not willing to share. But they can watch," Jared whispered close to her ear. "They can watch as I fuck you, as I drive my dick deep into your sweet pussy."

That did it. Whether it was the visual or simply the overwhelming sensations his fingers wrought from her body, Hope shattered, crying out his name over and over as she came on his fingers.

"How about we go someplace a little less adventurous for now?" Jared suggested. "Like your place so I can eat your pussy while you come on my face."

Yep, there was no doubt about it, Jared Walker's dirty, delicious mouth was going to make this more difficult than she'd thought. Hell, this was only the second time they'd been together. How was she supposed to survive another month without going completely out of her mind?

CHAPTER SEVENTEEN

BY THE TIME Wednesday rolled around, Jared was aching to see Hope again. Although he hadn't gone back to the ranch since the night he'd fingered her in his truck, then taken her home only to ravish her for another two hours, he was counting down the minutes until he could make that happen.

He had dedicated the weekend to Derrick, taking him to his favorite bounce house place just north of Austin on Saturday and then to the movies on Sunday. They'd had McDonald's for dinner on Saturday night and spent the evening with the whole family for Sunday dinner at Curtis and Lorrie's.

On Monday, he had hoped to slip out to the ranch to surprise Hope, but a problem with one of the jobsites had derailed him all day. Then on Tuesday, Jared got a response from Sable that had pissed him off for the better part of the day. It wasn't that he hadn't expected Sable to put a price tag on Derrick—she'd done it once already—but it had hit him at the exact wrong time.

According to Sable, Jared simply needed to wire her twenty-five thousand and she'd be out of his hair for good. If he opted not to, she'd take him for more than that when she took him to court. Sable was adamant that no court would keep a child from his mother.

Jared

Of course, Jared had forwarded it to Travis, and his cousin said he'd gotten a lead on something and would get back with him. Travis had also advised Jared to print the emails out so he'd have a copy. The lawyer would be able to use Sable's unstable messages to prove she was just that ... unstable. Jared honestly didn't think Sable was going to take him to court. However, he did fully believe that she would try to insert herself in his and Derrick's lives again, which would probably be the second-worst thing that could happen. The first, of course, being that Sable could take Derrick from him.

Because Sable had made his blood pressure skyrocket, Jared hadn't wanted Hope to have to endure his shitty attitude, so he'd figured that night wasn't good, either.

But those days were over and he was now looking forward to surprising her.

At least he was finally down to minutes.

Tonight, Derrick was going to spend some time with Lorrie and Curtis, along with Mason and Kate. The five of them were going to church, which meant Jared had a few hours to himself. He didn't waste any time, either. As soon as he dropped Derrick off, he hit the highway and headed toward Embers Ridge. He had told himself that the next time—after this—he was going to have Hope come to him.

At the resort.

Yeah, he'd gotten the impression that Hope was quite interested in finding out more about Alluring Indulgence Resort. When he had talked about it, he'd seen her hesitance, but then, during the text messages they'd exchanged over the past few days, she'd been the one asking him about it.

However, he wanted to take her there on a Saturday night, when they were in full swing. The weekdays could be hit or miss, with mostly die-hards coming out to play during that time. But on the weekends, things tended to get lively. Since Travis and his brothers continued to maintain the resort's invitation-only policy, Jared had had no choice but to approach his cousin with his request.

Travis had pretended to be shocked initially, but he hadn't asked any questions. Not that Jared would've told him why he wanted the invitation. He knew that his cousins didn't spend much time at the resort when they weren't working. Because they all had families now, they tended not to play as much at the resort anymore. Although there were those rare times when they went for the same reason Jared was going. For something out of the norm, a little walk on the wild side.

When Jared arrived at the ranch, he shot Hope a text, letting her know he was outside waiting for her.

Really? What a nice surprise. Come to the dining room.

He parked in the guest area, then walked around the porch to the back door that led to the oversized dining area where the guests came to have dinner.

The place was nice, with a homey, rustic feel to it. The interior of the house was bright, with dark wood beams on the ceiling, even a few posts on the floor. It had a log cabin feel that Jared liked. A lot.

Hope was waiting for him just inside the door. Her smile was wide, but it was clear she was trying to hide her hunger from him. He noticed it anyway, and he knew she wasn't craving whatever the kitchen had made for tonight's meal. Nor was he.

"Are you hungry?"

"I am," he told her, ensuring she knew what he was hungry for.

"In that case…" Hope turned to look around, probably wanting to make sure no one was watching her. She must've determined the coast was clear, because she nodded toward the door.

Jared followed her back outside.

"I've got something I want to show you in the barn," she said sweetly, grinning up at him.

Sweet jeezus.

Jared

He remained quiet as he followed her into the main barn. This one was clearly used to house equipment and hay but no animals. And just like in one of those cheesy pornos, Hope, dressed in a long-sleeve, body-hugging red T-shirt, and her boots, paired with very short shorts that showed off her incredible legs, headed right for the ladder that led up to the hayloft.

Jared followed, not bothering to hide the fact that he was staring at her ass.

Once they were in the loft, Hope took his hand and led him over to one corner, which offered quite a bit of privacy due to all the hay bales stacked there. That was when he noticed there was a blanket laid out on the floor. Ahh. The sweet woman obviously had something in mind.

He glanced at the blanket, then up to her. "You didn't know I was comin'," he told her.

She grinned. "No, but I figured sooner or later you'd show up. I put this here over the weekend."

"Pretty sure of yourself, huh?" he teased.

"I know you're a sure thing," she said, giggling.

Yes, when it came to her, he most definitely was.

"However," she said, still holding his hand as she went to her knees on the blanket. "Tonight I want to do things differently."

That got his attention, and perhaps made him a little weary of what she had in mind. This was a barn, after all.

"Get your mind out of the gutter, Walker," she choked out on a laugh.

Before he would let her lead them through whatever she had in mind, Jared went to his knees in front of her, then quickly took her down to the blanket, his body coming over hers.

Hope chuckled, the raspy sound going straight to his dick.

"You're always in such a hurry," he told her softly, pressing a kiss to her nose, then to her lips.

"If you came around more often, maybe I wouldn't be quite this horny."

Damn, she made him hot. He loved the way Hope said what was on her mind. She seemed to be as into this as he was. Sex with her was … off the fucking charts. However, Jared also got the impression that she was keeping this as impersonal as possible considering they were having sex.

Jared wanted something a little more intimate. Sue him.

But he wasn't going to worry about that tonight. They still had time for him to get everything he wanted from this woman.

He took his time kissing her, starting slow as he eased himself down beside her. While their tongues swirled, Hope began wrapping herself around him, rubbing against his thigh. Jared gave her what she needed, pressing against her, providing her clit with the friction she was seeking.

"How do you do that?" she asked, pulling back from him.

He stared down at her. Was that a trick question?

She must've read his mind because she chuckled. "You can rev me from zero to sixty in seconds. And I promised myself that the next time I had you, I would be the one making you wild."

"Honey, just kissing you makes me wild." It was the truth, and he watched her expression as those words registered.

Sure, he was more than willing to make this about sex. It had been a long time since he'd had it on a regular basis. However, since the day he'd met Hope, he'd known this was something unexpected. She could tell him all day that this was strictly physical, but for him, it wasn't. Not entirely anyway.

He enjoyed spending time with her, and they didn't have to be naked for that to be the case, either.

Then again…

"Holy shit," he groaned when her hand slid into his jeans, her fingers curling around his dick.

When she did that, Hope Lambert pretty much made it impossible for him to think about anything. Except for the fastest way to get her naked.

Jared

HOT DAMN, THE man smelled good.

The kind of scent that had every molecule in her body lusting after him. She wasn't sure what it was—cologne, body wash, or maybe even deodorant—but whatever it was, it worked on him.

It worked on her, too. Perhaps a little too well.

From the moment she'd received his text, letting her know that he had surprised her, an army of indignant butterflies had taken flight in her belly. And from the moment she'd seen him in the main house, her hormones had short-circuited. He was so tall, so broad he practically filled up an entire room. And when his eyes met hers, Hope had seen the lust sparking there. The same lust she couldn't seem to fight off when it came to him. So, instead of insisting that they have dinner—which truly had been where she'd been headed when he arrived—Hope had decided she wanted to have *him* for dinner.

Only now he was taking charge, and he was supposed to be the one receiving all the pleasure.

She would definitely have to do something about that.

It took some effort, but Hope managed to reverse their positions so that Jared was lying on his back on the blanket while she was straddling his thighs. She had worked open his jeans enough to free his cock, which she was still stroking, slowly, gently, while he watched her.

Since the night in his truck when he told her he wanted her mouth on him, she'd thought about little else. Well, when it came to him anyway. Admittedly, the man had taken up a lot of her head space lately. She wasn't sure whether that was a good thing or not, so she tried to ignore it.

For the record, ignoring Jared Walker was damn near impossible.

And now here he was, completely at her mercy.

Leaning forward, Hope slid her tongue over the head of his cock, watching his eyes widen as she did. His hands instantly threaded into her hair, holding it back from her face so he could watch what she was doing.

She liked that he wanted to watch, because that was hot in its own right.

"Oh, yes," he hissed, his voice barely above a whisper.

Clearly he knew that someone could come into the barn at any time. She doubted they would, but it was possible.

"Suck me, Hope. Put your mouth on my dick."

Oh, jeezus. She loved the way he instructed her to do what would please him.

Opening her mouth, she slowly slid her lips over the wide crest, down farther. He was so big he stretched her mouth, but she didn't mind. She liked the smoothness of him against her tongue, the way his cock jerked when she wiggled her tongue over the sensitive spot.

"Don't stop," he encouraged. "Slow, Hope. Keep going slow. That feels so damn good."

She watched his face contort with pleasure, and she felt the warmth between her legs. Her nipples were hard, her breasts sensitive, desperate for him to touch her. Only tonight wasn't about her. Well, in a way it was. Sucking him gave her this sense of empowerment. The way he looked at her, the soft growls that erupted from him, the way his legs tensed. All of those things made her hotter, made her burn brighter for him.

Jared's hands tightened in her hair. Not enough to hurt but enough for her to know that he was slowly taking control. And she let him. Hope continued to use her mouth on him while his hips thrust up, forcing him deeper until he was doing all the work, using her mouth, fucking past her lips. His groans were slightly louder, but she knew he was close.

"Can I come in your mouth?" he growled. "Please, Hope. Need to come in your mouth."

She nodded slightly, meeting his eyes, letting him know that was exactly what she wanted.

"Oh, fuck... Don't look at me like that, Hope. It drives me fucking crazy." Jared's hips were pumping faster, his hands holding her head tightly. "Hell, yeah... Fuck... Gonna come, darlin'."

His head fell back as his cock pulsed, filling her mouth. She wrapped her hand around his shaft while she swallowed everything he gave her.

Jared

If she thought that the night was over, that he was the only one who would receive pleasure, she was sadly mistaken.

However, Hope knew that *sadly* played absolutely no part in what Jared did to her over the next half hour. Right there in the hayloft.

Chapter Eighteen

"SHE WAS IN town today," Travis told Gage as they sat on the front porch, staring out at the night. It was one of those things they tried to do every Saturday evening. Hanging out at home, spending time with each other and the kids. Kylie had made a fantastic dinner, and after Travis and Gage had cleaned the kitchen, Travis had grabbed a beer and headed outside.

"Who?" Gage asked.

"Sable." Fucking Sable. It pissed him off to no end that the woman was resurfacing now. He'd received a phone call from Sid at the gas station, letting him know that there was a woman who'd come in asking about Jared. Apparently the woman didn't know where Jared lived. Luckily, Sid didn't, either. Not that Travis thought he would've said something, but with Sable, Travis simply didn't know how she might've tried to coerce the details out of him. The woman was known to do whatever necessary to get a man to see things her way.

It didn't take a rocket scientist for Travis to figure out she'd finally made it to Coyote Ridge because she was getting nowhere via email. He'd been expecting her.

"Please tell me you're not gonna get in the middle of this," Gage said, peering over at him.

"Not if I don't have to." So far, he'd simply looked into a few things, trying to find out what he could about the woman. He knew Jared didn't have the sort of resources Travis had.

Gage sighed. "Jared's a big boy. He can take care of himself."

True. Jared was a big boy. And yes, Travis knew his cousin could take care of himself. However, Jared was also family, and Travis wasn't going to sit back and let that woman take advantage of him again. It was bad enough that she'd taken his son away from him in the beginning. Although Derrick wasn't his biological son—Travis was having doubts about that since Jared had never had a paternity test done him but rather had trusted Sable's word and the papers she had provided him—the man loved him like one.

Travis had a hard time not interfering when it came to family. And yes, he'd been known to be a bulldozer at times. But that was who he was. He wasn't about to change now. Jared and Derrick had made their home here, and Sable was nothing but trouble.

"You should tell him," Gage said. "See if he wants to talk to her."

"He doesn't."

"Do you know that for a fact? Or is that what you want to believe?"

"I know for a fact. And she doesn't have good intentions."

"You know this how?"

Travis cocked an eyebrow at his husband. He couldn't believe Gage would ask him that.

Gage sighed again, this time deeper than last time. "You had her checked out?" He didn't wait for an answer. "Let me guess, she's flat-ass broke and looking for more money? Since Jared gave her twenty-five g's, she figures he probably has a little extra lying around."

"You should be a detective," Travis teased. It was meant to be funny since Gage had been an undercover police officer at one time. Travis had been the one to find that out about the man, accidentally. He'd also been the one to out Gage, something that had ultimately put them at odds and forced out the extreme emotions they'd had for one another.

He wasn't sorry about that.

"You can't keep her away forever."

Sure he could.

If he really wanted to.

"I CANNOT BELIEVE I let him talk me into this," Hope muttered to herself as she pulled her truck down the long drive that led to Jared's place.

He'd given her very clear directions because the house he lived in wasn't picked up on Google maps since he didn't even have an address. From what he'd told her, he was staying in one of the small cabins on his aunt and uncle's land.

Not only had the sweet-talking man talked her into visiting Alluring Indulgence resort with him tonight, he had also talked her into coming to his house first. He'd told her that his son would be staying with one of his cousins while they were at the resort and he'd be picking him up when they returned. They weren't staying at the resort, she'd been informed, because Jared hadn't found an all-night sitter despite his attempt. Apparently, the people who usually kept him overnight couldn't since they'd had things to take care of the following morning.

It was only then that Hope had given more thought to the fact that Jared had a son. A son Jared had been leaving with family members on the few occasions he'd come out to the ranch to see her. She figured it was only fair that she come to him this one time. And since his little boy was at someone else's house, she didn't run the risk of seeing him, falling head over heels for him, and then realizing Jared Walker had turned her world upside down again.

Truth was, Hope was probably a little bit in love with Jared already, and that was a big, big problem in her book.

Finding the cabin wasn't that difficult at all. She pulled in beside his truck and sat there for a moment. It took a few minutes to shore up her nerve. It was a little on the crumbly side—her nerve—but it was the best she was going to get, so she finally exited her truck and made her way up to the porch.

She knocked on the door and the next thing she knew…

"Hi! Who are you?"

Jared

Hope's heart chose that moment to jump into her throat. Her knees locked, and she probably looked shocked to the roots of her hair, which was exactly how she felt.

"Derrick…" Hope barely registered the chastising tone of Jared's voice. "I told you not to open the door, son."

Derrick. Derrick Walker.

The little boy was quite possibly the cutest thing she'd ever seen.

"I'm four," Derrick announced to Hope, holding up four little fingers.

She couldn't help but smile.

Jared pulled Derrick back and held his hand out, signaling for her to come inside. Forcing her feet to move, Hope woodenly walked forward, far enough for Jared to close the door.

"I'm goin' to Mason's house to pway," Derrick told her. "What are you gonna do?"

Hope's tongue was twisted; she couldn't seem to form words. She simply stared into the deep brown eyes of this cute little boy and prayed that Jared would save her. This was the very reason she hadn't wanted to come to him. It wasn't that she didn't like kids. She loved them. Hell, she'd be more content to sit on the couch and watch a Disney movie with Derrick than she would be going to the resort with Jared.

But that couldn't happen, because she wasn't supposed to meet Derrick. This was supposed to be a casual thing between her and Jared.

"We're gonna go out for a bit, big man," Jared told his son. "While you hang out with Mason, I'm gonna take Hope on a date."

"A date?" Derrick's eyes widened. "What's a date?"

"When two people who like each other go somewhere so they can spend time together."

"Oh." Derrick grinned. "Wike when we go to the movies? Or to McDonawd's?"

Jared chuckled. "Yep. Just like that."

"Okay." That seemed to satisfy Derrick's curiosity. "Can we go now?"

Hope realized Jared was looking at her while she'd been staring at Derrick, a ridiculous smile on her face. Was that question meant for her? She didn't know.

"You ready?"

She nodded, feeling like a bobblehead.

While Jared went to get whatever it was he went to get, Hope sent up a silent prayer that she would make it through this evening with the reminder that this was casual. She was not going to get seriously involved with Jared.

And more importantly, she was not going to fall—more—in love with the man.

Because that...

That would be really, really stupid.

JARED HAD INTENDED to have Derrick at Kaleb and Zoey's before Hope showed up. That had been the plan, only every parent in the world knew that plans changed all the time. It started when he and Derrick had gone to the grocery store to pick up a few things for the week. Derrick had had a complete meltdown in the toy aisle, of all places, because Jared wouldn't let him buy the toy he wanted. It had been a simple misunderstanding, but try telling that to a four-year-old.

"Dad, I think I need this truck," Derrick informed him, his tone sweet.

"Yeah? Lemme see."

Derrick shoved the bright yellow dump truck that he'd grabbed from the shelf toward him. Jared quickly peeked at the price tag.

"I think I can find a better one online," he told the boy.

"No!" Derrick spun around to face him, glaring in a way that only the cutest kid in the world could do. Jared fought the urge to smile. "I want this one. Right now."

Jared knew when Derrick started that way, he wasn't going to get far with him, so he shook his head. "No."

Jared

"Yes!" Derrick insisted, throwing the truck into the basket.
Jared calmly pulled it back out and set it on the shelf.
Derrick reached for it again.

"Don't," Jared warned, keeping his voice low. "We're leaving."

Derrick shook his head before throwing himself to the floor.

Rather than pay the ridiculously high price, Jared had intended to seek the toy out on the Internet, find it cheaper, and give it to Derrick on a day he did exceptionally well. Those days weren't as infrequent anymore, so he didn't doubt that his son would have his toy in the very near future.

However...

The instant Derrick started screaming and kicking, insisting that he get the toy right now, Jared told him it wasn't going to happen. And it wouldn't. Derrick needed to learn his lesson. It would've been so easy for Jared to give in to his son, to give him the moon if he could, but he knew better. Oh, sure, there were times when he did just that, but in cases like this, it never worked out in his favor. As a parent, he had learned from his mistakes.

From there, the day simply had gone downhill. Luckily, Derrick had taken a two-hour nap and had woken up a completely different kid. At that point, Jared had offered to take Derrick to Mama's Diner for a late lunch. The place had been unusually busy for the middle of the afternoon, and the few errands Jared needed to get done had been pushed back by a full hour while they waited for their food.

And that was the reason Derrick was there when Hope showed up.

Now, as he and Hope drove away from Kaleb's, Jared felt the tension. He'd noticed it as soon as he'd caught a glimpse of Hope standing in his doorway when Derrick had opened the door. She'd been completely shocked to see him, obviously.

"You okay?" he asked, reaching over and taking her hand.

Her fingers were stiff, but they eventually loosened when he linked his with hers.

"Good."

Yeah. Her smile was still forced. If he was lucky, that would change when they got to AI.

"So, did you do any research on the resort?" he asked, hoping to make casual conversation and put her at ease.

That seemed to do the trick, because he saw her chest deflate, as though she finally let out the breath she'd been holding.

"I tried," she said, grinning as she glanced over at him. "Apparently, people don't do a lot of talking about it."

"My cousins keep access to invitation only," he told her. "For that very reason. Not all people are open-minded when it comes to certain ... pleasures. In order to keep the hate to a minimum, Travis does his best to eliminate the problem up front."

"Makes sense." Hope glanced back out the front window. "Is this place going to scar me for life?"

Jared chuckled, then pulled her hand closer so he could kiss her knuckles. "I won't let that happen. Stick close to me and I'll keep you safe."

"How close are we talkin'?" she countered, amusement in her tone.

He glanced over, capturing her gaze for the briefest of moments so she could see the pure lust he knew was reflected in his eyes. "As close as you'll let me be."

Hope swallowed hard, and Jared fought the urge to adjust his jeans. They were getting uncomfortably tight.

They pulled into the resort, then drove down the winding entry, stopping under the portico. Ready to get the evening started, Jared hopped out and made his way around to the passenger door. Quite frankly, he was surprised Hope hadn't jumped out of the truck before he could get there. After all, she had done it the first night they'd gone to Marla's Bar.

Jared passed his keys off to the valet, then led Hope to the main doors. They were opened by a man wearing a tuxedo, and held so they could enter. "Good evening, Mr. Walker. Ms. Lambert."

"Good evening," Jared returned, smiling at Hope. She looked shocked that the man knew her name. Then again, they were on the guest list for tonight.

Jared

"I figured I'd give you a tour," Jared told her, placing his hand at the small of her back as they moved farther into the hotel lobby. "I didn't get us a room, but we've got full access to the entire place. Anything you'd like to see first?"

Hope turned to face him, and he could see the hesitancy in her gaze. She was nervous, although she was doing her best to hide it from him. It was one thing to claim to want adventurous sex, something else entirely to indulge in it.

Jared pulled her close, wrapping his arms around her, sliding his palms over her bare back. "We won't do anything you're not comfortable with," he informed her. "I'll show you around so you can see what it's like. There are two clubs here, both of which are nightclubs. Nothing different than you'd find anywhere else. If you want to go there, we can. They've also got a restaurant if you're hungry." He grinned. "There are certain parts that contain the play activity. You won't find naked bodies in the hallways, writhing on the floor." He cocked an eyebrow. "Okay, there have been some from time to time. From what I hear." He laughed. "But those are few and far between."

His words seemed to ease her somewhat, so he continued, "It's up to you. No pressure."

This time she nodded.

Jared knew he should've left it at that, but for some reason, he couldn't. Instead of fighting the impulse any longer, he leaned down and pressed his lips to hers. He trailed his lips along her jaw. "There are a million things I want to do to you, Hope. But we don't need an audience for that. I'm more than happy to take you back to my bed and spend the rest of the night feasting on you."

Her breath hitched, so he pulled back to look at her face. Her eyes were dilated.

"I'm intrigued," she finally said. "I mean, this might be a once-in-a-lifetime opportunity. I say we go balls to the walls tonight."

He barked out a laugh as his dick jerked behind his zipper. Those words ... said in that raspy, sexy drawl... Yeah.

Balls to the walls.

That sounded like a damn good plan.

CHAPTER NINETEEN

HOPE WASN'T SURE when she'd become so daring. If she had to guess, it was sometime between the first day she'd met Jared and now.

Sure, she'd been knocked a little off-kilter tonight, but the moment Jared's lips were on hers, all of her senses had awakened. As he explained to her they wouldn't be doing anything she wasn't comfortable with, her nerves had settled somewhat. Then it had occurred to her that she really did have a once-in-a-lifetime opportunity here.

Might as well make the most of it.

Now, as Jared led her through the hotel, showing her the many amenities the place had to offer, she realized that Alluring Indulgence Resort wasn't much different than other five-star resort hotels. They had a luxury spa, an exquisite gourmet steakhouse, many full-service bars, including a wine bar that served pretty much anything anyone could ever want. There was also a state-of-the-art health club that had been added last year, according to Jared.

"Five-star hotel, huh?" she asked, grinning up at him. "Honestly, I don't know the difference. I think I might've stayed in a hotel once in my life."

That seemed to surprise him. "Really?"

"Yeah. Don't really get out much."

Jared chuckled. "You've got your own resort to deal with. The rustic version."

"True."

Jared

Hope stopped when Jared did. "Okay, cowboy. So, you've shown me all the fancy hotel parts. But what really sets this place apart from any other five-star hotel?" After all, *something* had to be different. Since he'd referred to the place as a fetish hotel, she already had a good idea.

Jared reached for her hand, and she offered it, allowing him to lead her over to a railing that clearly overlooked a lower floor. He stopped there, stepping back so she could move closer to the railing.

When she put her hands on the wrought iron, Jared came to stand behind her. As in, right behind her. She could feel him against her back. His hands came to rest beside hers, fingers circling the rail, his arms caging her in. She noticed he smelled as good as he always did. It had to be cologne. If not, someone should definitely bottle the scent because... Holy smokes.

Speaking of holy smokes...

Hope's gaze traveled the open area below, and it took a moment to realize what she was looking at. There were black and red leather couches and chairs spread out below, along with tables that lined the periphery of the room. Large floor-to-ceiling windows overlooked what appeared to be some sort of garden. She looked up, noticing that the domed ceiling was also made of glass.

"How discreet is a place with all of these windows?" she whispered, more to herself than anything else.

"No one can see in," he said reassuringly. "One-way glass."

It was a nice touch. She couldn't tell now since it was dark, but during the day, she imagined it let in a lot of light.

Although the furnishings were impressive, they certainly weren't the main attraction.

No, the people were the ones doing the attracting. Many of them. In various states of dress and undress, some simply talking, others participating in a wide range of, yes, sexual acts.

"Does it scare you?" Jared whispered in her ear, his breath warm against her skin.

She shook her head, unable to find her voice. No doubt about it, she was captivated by what was going on. It surprised her a little to think that she could be turned on by this, but she definitely was.

"These people feel safe here," Jared explained. "Safe to explore their sexual appetites. Those who choose to come to this room are looking to either watch or be watched. They don't interrupt others, don't try to join in. It's not an orgy. However, there are private rooms that can be utilized for just about anything."

"Themed?"

"Some of them," Jared said. "When Travis first came up with the idea, he built the resort to suit his own needs and those of his friends. Since then, he has expanded, incorporated other fetishes that he hadn't thought of in the beginning. Two of his closest friends are ... well, she's a Domme and he's a..."

"Submissive?" Hope asked, peering back at him.

Jared chuckled. "No, he's a Dom, too. And they're married. Works for them, somehow. They've come down for various things, including classes they've taught. It's a constant work in progress, growing as time goes by. But this room remains the same as it's always been."

"So I take it you like to watch?" Hope realized she was breathless, her body humming from the sexual energy now fueling her.

Jared once again leaned in close to her ear. "I like to watch. I also wouldn't mind being watched."

Maybe it was the place, perhaps it was merely the man, but at the moment, Hope found she wouldn't mind it much, either.

UNABLE TO RESIST, Jared leaned down a little lower, kissing Hope's neck, lingering there so he could inhale the incredibly intoxicating scent of her.

"Does that bother you?" he asked when she didn't say anything.

She shook her head. "Not as much as I thought it would."

Jared

Hope's chest was rising and falling, her breaths a little louder. He knew she was affected by the sight of what was happening below them. It didn't surprise him, either. In their position on the second floor, the people below wouldn't see them. They probably felt eyes on them, knew they were being watched, but that was part of the allure.

For Jared, watching a man pleasure a woman or vice versa was extremely erotic. Although he'd considered it for some time, Jared had never participated at the hotel. He'd never brought a woman here, never hooked up with one here. Hope was his first.

The thought made him smile as he remembered her telling him something similar on the night they made out in the parking lot of the bar.

"Can we go down there?" Hope asked. "Just to ... watch?"

"Of course." Jared caressed her arms as he straightened, then took her hand and led her toward the staircase that spiraled elegantly down to the first floor.

They took their time walking down, allowing Hope the chance to take it all in. The décor was elegant, not at all tawdry as some might expect. The lights were low, allowing the illusion of privacy. The red, black, and chrome theme flowed throughout. From the carpeting on the floor to the furniture. Even the drapes that framed the windows—pulled back to the sides so as not to obstruct the view—matched.

As soon as they stepped foot on the main floor, a waitress came toward them. Jared ordered drinks for them both—Jack and Coke for him, red wine for Hope—then found a vacant seating area—which consisted of two leather chairs and a small table in between—that was tucked back near the stairs. It offered somewhat more privacy than the other seating areas, partly hidden from the room. Wanting to keep her close, Jared pulled Hope onto his lap, his hand on her lower back, his eyes on her face as she continued to watch what was going on around her.

Several feet in front of them, a man sat in a chair similar to the ones they were in, while a woman slowly walked around him. She trailed her nail over his shoulders, his neck, as she moved behind him. When she came around in front, she let her finger slide down his chest and over the evident bulge in his slacks. Those two were just getting started.

Against the wall on the opposite side of the room, a fully clothed man was standing against the wall, a naked woman pressed up against his chest. She was facing away from him because another fully clothed man was kneeling in front of her, eating her pussy while she writhed and moaned. If he had to guess, it was a fantasy being played out because the men were both wearing expensive suits while the woman wore nothing more than a diamond choker around her neck.

There were plenty of other couples sitting at the tables, having drinks, watching with interest as more and more play started. Some would probably join in; others would head back to their room, ready to ravage one another in private.

To each his own.

After the waitress brought their drinks, Jared continued to watch Hope, sipping his Jack and Coke. He placed the glass on the table beside him, then placed his palm on Hope's thigh, slowly sliding it beneath the hem of her dress. He wasn't going to push her, but he was willing to give her whatever she needed. Even if that meant having the valet bring around his truck so he could take her back to his place. He had no agenda tonight.

"What do you think?" he asked when her gaze slid down to his hand.

"I can see why people enjoy this." She actually blushed. "I mean, it makes me hot, I can't deny that. I never thought..."

"That you'd like it?" he finished for her.

Hope nodded.

Jared reached for Hope's drink, then set it on the table beside his. He slid his hand beneath her hair and pulled her mouth closer to his. He hadn't kissed her appropriately all night, and he wanted to taste her. She was quickly becoming an addiction. One he could ill afford but wasn't willing to deny himself.

Jared

When he pulled back, he leaned close to her ear. "From here on out, you have to tell me what you want from me. I'm not willing to assume anything. It's up to you." Jared pulled back and met her gaze. "And if you wish to sit here and simply watch, I'm completely on board with that, too."

Just being with her was enough for him.

And that, quite frankly, scared the shit out of him.

CHAPTER TWENTY

AS DARING AND as adventurous as she wanted to be, Hope knew she simply wasn't that woman. She couldn't have sex in public while other people watched. Sure, the idea that someone might happen upon them at any moment was thrilling, but she was fairly certain she would be mortified if someone actually did.

So rather than act on the incredible lust coursing through her veins, Hope had remained seated on Jared's lap for a solid hour, watching the action around her. This place was surreal and the people... Hope wasn't one to judge, so she couldn't say anything negative about these people. In fact, she considered them daring. Brave, in a way. And truly sexy.

It had to take tremendous courage to act out your fantasies, to give in to your baser needs. She had a feeling that the relationships these people shared were on a level so deep most people probably didn't understand.

And though she wasn't as courageous as they were, she was certainly turned on. More so because Jared was there with her. He made her feel safe. Never once did he try to cop a feel, nor did he try to seduce her with words. He merely sat with his warm hand on her thigh, his other arm around her back. When she would look at him, most of the time she found him watching her.

And wasn't that sexy as hell.

"I think I'm ready to go now," she told him, leaning in and kissing his mouth gently.

He nodded once, as though he'd expected her to say that.

"Are you disappointed?" she asked.

Jared

His eyes flared with heat, but there wasn't an ounce of disappointment reflected there. Although she sensed the man didn't say things he didn't mean, Hope had wondered. Being here made her want to do ridiculously salacious things, but beneath it all, her inner good girl won out. Although she still wanted erotic, mind-numbing pleasure, she wanted it in a place where there weren't any eyes on her. Except Jared's.

"Not at all. In fact, I'm more than happy to take you back to my place, where I can ravish you in private."

To think, the chemistry between them had been off the charts before... Hope wasn't sure what was going to happen when they did get naked this time. Hell, they might not even make it that far. Clothes be damned, Hope wanted this man, and sitting here, watching while men seduced women, women seduced men, men seduced men, and women seduced women—damn, it'd been hot, and now she was one spark away from going up in flames.

Thankfully, Jared seemed to be on the same page. He led her outside, where the valet retrieved his truck, and less than ten minutes later, they were pulling up to his house. This time she didn't wait for him to open her door for her. She was tired of waiting, and the sooner they got inside...

Three minutes later, they were standing in his living room, and Hope was pressed up against the front door, her dress pushed up, Jared's jeans around his hips, and he was thrusting into her hard and deep. Hope was soaring, her body ripping right in half from the incredible sensations slamming through her.

They had fumbled their way inside, hands groping, mouths feasting. Keeping her hands off him had been impossible the instant he had shut the truck off.

As she held on to Jared now, she allowed him to pump his hips, filling her to overflowing while she tried to hold still, which gave him better traction, allowed for more friction.

"Hope... Fuck, baby. I don't think I'll ever get enough of you."

She told herself not to think too much on that. Jared said it in the heat of the moment. He was referring to sex, because they both knew that *this*… Sex like this didn't happen every day. Once or twice, sure. But every single time they came together, it was magnetic, explosive. So damn hot.

"Harder," she pleaded, dropping her head back against the door as he rocked into her, going deeper with every glorious stroke.

"Hell yeah," he groaned, his voice rough, deep. "Come for me, Hope. Then I'm gonna take you to my bed and see how many more times I can make you come."

Before she was ready, Hope splintered, her body shattering as her orgasm ripped her to shreds, all thanks to that dark promise. She cried out his name, digging her nails into his shoulders. And when her body somehow floated back to one piece, she tucked her face into his neck and held on while Jared carried her to his bedroom.

AFTER STRIPPING HER dress and panties from her, Jared took his time removing his own clothes, enjoying the sight of Hope naked in his bed. No other woman had ever been in this bed. He'd never brought another woman back to this house. He'd never wanted to. Too much of a risk, he guessed. Introducing women to Derrick was a recipe for disaster, considering he didn't anticipate them being around for long.

Until Hope.

It should've freaked him out to have her meet Derrick, but it hadn't. He'd been intrigued by the way she responded, a radiant smile on her face as she spoke to him. She'd seemed both in awe and terrified.

Jared didn't want to think too long about what that might mean.

Jared

Instead of thinking, he crawled onto the bed after retrieving another condom, having tossed the first one because they'd been so rough. He wasn't taking any chances with Hope. If and when they ever moved in a direction to talk about kids, they'd worry about that then.

Not that he was thinking about a future with Hope, definitely not kids. They hadn't gotten that far. Or had they? The idea concerned him a little because it didn't bother him. Thinking about Hope pregnant with his child ... his heart rate sped up, but not from fear. That in itself was frightening.

He quickly shook off the thought.

Since she hadn't mentioned being on the pill, he wasn't going to ask. It was safer this way anyway. Not only from a physical perspective but from an emotional one as well. If and when he took Hope without a barrier between them...

Heaven help him, he couldn't even think about that now. He wouldn't last another minute.

"You know what I want right now?" Hope asked, her eyes opening to look up at him.

He shook his head, meeting her turquoise gaze.

"I want you inside me," she whispered. "And I want to feel you ... nice and slow."

Jared had no problem with nice and slow. That worked for him.

Leaning over her, he took her hands in one of his and pinned them above her head. He guided himself into the warmth of her body, leaned forward, and slid home. She was silky hot, her skin so smooth against his. He could do this forever and a day and never tire of it.

"Like that?" he whispered, brushing his lips against hers.

"Just like that."

Her hands clutched his, and he propped himself on his elbows, his free hand joining the other, linking their fingers together as he ever so slowly made love to her. He pushed deep inside, retreated slowly. Hot and slick, Hope's pussy clasped his cock. It was so damn good he had to think about math problems for a moment, unwilling to come too soon.

"Jared."

He loved the way she whispered his name. Pressing his lips to hers, he kissed her softly, then turned his head slightly, needing to deepen the kiss while he continued to move in and out of her. Air became scarce, the temperature in the room ticking up one degree, then another as they generated more and more body heat. Christ.

This woman seemed to be made for him. Specifically for him. They moved together in a rhythm that was unbelievably sexy, deeply erotic. Every single time their bodies came together … it was powerful, overwhelming, amazing. He could come up with a million adjectives, and none of them could come close to describing how abso-fucking-lutely amazing this was.

"Hope…" He pulled back, staring down into her face. "You're so beautiful… You steal my breath."

He felt her muscles flex as she shifted, her knees clasping his hips. He sank in deeper before retreating. Nice and slow wasn't working so well anymore. His body was humming.

"Ahh, yeah, Hope. Do that again."

At his urging, her inner muscles tightened, squeezing his dick as her body sheathed him.

"Your pussy feels so good. So tight…" His body was coated with a fine sheen of perspiration as he continued to penetrate her, deeper, harder. Jared tried to maintain a relatively slow rhythm, but it was becoming more difficult with every passing second.

Hope bit his bottom lip, a gentle nip with her teeth, but it was enough to make his body jerk, driving him into her harder than before.

She inhaled sharply, then sighed. "That… Do that… Need more."

Jared released her hands and leveraged himself up over her, still staring down into her face as he rocked his hips faster this time.

"Hope… Fuck, baby… You undo me."

The cry that escaped her was followed by her fingernails raking down his back. The erotically painful sting sent him soaring, her orgasm triggering his own.

Chapter Twenty-One

HOPE REALIZED SHE wasn't in her own bed as soon as she opened her eyes.

The sunlight spilled in through the blinds, illuminating the room, letting her know this was not her bed, not her pillow, not her... It was then she realized what she'd done.

Turning her head, she found the bed beside her empty. She instinctively grabbed for the sheet, pulling it up over her nakedness. Lifting her head slightly, Hope gave the room a cursory look. Nope. No devastatingly handsome cowboys standing around.

"Oh, shit," she muttered, keeping her voice low. "Oh, my God."

Reality was like a fist to the chest. She'd gone and done what she'd promised herself she wouldn't. She'd spent the night with Jared.

Not that she hadn't done that already. The making love until her brain was fuzzy, then falling asleep completely sated wasn't the problem. The problem was that this was *his* house. The house he lived in with his son. Jared had told her that he would be picking Derrick up last night, which meant...

Somewhere on the other side of that closed bedroom door were a four-year-old and his father.

"Double shit."

Sitting up, Hope glanced down at the floor, trying to find her clothes. She found them neatly laid out on the dresser. Her dress and her panties anyway. She remembered she'd lost her shoes sometime in the first thirty seconds they'd walked in Jared's front door. Last night.

Straining to hear, Hope slipped out of bed and tiptoed over to the dresser, snatching her clothes and pulling them to her chest. She didn't want to make a sound, didn't want Jared or—God forbid—his little boy to come into the room. Derrick was still young; he probably wouldn't know what was going on, but surely Jared didn't make a habit of bringing women back to his place.

Hope practically ran into the bathroom, closing the door softly behind her. Within two minutes, she had managed to use the restroom, wash her hands, brush her teeth with her finger and some of Jared's minty toothpaste, finger-comb her hair, and get dressed. Now came the hard part. How in the world was she supposed to sneak out the front door without either of them seeing her? There were two windows in his bedroom, but she'd probably make a lot of noise if she tried to go out that way. She glanced up at the small window above the shower. It didn't open, and even if it did, she wasn't small enough to get out of it. Hell, Derrick wasn't small enough to get out of it.

Taking a deep breath—

Hope shrieked when a knock sounded on the bathroom door. Instinct kicked in, and she slammed her hand over her mouth, trying to catch her breath.

"Hope? You okay in there?"

Her heart was beating a million miles a minute. "Yeah. I'm … uh… I'll be out in a minute."

Jared didn't respond, but she didn't hear him move away from the door, either. Which meant he was probably waiting for her to emerge from his bathroom.

Knowing she had no choice—locking herself in would seem incredibly weird—she took one last look at herself in the mirror, then reached for the doorknob. When she opened the door, she found Jared standing there, one hand propped on the doorjamb, a smile on his incredibly handsome face.

"Mornin'," he greeted.

"What time is it?" she asked, praying it was still early and that his son was still asleep.

"Seven."

Jared

Oh, thank God. At least she hadn't missed too many of her chores. As it was, she still had to drive the half hour it would take to get back to Embers Ridge, then she had to change. It would be closer to eight thirty before she could actually get started.

Shit. Her sisters were going to give her hell for this.

Hope met Jared's eyes, trying not to look terrified. "I'm so sorry. I must've fallen asleep."

"Don't apologize to me," he said, dropping his hand from the frame and pulling her into him. "I'm not complainin'."

"But Derrick..."

"He's none the wiser, I promise. He's still asleep. I just went to check on him. I was"—his smile held a devious curve to it—"gonna wake you up."

Heat flared inside her, but Hope ignored it. She would not be seduced by this man this morning. As it was, she shouldn't even be here.

"I have to get home," she told him, trying not to sound as though she was ready to run out the door. Which she definitely was. "I've got chores."

Jared nodded, then pressed his lips to hers. Hope thought he was going for sweet, but the kiss quickly morphed into something much hotter. She laughed, realizing how quickly he'd pulled her under his spell.

"I really do have to go," she told him.

"I want to see you this week. I'll come out to the ranch."

Hope nodded. She would like that. "Oh, wait. Shit. I don't know if this week's good. Gracie's bachelorette party is next Saturday. There's still a lot of planning to do."

She could see the disappointment in his eyes. Oddly enough, that made her feel good. She liked that he really did want to see her.

"But let me see what I can do," she told him as she leaned in and kissed him again. "But first, I really do need to go."

Jared's fingers slid into her hair, cupping the back of her head. She thought he was going to devour her, but he didn't. He just stood there, staring into her eyes as though he was trying to figure her out. Knowing he wouldn't be able to read her mind—if she was lucky—she smiled.

"Thank you for last night. It was interesting."

"The resort?" he asked, grinning. "Or what happened after?"

"Both."

His smile seemed less forced then. "Call me when you get back to the ranch. I want to know you made it safely."

God, this man was too good to be true.

She nodded, then managed to disentangle herself from his clutches, although as soon as she was away from him, she suddenly wished his arms were still around her.

Not wanting to tempt fate, Hope made a beeline for the front door, grabbing her shoes and her purse, which were both on the table by the front door, before smiling back at Jared and hurrying out of the house.

The good thing was, Derrick hadn't known she was there. A little boy wasn't going to spend the day asking his daddy questions about the strange woman in his bed. Unfortunately, as Hope was pulling out onto the main road, she was wondering what it would've been like to wake up to both of them. To have Derrick running into the room, telling them he was hungry. The cute little-boy giggle making them laugh before they followed him into the kitchen to have breakfast. Together.

She hated herself for wanting to get attached. She knew better.

And yet she couldn't seem to stop herself from thinking about it.

JARED STOOD IN his living room, staring at the front door after Hope left for probably a good ten minutes. He wasn't actually seeing anything, merely caught up in his own head, remembering last night, how he'd felt when Hope had fallen asleep in his bed.

Jared

She'd asked why he hadn't woken her up. Truth was, he hadn't wanted to. He'd wanted her to sleep there with him, to allow him to hold her through the night. So when she'd first fallen asleep, he risked leaving for the few minutes it took to go pick up Derrick. His boy had been sound asleep on the couch at Kaleb's, while Kaleb and Zoey were continuing to watch *How to Train Your Dragon 2*. The boys had passed out a short time before, but they had gotten caught up in the animated film, apparently. It happened. Jared knew. He'd watched more than his fair share of kid movies while Derrick slept soundly beside him.

After he'd tucked Derrick into his own bed, Jared had slipped back into bed with Hope, extremely grateful she hadn't disappeared on him while he'd been gone. Sleep had come quickly, her curled up beside him.

And when he'd woken this morning, seeing her there beside him...

He'd wanted.

Not only sex, either.

He'd wanted a million things that he knew he shouldn't want. Especially from a woman who had told him that a relationship couldn't be had.

Even now, as he stared at the door, he wished she was still there. Wished they would be having breakfast together with Derrick.

"Dad! Can I watch *Paw Patrow*? Pwease!"

Jared pulled himself from his reverie, glancing over at Derrick, who was carrying his blanket into the living room.

"You hungry, big man?"

"Yep."

"What would you like?" Jared asked, grabbing the remote and turning on the television.

"Marshmawows." Derrick looked up over his shoulder at Jared, grinning. "Pwease."

Jared laughed, then ruffled Derrick's hair before heading to the kitchen to get his boy breakfast. In their house, marshmallows meant Lucky Charms. He put on a pot of coffee, grabbed the cereal and a bowl, then went to the fridge for milk. He glanced at the expiration date. Still good. Thank God. He remembered the last time he'd let the milk expire and Derrick wanted cereal. No milk for the cereal was the equivalent of DEFCON 1 in his house.

After setting Derrick up with his breakfast on the coffee table, Jared poured himself some coffee, grabbed his iPad, and went to sit with his son. He didn't pay attention to what was on the television, his brain still drifting back to memories of last night.

He'd made love to Hope.

Made love.

That wasn't a term that was popular in his vocabulary. Never had been. And last night... He was fairly certain that he'd never before felt what he'd felt when he was with Hope.

Not that he thought she felt the same. He could tell she was trying to keep her distance, wanting to keep this casual, the way they'd agreed in the beginning. Easier said than done, in his opinion.

Pulling up his email on his iPad, Jared skimmed it. Of course he was looking for another email from Sable, even though he didn't want to. He figured it was the lesser of two evils. The worst possible thing would be for Sable to show up on his doorstep, insisting she be able to see Derrick. As it was, he didn't know what she was planning to do next. He only knew that he had an appointment with a lawyer on Monday afternoon. It was merely a precaution on Jared's part. He still doubted Sable intended to take him to court, but in the event she really had changed in two years and wasn't simply making idle threats, he intended to be ready. He had to cover his ass because no one—no one—was going to take his son from him. Nor was he going to give Sable another fucking penny.

Jared

He wished he could simply make it all go away, but he knew that wasn't possible. Paying the woman off would probably buy him some silence where she was concerned, but he knew that would only last so long. Obviously, it hadn't worked the first time. She was back asking for more.

His phone chirped from the counter.

"I'w get it!" Derrick launched to his feet, ran to the kitchen, retrieved Jared's cell phone, then tossed it his way, laughing.

I made it home.

Jared typed a quick message back. *I want to see you again this week. Let me know if you have time.*

I promise, I will. And thanks again ... for last night.

Jared grinned, surprised that Hope had actually responded with anything more than that she would look into it. He expected her to freak out a little. He'd seen it in her eyes when she opened the bathroom door. Something had spooked her, but he wasn't quite sure what it was.

He typed his response: *My pleasure.*

And it definitely was his pleasure.

One he hoped to bestow on her again in the very, *very* near future.

CHAPTER TWENTY-TWO

"I THOUGHT I might find you out here," her father said when he joined Hope on the back porch.

"I'm here," she replied, glancing over to see Jan following not far behind him. "What are you two kids up to tonight?"

Her father smiled, then adjusted one of the rocking chairs so that Jan could sit down. When she did, he took the one on the other side of her, turning it so he could see both of them and still look out over the ranch.

"Just hanging out," Jan said sweetly. "You look lost in thought."

She had been. It was a wonder she'd gotten anything done these past few days. Ever since she left Jared's house on Sunday, she'd spent more time thinking about him than anything else.

"What's weighin' on your mind, kiddo?" her father questioned.

Hope shook her head, continuing to gaze out at the twilight. "Not much."

Jerry chuckled. "I'm thinkin' that was her way of deflecting. What d'ya think, honey?"

Jan smiled. "Sometimes there're things a woman wants to keep to herself."

Hope smiled at the woman. She had come to love Jan over the years. The woman was good to her father, good to all of them. She didn't try to interfere, but she always let them know that she was there if they needed to talk. Hope had taken her up on that a few times. Jan was easy to talk to, much like her own mother had been.

Jared

But tonight, she really wasn't up for talking. She'd wanted to see Jared tonight, but when she'd texted him yesterday to see if he wanted to stop by, he'd told her he was in the middle of something, but if he could get away for a bit, he definitely would. This morning, he'd texted her and told her it probably wasn't likely.

Needless to say, she was missing him.

Aside from those texts, they'd been messaging back and forth repeatedly. Inane things, nothing important, but it made all the difference in the world. Since Sunday, Hope had been a little twisted up on the inside about a lot of things, mainly her feelings for Jared.

"Ladies," her father said, getting to his feet, "I need to go check on somethin'. Y'all need anything from inside?"

"I'm good," Hope assured him at the same time Jan said, "No, thank you."

When her father stepped away, leaving the two of them alone, Hope glanced over at Jan.

"Can I ask you something?"

The woman continued to gently rock in the chair, a warm smile on her face when she met Hope's gaze. "Of course."

"Did you ever want children of your own?" As soon as the words were out of her mouth, Hope felt bad for asking.

"I did," Jan said, seemingly unperturbed about Hope's insanely personal question.

"Why didn't you have any?" she inquired, unable to stop being obscenely rude, apparently.

"I never met the right man," Jan said. "I almost married once. Something kept niggling at my brain, telling me he wasn't the right one. Or maybe the universe was telling me it wasn't the right time. Either way, we ended up breaking up about a year later. He'd been sleeping with his secretary."

"That's so cliché," Hope said, trying to lighten the mood. "Guys and their secretaries."

Jan giggled. "Yep. And I guess from then on, I held out until it was too late for me to have children. But I never thought I'd missed out, honestly. My students ... well, they're like my children. From the time their parents entrust them to me until the final bell rings at the end of the day, I get to see their smiling faces, experience their joy and, yes, even their sadness. But I get to watch them grow. It's been an endless stream, year after year. It's been enough."

Hope wasn't sure that would ever be enough for her.

As usual, Jan didn't question Hope on why she was asking the question, but she remained where she was, silently letting Hope know that she was willing to listen.

"I met this guy," Hope told her. "He's got a little boy. It's just ... I've been burned before. Twice. I'm not sure I can go through it again. I don't want to let myself like him enough. And I definitely don't want to get attached to the kid only to have the relationship turn to ashes and I'm left once again wishing on something that's no longer there."

Jan's hand touched Hope's arm. "One thing I've learned," she began, "it's easy to compare everything to the past. We're human. We want to protect ourselves. Love's not easy. For anyone. But don't hold someone accountable for an action they haven't taken. It's not fair to them, and it's certainly not fair to you."

Hope smiled. "That sounds so rational."

"It is," Jan grinned. "Too bad it's much more difficult to get your heart to understand. But keep it in the back of your mind, Hope. This man and his son, maybe they are the very reason that your past relationships didn't work out. Maybe they were meant to cross your path, and you were meant to be there when they did."

Swallowing hard, Hope glanced down at the ground.

The sound of boots on wood sounded from behind her. Hope turned, fully expecting to see her father. Only the man coming toward her, slowly, wasn't her father.

"I think your father got lost," Jan said softly. "I better go check on him."

Hope nodded, but she never once took her eyes off the sexy cowboy heading her way.

Jared

"DID I CATCH you at a bad time?" Jared asked when he approached Hope. The woman she'd been talking to headed in the opposite direction, slipping inside the house. It looked as though he'd interrupted something important.

And when Hope said, "Not at all," he knew she was lying. Hope's eyes were big, the surprise on her face evident.

Jared stood there, glancing from Hope to the disappearing woman. "Are you sure?"

"I wasn't ... um ... expecting you. But this is a nice surprise."

"Last-minute opportunity," he told her, nodding toward the empty rocking chair. "Mind if I sit?"

"Of course not."

Jared felt Hope's gaze on him as he sat down, his eyes scanning the horizon. It was almost completely dark outside, and the exterior house lights made it difficult to see much more than a few feet in front of the porch.

"Something wrong?" Hope asked.

"Is it obvious?" Jared turned his head and looked at her, leaning his head back against the wooden chair.

"I'm not sure. It looks like you've got something on your mind."

"Ditto." He glanced back at the door to the house, then to Hope. "I really didn't mean to interrupt."

"You didn't," she said, smiling. It looked somewhat forced.

And yes, he did have something on his mind. The last three days had been hell. More so than the last two years of his life, ever since he'd divorced his crazy fucking ex and moved to Coyote Ridge. Of course, the hell he was living now was directly related to the crazy fucking ex, who was, yes, still fucking crazy.

He had wanted to come here to talk to Hope. To tell her all that was going on. See if she had any suggestions. More importantly, he'd wanted to share something about himself with her. Now that he was here, he wasn't sure he should. If they were supposed to keep this casual, it would only defeat the purpose.

"Talk to me, Jared," Hope urged, her voice soft.

He focused on the ground and sighed. "My ex-wife has decided to make a reappearance in my life. Normally, that wouldn't be a problem, except it is. A big one."

Hope was still watching him.

Jared swallowed, deciding to give her the full story. "Sable and I didn't date for long before we got married. It was all kind of a blur, I guess. Not long after we were married, she got pregnant. My life changed at that point. The only thing that mattered to me was that boy. He's my life." Jared glanced at her again, then turned his attention back to the darkness in front of them. "Turned out, I was the only one who was abiding by our wedding vows. Sable was stepping out. Not just once but constantly. When I'd finally had enough and called her on it, she told me Derrick wasn't my son."

Hope's sharp inhale was pretty much the same response he got when he told this story to anyone.

"In fact," he continued, "she didn't know who his father was. At first, she claimed it was one guy, but he insisted on a paternity test. Derrick wasn't his. But I'd raised Derrick, and we all know that blood alone doesn't make a family. Sable took him from me for a little while. I couldn't stay away, and I guess she figured out that I would do damn near anything in the world for him. So, not long before the divorce was final, she blackmailed me. Said if I wanted him, I needed to pay her." He looked at her, held her gaze. "Twenty-five thousand is a lot of money to some, but to have my son back, it was nothing. I would've paid ten times that much if I had to." He forced a smile.

Hope's eyes were soft with sympathy when she said, "I get it."

Jared

"So, finally, Derrick is back in my life, and we've moved to Coyote Ridge for a new start. Things are going great, and it's been almost two years now." He sighed. "Sable popped up again a few weeks ago. This time she sent an email, letting me know that she was going to take me back to court to get custody of Derrick. She'd originally signed away her parental rights, making me Derrick's sole guardian. Now she's telling me she wants him back."

"Can she do that?" Hope sounded horrified.

Jared shrugged. "The lawyer I talked to said it was not likely, but anything was possible. Said Sable would need a damn good case, which I honestly don't think she has. But she might win some judge's sympathy and at least get joint custody."

Hope didn't say anything, and Jared needed a minute to breathe. The idea of Sable taking Derrick away made his gut churn. He wasn't sure he'd be able to handle it.

"What I fear the most is that a judge will side with her because Derrick isn't biologically mine. When she told me he wasn't, I insisted on a paternity test. She showed me the DNA results, produced them almost immediately after I'd asked for them. Apparently she had been planning to use it against me for some time."

Again Hope was silent, but Jared knew there was nothing she could say. Hell, he didn't know what should be said at this point.

"My cousin Travis is helping me," he explained. "He's got contacts I don't have. He's good at digging up dirt on people."

"Sounds to me like it won't take much. Is she blackmailing you again? Does she want money?"

Jared nodded.

"How much?"

"Another twenty-five thousand." He glanced over at her. "And honestly, I'd give her the damn money if I thought it would get her out of our lives for good. But she's not going away. She'll only come back for more when she burns through it."

"What a bitch," Hope murmured.

That made Jared laugh. He hadn't laughed much these past few days.

"I'm sorry I laid all that on you," he told her. "I'm not expecting you to know how to fix it, but I..." Damn. How the hell did he explain this without freaking her out? "I wanted to talk to you about it. I ... wanted you to know."

"Where's Derrick now?" Hope asked.

"At Lorrie and Curtis's. They went to church. I told 'em I'd pick him up a little late."

Jared leaned his head back against the chair, continuing to stare at Hope. He wanted to know what she was thinking.

When she slid her hand over his, curling her fingers between his, he breathed a little easier.

"Thank you for telling me. I can't imagine how hard this is for you."

No, she probably couldn't.

And she probably couldn't imagine how much better he felt, just sitting here holding her hand.

CHAPTER TWENTY-THREE

"ARE Y'ALL READY?" Trinity hollered as she joined the rest of them in the recreation room.

Hope had been the first to arrive, making sure she had everything ready for Grace's arrival. After all, tonight was Grace's bachelorette party, which meant they were going out. And if they wanted to get to their destination on time, she knew they had better get going.

"We're ready," Faith answered for everyone.

"Where's Gracie?" Mercy asked.

"She'll be here in a minute," Hope told them. She'd stopped by Grace's on the way to the main house to ensure her sister was almost ready. She had been, but her men were experiencing some separation anxiety, or so she'd said.

Hope knew better since her men were going to be at the bachelorette party. But that was something Grace didn't know.

Getting everything together tonight had been somewhat of a challenge. For one, Mercy had suggested they talk to their cousin Cheyenne and see if she'd be willing to do a private concert. The idea was great, but the plan to make it happen had backfired at the last minute.

While Hope had gotten a go-ahead from Cheyenne, plans had changed because Cheyenne wouldn't be back home until tonight, and she'd been insistent that she stop to see her man beforehand since she would be in town for only one night. That was when Hope had another idea. What if they went to Cheyenne, rather than the other way around? So, instead of the local VFW hall, they had worked out a deal with the owner of Moonshiners, a bar in Coyote Ridge. As if it hadn't been hard enough to coordinate already, they'd switched the venue at the absolute last possible minute.

They'd managed to divide up the chores for the wranglers, and none of them were expected back on the ranch until bright and early Monday morning, which gave them all of Sunday to recover. With that in mind, Hope had managed to get rooms at the hotel closest to Coyote Ridge for her and her sisters.

Now, it was a matter of getting Gracie there without spilling the beans that it had become a co-ed party, since Grant and Lane had both insisted that they were not having a bachelor party. Their lame asses had forced Hope's hand. When Mercy had made the suggestion to combine it but to keep it a secret, Hope had figured what the hell.

"I'm here! Where's the beer?" Gracie yelled when she stepped into the room.

"It ain't here," Mercy told her. "But if you hop in the truck, we'll make it happen."

"I'm game," Gracie stated with a huge grin.

"But first," Faith intervened, "we've got a few things for you."

Hope stepped out of the way while Faith and Trinity accessorized their sister. They fixed some sort of tiara up on Grace's head, careful not to mess up her hair. Then they put a bride-to-be sash on her. And last but not least, they blindfolded her. Grace was a good sport about everything, insisting that as long as she was getting free beer all night long, they could do whatever they wanted with her.

Well, wouldn't Gracie be shocked to find out that she would be spending the night of her bachelor party at a sex resort.

Jared

Oh, Hope hadn't mentioned that one to anyone yet, but with a little more help from Cheyenne, she'd managed to snag an invitation to the resort for Gracie, Grant, and Lane. Hope figured tonight was a better option than their wedding night anyway. Although Hope had enjoyed herself and knew the amenities at Alluring Indulgence were fantastic, she wasn't sure a sex resort was the right romantic getaway for the newlyweds.

"All right, let's do this!" Gracie commanded, blindfolded and being led to the door by her sisters.

Forty-five minutes later, they were cramming into Moonshiners with a few dozen other people who had arrived before them.

Turned out, Cheyenne had extended an invitation to the Walkers—who, as Hope had suspected, were an oversized bunch. And by oversized, she wasn't necessarily referring to the sheer number of them. Although, there was that.

If she'd thought Jared was a big man, she hadn't seen anything until she was introduced to Jared's cousin Travis and Travis's six brothers. Of course, then there was Beau Bennett—Ethan's husband. That man was a giant in every sense of the word.

But Hope tried not to seem stupefied as Cheyenne introduced her to everyone. And when they finally made their way over to Jared, Hope's stomach was fluttering.

"I guess an introduction isn't necessary, huh?" Cheyenne said sweetly, mischief glowing in her green eyes.

"Nope, not necessary," Hope agreed, smiling at Jared.

"Hey."

To her complete shock, Jared pulled her against him, pressing his lips to hers instantly. The kiss was a shock to her system that nearly made her knees go weak. After their conversation on Wednesday, when they'd sat on the porch late into the night, doing nothing more than holding hands and talking, Hope hadn't known what to expect from the man.

She was pretty sure Jared's revelation was some sort of test. Although, what kind of test—and whether she'd passed or failed—she wasn't sure yet.

"On that note," Cheyenne said with a giggle, "I'm going to go get ready for my set. And you two lovebirds can sit back and enjoy the show."

Show?

Right now, Hope's brain was seriously scrambled. It took a minute for her to remember what show her cousin was talking about.

WHEN JARED LEARNED that Hope was moving her sister's bachelorette party to Moonshiners, he'd tried to play it cool. She hadn't invited him, but that wouldn't have stopped him from showing up tonight. Since Cheyenne *had* invited him, he hadn't had to crash the party.

And he certainly would have just to see that look of surprise and approval on Hope's beautiful face.

"What do you think?" Hope asked, standing close to him as she surveyed the room.

Unable to resist, Jared put his arm around her and shifted her so that she was standing in front of him. He put one hand on her hip, the other holding his beer. When she leaned back against him, Jared breathed deeply, loving the way she fit to him, as though she'd been created just for him.

"Was she surprised?" Jared asked, referring to Grace, who, according to Cheyenne, hadn't known that the venue had changed or that it was a co-ed party with live entertainment.

Hope nodded.

Jared had seen all of Hope's sisters for the first time when they walked into the bar. It wasn't surprising that all heads had turned, some more than once. The Lambert sisters were eye-catching, sure. But Jared's gaze had been drawn right to Hope, the prettiest of the bunch.

Jared

Tonight was somewhat unexpected, but Jared was happy to spend time with Hope. Especially in a setting that didn't involve them being naked. Not that he wouldn't want that later, but for some reason, this was better. It gave him a chance to see who Hope really was. Not only was she the sinfully delicious woman who'd rocked his world in ways he hadn't expected, but she was sweet and funny.

As he continued to stand behind her, people came over to her, thanking her for inviting them, letting her know how great this was, how they always enjoyed being with family. It was low-key—as low-key as it could be considering they were in a small-town bar with the West Texas Princess about to come on the makeshift stage that had been set up solely for this event.

"Hey, honey."

Jared turned in time to see Mr. Lambert approaching Hope. The man's stern gaze was on Jared, apparently curious as to what their relationship was.

Never one to back down from anyone, Jared reached around Hope and shook the man's hand. "Good to see you again, sir."

"Dad, you remember Jared."

"Of course I do." If Jerry was concerned that Hope was there with him, he didn't show it. Then again, his face was impassive. It would've been nearly impossible to tell what he was thinking.

"Jared, this is Jan," Hope introduced. "My dad's future bride."

Jared was pretty sure Jerry blushed more than Jan did. Wasn't that interesting.

"Jan, this is Jared Walker. Cheyenne's boyfriend, Brendon, is his cousin."

Jared shook Jan's hand. "Very nice to meet you."

"Likewise." Jan's eyes bounced between Hope and Jared before returning to Jerry.

"I'm so glad y'all decided to come," Hope said to her father.

Jerry put his arm around Jan. "Figured if my girls wanted to go out tonight, I better come along to ensure they don't get too far out of control."

Hope twisted her head back to look up at Jared. "We don't get out much."

Jerry laughed. "That's an understatement."

"Can I get you a drink, sir? Ma'am?" Jared offered.

"We're good, thanks. Wanted to catch up with Cheyenne before she went on stage anyway. She tried to disappear, but I think someone caught her before she could," Jerry stated.

Jared had asked around a little and found out that Cheyenne's mother was Jerry Lambert's sister. Unlike Jerry, who had raised his five girls and been a stand-up guy in the parenting department, Cheyenne's mother apparently hadn't received that gene.

"Well, we're gonna go mingle," Jerry said, his gaze once again meeting Jared's.

Jared figured the man was trying to warn him not to hurt his daughter. He could've assured him that would never happen. However, he was beginning to think the reverse might not be as true.

When they wandered off, Hope turned to him.

Jared brushed a strand of her hair back from her face, smiling down at her.

"I got a hotel room for the night," she told him.

He cocked an eyebrow. Part of him wished he could simply invite her back to his place so he could spend the night with her, but that wasn't an option. He could tell by the look in her eyes. He'd spent more time than necessary thinking about Hope's reactions that night. First when she'd met Derrick unexpectedly, and second when she'd been practically trembling because she woke up in his bed.

If he was right, Hope Lambert didn't know how to react around kids. That or she didn't like kids. He damn sure hoped it wasn't the latter, because that would put a serious damper on whatever this was between them.

"Think maybe you can come by for a bit?" she asked, her tone sugary sweet.

Jared

He wanted that more than anything. He'd purposely kept his visit to the ranch on Wednesday on a platonic level, letting Hope know that sex wasn't the only thing he wanted from her. However, sex was definitely something he wanted from her, and thinking about sinking into her body...

Yeah. It was getting a little warm in there.

Jared leaned down closer to her ear, not wanting anyone else to hear him. "I don't think a little bit will be enough time for all the things I wanna do to you tonight, darlin'."

When he pulled back, he noticed her cheeks were pink and she was smiling as she stared at him. He tried to read what she was thinking, but she did a damn fine job of concealing that from him.

"Unless, of course, you're not interested," he said, grinning.

"Jared Walker, where you're concerned, I'm definitely interested."

Yeah. The question Jared had was...

How interested?

CHAPTER TWENTY-FOUR

THE NIGHT WAS going far better than Hope had expected.

No bar fights, no out-of-control cowboys—or cowgirls—and all of the guests were more than thrilled that Cheyenne Montgomery had made a special appearance just for them. Hope could've told them all that Cheyenne was family and that she'd been honored to be included, but she doubted anyone wanted to hear that. They'd rather hear her sing.

Truth was, family was important to all of them, and from what she could tell, it was equally important to the Walker family. Throughout the night, Hope had been introduced to all of Jared's cousins and their significant others, along with Jared's brothers Kaden and Keegan—the twins. Jared had assured her that the rest of his family would be at the reunion. He also told her it was probably a good thing that she'd only had to endure the twins tonight because they were a handful in their own right.

Jared had been right about that.

For almost half an hour, Hope had sat back and watched Kaden and Keegan work their magic on some cute little brunette who had been hanging by the bar. At first, she'd thought she was seeing things ... watching as the two of them seemingly seduced that woman right off her barstool. *Both* of them. Yes, *two*, not one.

When Jared had caught her watching them, he had smiled.

"That's what they do," Jared told her, pulling her close. "For whatever reason, they share their women."

Jared

He said it so casually, like it wasn't unusual for two men to share their woman. Of course, Hope had some experience with that. Not personally, no. But Grace was with two men. However, Hope seriously doubted it was the same. In the twins' situation, it was clear they were in it to seduce and pleasure the woman. Grace's situation was quite different in that Grant and Lane also seduced and pleasured one another.

Hope had turned to face Jared, wanting to make sure she'd heard correctly. "Share? As in…"

Jared had pulled her closer, settling her between his legs. He was sitting on a stool but still much taller than she was. It allowed her to get close, to smell him. Yum.

"As in," he'd confirmed. "That whole salacious adventure thing… It runs in our family."

"Have you ever shared a woman?"

Jared shook his head, maintaining eye contact. "Never. And I have no desire to."

That was a good thing. Hope was all for experimenting with certain things, including the resort, but she definitely had no desire to be with two men.

"Have they always … done it like that?" She had chuckled at how that sounded.

"No," Jared had informed her. "They've always been ridiculously competitive, though. I remember numerous times they fought over the same girl."

Hope had glanced from Jared over to the twins.

"I'm not one to gossip," Jared had continued. "But my cousins Braydon and Brendon… Before Braydon got too serious with Jessie, they had shared her. They'd always shared their women. I think Kaden and Keegan took pointers from them."

"Really?" That had been a total shocker. That meant that Cheyenne's boyfriend had once…

"Well, not literally, I don't think. Everyone thought that Braydon and Brendon would eventually end up with the same woman. Sometimes, a man has no choice but to claim a woman as his. No matter what his desires are, the heart is often not interested in the same thing."

"Is that the way it is with Kaden and Keegan?"

Jared had shrugged. "They're thirty-two years old. From what I know, they have no interest in going solo now. The sharing thing works for them and there's less ... confrontation."

"Will they end up marrying the same girl?" She'd been too curious not to ask.

"No idea. You'd have to ask them. That's their story to tell."

Of course, Hope had no intention of asking the twins that question. But it had given her a different perspective on things. Then again, tonight she'd gotten plenty of different perspectives. She had learned that Jared's cousin Travis was in fact married to a man and a woman. No, not legally, but in the same sense as Grace would be married to Grant and Lane. To know that it wasn't so far out of the realm of possibility had been a surprise. She still remembered the day she'd found out that her sister was in love with two men and that those two men were also in love with her and each other. Talk about mind-blowing.

She had also heard that Jared's cousin Ethan was married to Beau. And that Beau was Ethan's brother Zane's best friend. As far as rumors went, she'd heard that Beau had actually been with Zane at some point—threesomes had been their thing—and that particular experience had cemented for him that he was in fact gay, not bisexual as he'd once thought.

Hope's head had been spinning with all the rumors and information she'd taken in tonight. She had enjoyed people-watching, asking Jared questions about who was who and answering his questions in return.

But now she was hoping the night was going to end soon. Gracie, Lane, and Grant were apparently gearing up to head out. Faith had surprised them with the resort information, and at that point, keeping them here seemed to be damn near impossible.

"Looks like things are winding down," Jared told her now.

"Hopefully."

Jared spun her around so that she was once again facing him. "Tired?"

She grinned. "Not in the least."

Jared

"Good." He leaned down and kissed her sweetly. "I need to call my aunt and check on my son. But after I do that, I'll be ready to head out when you are. If you'd like, I can drive you over to the hotel."

The reminder that he had a son was almost enough to dampen her libido. This past week had been difficult for her. Even after her conversation with Jan, Hope wasn't feeling particularly good about the fact that she was falling for a single dad. In fact, she'd come to the conclusion that Jared Walker was going to break her heart, even if she had to be the one to walk away. What was happening between them was far more than just sex, even though she was trying really hard not to let that happen. No one had ever warned her that keeping it casual was so much work.

"I'd like that," Hope said. "I'm gonna go check in with Trinity and Mercy real quick. I'll meet you out front?"

Jared nodded, his eyes searching her face for a moment. She wasn't sure what it was, but something had changed in him in the last few seconds. He was no longer smiling, but the heat she'd witnessed earlier was still there.

Had she said something wrong?

She followed Jared toward the front door, but she took a detour over to the corner, where Mercy, Trinity, and Faith were talking to Grace.

"A what?" Grace exclaimed.

Hope glanced up at Lane and Grant. The two men had just shared a look that said it was their lucky night.

Clearly, her sisters had just informed them they'd be staying at a sex resort for the night.

"Is that a real thing?" Grace asked, looking from one sister to the next, then her gaze landing on Hope.

Hope nodded. "It is. Surprise."

IT FINALLY OCCURRED to Jared that Hope didn't like the idea of kids. When he'd mentioned needing to check on his son, her eyes had dimmed significantly. It was as though the idea of him having a kid didn't sit well with her.

He knew that wasn't supposed to bother him. This thing between them was supposed to be temporary.

And that was the thing. It *shouldn't* bother him. It *should* be temporary.

Only Jared wasn't thinking much in the temporary sense right now.

Oh, no, he definitely wasn't thinking marriage or anything of that nature, but the idea of another man enjoying Hope, kissing her, talking to her, making love to her, even spending a night out with her... It was enough to send the green-eyed monster surging through his veins.

Grabbing his phone, Jared stepped outside, walking over to the right of the door along the narrow wooden porch. He dialed Lorrie's number and waited for someone to answer.

"Hey, it's me," he said when Lorrie's soft voice sounded on the other end. "Just callin' to check in. How's he doin'?"

"Perfect," she said, chuckling. "Aren't all little boys perfect?"

That made him laugh. She'd raised seven of her own. Jared found it amusing that she could still laugh about it.

"He had dinner, and we didn't let him get loaded up on chocolate, although he certainly tried. Right now, he's snugged in the recliner on Curtis's lap. They're watching a movie. If I had to guess, he'll be asleep in fifteen minutes, provided the phone doesn't ring again."

Jared laughed again. "Understood."

"Really, Jared. He's good. And feel free to call back anytime."

Not that Jared had expected any less. Curtis and Lorrie treated Derrick as though he were one of their own grandchildren. Although Jared's parents doted on him whenever they could, the opportunities just weren't there. With his parents in El Paso, Jared didn't see them as often as they would all like.

Jared

"Thanks, Aunt Lorrie. And I promise I won't call until morning."

After telling Lorrie good night, Jared stuck his phone back in his pocket. He turned toward the door only to come face-to-face with...

"Son of a bitch," he grumbled. "What the fuck are you doin' here, Sable?"

His ex-wife smiled, her dark eyes glittering as though she'd accomplished an impossible feat.

"I came to see you, of course."

Jared tried to move around her, but she stopped him with a hand on his arm. He didn't want to hurt her, but he damn sure didn't want her to touch him. He jerked away and spun around to face her.

"*Why* are you here?" He knew whatever her reason, it wasn't good.

"I told you." She tried to flutter her lashes, clearly hoping to seduce him, but it wasn't working. "I figured since the email thing wasn't working, maybe seeing me face-to-face would help move things along. Thought maybe we could get a beer."

"I'm leaving," he told her.

"Then how about coffee? It'll give us a chance to talk. And we do need to talk, Jared."

Yes, that was a definite threat in her tone, one he tried his damnedest to ignore.

"There's nothin' to talk about. Go back to El Paso, Sable," he growled. "Ain't nothin' here for you."

"*You're* here," she said sweetly.

Funny. She didn't mention Derrick. That would've been Jared's reason. Then again, Sable had never put Derrick first. Unless, of course, she was working a deal. Then she used Derrick at her leisure.

Jared leaned in closer. "No, I'm not here. Not for you anyway."

He knew she wasn't oblivious to his hatred; she simply pretended not to notice.

The door opened behind him, and laughter and conversation drifted out into the still evening air.

"Problem here?"

Shit.

Jared glanced over his shoulder to see Travis standing there with Gage beside him.

"No problem," Jared grumbled. "She was just heading back to El Paso." He met Sable's gaze, willing her to simply disappear.

"Oh, no," she said with a smile. "You're wrong, sweetness. I'm here to stay."

"The hell you are."

This time, Jared wasn't the one with the outburst. Jared had to step back out of the way as Travis damn near plowed him over. "You're not welcome in this town."

"You don't own it."

Well, technically…

Jared didn't bother to clarify that at one point, most of the town had belonged to the Walkers. It wasn't until Curtis inherited the land that he'd started selling it off to the small businesses who had established themselves there. Hell, Lorrie had been the one to name the town. And yes, Curtis had been the one to make that happen. From what Jared remembered, Curtis had renamed the town as a birthday present to her. No simple jewelry for that man.

And Jared knew that they still had a large share of the land, probably more than fifty, maybe sixty percent of it.

"You don't wanna go up against me, lady," Travis snarled.

Oh, crap.

Gage stepped in front of Travis, placing his hands on the man's chest. "Come on. We need to get Kylie home."

Travis looked at Gage, then back to Sable. He briefly swept his gaze in Jared's direction. It was evident Travis didn't like the idea of Sable being there. Jared was right there with him. Not many of his cousins knew the hell Sable had put Jared through, but Travis did. Jared had shared the details with him over a bottle of whiskey. And, of course, Travis was aware of the stunt Sable was attempting to pull now.

"I'd like to see my son," Sable said, practically standing up to Travis. Clearly she didn't realize the mountain she was up against.

Jared

"He's not your son," Jared supplied, getting angrier by the second. "And Travis is right. You're not welcome here."

"You can't keep me away."

"The hell he can't," Travis muttered, his eyes stormy.

"And who the hell do you think you are?" Sable countered. "This ain't none of your business."

"The hell it ain't," Travis snapped. "I'm family. And we take care of our own. Even when some two-bit—"

Gage slapped his hand over Travis's mouth. "Don't do that. This isn't your fight. Jared knows you're here for him. We're all here for him. Stay out of it."

"He's right," Jared told Travis. "I've got it under control."

And just like that, the shit storm that had been brewing settled. But only in time for something far more dangerous to move in.

"Is everything all right?"

Oh, shit. That was Hope's sweet drawl. She was stepping around Travis, coming to stand beside Jared. She clearly hadn't heard the conversation, because she stepped right up to his side, oblivious to the woman in front of him. Her wide blue eyes darted from one man to the other, then back to Jared.

She smiled. "My sisters took my truck back to the hotel. You ready to head out?"

Sable cleared her throat, and Hope glanced over, her eyes widening.

"You don't waste any time, do you, Jared?"

Jared rolled his eyes.

"Care to introduce your wife to your mistress?" Sable hissed.

Thank the Lord Almighty that Hope didn't fall for Sable's bullshit. She moved even closer to him, taking his arm as she smiled at Sable.

"Ex-wife," Hope clarified. "You don't get the honor of calling yourself his wife anymore."

"The hell I don't."

"Go back where you came from, Sable," Jared told her, putting his arm around Hope. "We're not doin' this."

"We need to talk," Sable said, her tone sweet once more, somewhat sad, but she was still trying to burn a hole into Hope with her angry glare. "And this thing here has no business in the conversation."

Ah, shit. He felt Hope bristle at being called a thing.

Hope leaned in closer to Sable but didn't release him. "This isn't the time or the place for this. I don't care who you are or what you think you want. Figure out a way to act like a grown-up, and maybe you'll get a civil conversation out of the deal."

Sable hissed. "In case you don't know, Derrick's my son. And that means I'll always be in Jared's life. Is that something you can live with?"

Jared was gearing up to silence Sable, but Hope beat him to it. She stood up straight, not that it helped in the height department. Sable was still several inches taller, but that wasn't as obvious once Hope spoke.

"I can live with a lot of things," Hope countered. "But a mother abandoning her child... Do you have any fucking idea the gift you were given? No, clearly not, because you turned your back on him. Not only that, but then you auctioned him off, like he was—"

Hope was shaking, so Jared pulled her back, wrapping his arms around her. He held her close, pressing his lips to the top of her head. "Let's go," he told her softly. "She's not worth it."

Hope nodded her head but didn't release him.

"Problem out here?" Sawyer asked.

Jared looked over at him. Great. Just what he needed. Looked as though every one of Travis's brothers had come outside. Not only that but their significant others were with them. The brothers were standing shoulder to shoulder now, an impressive show of solidarity. Jared had to admit, he liked knowing that they had his back.

"There's no problem," Travis said calmly. "Jared and Hope were just leavin'." Travis caught his gaze, nodding toward the parking lot.

"That we were." He knew when he was being given an out. In this case, he wasn't going to ignore it. "I'll check in with you tomorrow."

Jared

Travis nodded, and Jared, arm still around Hope, turned and led her toward the truck.

"Sorry, lady. They're not interested in company," Sawyer said. "Looks like you might wanna head on home now. To El Paso."

If Jared was lucky, that would be exactly what Sable did. Unfortunately, luck never seemed to be on his side.

CHAPTER TWENTY-FIVE

WOW. SO THAT was rather intense.

Hope knew that family stuck up for family, but she honestly hadn't expected that. Travis Walker clearly had some sort of protective thing going on, because he had looked ready to carry Jared's ex-wife out of there and dump her on the nearest bus.

Then again, Hope hadn't planned to go off the way she had. Every time she thought about what Jared had told her, how Sable had practically given her son away in exchange for money, it made her blood boil. Clearly the woman had no freaking clue what a gift a child was.

"I'm sorry about all that," Jared told her when they were pulling out of the parking lot of Moonshiners.

"No," she said, glancing over at him. "I'm sorry. It wasn't my place to say anything."

Jared reached over and took her hand. "I appreciate it all the same. You standing up for Derrick like that."

"Does it happen often? Her showing up uninvited?" After what Jared had told her about his ex-wife, it wouldn't be out of the realm of possibility. She sounded certifiable, especially if she could use her own child as a bargaining chip.

He shook his head. "I haven't seen Sable since…"

When Jared glanced her way, she knew he was trying to decide how much to tell her. The other night was an exception to the rule, she figured. This conversation, much like their previous one, dipped directly into the much-too-personal pool. If they were keeping this casual, she didn't need to know any more details than those he'd already provided.

She got the feeling they'd surpassed casual weeks ago.

Jared

"I'd like to know," she told him softly, wondering why she'd gone and crossed that line.

He nodded, as though resigned to talking. "Not since the divorce. We've exchanged emails these past couple of weeks, but I've been"—he sighed—"humoring her, I guess. I think she honestly believes I'm going to pay her off."

"Are you?" Based on their previous conversation, she didn't think he was going to go that route. Based on his expression now, he might've changed his mind.

"I don't want to, no." He met her gaze again. "Are you sure you want to hear this?"

She wasn't sure about anything. Shit. She'd spent the evening with Jared, hanging out with their families and friends, laughing and joking, listening to stories and sharing a few of their own. Honestly, Hope couldn't remember a time she'd had that much fun. Not in a long, long time anyway.

Being with Jared seemed natural. As though they'd known each other for years, not weeks. She liked being with him, listening to him laugh and joke. She enjoyed the possessive way he touched her, keeping her close.

Still, she knew she should keep her distance. It was much easier to convince herself of that when she wasn't around him. But when she was … it was as though all common sense fled and her heart was leading the charge.

"I'm sure," she said when she realized he was waiting for her answer.

"When I paid her off the first time, she told me that she was moving on. She had a new man in her life."

"The one she thought was his father?" Hope couldn't even imagine how hard that had been for Jared. In the little time she'd known him, Hope had learned one thing for sure. The man loved his kid.

"No. Well, not completely. I told you how she went runnin' to the guy she said was Derrick's father. She took my son with her. The fact that I had an ironclad prenup infuriated her. Apparently she hadn't thought things all the way through, because that guy asked for a paternity test. She provided him with one, and it proved that she was lying. Derrick wasn't his. Sable finally admitted she didn't know who the father was. However, while all of this was going on, she met *another* guy. One with money and time on his hands. Older guy. This one didn't want any more kids, his were grown, and Sable realized she couldn't be saddled with one and get what she wanted. When she said she would allow me to adopt him if I would give her twenty-five thousand dollars in the divorce, I didn't even blink."

Hope still couldn't believe the woman had sold her son for … for any amount of money. What mother did that? Knowing what she knew about this man, it wasn't at all surprising that Jared had paid it. Not that she blamed him. Hope would've done the exact same thing if she'd been in his shoes. He was absolutely right. Blood did not make family, love did.

"Everything went through legal channels. I haven't seen her or talked to her since shortly after I moved here. Not since Derrick came to live with me."

"What does she want now?"

"Money."

"She said she wanted to see her son."

Jared's expression looked tortured. If that was true, she wondered if Jared would let Derrick see her so the little boy wouldn't go without a mother. The thought made her chest hurt. It was a brutal reminder that Hope was an outsider in Jared's world. Even if she did spend time with Derrick, even if she and Jared had a serious relationship, she wouldn't be able to protect the little boy the way she would want to. It would always be up to Jared.

They pulled into the hotel's parking lot at the same time Hope's phone rang. She grabbed it out of her purse and hit the talk button. "Hey, Faith. Everything all right?"

"Well, if having to spend a night in *one* room with only *two* beds sounds all right to you, then yeah. We're just peachy."

"We're supposed to have four rooms," Hope assured her.

"Well, we don't. I even had Trinity lay on the charm. The guy at the desk said every single room is full. So, I just wanted to let you know since ... you know."

Hope glanced over at Jared. Yeah. She knew. She would be sharing a room with her sisters, which meant no privacy for them.

"Problem?" Jared looked concerned.

"We only have one room," she told him, trying to cover the mouthpiece on the phone.

"Hey, Hope," Faith said. "We're in room 317. I'll let you go. If we see you up here, we see you up here. If not ... don't do nothin' I wouldn't do."

Hope didn't have the chance to respond before Faith disconnected.

"Looks like tonight's just not meant to be," Hope told him, forcing a smile. "But I had fun. I'm so glad you were there."

Jared's eyes bored into hers, as though he was trying to find an answer to some unasked question. She expected him to lean over and kiss her, tell her good night, and send her on her way, so what he said next caused her heart to lodge in her throat.

"COME HOME WITH me," Jared blurted.

The instant the words were out, he saw sadness pass through Hope's brilliant blue-green eyes.

"I can't," she whispered. "You know I can't."

He didn't know that. "My son's not there. He's stayin' with my aunt and uncle tonight."

"That doesn't change anything," she told him, although he was fairly certain she did consider it for a moment. "I shouldn't've been there the other night, Jared. It's ... not what I want. I told you that in the beginning."

Perhaps he couldn't read every one of her expressions, but Jared got the sense she was lying. Yeah, in the beginning, she'd told him a relationship wasn't possible, but they'd been seeing each other for weeks. Things changed, people changed, what they wanted changed.

But Hope looked both sincere and torn, so he decided not to push the issue.

Rather than argue with her, Jared nodded. He would not be coming to her hotel room with her tonight, and she would not be in his bed. That alone was disappointing, but something else was nagging at him, too.

If he was right, tonight would be the last time he saw Hope until the family reunion. She was retreating right before his eyes. Ever since she'd gone off on Sable, then when he'd started talking about Derrick, she'd been slipping out of his grasp. After this incredible night, the fun they'd had... Apparently that wouldn't last for them.

Tonight had felt like they were a real couple. And it'd happened so easily. From the moment he'd seen her at Moonshiners, Hope had remained by his side. He'd touched her as often as he could, making sure the cowboys whose eyes had strayed to her knew that she was his. And he couldn't lie, he'd wanted that. For a while, he'd even allowed himself to believe it was a possibility.

Only he had a son who would come first, and Hope... God, he didn't even know what Hope wanted when it came to kids. One minute she seemed terrified of them, the next she was defending Derrick against Sable. She'd been so passionate, so angry.

Do you have any fucking idea the gift you were given?

When she'd asked Sable that question, Jared had paused momentarily, unsure what to think.

But if she had no interest in kids of her own...

Jared

No way would he chase a woman who didn't want kids, didn't want Derrick. Jared would never subject Derrick to that again. It was going to be hard enough explaining to the little boy why his mother wasn't there, why she wasn't a part of his life. No matter what Sable said, Jared knew it wouldn't be long term. If he thought for a second that she'd changed, that she wanted to be a mother to Derrick, he could very easily be persuaded to let her back into Derrick's life. But that wasn't Sable. She wasn't interested in being tied down to anyone or anything. Not even her own flesh and blood.

"Let me walk you up to your room," he told her, opening the door before she could argue with him.

He helped her out of the truck, took her hand, and led her inside. From there, she led the way. They took the elevator to the third floor, then wandered halfway down the hall, stopping in front of room 317.

"I really am glad you were there tonight," she said, her voice soft and sweet and filled with what he believed was regret.

Yep. This was the last time he would see her.

And because he knew that, Jared cupped her face as he leaned down and pressed his lips to hers. He slid his tongue along the seam of her smooth mouth, licking his way inside. It was then that the chemical reaction neither of them could deny gathered like a storm around them. The heat between their bodies intensified as Jared pulled her close, pressing against her as she clung to him. God, he could spend all night kissing this woman, tasting her sweetness, inhaling the fire he knew burned brightly inside her.

But he wouldn't be doing that, so he forced himself to pull back.

"Good night, Hope."

"Good night."

And then he forced himself to take a step back while she knocked softly on the door. A few seconds later, it opened, and Mercy stuck her head out, frowning at him before opening the door and letting Hope in.

Only when she was inside and he heard the lock engage did he head back out to his truck.

There were two weeks between now and the time he would go to Dead Heat Ranch for the family reunion. He only hoped that in that time, he'd be able to get over this woman who had somehow inched her way inside him in ways he hadn't expected.

Jared

Chapter Twenty-Six

One week later

HOPE SAT ON the bed in the room they had commandeered as the bridal suite. Trinity was working her magic, prettying Gracie up, doing her hair and makeup for the wedding that would take place just over two hours from now.

"So, what did you think of that resort?" Mercy asked, her question directed at Grace.

The soon-to-be bride grinned from ear to ear as a blush stained her cheeks. "It was ... different."

"Different good?"

"Oh, yeah." She swiveled her head in Hope's direction. "And oh, my God. I never knew a place like that existed. It was so"—Gracie turned back to face Trinity—"hot."

"Hotter than the loft in the barn?" Mercy asked, deadpan.

Hope felt her own cheeks heat at the memory of her and Jared in the hayloft. God, she missed him. The last time she'd seen him had been a week ago when he dropped her off at the hotel. Although neither of them had said anything, she had known that the kiss they'd shared in that dimly lit hallway that smelled vaguely of pizza and beer would be their last.

The man had invited her back to his house that night, but she had refused because she'd been a chickenshit. Too scared to indulge in something that could possibly lead to more heartbreak. Only she still experienced the heartbreak. Apparently she didn't do casual well. She'd found out the hard way that she'd become quite attached to Jared Walker.

But she had saved herself some pain because she'd only had the opportunity to meet Derrick briefly. She hadn't had a chance to fall in love with the little boy, just his dad.

"Definitely hotter than the hayloft, although seriously ... I love the hayloft." Grace giggled.

"I get the feeling other people love the hayloft, too," Mercy said, looking directly at Hope. "I went out to the barn one night after dinner and I heard these noises…"

Hope glared at her sister, silently telling her to shut her pie hole.

"How is Jared, anyway?" Mercy questioned.

"He's fine," she lied.

"Really?" Mercy lifted one golden eyebrow. "That's not what he said when he called today, trying to work out the final details for the family reunion."

Great. And now her sisters knew that she'd gone and fucked this one up as well. Not that it mattered what they knew. They already expected that from her. For the past week, she had buried herself in work, refusing to give up for the day until she was too tired to keep her eyes open. Only then could she give in to sleep and not have to worry about dreaming about a man she couldn't have.

"Oh," Faith added, "I forgot to mention that he's coming by on Monday. He's bringing his cousin Travis so they can check out the cabins and give us the down payment."

Hope would need to be gone on Monday.

"Okay, ladies," Grace said, a smile in her voice. "What do you think?"

"We think you need to put on the dress," Mercy offered.

Grace met each of their eyes, smiling. "I'm so glad y'all are here with me. This… I honestly never thought this day would come."

Hope fought the tears that threatened. Her sister did look beautiful, even without the gown on yet. And she looked so ridiculously happy. That smile met her eyes and lit her up from within.

At least one of them had found their true love. Or loves, in Grace's case.

"Okay," Grace squealed. "Don't go anywhere. I'm gonna put on the dress."

When Gracie stepped out of the room, Mercy turned toward her. "Did you ditch the cowboy?"

Hope frowned. "Of course not. He's still holding his family reunion here."

Mercy gave her one of those looks that said she was dumber than dirt. "I didn't realize that you were still tryin' to sell him on it. Based on the way you were with him at Moonshiners, it looked like a little more than that to me."

"It wasn't."

Mercy frowned. "He's got a kid."

Now Hope was frowning. "So?"

"Why are you afraid of kids?" Faith asked, joining in.

"I'm not talking about this," Hope muttered. "This is Gracie's day."

"Yep, and Gracie's getting dressed. It'll take her fifteen minutes to get into that dress," Mercy told her with a snort. "During that time, you can share some of your wisdom. What made you not like kids?"

"I never said I don't like kids."

"No, but you avoid them like the plague."

Hope twisted the bedspread between her fingers, refusing to look at her sisters.

"Do you not want kids, Hope?" Trinity asked. "Because it's okay if you don't. Not everyone wants kids."

"I *do* want kids," she said before she could stop the words from spilling out of her mouth. "I just ... can't have any of my own."

God, she did not want to tell her sisters any of this. It wasn't their business. It wasn't anyone's business.

No one said anything, and when Hope looked up, she found Mercy, Faith, and Trinity staring back at her. She could see the sympathy in their eyes. That must've been what sent her over the edge, because she started talking and couldn't stop.

"I was diagnosed with endometriosis when I was eleven." Hope focused on the comforter. "Mom knew because I'd had to tell her. When I got my first period, there was this awful pain."

"You started your period at eleven?" Faith asked, obviously shocked.

Hope nodded. "The pain was unbearable. Mom said it was normal, that cramps could be bad. All women were different. So, I spent years suffering through it. It was unbearable. But ... after Mom died"—Hope swallowed hard—"it seemed to get worse. I was missing school every month because of it." She sighed. "Needless to say, I finally went to the doctor and they told me what it was. They also informed me that because of it, the likelihood of me ever having children was incredibly low."

Hope had known they were being kind, softening the blow, so to speak. They'd meant that she was infertile and would never have children. Not only had she experienced so much pain for so long, she'd been told that the only dream she had in life was no longer possible. Hope had wanted kids. A whole houseful of them. But that would never happen for her.

"Did you have a hysterectomy?" Mercy asked. "I remember you had surgery. What? Four years ago?"

Hope shook her head. "No."

She'd been super secretive at the time, not wanting her sisters to worry about her. Since their mother had died, none of them dealt well with those things. With surgery came all the risks, even though they were small. She had sworn her father to secrecy, and apparently he'd held up his end of the deal.

"What about Ben? He had a kid," Trinity said.

Hope looked at her sisters' faces, but she didn't have to respond, because they all seemed to get it at the same time.

"You were hooked on Maddie," Faith said, sounding as though it was all clicking into place for her. "And then she was no longer here. Oh, gosh. That had to hurt."

"And that other guy..." Mercy said, her voice trailing off.

Hope glanced down at the floor again. Yep. They'd figured it out. And now, she had no desire to get attached to another man's child, because having to lose that in her life ... again ... would be too painful. It was easier to keep her distance. One day she would find a man who could make her happy. They might never have children, but she would learn to live with that. She had no choice.

"Hmm."

Jared

Oh, shit. That was never a good sound, especially when it was coming from Mercy's mouth.

"Let it go, Mercy. Today's Gracie's day."

"You're right," she said with a wide grin. "I forgot something I wanted to give her. I'll be back in a minute."

Hope lunged for her, but Mercy was too quick. She slipped out of the bedroom at the same time Gracie stepped out of the bathroom.

Hope's eyes instantly filled with tears. "Oh, Gracie. You look ... stunning."

Grace sniffed. "Don't make me cry. I'll ruin my makeup."

Trinity and Faith were also tearing up as they moved closer.

And just like that, Hope managed to push every other thought from her head while she focused on making today the greatest day of Grace's life.

AFTER GIVING DERRICK a bath, Jared tucked the little boy into bed before getting settled in his own room. He was tired. They'd spent the entire day with Kaleb and Mason, riding horses. Since the weather was damn near perfect at this time of year, they'd wanted to take advantage of it. Derrick had run him completely ragged.

Now, the only thing Jared wanted to do was sit down, watch some TV, then drift off into a dreamless sleep. He grabbed his phone, checked to make sure he hadn't missed any calls.

Nope. No missed calls.

Nothing from Hope. Not in the past seven days.

Damn, he missed that woman. Probably more than he should considering how little time they'd spent together. And he didn't just miss the sex. He missed the time he got to spend with her, seeing the smile on her face. He missed going out to the ranch.

Okay, it was time he got over this shit. He would see her at some point during the family reunion; that was a given. But he had to remain aloof and cool. If Hope didn't want kids, there was nothing he could do about that. It only meant that she wasn't the woman for him.

His phone buzzed.

Jared reached for it, glancing at the screen to see he had a voice mail. He hadn't even heard the damn thing ring. Then again, that happened quite frequently when he was at home. Not much cell service meant sometimes he didn't get the call but, instead, received the voice mail.

After using his thumbprint to unlock the phone, he pulled up his voice mail and hit play.

"Hey, Jared. It's Mercy Lambert. Here at Dead Heat Ranch. I was told that you were coming in on Monday to check out the ranch. I wanted to see if you could make it tomorrow instead. We've got a conflict on Monday. If you could be here around one, that'd be great. You can simply text back to let me know if this change works for you. Thank you."

Because Sunday was a better day than Monday, Jared quickly shot Travis a text to make sure his cousin could head out there with him. Within minutes he had his answer; a simple yes was all he received. He then pulled up the number Mercy had called him from and sent a text telling her that he'd be there at one. After church.

More than likely he would see Hope tomorrow. Then again, it was possible that this was simply Hope's way of ensuring she didn't have to be there when he arrived.

Nothing he could do about that now, though. He'd promised Hope in the beginning that he wasn't going to play games. If she wanted to avoid him, so be it.

That didn't mean he wasn't trying to remain positive. As it was, he wanted to see Hope more than he wanted his next breath.

Jared

Chapter Twenty-Seven

"YOU BEEN OUT here lately?" Travis asked from the passenger seat of Jared's truck.

"Nuh-uh," he said honestly.

He hadn't been here since the night he and Hope had spent sitting on the back porch of the main house. And he hadn't heard from her since the night he'd dropped her at her hotel after her sister's bachelorette party. One week ago. In fact, Faith Lambert had been the one to call Jared, asking him to come to the ranch to finalize the details of the reunion that would be kicking off in six short days, and Mercy had called to reschedule.

Not a peep from Hope.

It could've been a simple trip out to check out the cabins, but Travis had wanted to go along under the guise of handling the down payment and getting the details on all the costs. Jared figured it was more like Travis wanted to check up to make sure all would be the way he wanted. Didn't much matter to Jared. He'd meticulously checked off every single item on the list, even thinking of a few things himself, to ensure that this reunion went off without a hitch.

Every family had responded, including Jared's father and all five of his siblings. At last count, there would be a total of one hundred and four people in attendance, including all of the little ones being brought along. Quite the turnout, and an event that the entire family was eagerly looking forward to. Due to their sheer size, it was rare that so many of them could be contained in one area.

"So, a week on this ranch, huh?" Curtis called from the backseat.

Oh, and Travis's father had opted to come along as well. Turned out, Lorrie had something to handle at the church, so Curtis had some extra time on his hands. The man was curious as to what they'd be doing for a solid week on a dude ranch. Since Derrick had wanted to ride along, Jared figured having Curtis and Travis there to keep the kid entertained wasn't a bad thing. Then again, Derrick had been fully engrossed in whatever he was watching on his iPad for the past half hour.

"It'll be good, Pop," Travis answered. "Lots of time to spend with family. Plus, you'll get to sit back and rest."

"Rest? Have you *met* my family?" Curtis retorted with a snicker.

True. There were a lot of kids, which would mean a lot of energy to expend. But the good news was they were expecting mild temperatures. They should be able to hang around outside without issue. They wouldn't be using the swimming pool, but there were plenty of other outdoor activities to keep everyone busy.

Jared pulled down the dirt road that led to the ranch. Travis let out a low whistle as he looked around. "Even nicer than I thought it'd be."

Jared didn't bother saying anything.

After he parked the truck by the sales office, the three of them climbed out, and Jared helped Derrick out of his car seat before leading the way to the door. Jerry Lambert was once again front and center, greeting them with a warm smile.

"Welcome, gentlemen," he said jovially. "So glad y'all could make it down here."

"Mr. Lambert, this is my cousin Travis and his father, Curtis."

Jerry shook both men's hands, then turned back.

"And this is my son, Derrick," Jared introduced, putting his hand on Derrick's head.

"Are you a cowboy, too?" Jerry asked, squatting down so he was at Derrick's height.

Derrick nodded enthusiastically.

"Good to have another cowboy around here," Jerry said, chuckling. "You see, I have this hat…" Jerry stood, glancing around as though looking for something.

Jared

Jared saw the pile of children's hats stacked in the corner.

"Here it is," Jerry announced, grabbing one of the straw ones from the top. "I think it'll fit you just fine."

Derrick's smile brightened when Jerry set the hat atop his head. "Look, Dad! I'm a reaw cowboy now."

"You sure are," Jared concurred.

"Would you like a tour of the sleeping quarters while you're here?" Jerry offered. "We can't show you all the cabins since some of them are currently occupied, but you'll get the gist of it. You'll have to forgive some of the mess. My daughter Gracie got married last night, so we're still working on the cleanup."

Hope had been at her sister's wedding last night. For some reason, that irked Jared. Had she brought a date?

"That'd be great, Mr. Lambert," Travis agreed, pulling Jared from his wandering thoughts.

"Give me just a moment. If you'd like to step out on the back porch, have a look around."

After a polite thank you, Jared took Travis and Curtis out onto the porch that wrapped around the entire house. He explained a few things about the layout—where the cabins were, what trail they used for the horseback rides, what they could do at the main house—and was just finishing up when he saw Hope walking toward him.

Jared was pretty sure she didn't see him, which was probably a blessing since the instant he laid eyes on her, he felt a strange sensation flood his chest. She made it all the way up the stairs before she looked up, and the second their eyes met, he could see her shock.

"Jared."

He forced a smile, although it wasn't all that hard. "Hope, you remember my cousin Travis. This is Curtis Walker, Travis's father. Uncle Curtis, this is Hope Lambert."

Before either man could say anything, Hope's gaze slid down to where Derrick stood beside him. She forced a smile, that was clear.

"Hi, Derrick," she greeted softly.

"Hi," Derrick said cheerfully, his gaze drifting up to Jared's. "Wook, Dad. It's the wady you went on a date with."

Jared glanced back at Hope. She was blushing, her eyes instantly turning away from his and over to Travis.

Travis nodded to Hope. "Nice to see you again."

"Likewise." Hope then reached over to take Curtis's proffered hand. "Nice to meet you, sir."

"You must be Cheyenne's cousin." Curtis grinned.

"Yes, sir." She flashed him a bright smile. "And I've heard so much about you." It was clear to Jared that she was doing her best not to look at him. "I'm glad you chose Dead Heat Ranch for your reunion."

When she did finally glance back at him, Jared felt the need to explain his presence. Clearly she wasn't expecting them. "Mercy called me last night. Asked me to come down and finalize the details today rather than on Monday."

"Of course she did." She couldn't seem to look him in the eyes. "Please excuse the mess. Gracie's wedding took place last night. It went way into the night and we're still cleaning up." Her eyes cut over to Curtis. "Since she's on her honeymoon, I'm down my foreman and my head wrangler. She has two husbands..."

"No need to explain, sugar," Curtis said with a grin. "My boy's got one of each himself, so I'm quite familiar with how that works."

Hope blushed and Jared couldn't seem to look away from her. She looked incredible. Her jeans were dusty, her shirt damp from sweat, and her boots were caked with dirt, but still, she was the most beautiful woman he'd ever laid eyes on.

The door opened behind them, and all four of them turned to see Mr. Lambert step outside. "Oh, Hope. Just the lady I was lookin' for. Would you mind givin' these gentlemen a quick tour? You can show them the bunkhouse—it's empty—and cabin seventeen"—Jerry tossed a set of keys toward her—"so they'll have an idea of the accommodations."

"Sure," she said, sounding somewhat surprised by the request.

"Thanks, honey."

"You're welcome," she said to her father. "Gentlemen, if you'll follow me. We'll take the golf cart since it's a good trek."

"You're an angel," Curtis said reverently.

Jared

Jared wondered if Curtis knew just how close to the truth he was with that statement.

SHE WASN'T SURE if she was successful in hiding her surprise, but Hope prayed Jared hadn't seen it when she had stumbled upon them a few minutes ago. The absolute last person she'd expected to see on the ranch today was the sexy, Wrangler-wearing, orgasm-inducing cowboy.

Hell, for a minute, she'd thought he was a mirage, only there were two enormous men standing beside him, one of whom she'd never seen before. Granted, the family resemblance was uncanny. Without a doubt, these men were related.

And then, of course, alongside Jared was the cutest little cowboy she'd ever seen. It was clear that her father had given Derrick one of the hats Jerry kept on hand for that purpose.

"Are you and Cheyenne close?" Curtis asked from the seat beside her. Jared and Travis were riding in the back two seats, Derrick on Jared's lap, giggling uncontrollably every time they hit a bump.

Hope peered over at Curtis. "Not as close as we once were. She spent a lot of summers here as a kid. Her mom..." She cut herself off, realizing she was about to divulge personal information.

"No worries, darlin'. We're well aware of Cheyenne's parental situation. Just glad to know she has family she can depend on."

"Yes, sir." Cheyenne's parents hadn't been up for any awards, that was for damn sure. Not when she'd been a kid and certainly not now. "I didn't spend a lot of time with Cheyenne, even when we were young, because Cheyenne's Faith's age. With a seven-year age difference between us, I didn't have a whole lot in common with either of them, but because of Cheyenne's parents' problems, my dad's always kept tabs on her."

"I like the man already. So, tell me, what types of activities can we look forward to here on the ranch?"

Hope was thankful that Curtis changed the subject. While she wound her way through the ranch toward the empty bunkhouse that was currently being cleaned, she took the opportunity to tell them about the amenities. When they arrived at their destination, she gave them a quick tour.

"Who'll be stayin' in this place?" Curtis asked, his attention focused on Jared and Travis.

"We're rentin' eighteen cabins, the bunkhouse, as well as all the rooms in the main house that are available," Jared explained. "Figured all the single folks could stay in the bunkhouse, along with some of the older kids. Married ones'll take the cabins. Most will have to bunk together."

"Most of our cabins will sleep eight people comfortably. Several have two, even three bedrooms," Hope offered. "And, of course, the rooms in the main house are quite nice. May be easier for those who want to be closer to the activities to stay in the house."

"I like that idea," Curtis told her. "These old bones can't make this trek every day for a week."

Hope laughed. Curtis Walker looked to be in as good of condition as Travis and Jared. She doubted he'd have any problem making that trek, and the twinkle in his eye said he knew that she knew it.

"Yes, sir," Hope said, doing her best not to look at Jared.

"I can take you by one of the cabins if you'd like," she offered.

When the men nodded, Hope started back to the golf cart. They were halfway there when a little hand took hold of hers, swinging her arm as they headed into the sunshine.

"Do you wive here?" Derrick asked.

"I do," she assured him. "I've got a cabin here."

"I wish I wived here."

"Why's that?" She was too curious not to ask.

"'Cause I couwd be a reaw cowboy awe the time."

"Yeah?"

Jared

Derrick nodded as he grinned up at her. He had to lean back in order to see her from under the brim of the hat. Hope felt a tug on her heart, one she'd been trying to avoid all this time.

"Come on, boy," Curtis told Derrick. "You can ride in my lap this time."

"Yay!"

And just like that, their moment was over.

HALF AN HOUR later, after taking them to the cabin, then showing them the outdoor arena where they held dances and other nightly activities, Hope delivered them back to the house to hand them off to her dad so he could handle the financial details.

Knowing it would be disrespectful to dump them by the stairs, Hope shored up her nerves and walked them to the door, still not looking at Jared. It was bad enough that she'd looked at him when she noticed him at the main house. For the past seven days, she'd thought about him at least a million times. Not once had he tried to get in touch with her, though. Then again, she hadn't made the effort, either.

She had almost had herself convinced that the time they'd spent together had been a dream. Unfortunately, the second she'd laid eyes on him again, her body remembered all too vividly everything that had happened between them. No way could she have dreamed that.

"Thank you for the tour, young lady," Curtis told her. "We look forward to spendin' a week here. Just cross your fingers we don't do too much damage."

Hope chuckled. She liked Curtis. Hell, she figured by the time the week was over, she would end up liking the entire Walker family more than she already did. And that wouldn't necessarily be a good thing.

She made a mental note to keep her distance. That might be the only way she'd survive the week.

222

TRAVIS GOT THE feeling Hope was trying to avoid his cousin. He also got the feeling Jared was trying to pretend he didn't know her all that well, either.

It might've worked on someone else, but Travis was a highly perceptive man. He saw right through their pretend nonsense. Not to mention, Derrick had announced that Hope had been out to Jared's place. In order for him to know that, Derrick would've had to have been there. Travis was curious about that considering his cousin hadn't introduced his son to any of the women he'd dated—although dated wasn't really the right word for it—since he'd moved to Coyote Ridge.

And that meant Hope was special.

Whatever these two were trying to hide … it wasn't working. He'd bet his life savings that the two of them had gotten naked together at some point. Although he did have his doubts. He knew that Jared had asked for an invitation to AI, and Travis had offered it. He also knew that Jared had taken Hope there, but based on the update he'd received, nothing had happened between the couple the night of their visit. Nothing more than a little voyeurism anyway.

That didn't mean they hadn't gotten busy afterward.

And yes, Travis had expected that something was going on after seeing them at Moonshiners, but based on the way they were acting now, it was more than clear.

Not that it was any of his business. However, it wasn't a bad thing that Jared had taken a liking to the cute little cowgirl. Travis's cousin had spent far too much time being reclusive when it came to the opposite sex. Oh, sure, Travis completely understood Jared's desire to put Derrick first. The kid deserved that. Didn't mean Jared had to turn into a monk in the process.

Not that any of it really mattered. Travis got the feeling Jared's little cowgirl was just as stubborn, just as hardheaded as Jared. Or any Walker, for that matter.

Unless the stars aligned just the right way, it was quite possible that these two knuckleheads could very well let something good pass them by. And Jared wouldn't be the first Walker that'd happened to. Nor would he be the last.

Jared

Chapter Twenty-Eight

Six days later

"YOU READY, BIG man?" Jared asked Derrick.

It was a silly question considering Derrick was standing by the door, his small rolling suitcase right beside him, cowboy hat on his head, boots on his feet. He'd been ready to go to the ranch for a good hour now.

"Yep! Can we go? Can we go?"

"I think we can," he told his son, grabbing the handle of his own suitcase and wheeling it toward the door.

"Yay!"

"Come on, big man. Let's do this."

"Wet's do this!" Derrick echoed, jumping up and down when Jared opened the front door.

Ten minutes later, after getting their luggage loaded into the truck and getting Derrick strapped into his car seat, they were pulling down the drive to the main road. He passed Ethan's house, offering a honk and a wave to Beau, who was loading their stuff into their truck.

"Is Beau goin' with us?"

"He's goin' to the ranch," Jared told him. "But he's ridin' with Ethan."

"Is Uncle Kaden and Uncle Keegan gonna be there?"

"Yep."

"What about Gramma and Grampa?"

"They'll be there, too."

"And Aunt Eve?"

"Of course."

"Is Mason going to the ranch with us?"

"He'll be there, but he's ridin' with his momma and daddy."

"Why don't I have a momma?"

Screeeeech.

That was the sound of the conversation coming to a grinding halt. Not in a million years had Jared expected that one.

Okay, maybe he had been expecting it, but definitely not today. More importantly, he had absolutely no idea how he was supposed to answer it. He hadn't figured out yet if he should tell Derrick about his mother. He definitely didn't want the boy to know his mother had abandoned him. Or that she was threatening to take him back to court in order to squeeze Jared for more money. Based on the last email he'd received—which he'd gotten on Wednesday—Sable was pushing to get a temporary order allowing her to see her son. Or so she said.

Jared had passed the information off to his lawyer, who had told him not to worry about it. He'd also sent the email to Travis, who hadn't been quite as nonchalant as his lawyer had been. If Sable came up missing, Jared would know who to look at first.

Not that he thought Travis would do that. No, Travis would dig deeper to find the dirt necessary to keep Sable from ruining all of their lives. When Jared had offered to help, Travis had told him to stay out of it, but only because he wanted Jared to be able to say he knew nothing about it if things went south.

Whatever that meant.

So, as for answering Derrick's question, Jared knew he could make up a story, only he wasn't big on telling lies, regardless of whether they were better than the truth.

"You've got me," he told Derrick.

"Yep. And you got me!"

"That's for sure." Jared reached back and offered Derrick a knuckle bump, making his boy laugh.

And just like that, Jared was off the hook.

"Are we gonna see Hope?" Derrick asked.

"Maybe."

Jared

"Wiw she go on a date with us?"

Ever since Jared had explained dates, Derrick had been stuck on it. Based on Jared's reasoning—going to McDonald's—the little boy had obviously associated it with something a little more casual than the regular meaning. Jared didn't feel the need to correct him just yet.

"I need to stop and put gas in the truck," he told his boy. "Then we'll be off to the ranch for a whole week."

"'Kay."

Once they made it to the gas station, Jared pulled up to the pump and rolled down Derrick's window so he could stand there and talk to him while he filled up the tank. He was probably five dollars from being filled up when he heard a voice from behind him.

"Jared?"

His entire body went rigid, his heart slammed into his chest, and he instantly turned around and blocked Derrick from view.

"What are you doing here, Sable?" he asked his ex-wife, hoping the death glare he gave her was enough of a warning.

Her chin quivered, something she'd perfected over the years. "I wanted to see you. We really need to talk this out. Figure out how we can … be a family again."

A family? Yep, she'd gone too far this time. He knew she was full of shit considering they'd never been a family. From the day Derrick was born, Jared had been taking care of him. Even for the first eighteen months of Derrick's life, back when he and Sable had still been married.

Jared brushed off her comment. "Well, I don't have time to talk. We're headin' out for a while."

"Where're you going?" She tried to peer around him into the truck.

"Come on, Dad! Wet's get to the ranch!"

"The ranch?" Sable questioned.

"You shouldn't be here," he warned her. "You can't just show up out of the blue and…"

The gas nozzle clicked, signaling it was finished. He quickly turned to unhook it, putting it back in place but still trying to keep Derrick hidden from Sable. It didn't work, but thankfully, she didn't lunge for his son. He wouldn't put it past her to try and announce who she was and why she was there to a four-year-old.

"Oh, my goodness. He's gotten so big."

"Go home, Sable," he told her firmly.

"I've tried to call you, but your asshole cousin said he won't give you my messages," she informed him, her eyes glassy.

"I heard."

"I wanted…" She wiped an imaginary tear. "I wanted to talk to you. I need to apologize. I need to… God, Jared. I want to come home."

He frowned, lowering his voice as he said, "This ain't your home."

"But—"

Knowing she would keep pushing the subject, Jared opened the driver's door, rolled up the back window, and then climbed in.

And that was when the real Sable came alive.

"Jared Walker, don't you dare turn your back on me. I'll have you served so fast your head'll spin."

He cocked an eyebrow.

"You've got two choices," she declared. "Pay me what I'm askin', or I'm taking Derrick back."

Jared started rolling up his window because he knew what was coming. He turned on the radio, desperate to drown out Sable's next words.

"He's not your son, Jared! You can't keep him! I'll make sure of that!"

And just like that, Jared snapped. "I'll be right back, son," he told Derrick, then hopped out of the truck and closed the door behind him.

He took two steps, getting right up in Sable's face, but he didn't dare touch her. He knew better.

Jared

"This is the last time I'm gonna fuckin' tell you, Sable, go back to where you came from." Jared was seething, but he managed to keep his voice low, steady. "That boy is my son. No matter what you fucking say. He's mine. You will not take him away from me. I'm not giving you another goddamn dime, but let me tell you this, you think this is all fun and games." He pointed his finger at her. "Bring it on, Sable. Push me on this. I promise you, you'll regret it."

She stepped back, inhaling sharply. Jared didn't wait for her to respond. He climbed in his truck and pulled out of the parking lot.

"Daddy? Are you okay?"

Jared glanced into the rearview mirror. Derrick was staring at him, concerned.

"Perfect," he lied, forcing a smile. "You ready to go to the ranch? Maybe ride a horse?"

"Yeah!" Derrick squealed, reaching for his iPad. "Wiw we see Hope?"

Jared swallowed hard. God, he hoped so. "She'll be there," he told Derrick.

"'Kay."

While his son settled in for the drive, Jared took deep breaths, trying to slow his still-pounding heart. For so long, he'd sat back and let Sable walk all over him. From the day he met her, she'd pushed his buttons and he'd never fought back.

Well, he had news for her. This time, he wasn't going to put up with her shit. If she wanted to do this, she wasn't just going to go up against him. She was going to go up against them all. Despite his need to handle so much of this by himself, Jared knew there was a time to bring family in, to lean on them for support.

And one thing he knew about the Walker family ... they protected their own.

Sable didn't stand a fucking chance.

"WELCOME TO DEAD Heat Ranch," Hope said for what felt like the millionth time today.

"We're here for the Walker family reunion," one of the two identical young men said, a mischievous gleam in his eyes. She remembered them from the night at Moonshiners. They had the same sparkle in their eye now as they had that night when they'd been sweet-talking that woman into their arms. Probably into their beds, too. Well, single bed was likely more their style, but what did she know?

"And you are?" She didn't know them well enough to tell them apart.

"Kaden Walker, ma'am. I'm the handsome one." He used his thumb in his brother's direction. "The ugly one's Keegan."

Hope laughed, shaking her head.

She quickly put together the information they would need—a brochure with a list of the amenities, another paper that showed meal times, and one more that had the schedule of trail rides and times they could help out on the ranch if they opted to.

"You'll be stayin' in the bunkhouse," she explained, pointing to the location on the map.

"Bunkhouse, huh? You gonna put us to work?" Keegan teased.

"If you'd like to work"—she offered a wide smile—"I'm sure we can accommodate."

Kaden elbowed his brother. "Thanks. If you'll point us in the right direction…"

Hope pointed out the front window. "You'll follow that dirt road all the way to the back. The bunkhouse closest to the cabins is the one you'll be staying in. The other is for the ranch hands. If you end up at the wrong one, they really will put you to work."

"Thank you," Kaden said politely, chuckling.

And just like that, two more names were being checked off her list.

Jared

Because of the sheer volume of people coming in for the week, Trinity had insisted that they should all rotate at the main entrance counter to welcome the guests and show them to their cabins. Since their visitors were trickling in rather steadily and had been for most of the day, they'd spent most of their time running back and forth, taking the next set when they arrived. Based on the list of people the Walkers were expecting, they still had almost half to go.

Most of the people who'd arrived were the older set—Curtis and his wife, Lorrie; Gerald and his wife, Sue Ellen; Frank and his wife, Iris; Maryanne and her husband, Thomas. Hope knew they were still waiting for Joseph, David, Daphne, and Lisa, as well as the rest of the children and grandchildren.

Speaking of... Another truck pulled up front, but this time a younger couple got out. It took a few minutes for them to make it to the door, and once they did, they were carrying two little boys, one clearly a toddler, probably close to three if she had to guess. The other one was chubby and probably not walking yet.

"Welcome to Dead Heat Ranch," Hope greeted with a grin.

"Kaleb and Zoey Walker," the man said with a smile.

"I got this one," Mercy said, nudging Hope out of the way.

With nothing else to do for the moment, Hope slipped into the kitchen and grabbed a bottle of water. By the time she returned to the front, it was empty. Mercy had apparently taken the couple to their cabin, so the only thing left to do was wait.

She was settling in to do just that when she saw another truck pull up. While she waited for their guests to come inside, Hope busied herself by putting together the packet. It wasn't until the door opened and she looked up that she saw exactly who it was.

It was then that her heart decided to mimic the thump of a bass drum.

Hope swallowed hard, doing her best to remember to breathe.

"Hey," Jared greeted with a smile. It was forced, but she could tell he was trying.

"Hi," she said, the word coming out choked.

Her eyes instantly traveled to the little boy in Jared's arms. Her stomach dropped to her toes, and she held her breath.

"It's Hope, Daddy! We get to go on a date with Hope."

And sure enough, her stomach dropped again, making her a little light-headed. The grin on Derrick's face was one of pure delight. However, there wasn't a matching one on Jared's face. He looked ... grim? She had to refrain from asking if he was all right.

"Hi, Hope," Derrick greeted her directly. "We're gonna stay at the ranch and ride horses and swing on the swings and pway with the doggies we saw sweeping in the yard."

Her heart turned over in her chest, and it was then that Hope was grateful for the fact that she and Jared had severed ties before she ever had a chance to get attached to him. Even without knowing him all that well, this cute little boy had the ability to break her heart in a million pieces. And that was just from his smile.

Chapter Twenty-Nine

JARED TRIED NOT to look surprised to see Hope. He tried not to look as though he wanted to undress her, either. It wasn't an easy thing to do, though. He'd seen Hope nearly a week ago when he'd come to the ranch for the tour, but she'd somehow managed to elude him before he'd had a chance to talk to her. Seeing her again, without anyone else around... Suddenly he had no idea what to say.

"Were you gonna stay with someone in the cabins? Or would you prefer a room here in the main house?" Hope asked, her eyes never fully meeting his.

"Whatever's easiest for everyone. Doesn't much matter to me."

"I think you'll be more comfortable here. Plus, it'll give you a little more privacy for when Derrick needs to sleep. The cabins can get loud if there are a lot of people in there."

"Sure," he agreed.

At that moment, another woman walked up. Jared dug through his memory, trying to put the name with the face. He knew she was one of Hope's sisters, but other than Gracie, he didn't really know who was who.

"Trinity," the woman said, clearly seeing his confusion. "The prettiest sister."

Jared chuckled. "Yes, Trinity. Good to see you again." He peered over at his son. "And this is Derrick."

"Hey, Derrick," Trinity said, her eyes lighting up. "How old are you?"

"Four." Derrick held up four fingers.

"Wow. That means you're a big boy, huh?"

Derrick nodded, wiggling to get down from Jared's arms. Trinity looked back up at him. "You mind if I show Derrick around the play area in the main house while you get squared away here?"

"Pwease, Dad! I wanna see the pway area!"

"Sure," Jared told her, his attention turning back to Hope.

"Why don't *I* show Derrick around down here. You can show Jared to their room," Hope suggested to Trinity.

With a beaming smile, Trinity looked Hope right in the eye. "Not a chance."

"Yeah, that's what I thought," Hope mumbled beneath her breath, grabbing some papers from the counter and handing them over along with a key. "Right this way."

Jared hefted his suitcase in one hand and Derrick's in the other, then fell into step behind Hope as she headed for the staircase.

"We ended up having five rooms available. I'm putting you at the far end, which should be the quietest."

"Also the farthest from you, huh?" he muttered, trying not to stare at her ass.

He knew she'd heard him because she faltered for a second, but she clearly pretended that she hadn't as she continued down the hallway. When she stopped again, it was in front of a door. "This is your room. There's an attached bathroom. If you need anything, you can call the front desk."

Jared took the key she held out for him but managed to grab hold of her wrist before she could turn and bolt.

"Hey. What's goin' on?" he asked softly.

Small lines formed between her brows as she stared back at him. "What are you talking about?"

Jared unlocked the door and pushed it open, tugging her arm until she came inside.

"Did I do something?" he asked when they had a little more privacy.

"What are you talking about?"

Jared lifted an eyebrow. "I thought you weren't interested in playin' games, Hope."

233

Jared

Hope jerked her wrist free of his grip. "I'm not the one playin' games, Jared. I'm doin' my job."

"Yeah? Is that why you stopped callin'? You had a job to do?"

Hope narrowed her eyes. "I don't recall you blowin' up my phone, either."

"Is that what you wanted? Me to chase after you?" Jared closed the door to ensure no one could hear their conversation. He moved closer to Hope, then lowered his voice. "Why is it that every time I mention my son, you get this look in your eye? A look that says you're ready to turn and run as far and as fast as you can. You have a problem with me havin' a kid?"

"God, no!" she exclaimed.

"So, what? You don't like kids?"

Hope's gaze traveled to the floor and she kept it there. Jared knew he'd gone about this the wrong way, but he couldn't help himself. After his run-in with Sable, he'd been hanging by a thread. He was angry. At Sable. At the bullshit she was pulling. And at Hope. The more he thought about Hope, the more he missed her. And the more he missed her, the more pissed off he got that things had ended the way they had.

When she finally lifted her head, meeting his gaze, Jared leaned in even closer. Too close, actually. He could smell her and she smelled ... amazing. Like lavender or something. "Well, I thought if you wanted to talk, you would call me."

"Clearly neither of us wanted to talk," she quipped.

As though she just realized she was showing some emotion, Hope straightened and took a step back from him. "I need to get back to work. I hope you enjoy your stay here."

Knowing he wasn't going to win this one, Jared nodded, then watched as she backed out of the room.

Sure, he'd been a dumb ass. He'd had the best sex of his entire life with Hope, and he'd been secretly hoping for more. She hadn't promised him more. And she'd made it very clear what she thought of him having a kid.

So instead of chasing after her, Jared had convinced himself that taking care of Derrick was the most important thing, which meant he needed to forget about the woman who had captivated him in a way that scared the ever-loving hell out of him.

Sad thing was … he still wanted her.

OKAY, WELL, HOPE certainly hadn't expected Jared to confront her like that. Her heart was still racing, and she'd walked away from him nearly four hours ago. She wanted to believe she couldn't catch her breath because she'd been showing guests to their cabin or room, but that certainly wasn't the case. Her sisters had been pulling their weight, and none of them had been overworked.

Now that most of the guests were settling in—only a few more who would be coming in later tonight—Hope finally had a chance to relax a little. Dinner would be served in an hour, and her plan was to grab some grub early and slip out before any of the Walkers arrived. She had no more chores to handle for the night, which was the reason she had snuck in a shower early, wanting to be around for any of the guests who might need her. With Gracie, Lane, and Grant gone until Tuesday, things would be tight until then.

As she was moving through the recreation room, Hope heard someone clear his throat. Before she could process the male body standing only a few feet away, Hope felt herself being pulled toward the hallway.

She fought the urge to squeak her surprise when she looked up into those stormy blue eyes. "What are you doing?" she whispered fiercely.

Jared's eyes were fixed on hers, his big, hard body so close she could smell the sultry scent of him.

"I can't do this," he told her, crowding her back against the wall. He sounded tortured.

Her eyebrows darted downward. "Do what?"

Jared

He leaned forward, resting his forearm on the wall above her head as he stared down at her. His voice was so low, so serious when he said, "Stay away from you. It's killin' me, Hope. I can't do it."

Oh, heavens. The look on his face promised so many things, things she wasn't supposed to want anymore but did even though she knew better.

"I thought I could come here, pretend nothing ever happened, but I can't. It's only been a few hours since I heard your voice, Hope. I'm fucking dying for you. Even if the only thing I get is to hear you talk. I'm fucking crazy. I know it, but…"

Before she could respond—not that she had words to say to that anyway—Jared kissed her. It wasn't a sweet, simple kiss, either. This one was full of hunger, need. It drew an answering hunger from her as she ignored where they were, who might walk around the corner at any moment. Recklessly, Hope threw her arms around his neck, pulling him closer, crushing her mouth to his.

Jared groaned as he pushed her flush against the wall, his erection pressing into her stomach. This thing between them… It was explosive. Unpredictable.

"We can't do this here," she whispered when she finally pulled back. Her breaths were rushing in and out of her lungs, her heart racing.

"I can't stop myself, Hope. I just … can't."

It might make her a terrible person, but she loved that he seemed to be so enthralled with her that he couldn't control himself. She knew how he felt, because she felt the same way about him. Although she'd had few lovers in her lifetime, never had her need, her passion been this strong. Never.

"After dinner," Hope mumbled against his lips. "I'll meet you somewhere."

"My room," he told her.

She instantly shook her head. "Not with Derrick there. Not like that."

"He's staying with Kaleb and Zoey in one of the cabins tonight. Spending the night with Mason. I've got the room to myself."

"Too loud," she told him, surprised at how honest she was being. "I can't... With you..." She smiled, despite herself. "I can't seem to keep quiet when I'm with you. When you're..."

"When I'm buried inside you?" he whispered against her mouth. "When my dick's pushing inside your sweet, welcoming pussy?"

Hope nodded, her pussy throbbing with the need to feel him now. She didn't care where they were, who was around. If he kept talking like that, she'd be fucking him right here in the hallway that led down to her father's room. And wouldn't that be a stupid idea.

Jared pulled back, cupping her face as he met her gaze. "I can't stay away from you, Hope. I don't know what it is. I just ... don't want to. I know you don't like the idea of me having a kid, but I do have him. I can't change that."

"It's not that," she told him, putting her hands on his chest and pushing him back. She knew if he hadn't wanted to move, he wouldn't have.

She kept her eyes locked with his. She knew she had to tell him the truth. Whatever this was between them, she knew she wasn't going to make it through an entire week with him on the ranch without wanting to do this. He needed to know where she was coming from. What she was afraid of.

Swallowing past the lump in her throat, Hope held his gaze. "It's not that I don't like kids. It's not that I don't *want* kids. I—"

"Hey, Hope? Sorry to interrupt." Their chef peeked into the hallway, looking somewhat perplexed, more so apologetic. "I need your help in the kitchen if you don't mind. It's ... uh ... kind of an emergency."

"Sure, Jennifer," Hope told her, already moving away from Jared. She glanced back at him. "Let's talk. In a little while. After dinner."

Jared nodded, his eyes never leaving her face. She could see the heat that made his eyes glitter. He wanted her; there was no doubt about that. She should've been running, trying to hide, refusing to be anywhere near him, but unfortunately, she couldn't stay away from him, either.

Jared

Which meant, in about an hour, she would have to lay it all on the line. And either he would walk away for good or they could spend the next week doing what they'd missed out on when they'd both been too stubborn to call. Then, when he left the ranch, maybe—if she was lucky—she would finally have Jared Walker completely out of her system.

And if she said it enough, maybe she'd believe that was even a possibility.

CHAPTER THIRTY

TRAVIS STOOD ON the porch of the small cabin they'd claimed as their own. They'd lucked out getting a two-bedroom to themselves. With Kade only a month old and Kate about to be two, they had their hands full. So, getting two bedrooms—one of which would be used for Kade to sleep comfortably while his unruly sister got to have the sofa bed all to herself—was imperative.

"What's goin' through that head of yours?" Gage asked, coming to join Travis outside.

When Gage's warm hand slid over Travis's back, he relaxed a little, then said, "Just thinkin' about what's goin' on with Jared."

"With Sable?"

Travis nodded.

"Did you get the DNA test results back yet?"

Travis shook his head. "Expectin' them any minute now, though."

Although Jared wasn't aware, Travis had pulled in a favor from one of his contacts at Sniper 1 Security. He'd known that it would require a favor being called in from that point, but he hadn't cared. Something had made him question the accuracy of the paternity test that Sable had provided Jared. Perhaps it was simply because the woman was a snake, willing to do whatever she needed to in order to get what she wanted.

Jared

So he had enlisted his mother's help in the process. Under the guise of getting more family history from one of those genealogy websites, she'd requested a swab sample from everyone at the last Sunday dinner. Sure, it had seemed a little out there at the time, but thankfully, no one had asked questions. No one other than his mother anyway. Travis had broken down and told her his theory, instructing her not to say anything. She had reluctantly agreed, but only after telling him that she would squeal like a pig if this came back to hurt Jared or Derrick in any way.

Travis had assured her it wouldn't.

He wouldn't let that happen.

Only now he was getting a little antsy because he was waiting for the test results and waiting for some additional information he'd requested on some of Sable's history. If it all came together the way he expected, Sable was no longer going to be a threat to Jared or Derrick.

And quite frankly, Travis wanted to be the one to deliver that news to his cousin.

"I heard she stalked him today," Gage told him.

Travis frowned. "When?"

"When he was leavin' town. He stopped at the gas station. Apparently Braydon and Jessie were there. They saw it go down. Let's just say she's pushin' a little hard. I think Jared's finally reached his tipping point with her."

"Thank fuck," Travis said on an exhale. He'd been waiting for Jared to man up when it came to Sable. Sure, he understood his cousin's reason for being low-key. Jared didn't want to risk losing his boy again, but shit. He couldn't let that crazy bitch continue to run him over.

"You think she'll show up here?" Gage inquired.

Travis shrugged. He honestly didn't know.

"We need to tell people to keep an eye out," Gage stated. "That way there's no chance she can get to Derrick."

Travis glanced at his husband. "You don't think she'd snatch him, do you?" It was something he'd never considered. Sure, the woman was batshit crazy, but to kidnap Derrick…

240

"Who knows. Depends on how desperate she is. What I don't get is why now? What's going on with her that she needs so much money?"

That was another question Travis was waiting to hear back on. He was having her financials looked into as well. But until he got some solid answers, he couldn't assume anything.

"Just promise me we'll have some fun this week," Gage said. "Kylie and Kate've been lookin' forward to this, Trav. Let's enjoy ourselves."

Travis nodded, then turned to look into Gage's eyes. He gripped Gage's shirt loosely, pulling him closer so that he could brush his lips against Gage's. "Agreed."

JARED WAITED UNTIL ten. He waited until dinner had been served, eaten, then cleaned up. Until coffee was drunk, conversation was had, little ones were run ragged and they were practically begging for sleep. He waited until most of the people were tucked away in their cabins, no one hanging around to see him simply walk out of the main house and down to cabin four. During the ten minutes it took him to get there, he thought about all the things he wanted to tell Hope, knowing he wouldn't be able to get a single word out until he quenched his desperate thirst for her.

As it was, he'd been walking around with a rock-hard boner for most of the afternoon. Every time he got so much as a glimpse of her, his body hardened more. He hadn't been lying to her when he told her he couldn't stay away. He couldn't. He was trying. God, he was trying so fucking hard, but it wasn't working. It pissed him off to the point he wanted to put his fist through the wall, but violence had never solved anything.

Jared

And now, as he stepped up onto Hope's porch, he prayed for a little patience. Enough to get him through the door before he stripped the sexy little cowgirl down to nothing. His boots hit the wood at the same time the screen door opened.

And there she stood.

An angel waiting for him, her eyes so full of heat he knew she was battling the same urges he was. He stopped, simply staring at her. She didn't look away, holding his gaze.

"Once I come through that door, I'm not gonna be able to control myself, Hope." He figured she needed to know that.

Hope nodded.

"I've been counting down the minutes till I can bury myself in your body, to feel you wrapped completely around me. I can't wait another fucking second."

Another nod.

"You still want me to come in?"

This time, Hope held out her hand to him and he took it.

Part of his prayer was answered, because he managed to allow her to close the door before he backed her up against it and crushed his mouth to hers. He picked her up, and she wrapped those sexy little legs around his waist, her fingers digging into his shoulders as she kissed him back with the same unbanked passion he'd been battling for days on end.

"Christ, Hope," he breathed roughly.

She pulled back enough to stare into his eyes, her forehead resting against his. She was breathing hard, her hands buried in his hair.

Jared didn't waste time; he carried her into her bedroom and lowered her to the bed, coming down with her. He crawled over her, his knee pushing between her thighs, the steely length of his erection pressing into her hip. And still he kissed her. He was desperate to consume her in every way possible. He wouldn't lie to himself, he wanted more than this, but this was enough for now.

"Jared..." Hope ground her pussy against his thigh. "Touch me. I need your hands on me."

Jared pulled back, staring down at her as Hope lifted the thin T-shirt she was wearing over her head, tossing it to the floor. Beneath that she was completely bare, her rosy nipples puckered as though they were beckoning him. He lowered his mouth to one nipple, sucking and licking as he drew her into his mouth. She moaned, long and loud, her cool fingers sliding into his hair, digging into his scalp.

Hope cupped her other breast, holding it for him, and he shifted, gently biting her nipple before drawing hard and long on the pebbled tip.

"Oh, God, yes."

Testing her, he drew even harder on her, and sure enough, Hope's back bowed, her muttered cries filling the room. She liked that extra bite of pain. Goddamn, this woman was going to kill him.

When Hope started trying to tear his shirt off of him, Jared pulled back and offered her assistance. He quickly disposed of his shirt, then stripped the thin boxers off her legs, baring her completely.

"Oh, yeah," he groaned.

Knowing that once he got started, he wouldn't be able to stop, Jared jumped to his feet, discarded his boots, then his jeans while he watched Hope. She fished a condom out of her nightstand, set it on the bed beside her, then gave him her full attention once more.

Jared

He loved the way her eyes glazed over as her gaze traveled the length of him, pausing briefly at his dick, jutting up from his body, hot and hard and aching for her.

When he joined her on the bed, Hope pushed Jared onto his back, but he took her with him. She only thought she was in control. When she straddled his stomach, he took charge, jerking her hips forward, then depositing her directly on his face.

"Oh, yes!" Hope gripped the headboard while Jared slid his tongue through her slit, tasting her desire on her delicate flesh. He forced himself to slow down, wanting to savor her for as long as possible.

That only worked until Hope began riding his tongue, grinding against his mouth. He worked her clit as she cried out his name over and over. When she stared down at him, he suckled harder, thrashing the tiny bundle of nerves, wanting her to come on his face.

When Hope tried to pull away, he held her there, forcing her to give herself over to him. He wanted everything she would give him. And he wasn't going to settle on one orgasm. He wanted them all.

"Jared … oh, yes… Don't stop… Oh…" She jerked her hips; he held her tighter. "I'm… You're gonna make… Oh … hell, yes!"

And just like that, Hope was coming on his face while Jared continued to lap at her, loving the way she'd given herself completely to him. As she tumbled over to the bed, he quickly changed positions, coming down over her and melding his lips to hers, wanting her to taste herself, to understand exactly why he was addicted to her.

Her hands slid up his back, gently caressing him as he kissed her. The room cooled at least a few degrees although they weren't anywhere close to finished. "I need to be inside you," he told her.

Hope nodded. "Yes, but…"

He waited, brushing her damp hair back from her face, staring into those glittering eyes.

Her smile stole his breath, and the wicked gleam in her eye made his dick jerk. "But not yet. It's my turn."

His dick was screaming, "Oh, hell yeah!" at the same time his heart was moaning, "Better hang on for the ride, cowboy. You're probably not gonna survive this."

HOPE HAD KNOWN the instant Jared stepped through her door that tonight would be life changing. Then again, it had been that way the very first night he stepped through the door.

Although she desperately wanted to keep this on a sex-only basis, she wasn't wired that way. From the moment she'd met this man, she'd known he would be capable of destroying her. She should've been stronger, but she wasn't.

And here he was, and the only thing she wanted was to see those stormy blue eyes darken, to pull that rough, dark growl from deep inside him as she bestowed him with pleasure. He sure knew how to push her buttons; she wanted to learn every damn one of his.

With his hands tucked beneath his head, Jared stared back at her. She wanted to knock the wry amusement right off his face and replace it with undeniable pleasure. She straddled his hips, his thick, hard shaft pressing between her thighs. It would be so easy to take him inside her, to ride him until they both came undone, but she wasn't ready for that yet. Well, she was and she wasn't. First, she wanted to feast on him for a little while. It wasn't often that she had this type of sinful buffet laid out before her. No reason to pass it up now.

Jared

She plucked his nipples with her fingers, watching his eyes darken as she did. Adding her mouth to the mix, she teased and tormented the flat little discs until a rough growl escaped him.

"Fuck... Hope. Baby, that feels good."

Now he knew how she felt.

Hope nipped him, then licked the sting with her tongue before grazing her lips down his abs, over the soft hair that led lower. She had to move her body down as she went, sliding over the hard muscles of his body. She felt the coarse hair on his legs scrape the insides of her thighs. The sensation was erotic, making her nerve endings spark.

And when she licked the head of his cock, Hope once again watched his eyes, enjoying the way he was watching her. His lips were no longer quirked with amusement. No, Jared's expression was anything but amused. She could see the fire burning in his eyes, feel the heat of his hunger. He wanted her to continue, and she wanted that, too.

"Suck me," he ordered, his words deep, rough. "Suck my dick into your sweet mouth, baby."

Hope wrapped her lips around him, teasing him with her tongue. She didn't take him all the way, wanting to make him wait, to make him suffer the way she had all these nights she'd spent dreaming about him, wanting him.

"Oh, fuck, yes," Jared groaned, gripping his shaft, holding it still. "Right there. Lick right there."

Hope curled her tongue around the swollen head, licking, gently allowing her teeth to scrape over his sensitive flesh.

Jared directed his cock toward her mouth, and Hope took more of him. She drew on the thick head, slowly at first, then deeper, applying more suction. His fingers curled into her hair, but surprisingly, Jared didn't try to guide her. He simply held on while she attempted to blow his mind.

She was lost in giving him pleasure, loving the way he groaned, whispering her name as his eyes continued to watch her every movement. When he reached for the condom, she knew what he was thinking, but his next move took her by surprise. He reached for her, flipping her onto her back so fast she squeaked out her shock, laughing as he came down over her.

"As good as that little mouth is," he mumbled, his lips brushing hers, "I need to be inside you. Want to feel your pussy squeezing my dick."

Jared was quick to put the condom on, returning to his position over her. Hope spread her legs, expecting him to thrust inside, but he didn't. He hovered there, surrounding her. His mouth was mere inches from hers, one arm curled beneath her head as he propped himself up on his elbow. His other hand was brushing her hair back from her face.

This felt intimate.

Although they'd done this before, although they had shared some sort of connection, this felt deeper than that. Stronger. More powerful.

Jared tilted her chin up with his finger, claiming her mouth with his, and Hope gave in to the kiss. She still sensed his hunger, but the urgency was no longer there. He was savoring her, and Hope felt something stir deep inside. Longing, maybe. She wanted this man. She wanted his passion, his desire, his dirty, dirty mouth. But she also wanted this.

"Hope." Jared met her gaze as his hand slid between them.

She felt the thick head of his cock nudge against the entrance to her body. Wrapping her legs around his hips, she opened herself to him, her eyes drifting closed as he slowly filled her.

Heaven.

This felt unbelievably good. In a way she'd never anticipated.

Jared

"Open your eyes, darlin'."

Hope forced her eyes open, meeting his intense gaze.

Jared pressed his hips forward, lodging himself deep before retreating slowly. The slow glide of him inside her made her body tingle. He was making love to her. The knowledge of that choked her up. He must've realized it, too, because he shifted, moving her leg so that it was over his arm, changing the angle of his penetration.

"Oh, hell, yes," she hissed. Damn, that felt so good.

Jared had pushed himself up enough to watch where their bodies were joined. Hope watched, too. When his cock disappeared inside her, her pussy clenched around his girth, taking him deep, deeper still.

"More," she whispered.

As good as this was, she still needed more.

Jared gave her more. Then more still. He began thrusting faster, harder, deeper, still watching as he filled her. He put one hand on the back of her calf, forcing her leg closer to her head. His pelvis shifted and he drove in again, this time making her cry out with the exquisite intensity of the sensations building inside her.

"That's it, Hope. I want you to come for me. Come on my cock, baby."

He began thrusting harder, jerking his hips once he was halfway in, driving into her with such delicious power she thought she was going to lose her mind and her sanity.

"Jared..." Hope gripped his biceps, digging her nails into his flesh. She couldn't help herself. She was clinging to a very fine edge right now, so close. She didn't want to go over, though; she wanted this to last forever.

The way he made her feel, the way he looked at her with such... She didn't know what she saw in his eyes, but it was something deep, something powerful.

248

"Come for me, sweetheart. Don't hold back."

Jared moved, dropping her leg as he began slamming into her. He held himself over her, staring down into her eyes as he fucked her relentlessly. Hope groaned, trying to fight off the orgasm. It was overwhelming. It seared her senses, made her feel too much. He was pushing her too far, making her crazy with these overpowering feelings.

"That's it," he encouraged. "Milk my dick."

His dirty mouth did it for her. He knew just what she needed to fling her right over the rocky ledge and into the glorious black abyss that sent electrical currents racing out from her core.

"Oh, yes…" Hope bit her lower lip as her orgasm took her, rocketing her higher than she'd ever been before.

But Jared didn't stop; he continued to fuck her, filling her so completely until she was suspended somewhere between heaven and hell, a sensation so intoxicating she knew she was going to splinter into millions of pieces any second now.

"Hope." He growled, his voice dark and rich. "Damn, baby. That's it. Come for me, Hope. Aww, fuck yes."

She felt his cock pulsing inside her as his powerful thrusts became jerky. They'd reached that ever-prominent pinnacle together, and he was coming with her. That was enough to set off another less intense but still blissfully devastating orgasm.

No doubt about it, if Jared kept this up, Hope would forever be ruined by him. No other man would ever stand a chance.

Jared

CHAPTER THIRTY-ONE

JARED HAD LEARNED that holding Hope in his arms was one of the most incredible feelings in the world. Right now, as he tried to ignore his dick's eagerness to be inside her again, he focused on the soft sound of her breathing. They'd made love for the second time not twenty minutes ago, and still his body was desperate for her. He was thirty-six years old, for chrissakes. Not fifteen. Yet his little head didn't seem to realize that.

He was spooned around her, his nose buried in her sweetly scented hair. She was so warm and soft he should've easily been able to fall asleep, yet he didn't want to close his eyes.

"You awake?" she whispered, her hand sliding over his arm, up, down, up, down. A gentle caress that made his heart beat harder for reasons that weren't entirely related to sex.

"I'm awake. You?"

She giggled, as he'd expected. "Barely."

"You should sleep. I know you have to be up early."

Hope didn't say anything, but the soft sweep of her fingers down his arm didn't stop, so he waited, wondering if there was something on her mind.

"I'd like to spend a little time with Derrick," she said, her voice nearly too faint for him to hear.

With this surprising revelation, Jared found himself moving, rolling Hope to her back so he could look down at her. "You ... do?"

She nodded, a very subtle move of her head.

"Are you sure?"

This time she shook her head no. "Not at all." Her eyes lifted to meet his. "I'm terrified, Jared."

"Of kids?" How could anyone be scared of a kid?

Her eyes drifted toward the wall, but Jared continued to watch her, brushing her hair from her face. He could tell she was gathering her thoughts, and he absolutely wanted to hear her reasoning.

"I've wanted kids since I was young. Probably fourteen, I guess." She smiled but didn't look at him. "No, I didn't want kids *when* I was fourteen, but I knew I wanted them someday. A whole houseful of them. Then, when I was sixteen, my mother died. Heart attack."

Hope was silent for a moment. Jared moved closer, settling down beside her, his head resting on the pillow, his arm still resting over her torso.

"That was a tough time for us all. My dad was beside himself. My mom was the love of his life. When she died..." Hope sighed. "I knew from then on that I had to help with the ranch. My father needed help, needed someone who could make decisions when necessary, so I stepped into the role."

"At sixteen?"

"Yeah. But it didn't bother me. I was still in school, and so were my sisters. But I would get up before school to do chores, then finish them up after I got home. Faith was the youngest. She was six. Even at that age, she tried to help out as much as she could, but she's always been"—Hope chuckled—"a girl. She doesn't like to get her hands dirty if she doesn't have to. Trin didn't mind getting dirty, which was a huge help to me. But it was hardest on Gracie and Mercy. They handled our mother's death differently. Gracie just kinda stopped living for a while. And Mercy ... she was rebellious, always getting into trouble. She was a lot for my dad to handle.

Jared

"When I was seventeen, I desperately wanted to move out of the main house. It reminded me so much of my mother, and I missed her so much. I don't think he wanted me to, but my dad finally agreed. We'd started building cabins on the property back then, and he let me live in one. I loved being on my own, having a little space from my sisters. I closed myself off from them some."

She glanced over at him as though making sure he was listening, then continued, "When I was eleven, I got my first period. The pain was ridiculous. Really bad. My mother knew about it, and when it got to be too much, she took me to the doctor. They did some tests and said I had endometriosis. It's caused when tissue that usually lines the uterus grows outside of it." She smiled. "Sorry for the anatomy lesson, but I really do have a point."

Jared brushed her hair back, silently urging her to continue.

"I never told my father and I'd learned to live with it mostly. I had no other choice. I had too much to do to help my father. Both with the ranch and with my sisters. Being the oldest, I thought all the responsibility should fall on me.

"Plus, I was… I was a little embarrassed to talk to him about it. He's a man; I didn't think he'd understand. A lot of women have cramps, but mine were … really bad. I would throw up. It was brutal. Anyway, I didn't share the information with him, and when I was nineteen, I got to a point where the pain got to be too much. My dad found me on the kitchen floor, picked me up, dumped me in his truck, and drove me to the doctor. I had no choice but to tell him then."

Hope was silent for a minute, but Jared didn't push her.

"I also had to tell him that, because of it, the doctors had told me that I wouldn't be able to have kids. I was devastated."

Oh, damn. Hope had dealt with all that at once.

"And they were absolutely certain of that?" he questioned.

She shrugged. "The doctor I saw then reconfirmed it. I was embarrassed and my dad was there with me. I didn't want to talk about it or to deal with it. So I picked myself up, dusted myself off, and resigned myself to my fate. I would still be able to help with my sisters, help with the ranch. It was all I cared about, or so I told myself." Hope paused, took a deep breath. "In my mid-twenties, I did have surgery that made a significant difference. It helped with the pain, but I still can't have children."

"They told you that? It didn't fix the problem?"

"The doctor said it was highly unlikely." She shrugged, as though it didn't matter.

Jared could tell it definitely mattered.

"But before that, I met a guy. I think I was twenty, maybe twenty-one. Don't remember. His name was Brian. Nice guy. Single dad. I met him at the feed store in town. We dated for a few months, I met his son, fell in love with the kid almost instantly." Hope turned to smile at him. "It was hard not to. He was so cute." She turned back. "Anyway, we dated for a year and a half. Right up until he met someone else and… Well, you know how it goes. I was so attached to his son that it broke my heart to have to walk away."

Jared did not miss the fact that she said she'd fallen in love with the kid and not the man. Well, that certainly explained a lot.

Jared

"Of course, it doesn't end there. I wasn't stupid only one time. Two years ago, I started seeing one of the guests here at the ranch. It'd been a long time since I'd gone out with a man, so when he asked, I was desperate for company. I've spent all my time working, focusing only on the money-making aspect of this place, and I was lonely. His daughter, Maddie... Well, you can imagine how that went. She was the cutest thing. Six years old and so full of laughter and life. Again, I managed to get too close, started to care too much. There were issues between Ben and his ex-wife, things that definitely affected their daughter and needed to be addressed. He lived in Oklahoma, and we tried to make a go of things for a little while, but it didn't work. Once again, I'd let myself get too close to Maddie, and then next thing I knew, I was nursing a broken heart."

It sounded to Jared like Hope didn't fall in love with the single dads she'd dated, but she definitely fell in love with the kids. It made perfect sense because she couldn't have any of her own.

"Does any of that make sense?" Hope asked, twisting in his arms so she could face him. "It's not that I don't like Derrick, but I can't deal with more heartbreak. It'll be bad enough when you break my heart..."

Jared swallowed hard. He stared into Hope's eyes, desperate to believe what she was telling him.

"I won't," he whispered, cupping the back of her head and sliding his finger over her cheek.

And that was the truth.

"YOU CAN'T MAKE that promise," Hope countered. She wanted to believe him, but she knew there was no way Jared could say that with any kind of certainty. No one knew what the future held for them.

Jared leaned forward, pressing his lips to hers, his lips warm and smooth. God, she loved his mouth.

"But I can promise to do my best not to."

Hope pulled back slightly, peering into Jared's face. For once, she wished she knew what was going through his head. Was he starting to think long term like she was? How could that even be a possibility? They hadn't known each other for long. A month and a half. She didn't believe in love at first sight. However, after meeting Jared, she certainly believed in lust at first sight, and yes, she was desperately, madly in lust with this man.

She smiled. "I like you far more than I've let on." A whole lot more. "And I don't want this to end between us." She chuckled, unable to help herself. "And not only because the sex is freaking incredible, either."

Jared grinned, a sexy smirk that made her body heat all over again.

"But I need us to take things slow. I'll agree to spend some time with Derrick while y'all are here, and I want to spend time with the two of you. That doesn't change the fact that I'm terrified. And I still can't tell you that I'm ready for anything more than … this."

He nodded, surprisingly. Hope half expected him to try to reassure her. The fact that he didn't made her feel a little better.

"On top of that, you have your ex-wife to deal with."

Jared's eyes closed and he exhaled sharply.

"Did something else happen?"

"She's stalking us," he told her.

Stalking? That was a harsh word for the mother of his child. Then again, the mother of his child had given up her parental rights. Hope couldn't imagine ever doing that. Not for the reasons Jared had given her. No man, no amount of money would ever be worth her child.

Jared

"What'd she do?"

"We were leaving town. I had to stop for gas. She showed up there. I thought for a minute she was going to tell Derrick who she was. She would've completely waylaid the kid. He wouldn't know what to think. That's what scares me the most."

"Do you think she'd try to take him?"

Jared's eyes widened, and Hope saw honest-to-God terror reflected there. Apparently he hadn't considered that.

"Do you think she would follow you here?" Hope questioned.

He didn't answer that question, either.

"Maybe we should tell my sisters what's going on. And my dad. I'll make sure Grant and Lane know, too, when they get back. That way everyone can be on the lookout in case she does."

Jared nodded, but he was still unusually quiet.

"Should you call the police?" she asked, concerned.

Jared pulled her closer, kissed the top of her head. "No. I'll take care of it."

Hope snuggled closer to him, letting him know she was there. She closed her eyes, took a deep breath. The man smelled so good. She knew her sheets would smell like him for days to come. She only wished it was because he was in her bed for days to come.

If she wasn't careful, Hope knew that *in lust* would quickly morph into something much deeper, much stronger.

Much scarier.

Chapter Thirty-Two

"I THOUGHT YOU didn't know how to ride a horse," Hope teased Derrick, who was riding in front of her.

"I didn't say that," he told her, giggling.

"You didn't, did you?"

She kept one arm loosely wrapped around him, the other holding the reins while Ambrosia slowly walked down the hill that would lead them back toward the house. The trail ride had started a few hours ago, heading out into the gently rolling hills and to the creek that bisected the property. There were at least twenty guests in total, along with ten wranglers, and they'd all stopped for a picnic lunch, then loaded up and were heading back in.

On the way out, Derrick had ridden with Jared, on the gelding walking alongside Hope's horse. However, when they were packing up the lunch, Derrick had asked if he could ride with her. No way could she say no to that, even though her stomach was tied in knots. Jared had given her a sympathetic look, but she'd brushed it off, pretending she wasn't affected by it.

"I want to ride a horse every day, but Dad won't wet me."

"Well," Hope said, glancing over at Jared briefly, "I'm guessing you have to go to school, right?"

Derrick nodded.

"How do you ride a horse when you're at school?"

Jared

"I couwd ride a horse *to* school," he said, somewhat logically.

"True. But what if it was raining?"

Derrick seemed to think about that for a few minutes.

"So, what are you gonna dress up as tonight at the Halloween party?" she asked the little boy.

"A cowboy," Derrick said adamantly. "A reaw one."

"You're gonna wear your cowboy hat?"

"Yup. What're you gonna dress up as?"

Hope considered that for a moment. "A cowgirl."

"Do *you* have a hat?"

"Of course I do," she told him. She'd gone without the hat today because it was so nice out, the sun not too bright.

"Is it pink?"

Hope chuckled. "No, it's not pink. Why? Does your dad have a pink hat?"

Derrick giggled uncontrollably.

Hope tightened her grip on the little boy as she laughed, too. She glanced over to find Jared staring at them. He hadn't said anything, seemingly content to let her have this time with Derrick. She wasn't sure how she felt about that, but Hope had taken to the little boy, and she couldn't deny that. He was easy to talk to and fun to be with. A lot like his father.

By the time they reached the house, Derrick was leaning against her, obviously exhausted. Hope waited for Jared to come over and take him from her. As he was doing so, Hope looked up at the house to see what was going on, and that was when Hope spotted her.

"Uh ... Jared."

He looked up at her, a question in his eyes.

She nodded toward the house. "Is that ... *her*?"

Jared's eyes slowly scanned the area in front of the house. The growl that emerged from him was the confirmation she was hoping not to get.

"I'll take care of this," she told him, tugging slightly on the reins so that Ambrosia would move forward.

"Hope..."

She didn't look back at him. This was her ranch. It wasn't like she was doing something she shouldn't. Sable was not invited as a guest; therefore she needed to leave. Hope stopped in front of the woman, keeping Ambrosia directly in the woman's view of Jared.

"Hi. Can I help you?" she said sweetly.

"No. Thanks, though."

Hope cleared her throat, waiting for the woman to meet her gaze. "Can I help you with something?"

The woman's eyes narrowed. "I said no. I'm looking for someone."

"Well, you won't find them here," Hope told her. "This is private property. And you're"—Hope lowered her voice slightly—"trespassing."

That got the woman's attention, and she finally looked at Hope. Really looked at her.

"Oh, how interesting. You're the mistress."

Hope smiled. *And you're the bitch.* Of course, she held the words on her tongue, not willing to stoop to this woman's level. Hope glanced around, looking for the nearest wrangler.

"Hey, Rusty!" When he looked her way, Hope nodded for him to come over. "This woman is clearly lost. She needs to be escorted off the property."

Jared

"I'm not leaving without my son!" Sable yelled, damn near at the top of her lungs. "That man kidnapped him! Took him from me!"

Of course, that accusation gave Rusty pause, his eyes jerking toward Hope.

"Call the sheriff," Hope ordered him. "We're done here."

Hope dismounted, coming to stand in front of Sable while passing Ambrosia's reins off to Dallas Caldwell, another one of their wranglers.

"That's a pretty serious allegation," Hope told Sable, urging her toward the house. "I think it's best we take this inside."

The instant they turned toward the house, Hope stopped moving. In front of her was a line of men and women, all standing there, all watching. And they hadn't come out of the house to rubberneck it, either. These were some very unhappy people.

"Sable, are you lost?" Gerald Walker—Jared's father— asked. Alongside him stood Jared's brothers, Kaden and Keegan, along with the youngest, Wesley.

Yeah, this hadn't turned out the way Sable had hoped, apparently.

Hope knew not to get in the middle of this.

"You know exactly why I'm here, Gerald," Sable snapped.

"I do," he said, sounding oddly calm. "And just like before, Jared's not interested in whatever it is you want."

"I want my son."

Travis stepped out from behind Gerald, looking as menacing as Hope had ever seen him.

He looked angry enough that she took another step back.

"Is that really what you're after?" Travis asked. "Because I happen to have some information here that says otherwise."

Hope watched as he pulled a piece of paper out of his back pocket. He kept his eyes on Sable as he slowly unfolded it.

This time, Sable's eyes widened.

"I think it's time we talk," Travis told her.

Sable's eyes were wide, but she didn't try to fight him when Travis urged her up toward the guest parking area.

"Do you know what that's about?" Keegan asked her.

Hope glanced around, realizing everyone was still there. She shook her head. "Don't have a clue."

And she didn't really care. The only thing she wanted to do was go find Jared and Derrick. So she could make sure they were all right. She knew they weren't in any danger, but still, the protective instinct was one she couldn't shake off.

And while she was there, maybe she would try to explain why she'd gotten a little protective there. Perhaps she should start thinking of a reason, because *I love you* didn't seem like the right thing to say right now. Especially since she was having a hard time accepting it herself.

AT THE SIGHT of Sable, Jared's first instinct had been to get Derrick away from her. The woman had a screw loose, and he knew she wasn't thinking about Derrick's best interests. So, instead of following Hope, insisting that she not get involved, he had slipped away with a few of the others and gone straight to the main house. He'd passed his father on the way in, informing him that there was trouble brewing outside. Jared had kindly asked him if he could step in.

Jared

It wasn't that Jared wanted to run away, to hide, to have someone else fight his battles. That certainly wasn't the case. However, the one thing Sable wanted right now was access to him. If he didn't allow her to have that, then she would have no choice but to go away. Maybe not forever but for now.

Knowing that they were going to be up late into the night at the Halloween party, Jared had coerced Derrick into taking a nap. He'd been sitting in the chair by the window, overlooking the front yard, when a knock sounded on the door.

He quietly went to the door, and when he saw Hope, he let out a breath he hadn't realized he'd been holding. Rather than invite her in, he stepped out into the hall, hoping Derrick would sleep for at least an hour.

"Hey." He pulled her to him without another word, cupping her face and staring into her eyes. He wasn't sure what he was looking for. She didn't say anything, simply stared back at him. When he felt a little more in control, he put his arms around her and hugged her, resting his chin on the top of her head.

"Are you okay?" she whispered. "Is Derrick okay?"

"Yeah. We're good. He's asleep right now. I figured he better get a nap in or he's gonna be hell on wheels tonight." He forced himself to take a step back. "Is Sable gone?"

Hope nodded. "Travis took her to her truck."

Great. No telling what his cousin was going to say, but Jared figured whatever it was, Sable would be hell-bent for leather the next time he saw her. God, he wished he didn't have to see her.

"What do I do?" Jared found himself asking her. "I can't keep fighting her. Eventually, she's gonna get to Derrick."

Hope nodded, clearly understanding. "I think for now, you let all those people out there have your back. You did the right thing, not approaching her. She's trying to get a rise out of you; that's obvious."

Jared knew that. But this seemed hopeless.

He glanced down to see Hope staring up at him, her eyes glittering with what looked like sympathy, but also something else. Something more powerful. He didn't want to think too long on that. He didn't want to think that maybe she'd given in, maybe she was willing to give this a shot rather than run away.

But damn it, why would she want to? Why would she want to have to deal with Sable's bullshit? It could quite possibly go on forever. And worst-case scenario, Sable could take Derrick away from him. He prayed there wasn't a judge out there who'd side with her, but he honestly didn't know. His family had a good name; he knew that. But when it came to a mother and her child...

Hope's cool fingers slid over his jaw, and he forced himself to look down at her, holding her gaze.

"Stop thinking so much. She's gone for now. We're all here to protect that little boy. She's not gonna come back. Not tonight anyway. I'm sure your cousin's makin' sure she knows the wrath she'll receive if she does."

"But she will come back. Maybe not while we're here—"

Hope's fingers covered his lips, effectively silencing him.

"Not tonight. And that's what matters." She smiled. "I do have to go take care of a few things, but I wanted to check on you. Make sure you'd be down for dinner. And then at the party."

"Wouldn't miss it," he told her. "Derrick's lookin' forward to it."

"So am I," she said.

Jared noticed, for the first time, Hope didn't look completely terrified when either of them mentioned Derrick. He took that as a good sign.

"I'll see you tonight."

Before she could turn away, Jared grabbed Hope's arm and pulled her back, crushing his lips down on hers. He needed to feel her close to him. She was his anchor, the calm in the storm. He hadn't felt this out of control in a long time.

Granted, he wasn't sure what was making him feel that way. Sable's bullshit...

Or the fact that he was now absolutely certain he'd fallen in love with this woman.

Chapter Thirty-Three

MERCY SAT ON one of the tables, watching the little kids wandering from one station to the next, laughing as they were given candy, as their faces were painted, as some member of the Walker family blew up balloon animals—damn, was there anything these people couldn't do?

"A monkey! I wanna monkey!" one of the little ones hollered.

"How about a giraffe?"

"A horse!" another kid yelled.

While she watched, Mercy forced a smile, trying to pretend to be enjoying herself. She really wanted to go back home, fall into bed, and sleep for ... the next week, at least. But she couldn't do that because all of these people were sharing their love and laughter with one another while reconnecting after so much time away. Although she had to question how much time they actually spent away from each other. They seemed so familiar with everything that was going on. Which kid was whose. How old they were. How they'd spent their last birthday. And there were over a hundred of them.

And she knew from all that she'd heard that there were doctors and lawyers and secretaries and small business owners within this huge family. They owned cattle farms and grocery stores, and she was sure one of them was a bank president. And of course, the Spectacular Seven as she'd dubbed them—the Walker brothers someone called them—were owners of the freaking sex resort they'd built in their small but well-to-do town.

It was crazy to watch them, and part of her was sad that she wasn't part of it. But she was also sad that her mother wasn't here to share this with her, to sit beside her and people watch, to eavesdrop on the conversations. Such as the one good-looking guy—she thought his name was Ethan—talking to one of his cousins about places he could take his husband—yes, husband—for a surprise romantic getaway around Christmastime.

"Yeah," Ethan confirmed. "He mentioned the mountains. Snow."

"Ooh. I'd say Colorado," the woman said. Mercy thought she was Jared's sister, Eve, but she could've been wrong.

"Colorado?"

"Beautiful place. You could go to Aspen or Breckenridge or ... there are a dozen different places. Do you like to ski?"

"No."

"Well, you could always stay inside, by the fire."

Of course, Mercy pretended not to listen to that one because she felt as though she was invading their privacy, but in a rare moment, she found herself actually envying the big blond guy who shared his life with this man. Ethan and Beau. Happily ever after.

For fuck's sake.

Mercy didn't believe in happily ever after. Too much shit got in the way for that to ever come to fruition. For her, anyway. She'd come to accept that Gracie had definitely gotten her happy on big-time. And she suspected her father had now found his second chance in the love department, although anytime Mercy thought about that, her heart felt like a million bees were attacking it. She liked Jan, even if she didn't act like it. She simply couldn't wrap her head around her father falling in love again.

Why couldn't once be enough?

And then there was Hope.

Mercy had watched her the most tonight. From the time her sister had intercepted the crazy woman who hadn't been invited. She didn't know what that was about, and quite frankly, she didn't give a shit, either. But now, Hope was spending her time with Jared and his little boy—the cute kid with the chocolate-brown eyes and the cowlick. They looked ... happy.

Jared

It'd been a long time since Mercy had seen Hope happy. There for a while, she'd thought her sister was going to find something with Ben, one of their previous guests. But that had fizzled before it ever picked up any steam. But then Tornado Jared walked in the door and suddenly Hope was smiling again.

Secretly, Mercy hoped her sister continued to smile. She prayed to the universe—because she didn't believe in any sort of god, especially not one who would take her mother away from them when they'd all needed her the most. Nope, she prayed to the universe that Hope would find true happiness. Her sister deserved it more than anyone else. She'd always put the ranch first, put their family first. She wasn't selfish, even if she was a giant pain in the butt sometimes.

Still… As Mercy sat here, letting all this happy-happy-joy-joy bounce right off of her, she did want some of it to stick to Hope. Enough to make her sister smile a little every day.

"I THINK YOU wore him out," Jared told her as they walked into the main house, Derrick sleeping soundly in his father's arms.

It was a little after eleven, and most of the parents had started carting the little ones off to the cabins, desperate to put them to bed during the lull from the sugar high and tonight's festivities. It had been a good time, and Hope was pretty sure the Walker family had thoroughly enjoyed the fun.

But now, it was time for Hope to say good night to Jared and Derrick. She had to get up for work in the morning, even though she'd prefer to spend the whole day in bed with Jared.

"He's got a lot of energy," Hope told him now. "I think *he* wore *me* out."

Since Jared had his arms full, Hope unlocked the door to his room and held it open. She didn't plan to go inside but found herself being pulled in that direction when Jared latched on to her shirt, tugging her.

She laughed, trying to be quiet since Derrick had definitely passed out, Jared's shoulder acting as his pillow.

"Don't go anywhere," Jared commanded softly before heading over to the bed and depositing Derrick on it.

Hope watched while he removed Derrick's boots and socks, then tucked him beneath the blanket, setting Derrick's cowboy hat on the nightstand.

She kept her eyes trained on Jared as he came back over to where she was standing by the door. She thought for a second that he was going to kiss her good night and let her slip out. Apparently he had other ideas, because he took her hand and pulled her directly into the adjoining bathroom, closing the door as quietly as he could behind them.

Before she could protest, his mouth was on hers. Since this was the only place she wanted to be—maybe not necessarily in the bathroom—Hope leaned against the counter and let herself be kissed. Neither of them said anything as Jared began unbuttoning her shirt. The only sound she made was a gasp of pleasure when he placed his big hands on her ribs, then deftly slipped his thumbs underneath her bra.

Oh, God, yes.

She had to bite back another moan when Jared grazed her nipples with the rough pad of his thumb, sweeping across them over and over until she was hardly able to breathe.

"Shh," Jared said, pulling back and pressing his forehead to hers. "Don't wake the sleeping boy."

Hope nodded, not exactly sure why. She didn't want to wake Derrick. For one, the little boy needed to rest, and two, she didn't want Jared to stop doing what he was doing. She tried not to think about the little knock that could sound on the door at any moment if Derrick did wake up and hear them.

While she stared down at Jared's hands, she observed the way he deftly unhooked the front clasp on her bra, allowing it to fall open. Only then did he mold his hands—God, they were warm and rough—to her breasts, squeezing them gently, as he began lightly pinching her nipples.

She sighed, swallowing the cry of pleasure.

Jared

"Shh," he urged again as he lowered his head and took one nipple into his mouth.

Thankfully the light in the bathroom was on, because Hope wanted to see this, wanted to watch as he tormented her in the most exquisite way possible. Which he did for what felt like forever. When his mouth finally returned to hers, Hope kissed him, letting him swallow the sounds she couldn't hold back any longer. She gave herself over to him, barely aware that he was quickly unbuttoning her jeans, lowering her zipper, then slipping one hand down into her panties.

"Christ, you're wet," he said, the words barely audible. "So fucking wet. I want... No, I *need* to put my cock inside you. I want to feel you warm and wet around me, Hope."

As he spoke, he pushed two fingers inside. Hope had to bite her lip to keep from begging. He finger-fucked her while she urgently unbuttoned his jeans and lowered his zipper. She wanted to give him the same pleasure he was giving her, but Jared didn't allow it. Instead, he pulled his fingers from her body, roughly shoved her jeans down to her knees before doing the same with his own.

When he spun her around, one tanned arm sliding around her stomach to hold her to him, Hope knew that this was going to be the best Halloween ever.

JARED COULDN'T WAIT; he needed to be inside her. He felt like he'd waited an eternity for this. Every second he wasn't making love to this woman was torture. Bending his legs, Jared slipped his cock between her thighs, sliding against the smooth, warm lips of her cunt.

"Bend over more," he urged, whispering directly into her ear.

Hope did as he instructed, and Jared leaned over with her, continuing to hold her against him with one arm while guiding the head of his cock against the soft, wet entrance to her body.

"Fuck, Hope... Ahh, Christ..." The heat of her enveloped him, and for a second, he was sure he saw stars. The intensity was tenfold and he wasn't sure why that was. Sure, he'd been lusting after her for most of the day, blessed beyond reason that he'd been able to spend it with her and Derrick. Every time he'd looked at her, he'd thought about sneaking away so he could do this, push deep inside her and watch until she came undone.

He looked up into the mirror, capturing Hope's gaze and holding it while he slowly sank into her, pulling out only slightly, then pushing in deep once more. Her eyes were heavy-lidded, her kiss-reddened lips parted as she pushed back against him, taking him deeper.

With his mouth still against her ear, he said, "I could spend the rest of my life right here, Hope. Buried inside you, letting the heat of your pussy milk me."

Hope didn't respond, but he knew she wouldn't. She didn't have the luxury of being able to whisper in his ear.

"God, baby, let me... I need to..." He held her stare in the mirror. "Let me fuck you, Hope. I need to feel you come on my dick."

She inhaled sharply, and he released her, grabbing her hips with both hands as he began thrusting inside, deep, hard. He couldn't stop himself. She felt incredible. So hot, so fucking tight. But it wasn't like the other times. It felt different, better. And that was saying something, because every time he'd been inside her, it'd been fucking amazing.

He looked into the mirror once more, watching as she gazed at him, her heart in her eyes. He knew that Hope had been holding back on him, trying to keep herself distanced. Admittedly, he'd done the same, but it was futile. He couldn't stay away from her, didn't want to be without her. Hell, he wanted to spend every fucking night with her in his bed. He wanted to wake up every morning with her beside him.

"Jared..." The rough exhale wasn't loud enough to be heard outside the bathroom, but he could see she was worried she wasn't going to be quiet. She'd told him she couldn't when she was with him, and he fucking loved that. Loved when she told him she was coming. Loved the way she cried out his name.

Jared

He dug his fingertips into her flesh, doing his best not to hurt her as he slammed into her, mindful that he had to be careful. She was so small, but not at all fragile. Still, the lust she inspired in him was unlike anything he'd ever known.

Closing his eyes, he leaned into her again, pushing in deep as he reached around and slid his middle finger between the smooth lips of her pussy, seeking her clit.

Hope's hands gripped his arms, her fingernails digging into his flesh at the same time her pussy clamped down on him, gripping him as she came. It triggered his own release and only then ... only then did Jared realize what was different.

It wasn't the fact that he was completely and totally in love with this woman...

Nope. Not that simple.

Hope's eyes met his in the mirror, and he saw the recognition in her beautiful eyes. He waited to see how she would react. He held his breath, waiting, praying...

The smile that lit up her face wasn't what he'd expected. And when she turned to him, gripping him by the front of his shirt and jerking him down so that his mouth was on hers, Jared breathed again, his heart leaping into his throat.

"We forgot the condom," she breathed against his mouth.

He could feel her smile. It allowed him to breathe a little easier. He wasn't worried about it at all, and he prayed she wasn't, either.

"And I have to admit ... that was ... ah-fucking-mazing."

He couldn't have said it better himself.

CHAPTER THIRTY-FOUR

"WE'VE GOT A problem," Travis stated firmly, glancing down at his cousin who was sitting in one of the rocking chairs on the back porch of the main house.

Jared peered up at him, squinting. "What's that?"

Travis glanced around, noting all the people. There were a half dozen sitting in rocking chairs lining the back porch, others walking around as their kids played on the playscape, a group tossing a football not too far away.

Nope, they couldn't have this conversation here. As pissed off as he was, as much as Travis wanted to let everyone in on this to ensure they had the full support of their family, he knew he had to rein it in a little.

"Let's take a walk," he suggested, hoping Jared wouldn't ask questions.

Jared got to his feet. "You mind keeping an eye on Derrick for a bit?" he asked Zoey.

"Of course not," she said, her smile sweet, but Travis could see the concern in her eyes. She knew something was wrong.

And she was right. Something was very, very wrong.

Travis turned to lead the way off the porch and toward the front of the house, where he knew no one would overhear.

"What's up?" Jared asked when Travis stopped beneath a giant pecan tree.

"You know my brothers and I are taking turns this week going in to AI. We can't leave it for a full week without us there."

Jared cocked a brow. "Okay."

Jared

"I went in early this morning, but not before stopping by Pop's house to check things out. I drove through the property, making sure everything was good. Everyone's gone and the whole town knows it. Figured it wouldn't hurt to make sure everything was still locked up tight." Travis sighed. "All was well, except your front door was standing wide open."

Jared's eyes went wide. "The fuck? I know I locked it before we left."

"Yeah. It looked like you did. Especially since one of the back windows was broken. Whoever went in used the window but came out the front door."

"Did you call the police?"

Travis offered his best *are you serious?* look. "No. I went through the house, checked everything out. Temporarily boarded up the window, locked the door when I left. And yes, I checked it all out before that. The TVs are all there, laptop, stereo. Even your iPod, which was sitting on the kitchen counter. Whoever came in wasn't lookin' to rob you."

"Fuck."

Yep, looked like Jared had come to the exact same conclusion Travis had. It looked as though Sable wasn't quite ready to give up.

Then again, Travis blamed himself for that. When she'd shown up at the ranch three days ago, he'd held back some of the information he had. It was a lapse in judgment. His attempt at being a gentleman and not throwing her completely to the wolves. He should've known better. Sable wasn't going to quit until Travis shared the dirt he had on her.

No doubt about it, the information he'd been given this week would ultimately send Sable running hard and fast, as far as she could possibly get.

"What the fuck does she want?" Jared snarled. "I don't understand why the fuck she can't leave us alone."

"Well, first of all, I think she simply wants you to know that she found you. She knows where you and Derrick live." Not that they could've hidden that forever, but Travis admitted it was easier when she'd still been looking. "Not to mention, I'm sure she's jealous," Travis told him matter-of-factly. He actually knew she was based on their conversation.

Jared's brow drew up in a frown.

"Sable saw you with Hope, Jared. Back at Moonshiners. And since Hope was the one to approach her here, she put two and two together. She's crazy, not completely stupid. I'm sure she figures things are serious between you. That in itself is a problem for her. You might've divorced her, but that was only okay as long as you didn't have someone else in your life."

"She's been screwing other men," Jared said unnecessarily.

"She's a selfish bitch, Jared. What do you expect? She wants it all. But mostly, she wants … money."

"She ain't gettin' more fuckin' money from me, Trav. I'm done with this shit. Let her take me to court. Let her try to fight me. I won't let her have Derrick. She won't take him from me."

"No, she won't. But she doesn't know that yet."

Jared stared at him. "What else did you find?"

"A note. It was sitting on Derrick's pillow." Travis pulled a piece of paper from his back pocket, handed it to Jared. He watched as Jared read it.

> *Jared,*
> *You probably thought I wouldn't find out where you lived. But I'm smarter than you give me credit for. And while you're off with your mistress, I'm hiring a lawyer. You've got until the end of the week to figure this out. You know what I'm asking for. Surely Derrick is worth more to you than a little bit of money.*
>
> *Always yours,*
> *Sable*

Jared

When Jared looked up, Travis could see the man was fuming. The woman had been walking all over him for years now. She thought she had the upper hand, had the perfect way to control him because she could threaten the one and only important thing in Jared's life. Quite frankly, Travis was tired of watching it. His cousin deserved a hell of a lot better than that crazy, selfish bitch he'd married.

Which was what led him to this conversation in the first place.

Travis could finally give Jared some good news.

GODDAMN IT. JARED was so fucking tired of Sable and her bullshit.

The woman didn't know how to quit.

"Hey."

Jared turned at the sound of Hope's voice coming from several feet behind him. Despite the anger coursing through him, he felt something akin to relief as soon as he saw her.

"Hey," he greeted.

When she walked closer, he pulled her right into his arms, not caring that Travis was standing there staring at him. He hadn't seen her since she headed out this morning. When Jared's parents insisted that Derrick spend a couple of nights with them in their cabin, Jared had taken the opportunity to spend as much time as possible with Hope, which included spending the night with her both nights. After he'd made love to her this morning, he had waited for her to take a shower, then he had walked her to the main house, where they'd shared breakfast. Needless to say, it'd been a damn good morning.

"Go ahead," Jared urged Travis. "She can hear anything you have to say."

Travis didn't look so sure about that, but he finally spit it out. "After I left your place, I drove through town and found her at Moonshiners. We had another brief conversation. I was straightforward, asked her what it would take to get her to move on. To be honest, I was trying to be diplomatic. I don't need her input. *However,* she kindly stated that twenty-five thousand would no longer be enough." Travis shook his head, as though he couldn't believe it. "She's a whack job. She informed me that fifty thousand would make her reconsider, and she'd be on her way." Travis glanced at Hope briefly, then back to Jared. "She mentioned Hope, said that the additional twenty-five grand she's asking for is to help compensate for her mental stress."

"For the love of God!" Jared thought for a second his head might explode. Sable had completely gone insane. First it was twenty-five thousand. Now fifty thousand. And to think, the woman was only bluffing. She didn't even know if a court would grant her custody.

Then again, Jared didn't know if they would, either.

"It's bullshit, I know," Travis said heatedly. "But she's a fucking looney toon, man. What'd you expect?"

Jared swallowed hard, doing his best to focus on Hope's hand, which was pressed against his stomach, her other arm around his back. It was as though she was trying to calm him down simply by letting him know she was there. It was working. Having her next to him… It helped. Jared took a deep breath, tried to think.

"I have good news, though," Travis admitted.

Jared met his cousin's eyes. "Well, you could've fuckin' said so before now." He felt his face flame from the anger roiling through him.

Travis took a step closer, his eyes locked with Jared's. "We're gonna get through this. Sable's just graspin' at straws now. If she had a serious case, she would've done something by now."

Jared glared at Travis. "That's *not* good news."

275

Jared

"No, but you have to remember, Derrick is *your* son."

Jared frowned, the words not making a damn bit of sense. "Of course he is," Jared agreed. "I have full custody. He has my name. She can't take him away."

"You're right," Travis clarified. "He has the Walker name." Travis poked him in the shoulder. "Because he is a Walker. Not merely by name or simply by love. He *is* a Walker, Jared. You are his biological father."

"What?" Now his head was spinning. Jared stared at Travis, reading the man's expression, allowing the words to repeat in his head. *You are his biological father.* Yes, that was what Travis had said, but it... He was confused. "What are you saying?"

"That Derrick is biologically yours, Jared," Travis repeated. "I have the legitimate DNA test to prove it." Once again, Travis pulled another sheet of paper from his pocket.

When Jared went to reach for it, he saw his hands were shaking. He unfolded it and glanced at the top. Through blurry eyes, he saw *99.9%* and he felt light-headed.

Hope was staring up at him, and Jared could've sworn there were tears in her eyes. It was hard to tell because his vision was blurred by his own tears. No way was he going to cry. No fucking way.

Oh, hell.

And then it happened.

Jared couldn't hold it in; he broke down, sobbing like a fucking baby.

Hope wrapped her arms around him, her hand in his hair as she held his head close to her neck.

He felt Travis's hand on his back for a moment, and when it fell away, Jared pulled himself together.

He wasn't sure he wanted to know, but he had to ask the question anyway. "What did you have to do to make that happen?" No, he still didn't believe it.

Travis barked a laugh. "I'm good, man, but not that good. I can't simply restructure someone's DNA."

Jared let that process for a minute, watching as Travis's grin widened.

"I got nosy," Travis admitted, his lips curled into that mischievous smile he was known for.

"Ain't that the damn truth."

"Remember the DNA samples we all gave my mother? For her genealogy crap?"

Jared nodded. He had thought it strange at the time, but he also knew that it was something Lorrie would do. After all, she did have the family spreadsheet that even had the names of people's pets, past and present.

"I had a DNA test run on you and Derrick. You told me that Sable provided you with test results stating you weren't his father. You never said you had them run yourself. She's a liar, Jared. We all know that."

True. Why had he believed her? Jared wasn't sure. It had to have been something she said at the time. Or maybe he simply didn't give a shit because as far as he was concerned, Derrick was his son regardless. The moment Sable offered to give him back, Jared hadn't looked back.

"Now, I know you don't want me involved," Travis said. "And God knows, Gage doesn't want me involved, but I'm not gonna let this go. She's tryin' to fuck with your head. We need to put this to rest. If you try to pay her off—"

"I won't," he snapped.

"I know. But if you do, she's never gonna stop. She knows your weakness now. We need to use this against her."

Jared

Jared hated that Sable could do this to her own son. He wanted Derrick to have a mother, one who loved him unconditionally and didn't use him for her own personal gain. Clearly, no matter what he hoped, Sable couldn't be that woman.

"I'm gonna take care of this," Travis told him. "But from this point on, I'm leaving you and Derrick out of it. I need to talk to Reese. His brother works for Sniper 1 Security."

Jared nodded. "I know Z."

"Let's just say that I have a little bit of information that's gonna change Sable's world. With Reese's help, we'll let her know what that is. She can choose to do what she wishes at that point. But I seriously can't see her bothering you anymore."

"I'll believe that when I see it." Jared studied Travis's face. "What? Did she piss off her last sugar daddy or somethin'?"

Travis's eyes glittered. "Or somethin'. But seriously, Jared. I want you out of this. The less you know, the better."

"You don't have to do that." Jared was quite capable of protecting his own.

"I want to. You're family. Derrick's family. This shit stops now."

Jared knew he couldn't argue with Travis. Truth was, he didn't want to. He needed to protect Derrick from this, to shield him as best he could. Travis had a way of getting things taken care of without the whole town knowing what happened. The last thing Jared wanted was for Derrick to find out one day that his mother had tried to use him to blackmail his own father.

"Okay. Do what you gotta do. Let me know if I need to do anything."

Travis smiled then, his eyes darting to Hope, then back to Jared. He offered a curt nod, then disappeared.

Jared wasn't feeling steady enough to walk yet, so he simply pulled Hope closer, hugging her to him as he breathed deep. "I always knew he was mine, Hope. I always knew."

"That boy is one lucky kid," she said, her words muffled. "He's got your unconditional love. I don't think he needs much more than that."

He needs you, he wanted to say. *I need you, too.*

HOPE HADN'T BEEN sure what she had walked in on when she'd come to find Jared a little earlier. Finding him having a heart-to-heart with his cousin had been somewhat of a surprise. More so when Jared wanted to include her in the conversation.

Well, not that she contributed much, but having been there... Watching Jared break down when Travis told him that Derrick was his biological child... It'd taken a tremendous amount of effort not to break down in tears herself. Jared was such a strong, resilient man. To see him teary-eyed over that little boy... Yeah, she might've inched more toward the love side with that one.

Which, now that she thought about it, meant she was definitely standing beneath the *in love* umbrella more fully than the *in lust* one. Like, with both feet.

"You done for the day?" Jared asked, pressing his lips to hers before standing up straight.

With her hands flat on his chest, she stared up at him. "I am. I'm yours for the rest of the night."

"Mmm. I definitely like the sound of that." Jared's wicked grin caused heat to coil low in her belly. "I was thinkin' we could have dinner. Me, you, and Derrick."

This time Hope smiled. "I'd like that. A lot." And that was the truth. For the last few days, she'd thought about the time she'd spent with Derrick. Sure, she'd been anxious before, during, and even after, but she'd also been excited.

Jared

She wanted to believe that something was different this time around. That she'd fallen in love with Jared *before* she'd fallen in love with his son. More likely, it meant she hadn't convinced herself that she loved Jared because she enjoyed spending time with his kid. Which, she had to admit, was probably what had happened with her previous relationships. What she felt for Jared... Hope had never felt this before. This intensity that made her want to spend every waking moment with the man.

"What're we waitin' for, then?" Jared held out his hand to her.

Hope took it, linking her fingers with his as they headed back to the main house. When they walked around the corner, the sight of all those little kids playing on the playscape, along with all the adults sitting around, laughing, joking, and smiling made Hope feel welcome. This was the sort of family she'd grown up with. Although hers was considerably smaller, she remembered all the times when she was younger, her mother and father outside with her and her sisters running around. It was the type of family she wanted for her own one day.

"Dad! Dad! Come watch me!" Derrick hollered.

Jared tugged her hand, leading her toward the swings. Derrick was being pushed by a pretty redhead. Hope searched her brain, trying to remember the woman's name. Kennedy. Yes, that was it. Kennedy, who was married to Sawyer, another of Jared's cousins.

"Hope! Push me!" Derrick called out, his eyes sliding from her face to his dad's. The little boy looked sheepish but then tacked on, "Pwease."

Without hesitation, Hope wandered over beside Kennedy, who moved over to push Mason while Hope stepped behind Derrick.

"He likes you," Kennedy said, smiling.

"I like him, too."

Kennedy stepped closer. For a second, Hope thought the woman was going to make some disparaging threat. Something along the lines of, "You hurt them, this family will come down on you," blah, blah, blah. It wouldn't bother her if she did. She'd been expecting it.

"They *both* like you," Kennedy noted in a conspiratorial whisper, smiling widely.

Hope grinned, glancing over at Jared.

As she stood there, surrounded by all of those people, laughing, talking, and genuinely enjoying one another's company, Hope knew that this was where she was supposed to be. She'd kept herself closed off, secretly craving this all along. Convincing herself that the ranch was all she needed had never worked. And it wasn't the ranch that she loved so much. It was her family being there. The long days of hard work definitely appealed to her, but she knew it wouldn't be the same without family.

She held Jared's gaze for the longest time, unable to stop herself from smiling.

And when he mouthed three little words, she thought her heart was going to leap right out of her chest.

I love you.

She felt tears in her sinuses. It was hard to swallow as she tried to keep the smile on her face. She knew her eyes were watering, knew he saw everything she was feeling.

Had he really said it? Did he really love her?

Or … wait. Maybe he'd said something entirely different. Like, *I vacuum.* Or maybe, *olive juice.* Or *elephant shoes. Alligator food.*

Hope jumped, startled when Jared came to stand behind her. He planted his hands on her hips while she continued to push Derrick in the swing.

His mouth came to her ear, and very, very softly, he whispered, "I love you, Hope."

And she knew, without a doubt, that this time was definitely different.

Better.

Amazing.

Incredible.

She turned to face him, grinning. "I love you, too."

And right there, in front of all of his family, Jared leaned down and kissed her. It was embarrassing enough to know people were looking at them. So when they clapped, she thought for sure she was going to stroke out, her face flaming.

Jared

Thankfully, someone chose that moment to ring the dinner bell.

"Food!" Derrick squealed. "Wet's eat! Dad! Hope! Get me outta this thing!"

And the moment was over, or maybe it was just getting started, Hope didn't know. She pulled back from Jared, helped Derrick get out of his seat, and allowed the little boy to take her hand and tug her toward the porch while Jared walked behind them.

For the first time in her life, Hope felt free. The weight she'd been carrying around on her chest was gone. This was where she was meant to be.

Right here with this man and this little boy at Dead Heat Ranch, with her own family, as well as the Walker family, surrounding her.

Chapter Thirty-Five

JARED SPENT MOST of the evening in a fog. For one, he'd received the greatest news he could've possibly received. Derrick was his son. Biologically, of course. Because everyone knew that Derrick had been his son from the very second he'd breathed outside of his mother's womb. Blood or not, Jared had never questioned that Derrick was his son.

Only now, it was all the sweeter because Sable could no longer threaten to take the boy away from a man who wasn't his father. He wished he could be there to see Sable's face when Travis told her the news. Then again, he didn't want to see her ever again.

And on top of that mega-incredible news, Hope had told him she loved him.

Sure, it had been a risk mouthing it to her from across the small play area outside, but he hadn't been able to resist. Watching her as she pushed Derrick in his swing ... he'd had the urge to run over to her, drop to his knee, and beg her to marry him, to spend her life with him and Derrick.

"Hey, man."

Jared looked up to see Grace's husband Lane standing in front of him. "Hey."

"I wanted to thank you. For, you know, helpin' out while I was gone."

Jared knew that Lane was referring to the morning Jared had helped Hope with one of the calves. The little thing had wandered away from its momma and ended up getting caught up in some barbed wire. It was scraped up pretty good, but they'd gotten it out, and Hope had ensured it'd been cleaned up.

Jared

Jared shook his head and smiled. "Not a problem. I've got some experience."

Lane grinned. "Yeah, well. It sure beat comin' back from my honeymoon and listenin' to everyone bitch that I shouldn't be takin' time off."

"I'm just happy I was here to help out."

Lane held out his hand, leaning in closer. "If you decide to, you know, become a permanent fixture around here, just make sure I'm your second-in-command."

Jared frowned. "That won't happen, man. I've heard you're really damn good at what you do. Plus, I'm not lookin' to be in charge. I already have that headache. I'd rather let *you* boss *me* around."

Lane laughed, then clapped Jared on the back. "Don't think I didn't notice how you didn't deny becomin' a permanent fixture."

As Lane wandered off, Jared grinned to himself.

"You good, son?"

Jared turned to look at his father, a man he admired more than anyone on the planet. A father he'd always looked up to, always wanted to be like—still wanted to be like.

"Never better, Dad."

Gerald smiled, his gaze following Jared's as they watched Hope sitting with Derrick, Kate, Mason, and Joey—the ranch's chef's six-year-old son. She looked so happy as she sat there, talking to all the kids. Reid, Zane and V's son, along with Kellan, Kaleb and Zoey's second boy—both one year old and ready to be independent—were sitting in high chairs nearby, grinning and slobbering as only little ones did. Hope's sister Trinity was also with them. She was telling them a story about some magical, colorful horse. Jared hadn't paid much attention, choosing instead to simply admire Hope.

"It's serious, huh?" his father asked, clapping him on the back with one hand.

Jared nodded. "Definitely serious."

"Any chance we'll get the chance to really meet her?"

Jared grinned. "Of course. Just…" He glanced over at his father. "I've gotta take it slow, you know? I don't want to run this one off."

His father smiled, studying Jared's face. "Son, I've seen the way she looks at you. Even if you didn't think anyone noticed… Trust me, we did. Okay, your mother noticed," Gerald admitted with a chuckle. "But she pointed it out, and I definitely can see it, too. But don't take it too slow."

Turning his attention back to Hope, Jared was grinning when she looked up at him, their eyes meeting. She smiled warmly.

No, he didn't want to take it too slow. He wasn't sure where this would go, what direction they were headed, but he knew he couldn't stay away from her. He'd learned that over the last month and a half. Staying away from Hope Lambert was damn near impossible. But he didn't want to scare her.

"Mind if Derrick spends the night with us again?" Gerald offered.

Jared shook his head. "Of course not. He'll love that."

His father nodded, patting his back once more. "Good then. When they're done, we're gonna head out. See you tomorrow, boy."

"Night, Dad."

An hour later, after most of the family had gone in separate directions, some going back to their cabins to relax for the night, some heading out to the barn for some sort of contest that Mercy and Faith were handling, and others heading outside to enjoy the cool November evening, Jared waited for Hope to finish up.

He was perched on the edge of a chair in the recreation room, where his brothers Kaden and Keegan were trying to hustle Gracie's husbands at pool. From what he could tell, the hustlers were actually being hustled, but he didn't bother to tell them that.

"Hey."

Jared turned to see Hope standing at his side.

"Where's Derrick?"

"He's stayin' with my mom and dad tonight."

Jared

Her eyes glittered with understanding. He saw the heat swirling there, along with something else. Acceptance, maybe? Or maybe that was love.

Whatever it was, he wanted to spend the rest of the night lost in her eyes, buried deep inside her warmth, holding her close to him. He still hadn't wrapped his head around how this had all come together. How his life had gotten on this path so easily. It felt like he'd spent the past few years shielding himself from everyone, trying to find his bearings. And then Hope showed up in his life unexpectedly, and he was thrown off course once more, but this time, he knew better than to give up.

Hope leaned in, pressing against his side, her lips brushing against his ear. "So, your room or mine, cowboy?"

Jared turned, pulling Hope between his legs as he stared back at her. "Wherever you are, that's where I wanna be. That's the *only* place I wanna be."

He wondered if she knew that he meant more than just tonight.

WALKING BACK TO her cabin took forever. Or so it seemed.

Despite the fact that Jared held her hand as they made the relatively short trek from the main house, Hope couldn't wait to get inside, where she could get her hands on this man.

Literally.

For the better part of the evening, she'd disappeared into her own head, thinking about making love to him, waking up in his arms, smiling into his eyes and knowing—deep in her heart—that this was real.

And luckily, they were finally here.

She opened the door, paused briefly for Jared to shut and lock it, before she found herself once again lifted off her feet, her legs wrapped around his trim waist while he licked his way into her mouth. The wood door was hard against her back; his equally unyielding body was pressed against her front.

"Are you scared, Hope?"

His whispered question took her by surprise. She pulled back enough to look at him, trying to read his mind. She shook her head. She wasn't scared. Not of him, not of this thing between them.

"Good. Me, neither."

That made her laugh, but her chuckle quickly died when he crushed his lips to hers. She grabbed on to him, trying to press closer, trying to merge with him in a way that wasn't possible with this many clothes on. He clearly knew what she wanted ... what she needed ... because he carried her over to the sofa. He sat down, her straddling his lap, and Hope continued to kiss him.

They took their time, removing clothes, discarding them in a pile on the floor while their mouths and hands roamed, teased.

Her body was ready for him, desperate to feel him inside her, but Jared had other plans, and then she was the one sitting on the couch, her back against the cushions while Jared knelt on the floor in front of her. Stealing her breath right from her lungs, he speared her pussy with his tongue, feasting on her until she nearly came right out of her skin.

It was both shocking and so freaking good. She never wanted him to stop.

When his eyes met hers, holding her stare, his fingers pushing inside her while his lips sucked on her clit, Hope stopped trying to hold back. She slid her fingers into his cool hair, holding his head as she came, a cry tearing from her throat as the pleasure rocked her to her very soul.

Before she could say anything, do anything, Jared had picked her up and resumed his position on the couch, this time guiding himself into her as she straddled him once again.

"Oh, fuck, baby…"

Jared

Hope moaned as the sensations tore through her, as he filled her, stretched her. She kept her hands on his shoulders, her eyes locked with his as she began to rock astride him, taking him deeper. It was a slow, languid ride that she could've done for the entire night, staring right into his eyes, seeing everything he wanted her to see.

God, she loved this man. She'd never imagined that this was what love felt like. True, complete. Free.

And yes, she was scared, but not the way he thought. She wasn't scared of love, of this deep connection they clearly had. She was scared of what it meant for their future. How did two people combine their lives?

"Look at me, Hope," Jared urged, his hand cradling the back of her head. "Stay with me. Right here. You and me."

She nodded, forcing her eyes open as he began to rock his hips upward, driving into her.

"God, baby... You're so tight. I want to stay just like this for the rest of the night."

Hope smiled. She liked that idea, but she liked the idea of him losing control, coming as hard as she knew she was.

"Next time," she whispered. "Right now, I want you to make me come."

Jared's eyes glowed with what she'd come to realize was pure, unadulterated lust.

She smiled then, wanting to throw him for a loop. "Then I want you to fuck me harder, deeper," she whispered, her lips brushing his. "I want you to make me beg, make me scream your name over and over while you come inside me."

He growled. An animalistic sound that made her laugh. The next thing she knew, he was carrying her to her room, still lodged to the hilt inside her. He went down on the bed with her, never pulling out, covering her completely. He then sought her hands, linking their fingers as he pressed her into the mattress. Short, shallow thrusts were combined with deep, slow impalements until Hope was panting, her body tingling all over.

"Come for me, Hope. So I can make you scream for me, baby."

Jared released her hand, sliding his between their bodies, where he circled her clit, driving her slowly insane. He didn't stop until she was shaking, until…

"Jared… Oh, God, yes!"

He continued with his torturously slow pace until she rode out her climax. Only then did he begin fucking her hard, just as she'd asked. He kept his eyes locked with hers, watching her as he drove her right to the pinnacle again.

"Beg me," Jared commanded.

"Please…" She wasn't above begging. "Jared…"

"Say my name again," he insisted.

"Jared…"

"Tell me, Hope. Tell me what I need to hear."

As he continued to impale her, deeper, harder, faster, she held on, her fingers digging into his biceps, her knees locked on his hips as she panted and moaned.

"Jared… Oh, God, yes… I want to feel you… I want to feel you come … inside me."

"Tell me," he growled.

"Jared!" She was so close, hanging by a thread, ready to come apart simply from the look on his face.

"Say it, Hope. Tell me, baby."

Hope sucked in a breath, an orgasm cresting, sending her soaring to another dimension. "Oh, yes! Jared!"

He didn't slow down, and he didn't look away. Waiting. None too patiently, she knew.

And then, when her body fractured again, Hope smiled back at him, hoarsely saying what he said he needed to hear. "I love you, Jared. Love. You."

With an answering smile and a roughly groaned, "I love you, too, baby, more than you know," he gave her exactly what she'd asked for.

Jared

REESE TAVOULARIS WALKED into Moonshiners a little after nine. He'd purposely spent half an hour sitting in the parking lot, allowing the woman to go inside and get comfortable. He hadn't wanted her to get suspicious by him walking in right after her. When he'd assured his brother, Z, that he was capable of handling this without him driving all the way to Coyote Ridge, Z hadn't questioned him, he'd merely given Reese some tips, a few details of the story he was supposed to share, and then hung up and left the job to him.

And here he was, walking inside the dimly lit bar, the sounds of George Jones crooning from the jukebox filling the small, relatively empty place. It was a Thursday night, so he hadn't expected much of a crowd, which made this particular joint perfect.

"Beer?" Mack the bartender asked as Reese took a seat at the bar, directly beside the dark-haired woman. She was relatively pretty, although a little worn around the edges. As though she hadn't had her buff and shine done recently. Perhaps the reason she was looking to extort a shit ton of money from Reese's boss. Worse, she was willing to use her own kid against him in order to get what she wanted.

Reese nodded at Mack. "Definitely."

Mack went to the other end of the bar to get his drink, and Reese took the opportunity to introduce himself.

"Haven't seen you around here before," he said, making his normal twang a little thicker. It often worked with the ladies.

She smiled, somewhat shyly, but didn't say anything.

Reese knew, based on what Travis had told him, that he wasn't Sable's type. He wasn't wearing a three-piece suit, didn't sport a three-hundred-dollar haircut, wasn't showing off a Rolex on his wrist.

Nope, Reese was dressed down in Wranglers and a T-shirt, having left his jacket in the truck. The most expensive thing on his body was his boots, and even they hadn't cost more than a couple hundred bucks. Plus, they were at least three years old.

That didn't explain what Sable had seen in Jared. As far as financially anyway. Other than he was a Walker, and along with the name came the rumors. One of the rumors—although actually fact—was that they had money. But Reese didn't know who had what or how much. And the Walkers damn sure didn't flaunt it, didn't talk about it, didn't throw it around. Looked to him as though Sable had been willing to take her chances. In the end, she'd gotten some money out of the man, again, using her kid as a bargaining chip.

Reese offered the bartender another thank you, then turned his attention to Sable, as though he didn't have anything better to do than chat it up on a Thursday night. Well, that was pretty close to the truth. If he weren't here, he'd be at home, watching Thursday Night Football.

He extended his hand. "Reese."

Sable smiled, clearly willing to give him a chance. After all, she really didn't know what he had in his bank account until she took a chance, right?

"Sable ... Walker."

Funny how she added Walker, although she'd been divorced from Jared for years.

"Nice to meet you, Sable ... Walker."

Her smile was slow but seductive, which, again, he'd been expecting.

"What brings you to town?"

Sable's dark eyes lowered to the bar top. "I'm here looking for ... my ex."

"Ahh." He made it sound as though that made perfect sense. "He skip out on child support or somethin'?"

She looked at him as though she had never considered the idea of child support. Lord have mercy, she really was a snake.

A slow song came on the jukebox, and Reese glanced over at the open space behind him. It wasn't technically a dance floor, but it would work as one.

"Care to dance, sweetheart?"

Sable's eyes widened, but then she nodded, offering her hand as he held his out.

Jared

Reese walked her to the dance floor, then pulled her in close. Although she was several cards short of a full deck, the woman smelled good. Not good enough that he'd want to take her home—she wasn't his type. You know, the whole batshit-crazy part.

But none of that mattered tonight. He was here to do a job.

He allowed the song to play for a minute before he moved closer to Sable, making it appear as though he might want to kiss her. He cupped the back of her head when she rested her cheek against his chest.

And Reese chose that moment to speak. He kept his tone soft, with a hint of warning.

"Sable, I'm here with a message."

She tried to move, but he held her close.

"Shh," he told her. "Just stay right there. I'm not gonna hurt you. We're in a bar full of people. And trust me, I would never hurt a woman."

She stopped moving, but Reese kept his arms around her.

"I wanted to let you know that a paternity test was done. You know, one that wasn't tampered with. Funny thing, turns out Derrick really is Jared's son. Imagine everyone's surprise. Then again, you knew this already, so I'm not tellin' you nothin' new. However..."

Reese smiled at one of the old men looking their way, but then leaned in close to Sable again.

"We also learned another little secret of yours. Does the name Marco Moroso ring a bell, by chance?"

As he expected, Sable stiffened.

"Funny story, that," Reese continued. "See, my brother works for this protection agency out of Dallas. One of his co-workers has a brother-in-law. Some sort of mobster, from what I hear. Yeah, you know what I'm talkin' about. Well, it turns out, this Moroso guy is dead, and now, his little brother's gettin' out of jail. Of course, you know how it is. Those mafia guys are hell-bent on revenge."

Reese pulled back, cupping her face, staring into her eyes. He lost the good-ol'-boy attitude, going with dead serious.

"I think it's time you head on out. Make a new life for yourself somewhere else, Sable. There's nothin' for you here. And maybe, if you do, your name won't be whispered to Dennis. After all, I hear you and Marco were quite close at one time. You were what? Working for him? Secretary, maybe? The kind with benefits." He angled his head down. "And you know I'm not talkin' about health insurance, darlin'. So, when Dennis gets out, which I hear'll be really soon, he won't come lookin' for the secretary who disappeared on his brother. Right about the time a rumor started about a rat within the ranks. Oh, and yes, right when twenty thousand also went missin'."

Sable's eyes were wide, but she wasn't moving, she wasn't trying to push him away. Reese knew that the dirt Travis had worked so hard to dig up was true.

"See, there's this thing called six degrees of separation. Funny, sometimes, you don't even realize just how close you are to the people you're tryin' to get away from." He tilted her chin up slightly. "Do you have any questions?"

Sable shook her head, and Reese could see the real concern in her eyes. She should've known that eventually her past would come back to haunt her. From what Travis had told him, hooking up with wealthy men was Sable's MO. And apparently, she didn't really care what they did for a living or where their money came from. Or whether or not she gave up confidential information and risked the wrath of the mafia coming down on her. The last part proved she was crazy.

Reese purposely stepped back, waiting to see what she would say, what she would do. She glanced around the room, probably looking to see who was watching them, what they might know.

"Go on, now, sugar," he urged her as he turned back to the bar. "You disappear, all this information does, too."

Surprisingly, Sable turned and walked away. Right out the door.

Reese took his seat back at the bar.

Jared

Hopefully Travis's plan would work. Sable would be long gone. Oh, Reese knew that the woman had nothing to worry about when it came to the mob boss. The little brother knew nothing about the missing money or that Sable hadn't really sold them out, and apparently twenty g's was nothing in the grand scheme of things. Especially when avenging his brother's death was high on Dennis's list of things to do. Reese had told Z that he didn't need to know any of that. He merely needed enough to scare Sable.

Apparently, that'd been enough.

Grabbing his phone, Reese shot a text to Travis. *All done. Thanks.*

Reese smiled to himself, responding with, *Now you owe me one.*

And he fully intended to call in that favor one of these days.

Epilogue

Six weeks later

JARED PULLED INTO the ranch, heading directly for the sales office. It was a little after one, so he knew that lunch was over, which seemed to be a relatively good time to show up unannounced. After parking his truck in the visitor's lot, he headed for the office. When the door opened, Jerry Lambert's smiling face was shining back at him.

"Jared," he greeted, stepping back out of the way. "Is Hope expecting you?"

Removing his hat and holding it at his side, Jared shook his head. "No, sir. I ... uh... I actually came to talk to you."

That seemed to surprise Jerry, but Jared could tell the older man quickly tried to mask his expression.

"Is there a problem?"

A problem? No, he couldn't say there was. But he pretended to consider that for a moment, trying to gather his nerve.

"Sir, I came to ask you something."

"Is it about working here at the ranch?" Jerry perched on the edge of his desk. "Because Hope and I already talked about that. Since my daughters run this place, I leave the hirin' up to them. If Hope feels there's something for you to do here, something that you'll be content doing, then that's up to the two of you."

Interesting.

Jared

Hope might've talked to her father, but she hadn't yet talked to him. Not that he minded. It was one of the topics they'd been discussing as of late. Because there was no denying that this relationship was moving forward at warp speed, they'd talked about plenty of things. Where they might live when they decided to move in together. When, not if. They were so far past if at this point.

Jared had seen the concern on Hope's face when they'd talked about that. She'd told him she was scared to leave the ranch, but if that was what was necessary, she would do it because she was ready to build a life with Jared. She could compromise.

And compromise she would, he was sure of it. But not about that. He'd told her that where they lived wasn't important to him. Family made a home, not the house, not the county they resided in. None of that mattered as long as there was family.

They'd talked about Derrick, about getting him adjusted to living with Hope, to spending more time with her. Jared didn't worry that Derrick would have a problem. The only issue he seemed to be having right now was not spending time with Hope. When she wasn't around, Derrick wanted to know why.

"Sir, that's … uh … that's not what I came to talk about. Although, that's… Yeah. I'm glad Hope talked to you."

Jerry lifted his thick eyebrows, clearly waiting for Jared to continue.

Jared cleared his throat. "Sir, I would like to ask for your daughter's hand in marriage. With your blessing, I would like to ask Hope to marry me."

MERCY WAS PISSED. She couldn't find Hope, and she needed her sister to make a decision. After looking in the barn, the stable, even the main house, she couldn't find her anywhere. Now, as she jerked the door to the sales office open, Mercy came to an abrupt stop, the words she'd just heard echoing in her head.

I would like to ask Hope to marry me.

"Shit … uh … sorry," Mercy fumbled, staring at her father. The use of the S word generally got a rise out of him. He did not like his daughters to curse, but Mercy hadn't been able to help it.

Jared turned to look at her, grinning like a fool.

"Clearly I interrupted… I didn't … uh…" Mercy turned to go.

"Did you need something, girlie?" her father asked.

Mercy stopped with her hand on the door. "I was lookin' for Hope. I haven't seen her all morning. Have you seen her?"

She peered over her shoulder at her father. He was shaking his head.

"Okay, cool. I'll just … go somewhere else."

And that she did. Mercy darted out the door, grinning like Jared had just asked *her* to marry him. No, she hadn't found Hope, and she still needed to talk to her, but suddenly, Mercy could think of other things that needed to be taken care of first. She'd let Jared find her sister.

Until then, Mercy would…

She glanced over at the building where Cody worked on some of their equipment.

Nope. She would go anywhere but there.

A KNOCK SOUNDED on her front door, and Hope forced herself up to her feet. She hated this time of the year. Hated that the flu had been going around and clearly she'd gotten it. She kept waiting for the damn fever and body aches that came along with it, but it had been nearly two weeks now, and the only symptom she'd had to deal with was this damn nausea and vomiting.

Seemed everything made her want to puke.

Another knock. "Coming!" she called out.

Jared

Hope grabbed her toothbrush and quickly removed the foul taste from her mouth, fighting her stomach again. She'd known someone would come looking for her because she should've been working. She only hoped it wasn't that damned fool, Rusty, because she was pretty sure he'd given her the flu. He'd been sick with it for a week, then Dallas had gotten it. Then Lane. Only made sense that she was next.

"Hope! Are you okay?"

Hope stopped halfway to the front door.

Jared?

Crap. She did not want him to see her like this.

Forcing her feet to move, she made it to the front door and unlocked it before heading for the kitchen.

"Hey." He sounded concerned.

Looked it, too, the way he was watching her.

"You probably want to stay back," she warned. "I think I'm contagious."

"You're sick?"

"I think it's the flu."

"Do you have a fever?" He came to stand by the table, his hands resting on the back of the chair.

"Not yet. But I'm sure that's next. I've been ... nauseous."

"How long's this been goin' on?"

She shrugged, pulling a glass from the cabinet. "Couple of weeks."

Jared's warm hands came down on her shoulders as he pulled her back against him. He pressed his hand to her forehead, then turned her around to face him.

Hope pressed her hand to her stomach. She needed to eat something. Usually, if she ate a little bit, it helped.

"Honey," he said, tilting her chin so she had to look up at him.

"I'm warnin' you, Jared. I'm probably contagious."

"I've had the flu before, Hope. There's generally a fever associated. Chills, body aches."

"Vomiting," she told him helpfully.

"Did you get a flu shot?" he asked.

She nodded. "But that was back in September or somethin'. I'm sure it's worn off by now. Or this is probably one of those millions of strains they can't prevent."

When she looked up at him again, Hope saw that Jared was smiling. "What? You really should probably not touch me. I don't want Derrick to get this."

His grin widened, and Hope was beginning to think he'd lost his mind.

"Hope?"

"Hmm?"

"I don't think Derrick's gonna catch what you have."

"He had the flu shot?"

"Yes, but..."

Hope frowned.

Jared leaned in closer. "Baby, I think you're pregnant."

Her eyes widened as she stared back at this man. A million things started running through her head at once. She replayed the last couple of weeks, thought about the many times she and Jared had had unprotected sex—ever since their accidental incident in the bathroom nearly two months ago. They hadn't used condoms since because ... well, because Hope couldn't get pregnant.

Could she?

Jared was still smiling.

"I don't think that's—"

He put his finger over her lips so Hope quieted.

"Before we get into that and before I run up to the drugstore and grab a pregnancy test for you, there's actually a reason I came over here."

"To see that I really do have the flu?"

Jared chuckled, but as Hope watched, he went down on one knee right in front of her, pulling a box from his pocket and opening it. His expression turned serious, but there was so much love in his eyes she felt herself tear up.

Jared

"Hope, I want to spend the rest of my life with you. I already spend every waking moment thinking about you. I dream about you, dream about this life we have together. I don't want to be away from you any longer." He smiled. "Derrick is driving me crazy, honestly. He talks about you all the time. Wants to know why we can't go on another date, a longer one next time. When I tell him you're working, he insists that he's a real cowboy and wants to go to work with you."

Hope was crying now. She couldn't stop the tears from flowing down her face.

"I love you, Hope. I want more than anything for you to be my wife. Marry me. Make me the happiest man on the planet."

He seemed to be waiting expectantly.

Hope cupped his face with her hands, nodding as the tears dripped onto her arms.

After sliding the ring over her finger, Jared was up on his feet, his arms around her, holding her to him as he crushed his mouth to hers. Hope sighed, kissing him back, her heart full to bursting. After all, she'd warned him. If he got the flu, it was his own fault.

When he finally pulled back, he was smiling again.

"Oh, and when I went to ask for your dad's blessing, he told me it was up to you if you wanted to hire me."

Her eyes widened. Oh, shit. She hadn't talked to Jared about that yet. She'd wanted to see what her father thought. She still needed to talk to her sisters.

Jared chuckled. "I want to be where you are, Hope. Wherever you and Derrick are. That's home for me."

His hand went to her stomach, warm and gentle. Hope stared down at it, at the small but beautiful ring on her finger. She still couldn't believe that this man had fallen in love with her. And he'd done it despite the fact that she was as stubborn as they get.

Jared Walker was definitely a keeper. He'd made all of her dreams come true.

"Now, what d'ya say I run to town and grab that pregnancy test?"

All of her dreams.

♥□□□□♥□□□□♥

I hope you enjoyed Jared and Hope's story. These two took me completely by surprise. One day, I sat down to write and something was telling me that Jared and Hope were going to cross paths. And boy did they.

Want to see some fun stuff related to the Coyote Ridge and Dead Heat Ranch series, you can find extras on my website. Or how about what's coming next? I keep my website updated with the books I'm working on, including the writing progression of what's coming up for all of my series. www.NicoleEdwardsAuthor.com

If you're interested in keeping up to date on the Walkers or the Lambert sisters as well as receiving updates on all that I'm working on, you can sign up for my monthly newsletter.

Want a simple, *fast* way to get updates on new releases? You can also sign up for text messaging. If you are in the U.S. simply text NICOLE to 64600 or sign up on my website. I promise not to spam your phone. This is just my way of letting you know what's happening because I know you're busy, but if you're anything like me, you always have your phone on you.

And last but certainly not least, if you want to see what's going on with me each week, sign up for my weekly Hot Sheet! It's a short, entertaining weekly update of things going on in my life and that of the team that supports me. We're a little crazy at times and this is a firsthand account of our antics.

Acknowledgments

First of all, I have to thank my family for putting up with me. Especially, my amazing husband who somehow manages to live AND work with me every single day. I have been truly blessed.

I want to say thank you to my beta readers – Chancy and Denise. These ladies have given me so much input over the years, I honestly don't think my books would've been written without them. Not only do they give me input, they also push me to write.

I also have to thank my street team, the Naughty & Nice Posse—Jenna, Annette, Traci, Maureen, Alison, Karen, Missy, Joy, and Kathy—for all of their hard work and dedication.

I can't forget my copyeditor, Amy. Thank goodness I've got you to catch all my punctuation, grammar, and tense errors.

Nicole Nation 2.0 for the constant support and love. This group of ladies has kept me going for so long, I'm not sure I'd know what to do without them.

And, of course, YOU, the reader. Your emails, messages, posts, comments, tweets… they mean more to me than you can imagine. I thrive on hearing from you, knowing that my characters and my stories have touched you in some way keeps me going. I've been known to shed a tear or two when reading an email because you simply bring so much joy to my life with your support. I thank you for that.

♥••••♥••••♥

About Nicole

New York Times and *USA Today* bestselling author Nicole Edwards lives in Austin, Texas with her husband, their three kids, and four rambunctious dogs. When she's not writing about sexy alpha males, Nicole can often be found with her Kindle in hand or making an attempt to keep the dogs happy. You can find her hanging out on Facebook and interacting with her readers - even when she's supposed to be writing.

Nicole also writes contemporary/new adult romance as Timberlyn Scott.

Website
www.NicoleEdwardsAuthor.com

Facebook
www.facebook.com/Author.Nicole.Edwards

Twitter
@NicoleEAuthor

Also by Nicole Edwards

The Alluring Indulgence Series
Kaleb

Zane

Travis

Holidays with the Walker Brothers

Ethan

Braydon

Sawyer

Brendon

The Austin Arrows Series
The SEASON: Rush

The Club Destiny Series
Conviction

Temptation

Addicted

Seduction

Infatuation

Captivated

Devotion

Perception

Entrusted

Adored

The Coyote Ridge Series
Curtis

Jared

The Dead Heat Ranch Series
Boots Optional

Betting on Grace

Overnight Love

Also by Nicole Edwards (cont.)

The Devil's Bend Series
Chasing Dreams

Vanishing Dreams

The Devil's Playground Series
Without Regret

The Pier 70 Series
Reckless

Fearless

Speechless

The Sniper 1 Security Series
Wait for Morning

Never Say Never

The Southern Boy Mafia Series
Beautifully Brutal

Beautifully Loyal

Standalone Novels
A Million Tiny Pieces

Inked on Paper

Writing as Timberlyn Scott
Unhinged

Unraveling

Chaos

Naughty Holiday Editions
2015

55719935R00170

Made in the USA
Lexington, KY
30 September 2016